THE SECOND GRAVE

Ian Austin

THE SECOND GRAVE

ISBN 978-0-473-42770-2

Original cover art by Sallie Clough

Author photograph by Judy F Taylor

For Steve

"Before you embark on a journey of revenge, dig two graves."

Confucius. Chinese teacher, philosopher and political theorist, 551–479 BC

PROLOGUE

2007

Twenty something years' service done and dusted; two decades which came to define Dan Calder's life and made him the man he was. Good, bad and everything in-between.

"Do you feel it's rather an unsatisfactory ending?" the Human Resources rep asked, making it sound as unimportant as choosing the wrong coloured paint for the garden fence.

Dan just shrugged instead of telling the hook-nose bastard what he really thought.

"However, your department supervisor DCI Allen has written a rather splendid exit report. If you'd like to see?"

Dan didn't. Although genuinely shocked he let the revelation go without acknowledgment. Hook-nose immediately checked his watch and brought the salty meeting to an end.

Five minutes later, now ex-detective and newly appointed civilian 'Mr.' Dan Calder stood astride the Force's emblem engraved into the cold, grey concrete on the wrong side of Police HQ main entrance. He had no semblance of a plan about what to do next. He'd been wronged but what was new there?

Splendid exit report, he thought, and his eyes narrowed. Surely this was Jim Allen's idea of a last laugh, but he didn't see the funny side at all and subconsciously made a mental note as was his way.

Another fact was also stored away. Other people had been hurt or worse, emotionally, psychologically and physically. Their wounds were still weeping within him and it was unlikely they could ever heal now.

The police, his family really, although dysfunctional and therefore why he felt so comfortable being a part of it, would continue as if he and his collar number never existed. He was alone again, a second separation from dysfunctional circumstances.

He put one foot in front of another, every step carrying him further away from the police and towards an uncertain future.

CHAPTER ONE

January 1 2017

It was just a harmless and slightly boozy pact. Dan could not remember who first suggested the idea of making a New Year resolution for each other rather than the traditional "I promise et cetera, et cetera."

His resolution for Tara was for her to throw out one item of clothing or pair of shoes for every new purchase she made. "And that includes buying second-hand as well," he clarified victoriously.

"Pre-loved." She corrected him with a wet, alcohol-fuelled kiss.

Dan Calder and Tara Danes were having their first proper party in their newly renovated house. The guest list was select, but the good-natured conversation and loud laughter was worthy of far greater numbers. Harry Spiller and his wife Colleen were spread out on one sofa and their old neighbours Shelley and Paul were entwined on the end of another. Dan was slouched in his old faithful lounge chair with Tara equally comfortably slouched across him. The midnight hour came and went heralding in the New Year. After going outside for five minutes to listen to the ships' horns blaring out their own welcome from the Waitemata Harbour the friends returned inside to do justice to the remaining cheese, pâté, port and brandy.

The others had all given and received their resolutions for the coming year too, only Dan was left to get the good news from

Tara. As they all listened, Tara nestled herself into his lap even more comfortably before speaking.

"Dan Calder, you will not deliberately place yourself in danger or harm's way or do anything which should be the responsibility of the police or other official organisation."

As the others cheered and laughed Dan could only offer a grin of mock indignity and innocence.

"Thank God for that. I thought you were going to make me cut down on the coffee or something else really important," he said.

Harry pointed a chubby finger at them. "She's got your number my friend."

"Hey that's a cinch. I'm a reformed character now," Dan replied hopelessly. He turned to Tara. "My darling I promise."

October 19 2017

At that moment, Dan's focus snapped back from the events of the happy evening at his house ten months earlier. He could really do with a long black in the comfort of his old chair right now, or better still a brandy, but instead he was putting the finishing touches to his facial camouflage cream, tightening the laces of his assault boots and making final equipment checks before breaking into the highly-protected house of Detective Chief Superintendent James Allen.

Some resolutions, no matter how well intended they were at the time of making must be broken, and some vows no matter how dangerous their outcome could never be set aside.

"Ready?" he asked.

"Ready," Nick Hetherington replied before pausing. He grabbed Dan's elbow, stopping him in his tracks. "You don't have to do this, we've done some crazy shit in the past but that was always the job and we were the good guys. This will be so far over the line that the line won't even be a dot in the distance behind us."

Dan took a deep breath of cold night air. "Freddie Mercury once said that if a thing is worth doing, it's worth over doing."

"I don't think he had this in mind," Nick said, hand still vice-like on his friend's arm.

Dan looked down at the gloved hand at his elbow and smiled grimly. "Amber is more than reason enough."

Nick relaxed his grip and flexed both hands. "Okay, let's do this."

The close friends' original deal was struck one wet Friday in 2004; before he left the police and the UK, long before Tara and New Zealand and happiness. They were sat up in a supermarket car park waiting for their target to move for the umpteenth time that day. The surveillance team that they were part of had been following a group of cheque-kiters for a week. Their method was simple but very effective: having fraudulently obtained and stockpiled chequebooks they hit a big town or city on one day and bought as many expensive items as they could. The next day in another town they returned the goods for refunds at another retail branch of the store where the purchase had been made the day before. Both transactions took place before the bank could detect the fraud; the chequebooks for each account were only used once then binned. Today was a refund day and they were already up by over ten thousand pounds.

Annie and Mike, two other members of the team, were in an electronics superstore with the target and group leader now; watching, recording and reporting back to the team over covert radios. The duty log keeper for the day would be making a written record of their observations for evidential purposes. Dan and Nick had both been in two stores with the target or one of her two associates already and to save themselves from overexposure they were now responsible for the initial vehicular movement when she returned to her car and moved off.

As usual Dan and Nick's conversation was varied; they'd been crew mates for nearly three years now and knew each other to chat to for several years before that. Nick was older, a family man and the one person Dan could rely on for anything; Martini friends as the old advert used to say for the drink—'Anytime, anyplace, anywhere. That's Martini.'

Amber would be six in a few days' time. She was the apple of Nick's eye and there was a tennis racquet he wanted to get for her from the sports shop he'd been in with the target a few hours before.

"It's too late for me or Penny to be rich and famous so I'm relying on one of the kids to look after us in our old age. Amber's a natural, great hand-eye coordination and a determination never to give up no matter what the odds or how good her opponent is. She's been having lessons for a year at the local club."

Dan looked interested because he was. The Hetheringtons pretty much adopted him; he spent time with Nick, Penny and the girls and was the godfather to Amber's younger twin sisters Viola and Rose. His own family was so shit he tried not to dwell on it.

"Maybe you should get her into crime, it's one of the few boom industries left and judging by our little entourage, today alone she'd be able to keep you in gin and colostomy bags no problem."

It was obviously not meant to be a serious comment, but they never failed to be surprised by the willingness of some to make their livings dishonestly while honest citizens slogged their guts out.

"I know," Nick agreed. "Can you believe it? Whoever said crime doesn't pay was doing it all wrong. God help her or any of them if they ever get themselves involved in any of this though."

"Does it worry you? I mean do you and Penny think or talk about stuff like that?"

"I can't help it. Pen's still amazed about what some of these people are prepared to do but you and I both know there is nothing that can be imagined that some bastard somewhere isn't doing already."

Annie's voice came over the radio updating them on the target's current whereabouts and activity. It seemed Glenda Perham just increased her income by another eight hundred and was now heading for the exit. Dan and Nick put their discussion on pause as they waited for the next transmission from Mike or Annie. It was Nick's day to drive and he checked his mirrors automatically in case they had become boxed in by other vehicles and weren't able to take the first movement from the car park.

"Stand by, stand by." Mike's voice was pitched to concentrate the minds of all members of the team who were positioned around the near area. "Target is at the exit and out, out, out of the shop. She has obtained a refund on a Sony entertainment centre and Annie will approach the staff when the target is clear. Zero four acknowledge."

"Zero four yes, yes," Detective Sergeant Paul Rivers replied. He was the operational commander for this job and in his car were the log keeper and a member of the force's Banking Offences Unit who originally tasked the surveillance team to work for them this week and the next. Dan and Nick could not see the target or her car from their position, but they did not need to. The team was good, and they knew the member whose job it was to give the movement away would not fail. Nick turned the key and the engine fired.

Detective Constable John Woodward's voice came over the encrypted comms set secreted under Dan's seat next. "The target is approaching her vehicle; Associate One and Associate Two are still in the vehicle and have not moved since the target went inside the shop. Associate Two is still in the driver's seat; Associate One is still in the rear passenger seat. The target is in, in, in the front passenger seat; zero nine?"

Dan lifted the microphone slightly off his lap and turned to Nick to make it appear from the outside he was going to say something to him.

"Zero nine yes, yes we are ahead and waiting," he said.

Two minutes later, after John's detailed description of Perham's car moving through the car park, he gave its direction onto the main road and Nick brought his and Dan's car out into the flow of traffic with two other vehicles between them to give himself some cover from the target's view.

"From zero nine the target is ours," Dan said. "We are travelling west on Redoubt Road towards the motorway link at Bratton."

After another three hours and visits to five other shops, the surveillance team's day was done. Rivers terminated the job and the team travelled back to their office for a debrief session. It was almost 7:00 p.m. by the time Dan and Nick picked up the conversation from earlier over an end-of-the-week beer at The Archer, Nick's local.

"Amber's got tennis in the morning. After that I'll take her to the shop to check out that new racquet to see if it suits her. What are you up to over the weekend?"

Dan supped his beer, holding the malty ale in his mouth for a second before swallowing as if it would give him greater value for his money.

"Got to finish a vice training programme I've been working on for my Crime Squad courses. Hopefully I can get it done tomorrow and play golf on Sunday."

Nick took a swig from his bottled lager. "Vice; the one job I really don't want to do. Something to do with having a family of young girls I suppose."

Dan nodded sagely. "No, not everybody's cup of tea. So, what would you do if one of yours did get into something they shouldn't?"

"What! The sex trade?" Nick spluttered. "Are you kidding me?"

Dan rolled his eyes. "No, you know, what we were saying earlier about getting themselves involved in crime?"

"They'd have to be more worried about what I would do to them than if they got caught by the police, I can tell you that much."

"It must be every parent's worst nightmare," Dan conceded.

Nick considered the point for a minute as they drank and watched the flames dance on the oak logs in the fireplace. After draining his bottle and indicating to Becky behind the bar for two more of the same he said, "No, them being a victim of something would be the worst, especially something physical. I don't know what I would do if anyone ever laid a hand on one of them." He looked into Dan's face a second. "No, that's wrong. I know exactly what I would do. Prison time for them, that's for sure, if it came to it."

"I'm sure I'd be the same."

"You have to get yourself a family first and a girl one at that. You know what they say about being the parents of girls as opposed to boys?"

Dan looked blankly at his partner.

"With boys, you only have one penis to worry about, with girls you have to worry about all of them." Nick laughed and raised his new bottle. Dan finished off his glass and slid its replacement over but did not pick it up.

"I'd do the same for your girls too. All of you, in fact," he said deliberately.

"What's that?" Nick said, still smiling at his own joke.

"You, Pen and the girls; you are my family and I'd be right there with you if it came to it."

Nick became serious too. Spending hour after hour and day after day in the confined space of a car or a covert observations post you got to know your partner inside out and it had been a long time since they'd exhausted the banal conversation of new crew mates. They had touched on the subject of supporting each other on numerous occasions; not just one cop looking out for another but a deeper comradeship which they now both understood may mean blurring the lines of what was lawful if the need ever arose.

"Let's hope to Christ it never comes to it then," Nick said.

CHAPTER TWO

Only a week before Dan found himself back in England again with his best friend, his and Tara's discussions were no more dramatic than picking over the merits of a coffee table for the lounge to match the dining set they bought for the new house. He was quite happy not to have one at all, but Tara wanted this particular one as a place to put her favourite magazines and Dan's reference books on cameras. Since his business took off he could spoil himself a little and his camera collection now ran to six good quality pieces with a dozen more so far on his one-of-these-days list.

Two years had passed since his dealings with Katrina Mallinder brought them together and a lot had changed. Work was steady and good, challenging enough for him not to get melancholy, and after a difficult initial period they both got accustomed to Tara's wealth resulting from the inheritance of her dead brother's lottery winnings. The money hadn't changed her though; she was still athletic and down to earth, still fresh-faced with the cutest nose and that wonderful lopsided smile. Her energy was boundless but woe betide anyone who crossed her.

Neither needed to work yet they both chose to, she sourcing and buying for her vintage clothes shop and he as a security consultant and part-time visiting teacher to the National Police College where he taught new recruits how to take high quality evidential statements and record interviews. In any case, the thought of living off Tara's money offended him.

He was a happy family man—if Tara and Jet could be considered a family. Jet, a one-eared, liver and white mixed-breed arrived from the SPCA soon after moving into their house in Glendowie. The shy dog, little more than a puppy, needed a lot of care and attention to begin with. He'd been rescued from a bad start in life which drew Dan to him particularly. His and Tara's hours meant they could spend all the time with him he needed and after six intensive months Jet was a well-adjusted, obedient and loved member of the household.

The only constant shadows on Dan's otherwise good life were the ever present and unresolved matters in his past; the deaths of his mother and Tara's brother were always on his mind. He still had not finished his book either. It remained in a desk drawer occasionally calling to him or being brought out and added to in small wordy chunks. Tara never commented on the missing chapter fourteen even though she had read the manuscript a dozen times and regularly reminded Dan to get on and finish it. What grieved him still was how Katrina Mallinder did notice and recognised the significance of it. The pages of chapter fourteen seemed destined to remain concealed, and the events which led to its existence firmly anchored in his head and heart with no chance of being expunged.

Tara slid the low table around on the big Oriental rug trying to find the perfect spot for it between Dan's old chair and the two newer sofas. She thought about asking him to move it for her but decided to leave it until later. Dan watched on, diplomatically quiet, and Jet followed his master's lead from a safe distance curled up by the door. The lounge, and in fact the whole house, was a harmonious mixture of his, hers and theirs; Tara didn't mind Dan's old chair as, "It adds character and makes the sofas look even better," she said one day. It seemed a lot of Dan's stuff added character.

When the coffee table finally came to rest, Tara dropped herself down onto the nearest sofa and sighed contentedly. Jet ambled across the room and took a cursory sniff at the new addition before sitting on the floor between Tara's legs.

"See, he approves," she said stroking his forehead.

"Coffee?" Dan asked, already heading for the kitchen.

"Mm please, I've got some small tiles which will make good coasters," Tara replied. "Or… how about we don't have coasters at all and allow it to get stained and marked over time as a way of storing memories. You know, like remember when we had that great night and I spilled red wine here," she said, tapping a toe on the new table.

"That's a great idea," he said, returning with two steaming cups. He put them down on the table and settled next to her, causing Jet to stretch his head across Tara's left thigh onto Dan's right in order to maximise his patting potential. As Dan leant forward for his cup, Jet shifted backwards and jolted the table's edge; the coffee sloshed, and the slightly fuller contents of Dan's slipped over the rim and onto the table. He hesitated, waiting for the hot liquid to settle again.

Tara pouted and then smiled. "He's christened it," she said, patting Jet on the shoulder. "What a clever boy."

Jet's happy tail nearly took both cups off the table but Dan salvaged them just in time. As they sat sipping their drinks they both studied the virgin coffee mark on the light oak surface.

Dan tilted his head. "It looks like a ship," he said.

Tara frowned. "I see a horse's head. Whatever it is, it's our first memory, our very happy family." She took a sip from her cup. "Have you got plans for tomorrow?"

"I need to get the deck finished so if the weather is okay I'll be in the garden all day; in fact, I should be there now. Why do you ask?"

"Cathy wants me to do a couple of days in the shop as she has two days of hospital visits. If you're going to be busy I might as well."

Later that afternoon Dan was in the garden with Jet. The raised deck area he was building was intended to be a place they could sit, and where he could come and work when the weather was fine. Mentioning it earlier induced some guilty feelings and so he got his tools out instead of his golf clubs. The platform was in its latter stages of construction, already fitted with bench seating, an overhead canopy and a hinged table top, which could be folded away when not required. The concealed power points were yet to be connected to the mains supply, but the water pipe was in, which made watering the garden plants a lot easier and was also useful for mixing the concrete that supported the deck's ground posts.

Jet's role seemed to be advisory and he regularly came over to see what Dan was working on at that moment, resulting in pat or tickle, which kept him coming back for more and slowed Dan's progress. He did not mind a bit.

He was patting Jet when the phone rang inside. He waited to see if Tara would answer and momentarily heard her say, "Hello this is Tara."

There was a slight delay on the line; she somehow knew it was a long-distance call.

"Hi Tara, it's Nick here, Nick Hetherington... in England."

They had never met in person but saw and spoke to each other during Dan and Nick's regular Skype conversations.

"Hey, how are you? This is a nice surprise, but it must be the middle of the night over there."

There was a longer delay on the line before Nick answered and Tara knew it was nothing to do with the miles between them this time.

"Yeah okay; is Dan home?"

"He is, he's outside let me take you out to him."

"Thanks," Nick replied stiffly.

Tara did not bother speaking again in the few seconds it took her to walk across the grass to where Dan was now laying with Jet on top of him like a hairy wrestler.

"Dan, it's Nick for you. I think something's wrong," she said.

Dan levered himself up into a sitting position, keeping Jet on his lap and took the phone from Tara's outstretched hand.

"Hey buddy," he said, hopefully sounding relaxed.

His demeanour changed almost immediately. He gently placed Jet on the grass and then stood up. Tara looked and simulated an 'Is everything okay look?' Dan slowly shook his head and went to sit on the edge of his deck.

After a minute or so he glanced towards her; Tara felt something inside go cold. She turned and headed back inside with Jet in close attendance.

Nick was distraught and much of what he said at first didn't make good sense. Dan let him go on for a short while longer, allowing his friend to expel some of the emotion coursing through his body before interjecting.

"Okay I got it but tell me again one more time, so I can be sure I didn't miss anything." Dan felt Nick heave in a great gulp of air and then release it slowly.

"Amber was arrested and questioned a week or so ago. Pen and I didn't know anything about it until they let her go. We weren't allowed in to see her until she was bailed when we picked her up from Rodway."

"What did they arrest her for?"

"Regarding the death of a tom in south Nottingham," Nick said, sounding like he still could not believe it.

"Death?" Dan asked, the one word covering a multitude of questions.

"Unlawful killing definitely, murder possibly, sex and drugs also involved. There are articles in the papers and it's been on the news every night since it happened; national and local.

Obviously, she had nothing to do with it, but she's scared shitless and she thinks they want to pin it on her."

Dan's mind was racing, trying to compute what he was hearing and rationalise the ridiculous string of facts into some sort of order.

"How is she, you and Pen and the other girls? This is crazy. There must be some mistake."

"That's just what I said to start with but with what little she's told us I can tell there is something seriously wrong going on here. I didn't know who else to call. Pen didn't want me to call you, Dan, but I'm really worried about Amber, really worried."

"Why won't she tell you everything?"

"I think it's because," Nick paused, "because, and I can hardly believe I'm saying it, because the police have threatened her."

Dan could not believe that either. "What have they told you? Who's running the show?"

"Your old boss Allen; Detective Chief Superintendent these days. I haven't been able to talk to him directly, but I have spoken to a DI Binder and a couple of the DCs attached to the inquiry. They're saying that Amber was seen in the area where the girl was killed at the time and she got into a fight or argument with her."

At the mention of the name James Allen, Dan's heart skipped a beat. It was still a festering wound even after all these years.

"I don't know Binder, what's he like?"

"A yes man, on the accelerated promotion scheme with his nose firmly up Allen's arse." Nick spat out the reply. "Dan, Amber's told me a hundred times she had nothing to do with the girl's death and I believe her and not just because she's my daughter. I can see it in her face but she's too scared to tell me what she does know and she's going out of her mind. Penny's losing her grip too and I'm as useful as a chocolate fireguard to all of them."

"Are you still working?"

"No, they offered me compassionate leave which I took, but I'm starting to think that I should have told them to shove it. I'm firmly on the outside now and have the feeling that's just where they want me."

Dan juggled a number of inner demons; he looked back towards the house where he could see Tara sat in the doorway stroking Jet with long, slow rowing motions while staring intently back at him. She managed the tiniest of smiles and a nod which was more like a slow blink.

"I can be there in two days," he said. "If I let you know which airport once I've booked it, can you pick me up?"

"Hey, whoa there. Who said anything about you coming over?" Nick gasped. "I just wanted to talk to a friendly voice."

"We did, several times, years ago. It's what family do, remember. I'll look on the Internet at the various news articles now but email me anything else you think of, okay?"

"No Dan, you can't just leave New Zealand and fly back here. What about Tara? Penny will go berserk too."

"I'll talk to Tara, you tell Pen. End of discussion."

Nick sighed. He sounded relieved and concerned in equal measure. "I owe you. Let me know what time at what airport."

They finished their conversation soon after. Dan punched the end call button and stood up. Tara was waiting for him when he got back to the house.

"What's happened?"

"Amber has got into some trouble over the death of a prostitute and Nick thinks the police themselves are involved. He needs help and I've offered."

The hairs on the back of Tara's neck stood to attention.

"Offered what exactly?"

"To go."

Whatever reaction Dan was expecting it was not what he received.

"So, when do we leave? Do you think Paul and Shelley will have Jet?"

"We? I don't think it's a good idea for you to go," Dan said.

Tara crossed her arms firmly.

"Is that because you could end up getting yourself involved in something that you really should not?"

"Look, I have no clue as to what is happening. Nick is in such a state that I can't really take anything he said as one hundred percent gospel. His brain must be mashed just trying to keep his family together at this moment."

Tara was clearly in no mood for half-baked answers. "So, tell me exactly what he did say, then."

Dan related the information to her as best he could, leaving nothing out. He honestly did not want to have any secrets—on this subject, at least.

Tara had more questions, some of which he could answer and some he admitted he was guessing at. When she asked what he hoped to achieve by going he shrugged his shoulders.

"Just what I can I suppose. Apart from you they are the only family I have anywhere, and I know Nick would do the same for me if I was in his position. I know it's been years since I saw Amber, but she can't have changed that much from the girl I knew to being responsible for killing not just another person but a prostitute; that *does* alter the situation."

"How's that?"

"The world they live in T, how they live day to day, their priorities and even the area of Nottingham it happened in; they are all completely alien to how and where Amber would live her everyday life." Dan struggled for a suitable comparison Tara would appreciate. "It's like you getting into something in Dargaville. It's a place that you would have no reason to go to at any time for any reason and if you were there something just would not add up. Something is wrong!"

Tara's mouth tightened. She looked as anxious as a lamb in a butcher's shop. "So, what are the police doing about it? Surely they must be investigating?" she asked.

"They are, in fact the lead detective is James Allen."

As he said the name, something struck Dan as being odd. Nick said Allen was now Chief Superintendent, the head of Nottinghamshire CID. The odd part was not his rise to being the most senior detective on the force, but that the most senior detective would be taking such an active, hands-on role in any investigation.

"Not the same James Allen who you had the falling out with before you resigned?"

Dan nodded. "But..."

"So, that's it! You've seen a chance to get your revenge on him for what he did to you."

"No not at all." He tried to pacify her but it was too late. Tara was five steps ahead of him, albeit going in another direction entirely and too far gone to be brought back.

"Don't you dare try and tell me it's got nothing to do with it. I know exactly what you're thinking, Dan Calder."

The fact it had nothing to do with the historical chemistry between Dan and his last supervisor didn't matter.

"Tara, I promise you it had not even occurred to me." Dan spoke the complete truth; it hadn't registered with him, not until that moment. The air around him cooled. He took her and walked her over to his old chair where he sat and pulled her down on top of him. The uneasy silence did not last long as Dan desperately wanted to convince her that his only thoughts were for Nick and his family.

"Amber needs help and I might be able to do something. Don't you see I won't have a full understanding until I get there? Nick said it was in the papers and on the news over there. Why don't we both look and see what there is on the computer and go from there?"

Five minutes later they were poring over the screen in the study. The fullest written articles were in the national Guardian's regional news section and local Garstone Record. They read each of them twice, pointing out words or sections of interest before Dan printed them both off. Unsurprisingly the Record had Anna Rofe's death on the front pages for a week.

Anna Rofe was 26 when she was killed by blunt force trauma to her head resulting in massive brain injury. It was likely her death was instant although a post mortem would determine the details for certain and police would release information as and when they could.

As Dan read the next paragraph, two words jumped from the text and hit him between the eyes like an assassin's bullet—Mapperley Park!

He continued to read with a growing sense of apprehension. Anna had been a prostitute for at least four years, living and working in the area in and around Mapperley, Southey Street and Mansfield Road. She was known to the police as a drug addict too, with numerous arrests to her name. She had no known family and it was possible Anna Rofe was not even her real name but because she used it for so long and even possessed identity documents, it was her only current identifier.

Shit! It could only be Mapperley, he thought, maintaining a stony face for Tara's benefit.

Police were following several avenues of investigation but were still appealing for the assistance of members of the public who were in Nottingham's small but busy red-light district the night she was killed; especially Anna's clients, whose information would be treated with the utmost discretion.

There was an in-depth report about changes over recent years where the older street whores were now under pressure from younger girls, some in their early teens, openly touting for unprotected sex to pay for crack cocaine or methamphetamine, and the latest invasion by east European girls and women who were trying to establish a foothold along Southey Street.

Real details about Anna Rofe's killing were scarce, which was to be expected but the small pictures still connected like puzzle pieces in Dan's mind.

"See, she was killed by a single blow according to this, what does that say to you?"

Tara thought for a long moment. "That she was very unlucky. I mean I've heard of people being beaten to death."

"Good, and?"

"Maybe he is a professional and knew what he was doing so it only took one hit."

Dan smiled then realised it wasn't a smiling matter. "Two things straight away. You said he. Why?"

"I don't know. I suppose I just associate that sort of violence with someone stronger than her."

Dan was encouraged. "So, your instincts are telling you the killer is a man. Okay, second, you said she was unlucky."

"Of course."

"Right, think about that for a second and then try to expand on it."

Tara took her time. "She is standing on the street corner and either gets into a fight or is taken by surprise." Dan didn't react. He gave nothing away hoping Tara would continue to think it through like he was. "If it was a surprise attack then yes, it could have been a deliberate and calculated move, but if she was in a fight then it could still have been a deliberate blow or a lucky one which went very wrong. It could have been an accident in that case."

Dan sensed the need to speak. "Okay, here's Amber on the same street as Anna. What reason does she have to launch a surprise attack or get into a fight with her?"

Tara considered the new strings of information. "Not for sex, not as competition. What about drugs?"

"She could get hold of crack or meth in a million better and safer places than Nottingham's red-light district. Try again," he said.

Dan watched as she grappled with the jumble of thoughts in her head, her face contorted with the sheer effort. After a fruitless minute, she gave up. "I don't know. I can't think of anything. So, what is the answer?"

"No, you are dead right. There is no reason at all for the two of them to be in that place at that time and for Amber to have killed her. Unless there is a massive difference between what we know about Amber and what we know about Anna Rofe…"

Tara finished his sentence. "Then she could not have done it."

"So, all we need now is to find out why Amber is involved, and the rest will present itself."

"And what if that means you getting dragged in?"

"I'm already in Tara and there is only one way out."

CHAPTER THREE

It was a difficult evening. In less than an hour Dan booked a flight and packed a small bag while Tara and Jet looked on. Conversation was forced and at any moment it seemed like the atmosphere could combust again into a blazing confrontation of epic proportions. Tara knew Dan felt he must go and she hated him for wanting to. She also hated herself for not being able to be more understanding. She could see he was struggling with the thought of causing her pain which could be alleviated by simply staying at home and offering what support he could from there.

Jet stayed close to Tara, clearly deciding whose side he was on. When the taxi arrived to take Dan to the airport it was too late for emotional goodbyes.

"I'll call you as soon as I get in. I'm sorry I have to do this," he said.

As he went to hug Tara she prepared herself for the contact and the heartache which would undoubtedly accompany it. Dan mistook it for a rebuttal which made the embrace a slow and painful exercise, like pulling teeth.

"I suppose it would be stupid of me to ask you to be careful," she said.

"I will, and I'll be home as soon as I can. Try not to worry. I'll keep you posted about what I'm doing if that helps."

Tara's limp smile clearly explained it would not. "Yeah sure. I love you, that's all."

"Me too, more than you will ever know."

She went to say something but stopped and bit her lip as Dan walked purposefully along the path towards the waiting cab. Tara watched until the car was out of sight and then slowly went back inside their house. She felt an ache in her stomach and could not bear the thought of being alone; she picked up the phone to call Shelley. It was not until much later she noticed another new mark on the coffee table: a small heart in red ink.

Dan was pleased he booked business class. It made the whole journey slightly more bearable. The Air New Zealand 747 departed Auckland on time heading for a two and half hour stop in Los Angeles, and then on to London Heathrow where he was scheduled to touch down at 7:00 a.m. and hit the ground running.

He accepted the first glass of complimentary champagne but did not drink it and was rereading the newspaper articles again before the plane's wheels were off the tarmac. Despite the fully reclining seat, any deep and restful sleep would not be visiting before he saw the familiar green fields of England once more. Somewhere over the Pacific Ocean during the first leg he started to revisit some of the times and places of his past, and by the time he got off in LA for a welcome break, he was formulating strategies, collating information and preparing himself for the unknown as only he knew how. All the time one word kept intruding into all the others: Mapperley.

Tara slept courtesy of homoeopathic assistance and she allowed Jet onto the bed with her. He slept with one eye and his one good ear open.

She woke to a message from Dan but didn't open it and spent the day at her shop, which did not improve her mood. While she loved the clothes and especially the hunting for them, the shop part bored her and having the whole day to let her imagination run wild about what Dan was getting himself into again made things ten times worse. Jet stayed in his basket all day mirroring her dark thoughts. At the end of the day she delayed going home by visiting Paul and Shelley and accepted their offer to stay the night. As she got into the spare bed she guessed Dan would be arriving in England at any time and called for Jet to join her again.

She was only off by fifteen minutes; Dan's plane touched down ten minutes late, however his business class status and a quiet morning at Heathrow meant he was in an arrivals lounge cafe in less than an hour, sipping horrible coffee with Nick.

"Jesus it's good to see you," Nick said for the third time since they shook hands and then embraced each other like brothers at the arrivals gate. "Pen was livid to start with, but she's come around. I haven't told Amber yet; I'm hoping it will be a nice surprise."

"Tara was pretty pissed too. I don't know what I did to deserve her. She's far too good for me."

"Do you want to call her now?"

"No, she will probably be asleep. Tell me what the latest is."

Nick looked like he had not slept for a week. Apart from the fact they had not seen each other in the flesh for several years, his six foot, thee inch frame seemed considerably weaker too.

"The more I find out the worse it gets," Nick said. "And yesterday something happened which nearly sent Pen to an early grave."

Dan waited for his friend to summon the energy to continue.

"Amber disappeared for three hours and when she came back she was as white as a ghost. She's hardly said a word since."

Dan could not contain himself any longer. "What the hell is going on? Things can't have changed so much in just a few years. I remember you telling me how she was going to make her fortune as a tennis star not so long ago."

"I know I know. I can even remember us talking about me buying her a new racquet for her seventh birthday one day in the car. Up until two weeks ago, she was still that same girl, Dan. How could it have gone so wrong so fast?"

They sat in stony silence watching thousands of normal people going about their business oblivious to the torments Nick was being subjected to.

"Sixth," Dan said.

"What?"

"It was a racquet for her sixth birthday. Come on let's get out of here. You can tell me the rest on the way."

For some reason, it was easier for Dan and Nick to talk in the car. They were back in familiar and safe territory. In all honesty, not much had changed in the Hetherington household in the years since had Dan left the country. They were a stable, relatively happy family. The girls were growing up, Nick and Penny were thinking about slowing down and the future seemed to be predictably okay. Nick was into his twenty-fifth year and retirement was now in sight, and for the last eighteen months he had been attached to a crime unit investigating high value burglaries from building sites and shops throughout the county.

"I was really enjoying it, a good bunch to work with and with a bit of freedom to think for myself, you know. I was working on an idea about some of the burglaries where the alarms were off at the time of the offence, and the offenders maybe having some assistance from an official source in identifying premises. Then in the space of a few days all our lives have disintegrated into a hellish whirlpool where nothing short of divine intervention or some other miracle looks set to save us."

As they drove north, Nick continued to talk and Dan mostly listened. By the time they stopped at the Leicester Forest Motorway Services for a toilet break and more coffee, Nick had disgorged all he knew but there still seemed to be more questions than answers left hanging. What was as clear as daylight to Dan though, was the urgent need to get Amber to tell someone what she was so afraid of and to convince her that whatever it was could not be made better by her continued silence.

She was almost nineteen now, a young independent woman still living at home while she completed her university studies but with a passion for travel, which saw her visit three different continents in the last year alone, working two part-time jobs to save. That seemed a lifetime away from the girl Amber was when Dan last saw her. The fact they got on well back then was unlikely to have any bearing on how she would view his unexpected arrival later today.

Nick kept some recent photos of all his girls in his wallet. As was his routine ever since Dan first knew him, he updated them every year to keep their pictures current. Penny had not changed a bit and Amber, Viola and Rose were all more grown up than when he last saw them during a Skype talk a few months before. The twins were sixteen and had developed their own individual styles; Rose now sported dyed blonde hair while Viola's own look gave her an Egyptian princess appearance. Amber was still striking in her fresh and athletic appearance and from what Nick said, she never thought to use so much as a fleck of lipstick.

When they went back to the car Dan guessed they would be back in Nottingham within two hours and steeled himself for whatever might lay ahead. Nick seemed to have used up all the words he had and was quiet for the rest of the journey. Thirty hours travel took its toll and Dan eventually succumbed to the soporific motion of the car. He remembered seeing the motorway exit sign for Nottingham then the next minute Nick was waking him to say they had arrived.

There was no time to prepare; Dan opened his eyes to see the car pull to a halt in front of a black garage door and the open front door of the Hetherington house to its immediate left. As he blinked away the sleep he saw the familiar figure of

Penny Hetherington silhouetted in the doorway by the hall light behind her. Then the curtains in the adjacent window stirred and he saw two faces peer out, one topped with bright blonde hair gaped, Rose, and the other, more like a ghost or a shadow, was unmistakably Amber. Dan tried to smile as he levered his body out of the passenger door. Rose's face disappeared but quickly appeared again beside Penny at the front door. Amber remained motionless for a second or two longer until a flash of recognition passed across her face like sunlight on a cloudy day. The instant before her face withdrew behind the curtain, Dan was sure he saw the corners of her mouth move upwards slightly.

Penny stepped out in bare feet onto the paved area between door and driveway. She and Nick exchanged a brief hug and a briefer look that spoke volumes about their innermost feelings. Dan expected an equally cool reception but Penny flung her arms around his neck and held on as if her life depended on it.

"Thanks for coming." She breathed heavily into his neck before pulling away to get a proper look at him for the first time in many years.

"Hi Pen. It's good to see you."

Rose was still gaping. "Uncle Dan, is that really you? Nobody said you were coming."

"Hi Rose, well I was in the neighbourhood, so I thought I'd drop by and surprise you," Dan replied, feeling a little uncomfortable with the uncle label even though it had always been his title with the girls for as long as he could remember. They hugged each other, Dan noticing the lack of height difference between them now.

"Come on, let's get you in. You must be exhausted," Penny said. "Nick will get your bags."

A few minutes later Dan was seated once more in the lounge room where he spent so much of his time before emigrating. Very little seemed to have changed. He recognised several vases, pictures and ornaments in the same places they had always been, although the carpet and lounge suite were new to him. Rose went to make coffee and tea leaving Dan, Nick and Penny looking at each other with so much to talk about and yet not a thing to say.

"How's she been so far today?" Nick finally asked turning to his wife.

Penny heaved a sigh. "Same, quiet. I tried to talk to her again and for a minute or two I thought she was going to answer, but then when I said there was nothing she could do or say to stop us loving her, she clammed up again."

"Have you got any ideas yourself about what it can be?" Dan asked Penny.

"No. Nick's probably told you all we know and all we've been told. Whatever it is, how can it be so bad that she can't talk to us about it?"

Penny looked over from her chair to where Nick was and held out a limp hand before tears started to stream down her cheeks from already dark rimmed eyes. Nick dragged himself across the room and knelt at Penny's feet so he could rest his head in her lap. She buckled forward so her head was on his with her arms around his body. It was the saddest sight Dan had ever seen and then suddenly it reminded him of Jet sat by Tara.

"Is it okay to use the phone to call Tara quickly? I said I would."

Nick said a muffled okay and Penny told Dan to use the phone in their bedroom, or even the computer if he wanted to Skype instead. Dan knew the way and left the distraught couple to go and make his call.

"How was the trip?" Tara asked after she and Dan said hello.

"Long. Business class helped."

"Are you at Nick's now? What's it like?"

"Yes. Oh, Tara I've never seen him like this before, or Penny. They look like the living dead, like any moment the will to live could just leave them."

A silence stretched on between them as neither knew what to say next. Tara's eyes wandered the room and settled on the coffee table.

"I found your heart on the table. I'm sorry I wasn't more supportive."

Dan found a smile from somewhere. "I should be the one saying sorry and I am; for everything and for the way I get sometimes."

"What do you think you'll do? I suppose Nick has filled you in now on all that's happened," Tara asked.

"He has but there isn't a lot more than what we knew when I left. I need to sleep now but maybe tomorrow we can all talk some more, and I might try to talk to Amber too. After that and depending on what else happens in the meantime, I might try and track down a few old friends to see if I can find out a bit more."

"Do you think the police there are, well, you know?"

"It's hard to believe something like that could be true but it's too early to tell. Anyway, tell me how you've been."

"We're fine. It's a small consolation to me but Jet's behaving like you never existed already. I stayed at Paul and Shelley's the night after you left. I couldn't bear to come home to an empty house but I'm feeling a bit better today and our boy is looking after me. By the way, I've decided that while you're away breaking your New Year resolution mine doesn't count either, so until you get home I'm going to go shopping-crazy whenever I feel like it."

"I love you so much you know, and I'll be home as soon as I can."

"Right back at you. Please be careful and call me every day."

"I will, honey."

As he replaced the phone in its cradle Dan sensed her presence before he turned around. Although he was tired to the point of collapse he made sure his face conveyed nothing when he did turn. Amber stood at the doorway dressed in a white tracksuit with white socks.

"I can't believe you're here," she said in a hoarse whisper.

"Hi," he said back, allowing a small smile to form.

"You shouldn't have come."

"Would it be better for you if I hadn't?"

"Better for all of us."

"Do you really believe that?"

Amber Hetherington was a ghost of the strong, effusive girl he knew. If her father looked like he had not slept for a week, Amber appeared not to have for months. She shrugged and leant against the door frame.

"You can't do anything."

"If I could, what would you want me to do?"

Amber's resolve foundered and she started to weep uncontrollably, only staying upright thanks to the door frame. Dan didn't move but kept his quiet, steady gaze on her until she looked at him again, still crying. He held out both arms; she had to come to him, make the voluntary move to allow him inside her outermost layer. Whether he would be able to get any further inside, only time would tell. It took an agonising few moments but when she did, it was like the troubles of the world were shifting slightly. She was as tall as him now but felt like a fragile stem of a flower in his arms. She cried as if her heart was going to break and Dan just held on to her. He would hold on all day long if necessary.

CHAPTER FOUR

When Amber woke up the next morning she felt like her whole body was emerging through a meat grinder again. There was not one part which did not ache, even her tongue when she tried to lick her dry lips.

Dan had held on to her as she cried by her parents' bed for ten minutes or more without saying a word the day before, and then she retreated to her bedroom again for the rest of the day. In all the time since she had been arrested it was the first time someone didn't try to talk to her and it had been a blessed relief.

The house was quiet and still; the light through her bedroom window gave no hint of the hour and she reached into her bedside drawer to find her alarm clock to see the time. It was almost 10:00 a.m. which meant she had slept for eleven hours. She got out of bed and put her white tracksuit on again. She had worn it for the last two days but didn't care. How she looked was the least of her problems at the moment.

It was not until she was downstairs that she heard the first sounds of human life coming from the back garden. When she got there her parents and Dan were sat around the patio table with a large cafetière and assorted cups between them. Penny moved to get up but Nick's hand on her wrist kept her in her chair.

"Morning love. Have you actually slept all this time?" Nick asked.

Amber was alert enough to feel relieved her parents' first moves of the day were not to smother her in the sickening truth of the current situation or envelop her with anxious affection.

"Mm yes," she mumbled.

Only ten minutes before, Dan finally convinced Penny to try and be normal just for today to see if it might help in some way. Dan was wearing his sunglasses, force of habit in New Zealand because of the brightness of the light there. He slowly and deliberately removed them so as to make sure Amber saw him revealing his face.

"Good morning," he said.

"Hi. I thought for a second when I woke up that I dreamed you being here. What are you doing here?"

Lying was pointless, as was a sugar-coated explanation.

"I wanted to come when your dad called a few days ago," he replied in a measured tone. "You've changed, so have Rose and Viola."

"You haven't."

"Hey, I've lost weight and run two marathons I'll have you know. Still a coffee addict though," he said, moving cups around on the table. "Want some?"

The fourth chair at the table had been deliberately placed. Amber walked hesitantly over and sat between Nick and Dan, so Penny was opposite, and she would be able to see the garden sculpture she made in college over her mother's shoulder. The Indian summer was still lingering, therefore this late October morning was as warm as any July day.

As Penny poured a cup of straight black for her daughter, Amber looked at her knees. Dan and Nick talked as though continuing a conversation they were having before she arrived; it was a full two minutes before there was a sufficient gap for Amber to interject.

"Thanks for coming, Uncle Dan."

"You should thank Mum and Dad for letting me. Makes me really feel part of the family again."

Amber looked set to ask another question, hesitating before she did. "Where are Vio and Rosie?"

"Gone into town. They said for you to call if you wanted to go and meet them later," Penny replied.

Amber managed a weak smile as she sipped her coffee and then tilted her face back so the sun was on it. Her skin was pale and unhealthy looking, and her grubby tracksuit did nothing to improve her overall appearance.

It was more than Penny could stand and she got up to go inside. Dan quickly pushed the near empty coffee pot over and said, "Great idea, I'll have another."

His look of encouragement to Penny was just enough for her to keep playing the game.

"Okay. Nick, Amber would you like another? I'll just go and make the beds and then do another fresh pot," she said before making her way back to the kitchen.

"I've got to go and get something for the car in a while. How about a drive out and maybe a pint at The Archer on the way back?" Nick asked Dan a minute later.

Dan put his sunglasses back on and was able to watch Amber's subtle facial movements without appearing to stare at her. She blinked and flashed a look in his direction, so he knew she was interested in his reply.

"Maybe later if that's okay. I'm still pretty spent after the flight and didn't sleep much. Still on Auckland time probably."

Amber's right eyebrow shifted, and the corner of her mouth creased.

"You go and sort the car and I'll sit here in the sun with my coffee for a while. Perhaps we can have that drink later?"

"Yeah, okay. Are you sure you don't mind me leaving you for a while on your first day?" Nick asked, but was already making to get up.

When they had been alone for five minutes, both ostensibly enjoying the sunshine Amber spoke without looking at Dan.

"Was that all for my benefit? Dad going out, so we were alone, and I'd tell you everything."

"Of course."

"I'm not stupid, Uncle Dan."

He leaned forward and removed his glasses again, this time sliding them up on top of his head.

"Do you think you could dispense with the uncle? It's all a bit creepy now."

Amber giggled without meaning to. "Thank God for that, I never liked calling you it."

There was a palpable release of tension in Amber's demeanour, as if her laugh was the first time she had allowed herself not to be terrified in a long time, but she soon remembered where she was and shrank back inside herself. Dan knew he must act then and there before she was out of reach again.

"Did Dad ever tell you why I left the police?"

Amber shook her head.

"I got shat on by my boss and then punished again for saying I got shat on." To his knowledge, it was the first time he ever used coarse language in front of any of Nick's daughters and it was a very uncomfortable feeling. "In the end I just thought, enough is enough."

If Amber was offended or surprised it did not show. She merely looked at Dan with interest and took another sip of coffee. Dan considered saying more, decided not to and then changed his mind again.

"It's only now I realise I did it all wrong. What I should have done was say nothing and bide my time until I was in a better position to deal with him."

"If this is all still for my benefit then you're wasting your time."

"Okay, Amber. I can see you've made your mind up. I'm okay now too. I can't think of the last time I thought about Detective James Allen anyway."

Amber's hand stopped with her coffee cup close to her lips. She looked like somebody had put a ball and chain in her cup;

Dan froze. He started reciting the Desiderata poem in his head as he always used to, taking up time to outwait another. It proved to be more difficult than he imagined; the other used to be a suspect under interview or a witness providing a statement.

"Did you say Detective Allen?" Amber asked, rescuing him from his pain.

"Yes, he was a Detective Chief Inspector in those days, my boss at Garstone. I'm sure his version of events would differ from mine."

"What did he do?"

"Messed up an investigation I was involved in and then made it worse by trying to cover up what he'd done. Unfortunately, the only one left high and dry was me because he had the rank to make things happen and other things disappear. If I knew then what I know now, I think the results would have been different."

He noticed her interest. "I don't understand," she said.

"It's all a game being a policeman Am, like cowboys and Indians for adults, but when it comes to one of the cops against another, the rules of the game change. I was too naïve then, even after twenty years of doing the job, to see I should've been playing the game like he was. That's the only reason he came out of it okay and I got shafted."

"James Allen is a name I heard from another detective the day they arrested me. I think he was telling this detective what to do with me."

Dan was elated. "I know. Do you want to tell me about it?"

"I'm scared. They said if I said anything they would do something terrible to Dad as well as send me to prison. They want me to lie or they're going to say I killed that woman. They're the police, Dan. They threatened the whole family."

Dan's elation was not only caused by Amber confiding in him. The news that Allen was in some way involved was a vindication of every contemptuous feeling he had had in the last five years.

He uncomfortably remembered what Tara said to him but hid it from Amber.

"Jesus, Amber I am so sorry. It must be hell for you trying to protect everybody else while they're all pleading with you to tell them what's going on."

She wasn't crying now and there was no hint tears were going to be coming again soon.

"I have to. Mum will die if anything happens to Dad or the others. I've just been thinking that whatever happens they can't possibly convict me of something I didn't do. I'm not going to lie about what happened, I decided that on the first day. Fuck them!"

Dan was never prouder of any single person in his entire life. He touched her cheek with his palm and then took a hold of her hand.

"If there was a way I could help, would you let me? Even if it meant telling your dad?"

Amber shivered a little but the steel in her eyes Dan remembered from years before was present again.

"Will it be dangerous for Mum and Vio and Rosie?"

"I don't know yet, Amber, but I like the odds of you, me, and Dad together more than you on your own."

"It's not cowboys and Indians, though is it? Not anymore." She managed an ironic smile.

"No, it's cowboys against cowboys now and we are going to be making the rules from now on."

"Can't I tell you before we tell anyone else? Once you have heard you might not want to help and I'd still prefer Mum and Dad were kept out of it."

Dan adjusted his sunglasses once more. "I'm all ears."

Amber cleared her throat and looked back at the house to be sure both Nick and Penny were not in sight. "It's just so mad. We were supposed to be going to the movies."

Dan went into sponge mode, absorbing every detail of every word so he need not interrupt her, and at the same time, registering queries and questions he would need to clarify later. Amber seemed to gain strength just by virtue of sharing the awful secret and with every sentence it became easier to relate the whole story.

"We—sorry, my friend Stacey and I—were going to go to the movies to see the new Matt Damon in Nottingham. It's a long way to go but the cinema is so much better there than Garstone's old flea-pit. She got her new car which she only picked up earlier that day and she wanted to have her first proper drive in it, so we went for a spin around before. It was my fault because I suggested we go around Mapperley, but we got stuck on the one-way system and ended up taking a few wrong turns to get off. In the end, we were lost so we just kept taking rights and lefts hoping to get back on a road we knew again. It was all a joke at the time."

That word again. That place, Dan thought.

"At about eight we found ourselves on this street with big old houses on both sides. Stacey noticed them first, the working girls, some looked really young." Amber took another peek at the house before continuing. "She dared me to ask one of them for directions if she stopped and we laughed that they might want to charge us if we did. Anyway, on the next corner we stopped for traffic and I opened the window to talk to this girl. She sounded German or Russian or something like that and had no idea, so we carried on. By that time Stacey was almost in hysterics, laughing about us finding a Russian prostitute in the middle of Nottingham. On the next corner, I saw this other older girl, she was talking on her phone and obviously local, so I got out to talk to her. She's the one who got killed."

Dan said nothing but maintained eye contact and kept up his non-verbal communications, encouraging Amber to continue.

"She said we were miles off track and started to tell me which way to go when this guy came up to us. He was acting as if he was a rock star, preening and strutting about and trying to talk posh although it just made him sound like a wanker. She knew him; he wasn't a customer because of the way she started talking to him straight away. She was quite agitated, and he was pretty pissed off with her about something—he even grabbed her hair. Then he changed and was all nice and laughing and even playing with her hair; she had long red hair in a French plait. Then he came over to me and asked if I was on the game too. I think the girl wanted us to get away now because she was sort of shooing me away without him seeing. When I didn't take the hint, she walked off and I followed her because that's what I thought she was indicating me to do. He followed us, and we ended up around the corner. She told him to leave me alone but then he wanted to know if I did any sort of drugs. He didn't say but I thought he was maybe selling them." Amber appeared to be in need of a rest and slumped back in her chair.

"I'd forgotten that in the time I've been away you, Rose, and Viola have grown up," Dan said. "You're not little girls, anymore are you?"

"Tell that to Mum. She's still mortified when we accidentally swear in the house."

"How are you feeling right now?"

"Freaked out to the max but better than an hour ago."

"Do you want to continue?"

"I told him to go fuck himself and if I wanted anything I wouldn't get it from a lowlife like him who went around pulling women's hair to frighten them. I said I'm a Daddy's girl not a Mummy's, in case you didn't know."

It was Dan's turn to laugh. Amber Hetherington was his sort of person.

"She laughed too which really pissed him off again. That's when I realised I couldn't see Stacey anymore. She was still in the car. I wanted to get back to her then, so we could go. I asked the girl if she was going to be okay and she said no problem. The guy was standing between me and her, so I went to walk around him, he stepped in my way again. The girl told him not to be a prick, but he ignored her and tried coming on all Casanova with me. Then he said something really bizarre. I can remember it exactly. 'A thing of beauty is a joy forever. Its loveliness increases so come back and see me some other time gorgeous.' I nearly threw up on the spot and told him that you can try to polish a turd and even roll it in glitter but it was still a turd. I pushed him out the way and ran back to Stacey.

"We joked about it all the way back into town and made it to the movie just in time. After it finished, when we got back to the car, a policeman was waiting for us. He said a girl had been attacked and our car was seen in the area and we needed to go to the police station to give a statement. That was okay but when we got there we were taken to different rooms and then everything turned upside down. Before I knew it, I was being accused of attacking the girl for her pills, and when I said I wanted to talk to Dad or a lawyer it all got unbelievably worse."

"I can imagine," Dan said, thinking that really, he could not.

"That's when Detective Binder came in and started threatening me with all sorts of shit. It went on for hours. In the end, he took another phone call and then let me go."

"The day before yesterday when you went missing for a while, were you at the police station?" Dan asked, expecting an affirmative response.

"The detective collected me from uni. He told me we were going there but then took me to an old warehouse behind the supermarket in Garstone."

"Fuck, Amber, this is unbelievable," Dan said, unable to control his feelings or his language.

"I know. If you think that, imagine how I'm feeling about trying to make people believe me! Including Mum and Dad.

He gave me the third degree again and this time said they had enough evidence to prosecute me, but might settle for a statement if I said what they wanted me to say."

"This may seem like a stupid question, but why didn't you just agree? Anyone would have been more than tempted under that sort of pressure."

"Dad always said I was stubborn, even when I was younger, and he sent me to tennis every week. He always wanted me to play the girls older and better than me. You can blame him."

Dan's admiration for his best friend's daughter took another leap and he shook his head in disbelief. "I hesitate to ask you what you were planning for your next move."

"To see what they do next. I thought that once they tell me what their bullshit evidence was I'd be able to prove I was at the movies at the time or do something else to show it wasn't me. He said he would contact me again next week." She tousled her hair and adjusted the zip of her tracksuit top. "What do you think?"

"Can you give me a few minutes to let it all sink in? I think you should come to the pub with me and your dad later. How would you feel about not saying anything to your mum for a while longer though?"

"I need a bath and a change of clothes. I feel terrible about putting them through all this, but can't you see what might happen, what they might do if I did tell them? You know what Dad's temper can be like."

"I can. To be honest I think I'd probably have done the same to begin with, but you're going to have to tell them sooner or later for the sake of their sanity."

Amber glanced at the house. "Please don't tell them but I know Mum and Dad have been having a few problems. She told him to leave a few months ago but Rose got sick and that brought them together again."

Dan hid his shock. "He hasn't mentioned it to me."

"You know what he's like. I thought this, well, you know."

Dan did.

Penny was fussing in Amber's bedroom, putting more finishing touches to the already perfectly made bed when her daughter came in and her put her arms around her.

"I'm sorry, Mum. I'm so sorry."

Penny hugged her back even harder, fighting the urge to blurt out all the maternal words that naturally rushed into her head. Amber was different than she was an hour before, but she couldn't put her finger on exactly what had changed. All she knew was Dan had asked her to be normal and it had somehow affected Amber. That was good enough for the time being at least, so she kept her words to herself.

When Nick came home a while later Dan was working on his laptop in the lounge.

"Hey?" It was a question as well as a greeting.

"Did you get the car sorted?" Dan asked, looking up.

In the space of a few hours, more of the old Nick had returned in terms of appearance and attitude. Dan welcomed the improvements; he felt sure they would be tested soon.

"Yes, it's fine. You know what I'm like about always having the car in A1 condition."

"I certainly do. You were always more anal about that than anything."

"Anal! It saved your arse on more than one occasion if I remember rightly. Like that night in Birmingham when Rivers put his in a ditch and we drove two hundred miles with five people in the back." They shared the pleasure of reliving the moment for a second and then Nick said, "How did you go?"

"Good. Pub this afternoon and you'll need your 'what the fuck' ears on," Dan replied, reverting to police speak.

Penny was utterly crestfallen when Nick told her he was going out to The Archer with Dan and Amber a few hours later.

"Trust me, Pen, please," he said, putting a gentle arm around his wife. "It will be okay. I promise."

"What have I done?" she moaned.

"Nothing love, nothing at all. She just wants to tell me something first and I don't even know what it can be yet. I'm sure I'll be able to explain when we get back."

Although she was absolutely gutted that Amber felt she could not talk to her for whatever reason, she had no choice but to let them walk out the door. Rose and Viola were still out, and she was left alone in the house with nothing to do but sit and wait.

The Archer was the same as ever, even the jukebox was still playing the same eighties and nineties tracks it did when Dan was last there. While ordering the first round of drinks he noticed the stunning new barmaid and then realised it was Becky whom he ordered his last pint from all those years before. If the pub had not undergone any redecoration or restoration then Becky certainly had. Everything from a nose job and new hairstyle to fake suntanned legs and manicured toes in six-inch heels. She was obviously used to the attention too, and liked it. Dan couldn't help but notice the way she bent down in front of him to get Nick's bottled lager from the chiller cabinet. After paying, he carried the drinks over to the corner booth where Nick and Amber were seated. He was holding her hand, but neither were talking.

Dan took a long swallow and savoured the taste of a good old-fashioned English beer; nothing in Auckland came close. He was ready to engage in a little small talk, but Nick looked like he could have a seizure at any moment, such was his anxiety to find out what was going on and what Amber was going to say.

"I think you should just get it over with, unless you'd rather I tell him?" Dan said to Amber encouragingly.

"No, it's okay," Amber replied, spinning the straw in her vodka and tonic, making the ice play a tune on the glass. "Dad, you have to promise not to freak out or go and do anything stupid."

"Oh, for Christ's sake, Amber, just tell me," Nick pleaded.

"Just promise."

"Okay, I promise."

Over the next forty minutes Amber recounted the story she told Dan earlier. He noticed a couple of extra details she must have forgotten to mention to him, but they were minor, and he was pleased to note his recall was pretty well spot on.

Nick spent most of the time battling with himself not to interrupt and gripping the edge of the table as if he were about to snap it in two. After ten minutes his drink was still untouched but when Amber got to the part where the man first approached her and Anna Rofe, he drained the whole bottle in twenty seconds. Dan left them alone with Amber still talking to get more drinks and when he returned Nick's face was a dark shade of red as Amber was telling him about her first interview at the police station. When she stopped to take a sip of her second vodka, Nick looked hard at Dan.

By the time she finished, the scarlet covered her father's face again and Amber was trembling. There was a moment when Dan did not have a clue what was going to happen next and he was readying himself to wrestle Nick to the ground if he erupted. He was as relieved as Amber when Nick slid along the bench seat and embraced her as if she were a returning hostage.

"You should have told me. You should have told us both," he cried.

"I couldn't. Can't you see?" she cried back.

After a few more minutes of shared "I love yous" and "It will be alright somehows" Dan felt it was time to address the issue of what next, but Amber excused herself to go to the bathroom before he was able. As soon as she was out of earshot the volcano did erupt.

"I'm going to fuckin' kill that bastard Binder and I'm going to beat him to death with the severed head of James bloody Allen. I know you hated him with a vengeance, but to be honest I always thought Allen was a reasonable bloke and a decent boss. In fact, most people except you do."

That Nick said it in little more than a whisper took away none of its feeling and impact. "I cannot believe this, can you?" It was the rhetorical question to end them all and he left no time for Dan to reply. "How the hell can they think they can get away with it? The daughter of a fucking police officer for Christ's sake. It's not the nineteen frigging sixties anymore. Police corruption was supposed to be a thing of the past, not alive and well in bloody Nottingham of all places."

"Calm down, you'll have a coronary," Dan implored his friend. "That's just the reaction that will make this a hundred times worse. I convinced Amber she needed to tell you what happened because she was trying to prevent you from doing something stupid. You have no idea how smart and brave she's been if you go off your head now."

Nick's facial colour slowly returned to normal but Dan could tell his blood was simmering below the surface.

"Try to understand why she felt she couldn't tell Pen? You're supposed to be the strong sensible one most of the time."

"Did you not hear what she just said?"

"Of course, and look at your response now, as if you're ready to commit bloody murder. I have heard it twice and it does not get any better the second time, I can tell you. Try and think about it. Look what happened to me."

"What do you mean 'what happened to you'?"

"We'll sort it. We can and will get them but without collateral damage on our side. Amber is too young and too important to all of us to put her safety at risk. Think about it, trust me. I know Allen. We will get him Nick, and Binder too."

Nick's face hardened with the thought. "What am I going to tell Penny? It's not been hearts and flowers with us for a while."

Without further consideration for the promise he made to Tara not to keep secrets from her, Dan said, "Just enough to stop her from killing herself with worry. Enough to make her feel better until we can sort it all out."

By the time Amber returned her father was much more relaxed which made her feel better about having told him. As she settled back into her seat all three of them were sharing the same thought: *What next?*

CHAPTER FIVE

Edward Parker the younger was holding court at the Right on Cue snooker and pool club in Charlton Mews. A baseball cap and baggy jeans-wearing band of black and white youths surrounded him at the bar while he described the finer points of his newest BMW seven series he'd picked up the previous week in lieu of a gambling debt owed to him by another of Nottingham's upwardly mobile.

Teddy Parker was the son and heir to the building and renovations empire which was his father's business. "Empire" was how Edward Sr. described the company which he had built up from scratch with a mixture of hard work and hard conduct towards those he'd encountered along the way since leaving school in 1972 at fourteen years of age. Teddy inherited some of his father's work ethics—in particular the hard conduct towards others in order to advance.

Teddy Parker was also a nasty individual, possessing enough money with which to exploit it to the fullest. A lack of proper parental guidance in his childhood, intelligence combined with laziness and a desire for the good things in life were a recipe for trouble. But what made him so much worse was he enjoyed degrading people he did not like or who failed to meet his expectations and requirements. Not just upsetting them, but breaking their sense of being.

Teddy's other appetites, particularly sexual, were voracious too, often fuelled by drink and drugs. Living in a night-time world of clubs and seedy streets provided all of the above like they were on tap. When he couldn't pick up a girl at a bar or on a dance floor he could choose from dozens walking the red-light district around Mapperley, which he largely controlled.

Teddy's second in command, an imposing male called Flick, stood tall amongst the gathered pack. Nobody could remember if he acquired the nickname due to his real name being Felix or because of the knife he habitually carried in his trademark Timberland high-top boots. Flick's immediate mixed heritage of West Indian and Scottish Borders resulted in him being physically big and strong as well as impossibly good looking. All pleasing traits ended there.

"You tha bomb, Teddy," Flick said, high-fiving another of the group.

The nearest he ever came to the Bronx or Harlem was the MTV music channel on the giant plasma at home, but that fact did not seem to matter to him or anyone else stood around in the gloomy light.

"Hey what can I say," Teddy replied, revelling in the occasion. "A man in my position has to have the right wheels, right? The funniest thing is he's left his passport in the glove box."

Teddy liked the best of everything; his gang rarely saw him in the same suit twice. The fact he was a good looking young man by anybody's standards, with the smile to go with it, only made his poisonous character even more of an anomaly. Teddy Parker was powerful in the circles he moved in and that power further corrupted him.

If his father did not have the fortune to afford the best of the best growing up, he more than made up for it with the attention he lavished on his only child. Teddy went to the best preschools as a child and in turn, Nottingham's finest private Grammar before Edward Sr. bought him his way into Durham University on an English Literature degree course. Teddy was expelled at the end of the first year when one of the students he supplied an ecstasy tablet to almost died. More deals were done so the police did not become officially involved and Teddy's reputation did not suffer. Partly due to his silver tongue and partly because of sheer bloody-mindedness in his father's eyes, Teddy could do no wrong and it was the responsibility and fault of everybody else except Teddy for the predicament he became involved in.

When Teddy returned home he took up an executive position in the family business which, in reality, meant he got paid for doing nothing and so was able to concentrate on developing his own enterprise which spanned drug dealing to the weekend clubbers and prostitutes around Mapperley to high value thefts and handling stolen goods. He preferred to believe he was more akin to Nottingham's most famous son Robin Hood, with Flick the leader of his Merry Men.

Teddy's literature studies were not all in vain and he quoted biblical texts or lines from the great poets frequently. One day he convinced a group of friends that robbing people in the neighbourhood was how the bandit of Sherwood Forest really got his name and soon after that, he gave Flick and his other subordinates their own catchphrase. "Steal from the rich… and that's it."

Today was an off day for the group. Teddy wanted to lay low for a while after the incident with the prostitute, and the night before, two of Flick's associates got themselves arrested when they unhappily attempted to roll a black-belt in taekwondo in the street as he was walking back to his car. Teddy was not unduly worried. That situation was under control and could easily afford as many days off as he wanted; taking his substantial cut from Flick's group's crimes was small change in comparison to the money he was making providing crack, pills and crystal meth to the street whores and weekend clubbers. He could, in fact, have bought a fleet of brand new BMWs if he wanted.

When his cell phone rang to the tune of *The Godfather*, he opened it with a long swipe and put it to his diamond studded left ear. Teddy didn't answer but waited for the caller to speak.

"What time?" he said after a moment, then, "I'll swing by in an hour." He ended the call with an equally extravagant flourish and replaced it in his Armani jacket pocket. He then took out a wad of bank notes from his trouser pocket and peeled off four fifties, which he casually put on the bar.

"Have a few games," he said to his crew. "Be in touch."

With that he left the club and the others to their own devices as he headed out into the sunshine and his new seven series.

Dan walked back from The Archer to give the Hetheringtons some time on their own. Nick would know how much to tell Penny. He and Amber also needed to do it without him being around.

As he walked along familiar streets in the late afternoon sun he ran various scenarios through his mind. Some were of jobs or training exercises he'd been involved in the past, and some were new what-if's and would-this-work ideas. Prior to Nick's call there was no possible reason to think that in the space of less than a week he would be contemplating locking horns with his policing nemesis once again, and yet that was exactly what he was thinking. A woman walking a dog in the opposite direction passed him and they exchanged a polite hello. Seeing her made him think about Tara and what they had been through together in the last two years and how she would be at home now with Jet. He tried to force the guilty thoughts from his mind, but it was of no use.

"You're a bastard, Calder," he said to himself. "A very bad bastard indeed."

Whatever Nick and Amber said to Penny worked a near miracle. When Dan walked in through the open back door it was just like old times. Penny was emptying the dishwasher while sharing a joke with Amber about the state of her white tracksuit, which badly needed washing. When Dan appeared they both went tense and quiet before relaxing again and finishing the conversation.

"I was going to do fish for dinner, Dan, is that okay with you?" Penny asked with her head still in the dishwasher.

"Great."

"I suppose the fish in New Zealand is tons better is it?"

"Different. Probably a bigger selection than here. My favourite is called tarakihi."

Penny's head reappeared, grimness still etched across her face, but whereas before it was laced with despair, a determination was visible now.

"Don't let them hurt my baby."

Dan was taken aback for a second. "I won't, Pen."

"I'm sure they have only told me part of the story and I know what Nick thinks I'm like, but no one has ever tried to harm one of my girls before." Penny's eyes grew wider. "So I am telling you Dan, do not let anything happen to Amber or you will have me to deal with as well, and I'm telling you right now, compared to me any one of these pieces of scum will look like kittens. Is that clear?"

"Yes, Penny."

She touched his shoulder and the warmth returned to her features.

"Good. I got haddock and plaice, which would you prefer?"

"You Hetherington women are full of surprises," a shocked Dan replied.

"And don't you forget it. Nick's in the lounge. I'm guessing you two need to talk."

Dan found Nick alone in the lounge, sitting on the sofa but staring at the ceiling as if in a trance. They had been best friends and work colleagues for so long that both knew each other inside out. That it had been years since they'd worked together was completely inconsequential.

"Information?" Nick began, automatically listing their operational order's priorities.

Dan sat in one of the two big armchairs. "Yes, we need to sort a few things before we can make a plan."

"Intention goes without saying."

"Agreed."

"Method is all yours as usual. I'll handle the ancillaries." Nick lowered his head to look at his old friend. "This isn't your battle."

"It shouldn't be a battle for either of us, but people like us don't seem to get to choose their battles, do they?"

"Like you and Allen?"

"Mm, yeah."

Nick sniffed and let his green eyes rest on his old partner's face. He rubbed his chin with a rough hand, displaying the chewed fingernails he maintained ever since Dan first met him. "You can't let it affect getting Amber out of the shit. I can't let anything or anyone, including you, affect that."

It was not intended as an insult or a warning. Just a simple statement of facts.

"Can I use the car tomorrow? There's quite a bit of running around to do and I have to catch up with some old acquaintances," Dan asked, acknowledging Nick's previous comment.

"You better call Tara as well."

It was not a subject that filled him with joyful expectation, but Dan knew Nick was right. It was what couples did.

"I'll phone tonight," he said.

"Why am I not surprised?" Tara sighed.

They had been talking for twenty minutes and Dan had explained most of what had happened without going into any detail about what he and Nick were planning for the days and nights to come, save to say he wanted to stay and try to help in whatever way he could.

Dan stared at the screen blankly. “What do you mean? We don’t even know what we can do yet.”

Tara smiled wearily; the Skype call meant they could see as well as hear each other. “Help in whatever way you can, you say. I pity whoever gets in your way.”

CHAPTER SIX

Dan left the house early the next morning. If they were going to be able to dig Amber out of the hole she was in before the following week's deadline appointment with DI Binder, there was no time to lose and no point in prevarications.

His first port of call was the bank; funds were required. Armed with an impressive stack of cash he then headed into Garstone town centre to do some shopping and catch up with a number of characters he thought he'd seen the last of when he handed in his ID.

The Divisional Police Headquarters building on Garstone's eastern fringe comprised of a six story grey concrete tower fronted by a two hundred space car park, surrounded on the other three sides by various other buildings and Portacabin offices. The whole complex was ringed by a wall and fence, providing security for those within. The fourth floor of the main building was home to senior officers, their assistants and other administration functionaries.

In a large corner office, James Allen replaced a file in his desk drawer and locked it with a key attached to an extending chain clipped to his belt. He gazed out of the window facing the ugliest industrial part of town and contemplated the eleven months left before retirement. He had gone as far as was possible in the job without becoming chief constable of a whole police force or one of their deputies. Time had been mostly kind during the previous thirty-one years and he felt ready to put his feet up and make the most of his pension while he was still fit and healthy.

That being the case he wondered, *How the hell things could have got so out of hand in the last ten days.*

He picked up the phone and called home. He and Gwen had been married for thirty years and were looking forward to retirement away from Nottingham in the more temperate southwest where he could grow roses and she could spend his pension. Their marriage was a cocktail that worked, when to the ill-informed it seemed unlikely. She had an eye for lovely things and it took him a number of years to appreciate everything she did was with him and them in mind. Spending money as it came in meant they could enjoy the luxuries they could afford.

Circumstances around their son leaving home to chase a dream which never materialised left an indelible mark on them both; it brought them a closeness others never got to see and a love and appreciation for what they gave each other day by day.

"Morning love, what are you up to?"

"Hello Jim, this is a nice surprise. I'm making banana cake."

Hearing her voice made him feel a little better. He looked at his closed top drawer, thinking about the brochures inside.

"What do you say to a few days away next week? I thought we could drive down to Devon and look at some houses, you know actually start looking properly."

They moved into their newly-built house a few months before; Gwen already loved it for the furnishings and decorations she'd already added, he disliked it with equal fervour for other reasons.

"Oh, Jim that sounds wonderful. Is everything okay? You don't sound quite right."

"Fine, just one of those days when I wish it was all over."

As if on cue his telephone console chirped into life.

"Sorry pet, my other line is ringing now. I'll talk to you again later. I'm looking forward to that cake."

He hesitated before picking up.

"Good morning, Allen speaking," he said with practiced ease but feeling less so.

"I hope it is James, I hope it is."

Allen slumped in his chair. "I've got a meeting in fifteen minutes, so you had better make it quick."

"We need to have another talk sometime. Tomorrow would be okay but today is better. Why don't I come around to your place after work?"

"You can screw yourself if you think I'm letting you into my house. I'll meet you here," Allen sneered.

The laugh on the end of the line turned into a cough and Allen had to wait for the caller to get his breath back.

"You've hurt my feelings, James."

"My secretary leaves at four thirty so come at five. I'll meet you in the reception area." Allen clicked off to terminate the call and double-checked his desk drawer was locked.

If Dan was having a productive morning out Nick was trying to do the same at home. With his entire family around him in the kitchen, he told Penny and the girls what was going to happen and giving instructions. He was in no mood for a discussion or debate.

"If I could make Amber go with you too I would, but she has her bail to answer. I've arranged it so a friend of mine will collect you at the railway station when you arrive and he'll take you to his place. I'm sorry darling, but with you away somewhere safe I can concentrate so much better."

Penny, Rose and Viola were vocal in their objections to leaving but Nick's do-as-I-say side ended matters. The friend was ex-army, Special Ops. He now operated an outward bound and team building enterprise in the wilds of north Wales where there was ample accommodation on a secure fifty-acre site. When Nick called and explained, Martin first offered to come to Nottingham and lend his considerable expertise to the cause but was then more than happy to supply safe haven to Nick's family along with a blood oath to protect them.

"And just what is it you and Dan have planned? This isn't a game, you know. This is our daughter's life you're talking about," Penny said in desperation.

"He's right, Mum. Please just go and be safe. I can't cope with worrying about you as well as myself," Amber pleaded.

Rose and Viola wanted to have their say too but Nick put a sudden and final stop to the whole conversation.

"Pen, this is not going to change the longer we talk about it. You two go and pack a bag each, a small one! I want you ready to go in thirty minutes. Penny, I love you and I have never told you to do anything in all the time we have known each other, but I'm telling you now, darling. Go upstairs, pack a bag. You're leaving in an hour."

Rose started to protest again but Penny's look silenced her.

"If we go I don't want to know what you and Dan do apart from taking care of Amber. You call me every day and if you don't, I will be straight back here. If anything happens to her I will never forgive you, and you call me the minute it's over."

Nick put his arms around her and they hugged, sealing the agreement. Penny then gave Amber the same and quietly said to her eldest daughter, "Look after your dad for me too, okay?"

"I will Mum," she whispered back.

In accordance with Nick's instructions, Penny, Rose and Viola were in a taxi before the hour was up. He told his wife to pay for the taxi fare and train tickets in cash to prevent any chance of credit card details being traced—he was that paranoid.

"I'll give you time to get to Martin's place and call you tonight. Don't worry, it will be alright." Those were his last words as he closed the taxi door and tapped the roof indicating for the driver to go. As he was walking back into the house his mobile rang; it was Dan.

"How much longer do you think you will be?" Nick asked.

"I'm on my way now. I've got a fair bit to tell you, so I'll give it to you in full when I get back."

"It really is like old times," Nick said, scooping another spoonful of lamb madras onto his plate.

"You can say that again. I don't think Amber and I have had half of what you've eaten on your own," Dan chided back.

Amber seemed more relaxed now than at any time in the two and a half days since Dan had been back. He was even more impressed with her guts and spirit than the day before when she first confided in him, and he hoped it made their options a whole lot easier.

"You two must have had a great time working together," she said.

"The best time of my career," Dan replied.

"I remember you talking about some of your jobs every now and then, Dad, but not the real specifics. You were on the surveillance squad I know, and both detectives at different points in time. Do you think you can really sort this out? I mean, my idea of being able to prove I didn't do it because I didn't isn't so bad, is it?"

Nick put his fork down and wiped his mouth with a paper napkin.

"I'm not so sure it's that easy now. If somebody told me two weeks ago the police force I work for was capable of employing people who could set up anyone for a murder, let alone my own kids, I would have said they were crazy." Nick pointed his fork at Dan. "And yet here we are. What did you find out today?"

"Please don't take this the wrong way Amber," he began, "but I wanted to try to see if you had all your facts straight." He felt Nick bristle, but ploughed on. "No listen. It's like you just said, almost too fantastic to be credible, but you were right about everything. I got to talk to one of the jailers at Nottingham Central this morning, an old mate I've known for more years than I can remember."

Amber was confused. "But I wasn't taken there. They took me all the way out to Rodway."

"It's the jungle drums. If you want to know about anything going on in the police you ask the cleaners, the drivers, or the jailers. It doesn't matter where you were taken or questioned; between them there is not a thing you can't find out. Roger told me the Rofe girl was a regular with convictions for possession as well as prostitution, so I reckon you were right about this man being a supplier.

"He also said that you going to Rodway was really bizarre because it's the only station left in the whole force which doesn't have an electronic custody centre and nobody gets taken there nowadays. I remember it being old when I was still in the job."

"So why would they take me there then?"

Dan could see Nick knew the answer already.

"In the modern centres, just about everything is automated," Nick said. "If you went to Central for example, a digital record of your arrival would be made and you would be on film from the moment you stepped inside. Out at Rodway it's all still handwritten records and therefore dates, times or anything else can be written to suit. Come to think of it, your bail sheet was hand written. I didn't even think about it until now."

"Roger's going to see if he can get hold of some copies for us," Dan said, and seeing Amber's incredulous look added, "Don't ask. He's a good old friend. I suppose now is as good a time as any to tell you a few home truths about the situation."

After witnessing the strength of Amber's character first-hand, he made a judgement which, if he was wrong could jeopardise her safety and liberty, not to mention his relationship with Nick and all that entailed. He was grateful Nick had given his tacit blessing to what he'd planned by persuading Penny to take the twins and leave Garstone, but...

There was still the 'but.'

"Your dad and I have known each other for a long time. He is my best friend and I think I am his. There is nothing in the world I wouldn't do for him, or you. What I'm going to tell you is the plain truth because I know you can deal with it." He sniffed loudly. "But when I do, remember I am the best person there is to make it right again. You are going to have to trust me, and so is he."

"Trust you! You're scaring the shit out of me," she gasped.

Nick looked at his daughter. "He's right, my love. You can't deal with this on your own and I can't do it either. If I had to bet my life on someone to help us, it would be on Dan. Let him help us. Let him help you."

Dan saw understanding dawn on Amber's face. Her belief that justice would prevail was not good enough. The one person in the whole world she trusted and relied on the most was telling her so.

"What are you going to do, Dan?"

"We have seven days until you're due to answer your bail. That's one week to find the real killer and the reason why the police don't want him found. If we work together we can do it, but it's not going to be easy. I might need you to do some things you don't want to do. I'm almost certainly going to break the law and ask you and your dad to do the same. You might meet some scary people and get in some scarier situations, but we will be looking after you at all times. How does that sound so far?"

Amber looked at Nick, who had not moved or made a sound. "Like a Bruce Willis movie."

Dan offered her an encouraging smile. "So, do you want to hear what else I did today?"

Over the next hour, Dan spoke while Nick and Amber mostly listened. Amber could hardly believe how much Dan had discovered in a few short hours and even Nick was impressed by his old partner's compendium of results.

"After sharing a bacon sandwich with Roger, I went to visit Josephine Lamas. Josie must be in her late sixties now at least, but in her time, she was the Queen of Mapperley Park. She ran the biggest and best brothel for a hundred miles and was famous for looking after her girls and her clients. There were some famous names who visited and as far as I know, not one of them ever got identified."

He declined to mention his walk to her house deliberately circumnavigated the area of Powton Road, indeed, it took all his courage to go anywhere near the area at all.

"I've always seen what the likes of Josie do as providing a public service. If I had my way, there would be proper council-run places. That would clear up fifty percent of all crime overnight. Anyway, I helped a few of Josie's girls a number of times and also had an arrangement with her where I would occasionally turn a blind eye to a girl using her house as a bail address, even though strictly speaking it wasn't suitable. In return she gave me the heads-up on some of the real criminals in the area."

Nick looked surprised. "You really are a dark horse, you never told me about her. I can understand some of your collars now."

"You have to have one or two secrets, buddy. Without Josie's help, you would have left me for dead in the arrest stakes."

Amber grinned. "So, what did she have to say?"

"She's been retired for years, closed the business down when the street girls arrived in numbers and became more interested in earning money for drugs. Fortunately for us though she is still a fountain of knowledge and discretion when it comes to what's happening in Mapperley.

"She knew Anna Rofe, not as one of her previous employees but as a local tom for at least three or four years. She said Anna was okay until she got hooked, just like so many of the others. She didn't know what her drug of choice was but thought it must be either coke or meth. Anna worked for herself, that is, she didn't have a boyfriend or a pimp leeching off her, and she lived locally too. I told her about the man who you saw and described him how you said to me. Straight away she asked me if his name was Teddy Parker and if he had a big diamond in one ear."

Amber nearly jumped off her seat. "The earring yes, oh my God yes, that's just what he wore in his left ear. I never heard her say his name but he had this disgustingly big diamond."

"Great Am, that makes our task a lot easier."

"Come on then, share the good news," Nick said.

"After I left Josie's I went shopping for a while and then went to the Registrar's Office."

Nick spluttered. "Not Arthur Mountfield?"

"The very same."

"Who is he?" asked Amber.

"A filthy pervert Dan locked up years ago, but was never prosecuted. We always thought Allen had something to do with why it never went to court," Nick explained. "Maybe they were in the same club and shared a funny handshake."

"So why would you go to see him?"

"After the case went belly-up I kept hold of some of the evidence I gathered. When I needed information, I could use it to get what I wanted out of him. Sorry. I told you some of this wasn't going to be pretty."

"No, it's alright I understand," she said. "If he is a criminal I'd want to make his life hell too."

"You really are your dad's girl. Mountfield nearly collapsed and died when I walked in. A couple of years ago I did this thing in Auckland and I bled him dry for information in return for telling him I'd never darken his door again."

Nick could not help but interrupt Dan's flow, as if needing to further demonstrate his credentials to Amber. "This Auckland thing involved trapping a serial murderer and using himself as bait to catch her."

"I take it all back. Bruce Willis has got nothing on you," Amber replied, shaking her head.

"This time I needed to bring some stuff with me to persuade him to play ball. All the stuff I kept about him in fact, to hand over before I could get what we needed."

"You mean all the evidence you kept from his case?"

"Yes. Videos, documents and some other bits and pieces. When he recovered from seeing me I told him I wanted to know if he and Allen were ever friends, and who else Allen might know called Teddy. I wish all police work was that easy; you know who the scumbags are, so you squeeze them until you get what you want. Unfortunately, it's not and I probably broke half a dozen laws this afternoon so what I found out you could never use in a court to prove your innocence."

Dan opened his newly acquired black canvas holdall and took out a sheaf of papers. "One or two photocopies courtesy of Arty Mountfield."

Amber's jaw dropped open. Nick smirked and playfully punched Dan on the arm. Spreading the papers out on the floor, Dan continued.

"Mountfield and Allen were associated at one time, but he said they hadn't spoken to each other for years; that may or may not be true. He didn't know anyone called Teddy but then suggested Edward Parker, who Allen has known for ages. Parker is a builder and built Allen's house for him, some huge monstrosity out in the country. That got us going on the right track. Here are all Parker's birth and marriage certificates, and this is his wife's."

"Gathering information means leaving no stone unturned," Nick said for Amber's benefit.

Dan agreed and pointed to another copied birth certificate.

"That's right, which then brings us on to the Parker children, or to be precise, only child: Edward Francis Parker born in 1991. Edward Junior." He paused while searching for the right document in the mass of paper and then held it up for them to see. "Edward Junior, or Teddy to his friends, is one very interesting little boy."

The document was a page from a school year book dated 2006 and showed passport-sized photos of about twenty male youths in identical school uniforms with a few lines of script underneath. On the third row from the top under the picture of a surly looking boy with spiky black hair was written, "Teddy Parker, Cromwell House 2005–2006. Represented in cricket and hockey. Member of the National Schools Expedition to Brazil in 2006 to improve awareness in the Western World of emerging countries even though he had to overcome a fear of flying to participate."

Amber was out of her seat again. "That's him!"

Dan grinned this time. "The wonder of the Internet. Once I got the name and date of birth, social media took care of the rest and it was easy. That and the contacts with other agencies and databases registrars have these days. That picture was of him when he was fifteen at St. Patrick's private school. He was a part-time boarder even though the Parker house was less than an hour away. After St Pat's he went to Durham University but left before the end of the first year. The interesting thing about that is I could not find the reason why he left. There was a little note saying he left before the end of the year for personal reasons and that makes me suspicious. The other interesting fact is he was doing an English literature degree."

Dan waited but could see the relevance escaped father and daughter. Although he knew it was wrong given the circumstances, he was enjoying the moment. "When you told me about the night he approached you, you said he said 'a thing of beauty is a joy forever: Its loveliness increases.'"

Amber's eyes widened. "Bloody hell Dan, how did you remember that?"

"I know, he's a freak. He's always done stuff like that," Nick answered.

"It's a quotation from a famous poem by John Keats. Just the sort of thing an English literature student would know."

Dan sat back to temporarily bask in the glow of certainty and was happy to see his friend and his friend's daughter show some signs of hope and happiness at last. The moment did not last.

"That doesn't actually prove anything, does it?" Amber said quietly.

"Small steps. We know you had nothing to do with it and it's only because you happened to be there. That in itself tells us something."

"Then tell me, for God's sake."

"The daughter of a serving police officer is not the ideal candidate for setting up so whoever did it was in a hurry. Whoever did it also has the nerve to believe he or she can get away with it and has the influence in the right places to get away with it. That narrows the field down. Your experiences tell us at least one policeman is involved, but why would he need to be unless it was in his interest or he was being forced to? As far as I can see, Allen would have no reason on his own and nor would this other Detective Binder, so they must be being pressurised. The question is by who and why.

"We know Allen is associated with Edward Parker and we know Teddy is Parker's son, so there's a link and a reason. Sherlock Holmes had a saying…"

"Oh no, not bloody Sherlock Holmes again." Nick groaned in mock frustration.

Dan laughed. "Take no notice of your uneducated father, Amber. Sherlock Holmes was a great man and he said, 'When you eliminate the impossible, whatever remains, however improbable, must be the truth.' It might seem improbable at the moment, but I bet you Teddy has somehow been able to get either Allen or Binder or both to cover up him murdering Anna Rofe." Turning to Nick he added, "Show me I'm wrong!"

"See what I mean Amber? A freak!"

Amber's jaw was on the floor for the second time in as many minutes.

"You really are Dan, but I'm really glad you're our freak and no one else's. Have you thought about what we're going to do next?"

"Cowboys and Indians Amber, cowboys and Indians," he replied.

While Dan was outlining his plan to Nick and Amber, Allen was giving his own briefing about the current status of the Anna Rofe murder investigation to his after hours visitor.

"The girl Stacey Briggs gave us another statement earlier today, which locks up her entire evidence chain nicely. It also ties in with the two witnesses we found in Ketch Street who saw her in the car and the Hetherington girl with Rofe. It's a bonus we found two of them who saw them before Teddy arrived on the scene.

"The Ukrainian will say and do exactly what she's told. It's second nature to her and she wants to help as she thinks it will also help keep her in the country."

"I'm still a little concerned about Briggs."

Allen sighed. "No need. She's crapping herself. Of course, she doesn't want to believe her friend gave Rofe a wallop, but she didn't see them when they went around the corner. The thought she might be implicated in Hetherington's escape by driving her away is more than enough to outweigh her wanting to believe her friend. What else can she say anyway?"

"Okay, what about forensic evidence?"

"Thanks to Teddy trying to rip the tart's hair out, you got several strands of her distinctive hair, which were put on Hetherington's clothes at Rodway. It got bagged up by the Scenes of Crime when they attended and seized her outer clothing. That plus Hetherington's statement she never came into contact with Rofe will do fine."

"Okay. Well it seems like you have it all under control."

"I have, don't worry. I've been doing this for long enough to know all the tricks. Even her father is out of the equation now he's been sidelined. There's no one who can help her."

"Very good, James. You've done extremely well."

"Save your congratulations for someone who cares and remember why I'm doing this for you."

CHAPTER SEVEN

Martin reminded Penny of the Boy's Own comic heroes her older brothers used to try and copy in the fields around their home when they were kids.

He picked them up in a black Land Rover dressed in army fatigues and a waxed jacket any poacher or gamekeeper would be proud to sport. Martin was tall enough that his head almost touched the ceiling of the car and the ampleness of his clothing concealed his muscled physique. He spoke in clipped sentences, as if every word was rationed, and his steely grey eyes gave no indication as to what he was thinking. Penny would have felt the epitome of safe in normal circumstances, but she hadn't heard from Nick so was unable to settle.

The drive from the station to his establishment was through rugged terrain where the roads seemed to have been ripped from an alien landscape and deposited here by giants. Martin gave Penny and the twins the option of separate bedrooms, but Penny preferred the small dormitory which catered for up to ten so they could stay together.

Nick finally called just after nine.

"How's Amber?" she asked without saying hello.

"She's fine, Pen. How are you?"

"It's like Colditz here Nick. I hate that you made me leave."

"I'm trying to do what's best."

Penny could not help herself and allowed a degree of poison to enter the conversation. "Well, we have a different idea about what's best sometimes, don't we," she said, regretting her tone instantly.

Nick went quiet, she guessed he was thinking about their recent troubles over her view of his apparently domineering attitudes.

Penny tried to lighten the mood. "I can hear him outside. We have to have a serious talk about some of your friends one of these days."

"I told you it would be okay with Martin, didn't I?"

"I get the feeling he's patrolling with a machine gun," she joked, easing the tension a little more. "So, what are you up to?"

"I'll spare you some of Dan's details. The police are involved somewhere and that's why we can't go to them yet. Amber was reluctant to tell us at first but she's an amazing girl, Pen. Tomorrow we're going to try and find out a bit more about the whys and wherefores. I honestly think it will all be over in a few days."

"Okay, I suppose."

"You should try some of the facilities at Martin's place. I've never been but some of the things he told me about sound really good. Get Rosie and Vio out in the fresh air too."

"Maybe tomorrow. I can't even think about things like that right now."

"Okay love, I'll call you about this time tomorrow?"

"Just take care of Amber and yourself, Nick."

"I will. I love you Pen, give the girls our love too."

"Yes, you as well."

When Nick clicked off he handed the phone to Dan.

"Your turn; Tara. Good luck with that."

He called from the hallway. "Hi T, it's me. How are you?"

"Dan, hi. I was just wondering when you were going to call. We're okay, no new news." She sounded tired. "So tell me all about your day?"

He didn't lie but was economical with some of the facts. The name of Arthur Mountfield did not come up in the conversation but he did tell her about all the other names he Nick, and Amber came across most recently. Mountfield—even the thought of him—revolted Tara. She had learned all she wanted to know about him during Dan's dealings with Katrina Mallinder.

"Sounds like a very productive day. Are you planning something only moderately dangerous for tomorrow or ridiculously so?" she asked, trying to sound okay with what he was doing.

"Moderate tomorrow. I was right though. Allen has got his poisonous fingers in the pie somewhere along the line. It's going to be a pleasure to see him crash and burn." The split second he said it Dan knew it was a huge mistake. "What I mean is…" but it was too late.

Tara exploded just like Nick did in the pub, but without the silencer attached to her voice.

"I bloody knew it. You absolute arsehole! Dan, when are you going to learn you're not the saviour of the whole world and can't go around causing all sorts of mayhem and putting the life of yourself and others in danger to satisfy your damned desire for revenge?"

"It's got nothing to do with revenge! I didn't ask for him to be involved."

Tara was not going to be dissuaded. "Don't give me that bullshit. I bet you almost pissed yourself with pleasure when you found out. Don't you care about anybody except yourself?"

"Tara, honest, you have to believe me."

"I'll believe it when you get on a plane and come home. You have a family here to consider," she said.

Dan tried to calm the situation a little. "I know, I'm sorry. How is Jet?"

Tara's delayed response stunned him into catatonic silence. "Not Jet you prick, I'm pregnant. I was going to tell you on the day you left." She sighed. "You know there's an old saying about the thing with vengeance, when you start off on that journey you better be prepared to dig two graves. Call me tomorrow. I don't want to talk to you anymore now."

Dan was left holding the disconnected phone. Stunned he went back into the living room.

"Are you okay, Dan?" Amber asked. He surmised she and Nick must have heard Tara's volume and tenor if not the words of the conversation. It took him a full minute to regain enough of his senses to pass on the news of his impending fatherhood.

It took even longer before Dan was able to continue. Nick encouraged him to call Tara back straight away and he almost did, but ultimately decided to do as she instructed. In truth, it felt more like cowardice. There was nothing he could do right now. He was on the other side of the world and Tara wanted nothing to do with him. There was something he could do though, help Amber. When his focus returned, he had a list of jobs for all three of them.

"Tomorrow's project for you and me, Amber, is to dig into Teddy Parker's recent past and see if the direct approach might be possible. Then if there's time, go back and see Josie. Nick, you'll be doing some house-to-house and then having a look at this DI Binder. We'll leave Allen and Edward Parker until we have a bit more on the people around them. At the moment, we must assume they are the keys to this whole mess but by this time tomorrow we'll have an even better idea."

"Don't you think you should be concentrating on Tara and home? We won't hold it against you if you want to go back, you know," Nick said.

"Of course, not," Amber added. "You've helped so much already."

Dan's mind was in a whirl but he was still able to control his many thoughts. "Thanks, that means a lot. I'll talk to her again soon but in the meantime, we have a job to do."

Tara was feeling as bad as Dan. She let her annoyance dictate the way she talked to him and knew she struck a raw nerve by deliberately taking aim at his emotional weak spot. As she sat with her feet up on the coffee table tears welled up in her eyes. Jet was nowhere to be seen and she felt miserably alone. So far, the dreaded morning sickness remained a non-issue, but she was definitely recognising some changes in her mood patterns.

"Bloody hormones," she cursed, wiping away the first tear.

CHAPTER EIGHT

Instead of a usual night out in the clubs or on the streets working, Teddy Parker was spending the evening at home for once. He had been summoned to the family residence by his father. Normally, he would have chosen whether he was going to show up but tonight was one of those occasions when there really was no choice.

As his mother skated around the gleaming granite kitchen preparing something Italian with an imported cheese that cost the same as the joint of meat it was dressing, Teddy was in the lounge with Edward Sr. and a twelve-year-old single malt.

"Nice," Teddy said, holding up his crystal tumbler in a salute to his father.

Parker Sr. was unimpressed. "I talked to James Allen today. He says the investigation into the Hetherington girl is going according to plan. He didn't want to talk to me at all but in his position, he has no choice."

"I could have told you it was all cool," Teddy sneered.

"Don't be smart with me. I'm not one of your gofers, and remember your place in this house."

Teddy puffed out his chest. "I didn't ask for your help in the first place. I could have handled it."

"Keep your bloody voice down. The last thing I need is your mother giving me earache too. You handling it would probably have ended with the copper's daughter in a ditch as well as the prossie dead. I want to keep the body count down to one. This way we get shot of the one person who can put you there at the time and put enough flies in the ointment to make any investigation into you impossible even if she doesn't get convicted—all that reasonable doubt stuff."

Teddy smiled. Edward Sr. had no idea how in control of everything he was, but he was happy enough to let his father bluster on until he was good and ready to tell him. In the meantime, he would keep drinking his father's scotch and keep eating his mother's God-awful dinners when he came back to the house.

When his cell phone rang, he waved it in front of his father. "Gotta take this."

In the large black and white tiled hallway, he put it to his ear and waited. "Good work my man," he replied. Dinner just became a little more palatable.

CHAPTER NINE

The Indian summer was officially over. The next morning was cold, wet and miserable, reminding Dan of why he left England and why New Zealand felt so much like home. A bad day there was somehow better than most good days in the country of his birth.

Amber's new toughness was demonstrated at breakfast when she insisted she play her full part in "doing whatever it is we are doing."

Nick left immediately after downing double helpings of tea and toast and confirming again that Dan need not stay if he wanted to head back to Auckland. Dan remained stoic. He and Amber finished off their preparations for the day ahead and they set off for Durham an hour later. Amber drove the 120 mile trip to Durham University; it was the first step into discovering exactly who Teddy Parker was. Nick's in-car satnav made the journey stress free and they arrived well before midday.

When they walked into the main administration building in search of information about degree courses in English literature, they were no longer Dan and Amber.

Mr. Cliff Riley and his daughter Lucy were hopefully prepared for whatever might come their way. The Rileys were from Oxford, but Lucy wanted to get a little away from home as she began her adult life. Durham's English Literature reputation was among the best in the country and suited her requirements very well.

After completing enough applications and sundry documents to stock a filing cabinet, Dan and Amber as the Riley duo were keen to see the accommodation blocks. As they had come so far, they were issued with day passes and given directions by the helpful staff who hoped Lucy would enjoy her time at Durham if she was accepted into the next academic year's enrolment.

The only accommodation block they were interested in was F14 at the far end of the campus, so they drove the few minutes to get there, giving time for Amber to regather her composure after committing her first ever fraud and deception offences.

Teddy Parker had been a resident in F14 between two and a half and three and a half years before; there was a remote chance some of the current residents would have been there when he was, but they were secondary targets. It did not take them long to find a priority target cleaning the corridors and emptying the rubbish bins on the second floor.

"Hi, I was wondering if you could help us please?" Amber asked the middle-aged woman in jeans and a blue knit sweater.

"If I can darling," the cleaner replied.

She wore an ID tag on a lanyard around her neck, which gave away her name as Claudia Bennett. She looked at Amber's day pass and then Dan's.

"Let me guess, Lucy Riley, your dad wants to know if it's safe for him to send you here to live?"

Amber giggled. "Got it in one."

Claudia's mild manner was so good she could have been a United Nations ambassador. "It is mixed boys and girls, but everybody gets on. I wouldn't mind if my kids came here."

The Rileys were pleased. They chatted with Claudia for several more minutes in which time she told Lucy about the local entertainment venues and the ones to be avoided, the best fish and chip shop and where to buy good-quality second-hand reference books.

Cliff and Lucy seemed convinced and were about to leave when Lucy broached the subject of a rumour she learned from a friend who was also thinking about Durham.

"I heard about a girl a few years ago who nearly died of an overdose, and a boy who was chucked out for supplying. Is that true?"

Claudia did not blink before replying. "That was all very hush hush. I'm surprised you heard about it."

"So, it's true?" Lucy whispered.

"Don't tell anyone I told you but yes, it is. The poor love was taken to hospital and had her stomach pumped but the drugs were already well into her system. She was in intensive care for two or three days and she didn't come back here for a month. I'm actually surprised they let her back at all."

Cliff Riley appeared to be less keen on Durham as a place for his daughter to study than he had been a few minutes before.

"I don't like the sound of this Lucy," he said.

"Oh, Dad please don't be like that. What happened to the boy who gave the stuff to her?" Amber plaintively asked just as they had rehearsed it earlier.

"He left, quickly and quietly. Nobody wanted to make a fuss or for it to get into the papers and so on. I heard that his family paid the girl off not to make an official complaint and they might have even made a big donation to the university itself. I'm not saying that's right you understand, but there has never been a hint of trouble like that ever since."

When they got outside Amber was buzzing like she had taken something pharmaceutical and it was all she could do to keep a lid on her emotions until they got back to the car.

"Oh, my God that was amazing, Dan. Did you hear what she said? She just knew everything. I cannot believe how easy it was to waltz in here and, and, oh my God I think I'm going to pee myself."

Dan could see his latest protégé revelled in her role. He was pleased she came through the initiation so well, but it was important Amber did not get carried away with her maiden success.

"You were great but remember, we're still on campus. You don't know who could be watching us right now, so you have to stay focused."

It was better than telling her to calm down. He didn't want to deflate the way the poor kid was feeling after all she had been through.

"Yes of course. Stay on track," she enthused.

He looked over and patted her on the knee.

"Good fun, though wasn't it?" he said, winking.

Once they were clear of the university buildings and on the ring road following the satnav's directions for the motorway they went over the newly discovered facts.

"Surely it can't be so simple all the time?" Amber enquired.

"Definitely beginner's luck. I think I can count on the fingers of one hand the times I was able to complete all the components of a task so quickly. That's jailers and cleaners. All we need now are drivers and then we'll have the whole set."

If Dan and Amber's early success was total, then Nick's day had been a total failure so far. He too was probably breaking at least one law and most certainly contravening several police regulations by conducting house-to-house investigations in the roads around where Anna Rofe was killed, using his police ID and asking questions of residents while he was officially on compassionate leave and not permitted to be involved in operational inquiries.

Of the numerous people he talked to, none could offer any morsel of information that might assist Amber's cause. It was obvious that in this part of Nottingham the decent upstanding residents kept their thick curtains closed and did not look out at night-time, while the more degenerate members of the community had no desire to help the police, bogus or otherwise.

Detective Inspector Ben Binder had some business to attend to in Mapperley. He had finished 'interviewing' the two robbery suspects some time earlier. Having to sort out Teddy Parker's screw-ups was part of his everyday job these days and occasionally he felt it was more trouble than it was worth, but then he always considered it was worth a hell of a lot.

Flick's two morons chose the wrong man to rob and paid a heavy price; one receiving a broken nose and dislocated shoulder and the other so bruised in a certain area that he would not be welcoming his girlfriend's advances for weeks to come.

Binder had coached them both quickly and efficiently before he turned the recording tapes on to say their intention was to rough the man up a little as one of them mistook him for a rival and it quickly went very wrong; there was no intention to steal from their victim. According to the law, if there was no attempt or intent to steal then the offence of robbery could not be complete. In the end because they came off so much worse they were both given an official police caution and sent on their way. Binder was pleased to have another pair of locals more in his debt even if they were part of Flick's gang.

He was a perfect specimen of the modern police officer: articulate, big enough to command respect, attractive enough to look good in a suit or a uniform, liked by his supervisors and his subordinates.

Now as he drove along in his police issue unmarked hatchback, he ran through the current situation. Most importantly he was clean, secondly Teddy Parker was still okay, and thirdly the other interested parties were still under control even if they did not know they were. Turning into Cutter Road he nearly didn't see the man coming out of number 24, but when he did, he recognised him instantly. Binder's many skills included having an eye for names and faces, unfortunately for Nick. The instant he placed Nick's face, the father of Amber Hetherington, the man who collected his daughter from Rodway, he stamped down hard on the brake and leapt out.

"DI Binder from Nottingham Central," he said fiercely, striding up to Nick within a few yards of number 24's gate. His voice sounded like it should be followed by a flash of lightning. "What are you doing here?"

"Oh, sir, hello there," Nick said apologetically, showing his ID badge. "You have me bang to rights. It's me Nick Hetherington, Amber Hetherington's dad."

Binder was one of those people who exuded authority and although Nick was not normally prone to be nervous, being in Binder's presence made him break out in a sweat.

"I said what the bloody hell are you doing around here?" Binder replied, taken aback by Nick's guilty admission but pleased it seemed the Hetherington girl had not told him all the details of their interview.

"You know what it's like. My girl is in trouble and I want to help her. I can't sit at home all day doing nothing. My wife told me not to get involved, she said leave it to the incident team to sort it out and everything would be okay, but here I am. She'll kill me when I get home. You can understand, though can't you? Wouldn't you do the same if it was your kid?"

Binder saw the anxiety on Nick's face and had to admit, if he was a father and if it was one of his own he would want to do something about it too, but this was all too close for comfort and he needed to make sure there were no loose ends.

"I could have you locked up. You're supposed to be on leave, what do you think you're going to achieve charging around like the Lone Ranger, stepping on the investigators' toes and upsetting the locals?"

"I know, I know. You're right but try and see it from my point of view. I'm on the outside looking in here. Nobody is telling us anything. You're on the team, can't you tell me?"

Binder clenched his fists. "I'm not on the bloody investigation team. I just happened to be the duty DI on the night. I know as much about this case as you do.

"Oh, sorry I just thought…"

"No, you didn't! You did not think for one second about what you were doing and what situation you have put us both in now."

"Sorry, sir. You're dead right."

"I should put you in the car right now and… Oh, what he hell. Listen to me, you get yourself out of here and go home. When you get there, you do nothing and let the investigations team do their job. Do you understand me? If you keep your mouth shut about today, so will I."

"Yes, sir. Thanks."

Binder strode off, feeling this particular fire had been extinguished.

Nick stalked back to his car. The only good thing to come from the unfortunate meeting was that he could tick off one of the jobs Dan allocated to him: make contact with Ben Binder. He wanted out of Mapperley now to see if he could find out any more about Binder, which meant a visit to an old friend.

Des Shand was old school in every way. He had worked for police recruitment and then the complaints and discipline departments for years after completing his time in Her Majesty's Royal Navy. If Des had his way, every new recruit would be required to serve at least ten years in the armed forces before being allowed anywhere near a police uniform. Nick was a Navy man too before he joined the police and luckily for them both was Des' son's Tutor Constable when he joined the police in the early 1980s.

It was over an hour's drive out to Des' house in Penny's old runabout car and Nick had not called ahead. Fortunately, the Shands were at home.

"Nick! Get your bum in here. It's great to see you," Des near shouted when he opened the door.

A few minutes later, with one or two formalities out of the way, Nick got down to business. Though Des had retired a few years before, he was still a mine of stored information. He had not heard about Amber but seemed to take Nick's word as one hundred percent accurate.

"I need to know anything you can tell me about a DI Ben Binder and also Jim Allen, whether they have any connection to each other or to a family called Parker. Edward Parker is a fairly big builder in Nottingham and he has a shitbag of a son also called Edward, but he goes by the name of Teddy."

Des listened intently, sipping his tea as Nick spoke and nodded acknowledgement to at least some of the names.

"Right, first off I take it we're talking about James Allen *the* Det Chief Superintendent. We at discipline all liked him because he was forever trying to look after his staff." He handed Nick a pad and a pen. "You might need this. Ben Binder I know well; he transferred down from Northumbria. If he had been a footballer he would have been a multimillion-pound signing, a real golden boy. I don't think Northumbria was his first force though and he'd only been there for a short time before he came to us; he was obviously looking for promotion as fast as he could. As far as him and Allen being connected, I don't know but with Ben's eye for advancement he would be the type to ingratiate himself in with the bosses."

"Did he have any run-ins with your lot in complaints?"

"No, when I say golden I mean it. As far as I know, the sun really does shine out of his backside."

"What about the Parkers?"

"I'm sure I know the family name but that may just be because of the business being in the area. It doesn't ring any bells together with Allen or Binder. Do you think they're all in it together? I just don't see Mr. Allen like that."

"Honestly, I'm not sure. Dan and I think so but without any concrete evidence so far. Binder for sure is up to his neck with Teddy, but I'm not betting the house on all four of them quite yet."

"Talking of houses, I heard the new Allen mansion is quite something. A brand-new castle out in the sticks somewhere and you can bet your bottom dollar the formidable Mrs. A has got it just how she wants."

"Never met her but heard enough not to want to." Nick laughed.

"Dan—not your old sparring partner Dan Calder? I might have known."

"He's helping and right now I need all the help I can get."

"Now he was a regular visitor to discipline, wasn't he. He got really shafted by HQ, a bad business that should never have happened and not even Mr. Allen could dig him out. Pass on my regards. He went to Australia or New Zealand, didn't he?"

Nick was jotting notes and answered spontaneously without taking in Des' whole comment. "Yes, NZ. He's doing alright, got a training business of his own, a girlfriend and a baby on the way."

Before he left, Nick asked Des to do any more checking he could and call back as soon as possible.

"Time is of the essence. I'll owe you big time."

"Leave it with me for twenty-four hours. I'll do what I can," Des replied.

Feeling a little better, Nick headed back to Garstone.

Once home he made a call to Penny. "I wanted to talk to you without Amber being here; she and Dan have been out all day."

"I'm so worried, Nick. Martin gives me the creeps, but in a good way. I get the feeling he could and would do anything if someone turned up here. This sort of thing doesn't happen to us."

"It's for the best, Pen. Amber will want to call you later; can you just try and be as normal as possible?"

"Rose and Viola are making me crazy too," Penny said, not acknowledging Nick's request. "They know it's not a game, but you know what they're like."

"Ask Martin to get them outside for the day tomorrow. He will work them so hard all they will want to do is sleep. I'm sure they will calm down after a day or so."

"It seems wrong to be here with you there."

"We need to be able to do what we have to without me worrying about you and the girls. I told you I would keep Amber safe and I'll get you home as soon as I can. Believe me, I don't like it either."

On the way back from Durham, Dan and Amber stopped for refreshments at a service station. He wanted to explain what was going to happen when they went to Josie's.

"You will be okay because you're with me, but be careful about what you say and do. Josie is a lovely old lady, but she has got as old as she is by being ultra-careful. She's one of my best ever contacts but she would drop me like a stone if she thought any trouble was coming her way."

"Might it be better if you talk to her alone. You could drop me off at home."

"No, she's got where she has by looking after her girls all those years. When she sees you I'm hoping she will have all the same feelings again, which will be to our advantage."

"Oh, I see, so you want to use me to get more info," she said light-heartedly.

"Amber, don't think I won't do whatever I have to. It's not a game despite the fun we've had this morning. Sorry, but that is the reality."

She was not upset; the reality check did her good and she finished her coffee in silence before they hit the road again.

"Dahlings," Josie cooed, ushering Dan and Amber inside. She was dressed in a long silk dressing gown and mule slippers covered in pink fur but still had her elegant grey hair made up in a style as if she was ready for a night at the opera or theatre. She held a palm-sized Bible, which she laid gently on the hall table to leave both hands free.

"My sweet Lord isn't she gorgeous? Look at her skin, flawless," she said, touching Amber's cheek as they moved into the lounge of the large Victorian house. Amber found her instantly likeable.

"Thanks for seeing us again," Dan said.

"Anything for you Daniel my sweet, and you too," she said, looking at Amber and aimlessly thumbing a small silver cross and chain around her neck.

"I really appreciate it."

"Amber, is it? A beautiful name. Daniel told me all about you and of course I still keep my ear to the ground. I can see you could no more harm poor Anna than you could hurt a fly."

"I'm sorry Josie, but we haven't got time for small talk today," Dan said.

"Quite so, Daniel. Let me see what I have for you." Josie rearranged her robe. "You got me thinking yesterday. Once the really young girls started arriving on the streets the pimps and dealers were not far behind. Within a year, the whole of Mapperley was overrun with greasy men in cheap suits trying to sign the girls up and then get them onto powder and pills. I knew then my time and style of service were on borrowed time. A quick, cheap liaison is much more preferable these days."

"Is this going anywhere Josie?"

"Patience, Daniel, the scene must be set. Just when I thought things could not get any worse a knight in shining armour appeared. I thought you were the only understanding policeman until Mr. Binder arrived."

Dan and Amber both stared but Josie hushed them before they could speak.

"Or so it seemed at first. He was a new detective in the area and in no time at all he cleared away virtually all the pimps and pushers by locking them up. It was obvious to us then, somebody must have been helping him, but I imagine his superiors would not have cared a jot seeing the results. Whatever he did worked because they did not come back. Most of the girls stayed, even the ones who were on stuff before and they always got their needs met; it only occurred to me yesterday when we were talking. I made a call when you left. I bet you can't guess who is left to be the one and only supplier to all the girls now?"

"Teddy Parker."

"Got it in one, Daniel. I think young master Teddy must be very lucky indeed if the good Mr. Binder has not been able to sweep him away with the others."

Amber was still listening with rapt attention, but she was unable to contain herself any longer. "Unless they're partners in crime. Binder clears the way for Teddy to be the only dealer and they share the profits."

"So, young. So innocent and naïve." Josie sighed. "Yes, sweet thing. Yes, yes, yes."

"Dad, you won't believe what sort of day we've had," Amber said before they were even properly inside the house. Nick and Dan exchanged a look in which they shared a whole conversation.

"Come on then, you tell me your news first and then I'll tell you mine, good and bad," Nick said.

The takeaway of choice tonight was pizza. Nobody felt like cooking nor would have the time even if they did.

"I can see why you cops could end up like elephants," Amber commented between mouthfuls.

The dinner time debrief confirmed facts and answered questions. A timeline emerged from when Teddy was at Durham University until now. There were still more gaps in it than entries, but it was a whole lot more than they knew at the start of the day and gave them fresh impetus for what lay ahead.

Nick ran over the salient points one final time before they focused their attention on what they needed to accomplish next.

"Teddy Parker supplies a dodgy pill to a fellow student and it all goes horribly wrong for everybody. In the aftermath, his father comes to the rescue, paying off the girl and the university to keep his son out of the crap and Teddy returns to Nottingham.

"Soon after that he's back to his old tricks courtesy of Ben Binder who clears the way for him to be the main man in Mapperley. The obvious conclusion is for their mutual financial gain. Chances are, old man Parker is aware and may also be involved, but we don't know that Allen is.

"Allen is connected to Binder by way of the Rofe investigation. Binder spoke to Amber and Allen is leading it, but we can't connect Allen to the Parkers, apart from the house. Is that it?"

"I think so," Amber replied. "It doesn't actually sound like much now."

Dan finished chewing on a pizza crust.

"Well we still have to hear back from Josie and Des again, so you never know. I'm feeling it is all there for us to discover, we just have to keep looking in the right places. Let's talk about tomorrow. Nick, are we compromised by your meeting with Binder today?"

"No, I don't think so. He was glad Amber appeared to have kept quiet because I didn't mention how he threatened her or tried to tear his heart out. Believe me, I wanted to."

"Plus, we now know he isn't actually on the investigation team unless he lied to you about that, Dad," Amber added.

"True, he's got a bloody lot of nerve."

"Good. I think we really need to see how much Allen is involved with the others. He's the one driving the police investigation and until we know one way or another we can't risk going to them and making allegations about a conspiracy. I've been giving it some thought," Dan stated.

Before he could let them into what those thoughts were exactly the home telephone rang. Dan's heart fluttered as he imagined Tara on the line. Nick answered and immediately raised his hand for their attention and silence. For two minutes, he kept his hand in the air and said nothing. When he finally spoke, he sounded shocked.

"Des, you are a beautiful man. Give my love to Brenda. We'll have a proper catch up when this is all over. Take care and thanks again." He hung up. "Hold on to your horses, have I got news for you," he triumphed, playfully pulling Amber's hair.

Dan grinned. "Allen, Binder, or the Parkers?"

Nick grinned straight back. "Two outa three ain't bad but a full house is even better."

Once a degree of calm diluted the excitement, Nick told them the latest.

"Des has really come through for us. It seems that Ben Binder was somewhere else before Northumbria. County Durham!"

"No way!" Amber cheered.

"Oh yes, he was there for the first five years of his service and was a detective constable in Durham when Teddy Parker was poisoning students. But it gets better. In 2005 Teddy got into a scrape at school and kicked a younger boy's head in. That sounds quite nasty, but he was only cautioned by the police for it. If police procedure was then as it is now, the local head of CID would have the final say on prosecution for an assault like that. St. Patrick's School is in Delta Division's area and Jim Allen was head of Delta CID in 2005."

Dan took up Nick's line of thinking. "There are no coincidences in our work, Amber. If Binder was there, I'll bet you anything he was there in Durham when the deal was done for Teddy not to be prosecuted."

Nick said what they were all thinking. "It would be a perfect way for them to get introduced and to have a history when Binder came to Nottingham. It would only be a matter of time before Binder became linked to Teddy here again and probably Allen, too. Shit attracts maggots!"

Amber grinned. "So, by my reckoning that now links all four of them together in one way or another. I don't know what you were thinking of for tomorrow Dan, but you may need to reassess it already, but before you do any of that, don't you think you should call Tara? I'm going to call Mum."

Dan's other current situation came into sharp relief.

An hour later he was sat at Nick's computer still waiting for Tara to come online. When she did he punched the Skype call button immediately so as not to have time to back out. Tara answered immediately.

"Hi, thanks for answering," Dan said.

She looked tired. Even though it was only 8:30 a.m. in Auckland, it was still well after her regular wake up time on a work day.

"Hi."

"Tara, I don't know where to start."

"Pick a place."

"If you ask me to come home now, I will. I wish you told me about the baby before I left."

Tara viewed him with suspicion. "Would it have made a difference to you, Dan?"

"Maybe."

"Well at least that's an honest answer. If you had said yes I might not have believed you; if you said no, I would have hated you. Well, maybe I could have told you differently too. I was waiting for just the right time and then on the day I was going to, you took off."

"Tara, I'm so sorry, please forgive me. I wish I was different and I know I'm hell to live with."

She almost smiled. "Jet misses you. He's turned traitor on me."

"See, men, we are all hopeless."

"It was a surprise for me as well you know. We've never really talked about it and we did take precautions. How do you feel?"

"Honestly? Shell-shocked. I've never thought about us being parents. You will be fantastic but with my age and everything, what about me?"

"What about your age? You keep telling me how young you feel inside. I'm sure you'll still be able to teach him or her how to swim. Are you happy about the prospect? That's all that matters."

"I could not be more so."

Tara peered into the screen. "Really?"

"Really." He drew a cross over his heart with a finger.

Tara smiled properly for the first time and the invisible layer of ice on the monitor screen thawed a little. "What am I going to do with you, Calder? I suppose I will just have to keep working on you until I get you right."

"It could be a lifetime sentence."

"Don't remind me or I might change my mind."

"So, please tell me about our new addition?"

Tara explained she missed occasional periods in the past and did not think anything of it, but two was unheard of. After missing two consecutively, she went to see her GP and within a few minutes the pregnancy was confirmed.

Dan was shocked. "So just how many weeks are you?"

"Eleven now, nearly twelve."

"That's three months!"

"Congratulations on your maths. He or she is due around the second week of April. What do you think?"

"It's amazing, wonderful. I love you so much, are you okay? I wish I was there."

Tara was happier, that was plain to see but Dan's last comment tested her belief. "Do you really? Don't bullshit me Dan, what's happening there?"

Crunch time, he thought. "If I could spend every minute of every day with you for the rest of my life I'd never be unhappy. Having said that, what is going on here is almost beyond belief."

She listened intently as Dan took time telling her how the last few days had brought a series of events that tested even his imagination.

"Amber must have been absolutely terrified, in fact all of them," she said when he took a breather.

"She was, but she reminds me of you in the way she's faced up to it all."

"When will you go to the police, that is, someone you can trust in the police?"

"That's the million dollar question; as soon as we can."

They talked for another hour until both were back on an even keel with each other again.

"You have to see this through," she stated before they finished.

"Yes." It was a calm and determined response she heard many times before. She could feel the sense of cause in him and it was a reply which filled her with trepidation.

"I'm going to have a few days away with Shelley; I'm treating her to a mid-week spa and want to break the baby news to her. Did you know they've been trying too? Let me call you when we get back okay?"

"I'm always okay if you are. Say hi to Shelley and Paul from me."

CHAPTER TEN

Teddy met Flick inside the snooker club at 11:00 p.m. to discuss business, but in the confines of the club, time did not matter. They could talk safely whilst playing pool as most tables were empty and all the other patrons knew better than to look like they were interested in Teddy's business. Their ad hoc meeting followed the usual format. Flick handed over a large amount of cash in respect of recent jobs his boys completed, Teddy then gave him details of vulnerable residential and retail premises he should be looking to target next—the information coming from Ben Binder. Finally Flick updated Teddy with other current news or "tha word from the herd" as he put it.

Flick was the self-appointed leader of his gang. They spent their days hanging around on street corners, intimidating local children for small change and dabbling in petty crime with mixed results, until the day Teddy introduced himself into the group. When he began feeding them with information, their professionalism and success expanded overnight. Flick's leadership solidified, as did the gang's reputation.

Flick viewed the relationship as a lucrative partnership. Teddy viewed it for what it really was: a cheap and efficient way for him to command the area around Mapperley while insulating himself from threats and competition with an army of tame thugs. The financial rewards were a pleasant bonus. Business grew steadily over the following two years.

Flick did not know how Teddy got his information about which big houses would be left empty by holidaying occupants, or stores where the alarms would be off overnight for maintenance. All he knew was he and Teddy were tight and he was Teddy's lieutenant. Ironically, Teddy also thought he was in a partnership with Detective Inspector Ben Binder. They were both wrong.

"Ma boys walked outa the police station free and clear," Flick said as they discussed the botched robbery. "Your detective man friend do just like you said, huh?"

Teddy intervened when the two members of Flick's gang were locked up, asking Binder to sort it out as a favour to a friend.

"I look after my own. You remember to tell them, too. It's a favour I will call in one day," Teddy said, nailing the four in a corner pocket.

Flick grinned, flashing a jewelled tooth in his lower jaw. "It's all good."

Teddy slammed his cue down on the table.

"No! It's not fucking good if you can't control your boys and they get themselves noticed by being arrested. Next time they can rot their arses off in there."

Flick hopped on the spot at the sudden outburst, making his gold chains rattle. "Sure thing, Teddy."

"That's the difference between me and all your homeboys Flick. I have a brain and I use it for more than ordering different flavour pizza. 'One man that has a mind and knows it can always beat ten men who haven't and don't.' George Bernard Shaw."

Flick's bewildered look proved to Teddy how right he was. The meeting was over.

CHAPTER ELEVEN

Amber slept in the following morning; it was a rare and comparatively restful night with her only waking up once. Dan and Nick were at the breakfast table when she came down. They had finished eating some time before and were in heavy discussion about the previous day's findings and today's action plan. They were running out of time; Amber was supposed to be reporting back to the police station in five days and while they knew a lot, they did not know enough.

"Morning love, did you sleep? You were talking to Mum for ages last night," Nick said.

She kissed him on the cheek. "Yes thanks. You know what she's like. Is there any tea left?"

Dan shifted the teapot in her direction. "You're looking better."

"Morning, Dan. What have we got on the agenda today?"

"We were just discussing that. I need to know if you feel like a bit of surveillance training. Nothing too heavy but it would help if you wanted to. Dad's okay with it but only if you are."

"Definitely!"

The transformation from trembling and downcast to bold and resurgent in the space of two days was astonishing. This morning her fresh, natural complexion was back.

The night before when Amber called her mother on her cell phone before bed, she made Penny cry again but this time with sheer joy and relief, and that made Amber cry, too. With what they had accomplished already, she could see a way forward.

With their positive results, she felt her personality strengthening, if not already fully restored.

For the rest of the morning Dan worked with her on a fast-paced one-to-one, the subjects being perimeter security and log keeping, while Nick went into Nottingham with a shopping list of items they needed for later.

At 12:45 p.m. they broke for a snack, which Amber volunteered to make. While she was in the kitchen Dan remained at his laptop in the lounge but could not help himself thinking about her transformation over the last few days. She had only been out of the room for a minute when he heard the sound of a car door closing out on the road. He looked out of the window and his blood ran cold. The partly hidden figure coming towards the house was unmistakable. He jumped up and went to the kitchen door. Sticking his head around it he said, "Amber stay here, not a sound. Do you understand?"

"What is it?"

"Police. Not a word, okay."

Amber acknowledged him, but he was gone before she finished the sentence.

Dan got to the door as it was knocked from the other side and for once he had no idea about what was going to happen as he opened it.

The piggy eyes and thin lips were just as he remembered.

"Well well, Dan Calder."

"Jim." Dan chose the greeting deliberately to antagonise.

"At first I didn't believe it when I heard you were back, but here you are," Allen said tightly. "Aren't you going to ask me in?"

"No."

"I see your manners have not improved over time."

"Your pet paedophile obviously told you I was in Garstone, but how did you know I was here?"

"Who? What?" Allen said, clearly confused. "It doesn't take a lot of working out to know where to come. Your oldest and dearest friend, and let's face it, there aren't many others to choose from, is in trouble."

Dan's skin prickled. "So, you are a detective after all. You fooled me for so long."

"What are you doing here, Calder?"

"I'm sure Mountfield has already filled you in on that."

Allen sniffed. "No idea what you're talking about and you haven't answered my question."

"Arrest me if you want me to answer anything."

"What makes you think I have any interest in you anyway? You're old news. Are the family home?"

"No. Why don't you go back to where you came from? It will be better for everybody."

Allen's neck reddened slightly, and it was not lost on Dan.

"Be careful, Calder, you're a civilian now."

"Is that a threat? Oh please God, tell me that was a threat." Dan's eyes flashed with a determined fire as his rage rose too.

Allen hesitated. "I need to talk to Nick Hetherington. If he's here, that means now."

"I told you he's not. I'm sure you can find his mobile number so call him and make an appointment."

"I hear you're quite the star in New Zealand." Allen's sudden change of tack took Dan by surprise, his mouth opened to reply but nothing came out. "A word to the wise. You might be a big fish in that little pool but here you are just fish food. If I were you, I'd go back to the little pool as soon as I could."

"More threats. When did you become the mafia king of Nottingham?"

"Just some friendly advice. Tell Nick I called to see him and tell him to get in touch or I will be coming back to arrest him next time. Interfering with an investigation is a serious matter."

Dan instantly compared risk against reward in following the line Allen just introduced.

"How can you live with yourself, look at yourself in the mirror every day without wanting to puke? Amber Hetherington is no more guilty of killing that girl than I am, and Nick is only doing what any caring father would do. If you did your job properly, Nick wouldn't have to do it for you."

Allen's neck changed to puce and Dan leant forward to drive home his point.

"If you still haven't worked out she's innocent then get someone on the job who is more capable than you or your trained monkeys. If you know she didn't do it, then there must be something in it for you and you have a shit load of trouble coming your way. I'll say hi to you from Nick, you say hello to the Parkers from me."

Dan switched all his senses into overdrive in order to memorise every part of Allen's reaction. It would all come together and be over in the blink of an eye, therefore, he knew not to blink. What Allen said would only be a small part of what he was actually communicating.

They were almost nose to nose; Allen wavered first. "I'm warning you. Watch what you do and watch what you say. Get him to call me." With that Allen was gone, spinning on the heels of his black Oxford brogues and heading purposefully towards the gate and out of sight. Dan watched, still soaking it all in.

"Got you, you slippery bastard."

"Dan?"

He jumped and turned around. "Amber! You scared me."

"I doubt that very much. What did he want?"

"He said to see your dad but I'm sure he came around for a lot more than that."

"I heard what you said about getting him. What is that all about?"

"Come on, I'll tell you. Have you ever heard about NVCs before?"

The earlier lessons were put on hold and for the next hour Dan told Amber all about the concepts of fear and non-verbal communication.

"What is fear?" He asked it like a professor in front of an eager class.

Amber shrugged.

"It's not being afraid of someone or something. Fear is a chemically induced chain reaction which starts in the brain and cannot be prevented, faked, hidden or deliberately brought on. When we experience fear it's with all our senses. Your mouth goes dry, your heart races or you get goosebumps."

She nodded.

"If you open all your own senses to someone else you can read them like a book."

"Is that what you did with me the first day you came?"

"I'm sorry to say it was, not in a bad way though, if you can understand."

"No, it's alright. I knew you were doing something, but I couldn't tell what or how. So, you just gave Mr. Allen the once over, did you?"

"Yes, so to speak. Some people are easier than others."

"What was he easy or hard?"

"He's always been easy."

She leaned forward grinning. "So, tell me."

"I don't know how much you overheard but I mentioned the Parkers to him and I also insulted his police skills. I told him if he already knew you were innocent and had something to hide, he better watch out. I wanted to provoke him."

"No shit! I would love to have seen his face."

Registering her excitement, surprise and almost arousal all at the same time, Dan grabbed her by both arms. "Exactly Amber!" he exclaimed.

"My God, you are a genius."

"You have to be really switched on, you know, be ready to see, hear and feel it all in three seconds, sometimes less."

"So, what did he say?"

"He warned me off getting involved and said for your dad to contact him."

"And what did he really say to you?" Amber was an exceptional student.

Dan grinned at her, allowing them both to feel the momentary pleasure of knowing what someone does not want you to know.

"When I said that to him the neck around his collar went bright red and the big vein pumping blood to and from his brain swelled. At the same time his eyes dilated, which is an involuntary reflex action and a symptom of what's called fight-or-flight."

"Meaning what?"

"Meaning I confronted him with something he didn't know whether to challenge or run away from. His blinking patterns changed and I could tell he wanted to dismiss any knowledge of your innocence but could not bring himself to challenge me on it. Did you notice his clenched fists as he walked away?"

"No," Amber replied.

"Well that was the last sign. He was enraged by me suggesting he's not capable, and even more so when I mentioned the name Parker. At that moment, he caught the breath in his mouth and then he started to breathe much faster to compensate. The fact I knew the name Parker and inferred I knew there was some dodgy link between them scared the pants off him, meaning obviously, there is a dodgy link. There was more but I can see you get the idea."

Amber was amazed. "More. How can you possibly see all that in a second or two, let alone more?"

"Not just seeing. Remember what I said, use all your senses. It takes practice and maybe a bit of natural ability too, but if you can allow yourself to listen to his change in breathing, almost feel the change in his body temperature—did you notice I leaned forward when I challenged him?"

"No, I missed that."

"He probably thought it was to scare him, but I needed to be that close to hear and feel him too. I swear to you Amber, sometimes you can taste and smell it as well."

Dan went back to his laptop, mulling over the confrontation with Allen but could not help a smile at Amber's reaction to their impromptu lesson. Hers was the opposite to Tara, who would tell him off for seemingly reading her mind. He would not to tell her about Allen's visit next time they spoke.

As he tapped the keys he was struck by another thought, more like an acknowledgement of something else that passed between them during Allen's brief visit. It made no sense, but he could not shake the feeling that Allen felt sorry for him.

Tara and Shelley stayed at a country park house on Auckland's North Shore. It still felt weird but also nice using her brother's inheritance to indulge herself and friends with a night out or a day or two away every now and then.

"Please don't be too angry with me Shel', I know you guys have been trying for ages," she said over dinner the first night.

"I'm not angry, you idiot, jealous definitely. I should have guessed when you wanted sparkling water instead of wine when we arrived." Shelley held up her wine glass. "Congratulations, here's to you, Dan and your baby. What does Dan think?"

"He's still bewildered. I wish he was here, but you know what he's like."

"Mm I do. It sounds pretty horrible what he has got himself involved in again."

Tara nodded. "I know but from Amber's point of view, who would you want helping out if anything like that happened to you?"

"Dan absolutely. How long do you think he will be away for?"

"A week or two."

"Right. Until he's back, I'm in charge," Shelley said. "I am going to be godmother after all."

Nick returned halfway through the afternoon loaded with supplies as Dan and Amber were finishing their improvised training day. He was keen to know how the lessons went but they had much more to tell him.

During a moment alone, Nick and Dan discussed Allen's unexpected visit and decided to test his resolve by Nick not calling back.

"Let's see if he has got the balls to try and lock me up. Somehow I doubt it," Nick said. "Are we still on for tonight?"

"If you're okay with it. What about Amber?"

"How was she today?"

"Good. I'd trust her."

"Okay then. I'll ask her if she wants to come with us," Nick said, rising from his seat.

When her father floated the idea of some night-time surveillance work, Amber jumped at the opportunity.

"I thought you'd say that. Here, try these on for size." He smiled, throwing her a bag containing articles from his shopping expedition.

Amber turned the bag upside down allowing the contents to fall out. Five minutes later she was stomping up and down the hallway in her new heavy-duty cargo pants, polar fleece top, beanie, and assault boots, all in black.

"This is so cool, Dad."

"Just remember two things: it's not a game and do not tell your mum."

Amber could not keep the grin off her face and even though he knew better, he could not prevent a smile either.

"And here was me thinking black wasn't your colour!" He chuckled.

At 10:30 p.m. they left the house. Beneath coloured topcoats they were all similarly dressed in their new black garb. Dan insisted on a briefing before committing to the operation and between him and Nick emphasising the security measures above all else, Amber was ready for the night ahead. In years past the two friends would have been wearing covert radio packs and earpieces; tonight, thanks to the wonders of modern telecommunications, they were all equipped with new pre-pay mobile phones with conference call facilities and hands-free earpieces. Their amazement at the quality of reception during a ten minute test was only matched by Amber's incredulity.

"Welcome to the twenty-first century," she teased.

"It will probably take the best part of an hour to get out to Allen's house. We'll have to park up and walk the last bit," Nick said, repeating part of the briefing. "Tell me again what you do when we get there?"

Although they'd been over the plan a number of times before she understood why Nick was asking and replied in a focused and sombre voice.

"I will become the driver and log keeper for the time you are away from the car. I will wait for your comms test before moving away to the agreed pickup point. If for whatever reason it is not safe, I will go to the reserve pickup point and report my position to you. If you call I will make a written record of your observations and also note any vehicle or persons' activity I see. If I do not hear from you at any time within a ten minute period I will conduct a comms check. If you do not respond to two consecutive checks I will leave and go straight home and then call you again." She hesitated and Nick looked at her encouragingly. "If you don't respond to the call from home, I call Mum."

"Good girl. What else, Amber?"

"If I am compromised I go home and call you."

"Okay, how are you feeling?"

"Nervous now for the first time to be honest."

Dan quickly looked over his shoulder. "That's good, nervous means you'll be careful. Anything else and we would probably be going back home."

They spent the rest of the journey failing to find adequate small talk to fill the silent minutes and preparing themselves for what was to come.

When they arrived at the drop-off location there was nothing else to say. Nick gave Amber a peck on the cheek. "See you soon."

He and Dan took their compact black backpacks from the boot and once on, checked each other's fastenings. Nick then produced a small tin and smeared some of the black contents across his face before handing the tin to Dan.

"It is a Bruce Willis movie," Amber said nervously.

When they were ready the trio completed a final comms check before Dan and Nick moved off into the still night. Amber peered after them but they were invisible within a few seconds; in the countryside, the lack of artificial lighting took a little getting used to. A minute passed, followed by another during which Amber toyed nervously with her pen-torch, another purchase made by Nick. Finally, she received her first proper transmission from Dan.

"Amber from Dan, all okay here."

She sighed loudly and allowed herself to relax just a fraction.

"Dan from Amber, loud and clear; likewise, here," she replied, breathing deeply.

"We have the house in sight; the front of the house is north facing, there are lights on in the entrance and in the hallway only."

"Got that." She wrote Dan's comments down with her pen-torch in a new A4 exercise book.

Dan continued along the public footpath to the north of the Allen residence, scanning the area ahead for potential hazards, and occasionally behind to be sure they were not being monitored. Five steps behind, Nick duplicated his friend's actions. Conversation was minimal; they already knew what their objectives were, and both trusted the other's ability to react as necessary to any situation.

When they reached the drystone wall that formed a boundary around the Allen premises they stopped to assess and complete their second, and final equipment check. Once over the wall they were officially breaking the law. Their behaviour up to this point was criminal but difficult to prove, but once they were in the Allen garden, all the ingredients were present for them to go to prison for up to ten years if they were caught and convicted.

"Ready?" Dan asked.

"Ready," Nick replied before pausing. He grabbed Dan's elbow, stopping him in his tracks. "You don't have to do this, we've done some crazy shit in the past but that was always the job and we were the good guys. This will be so far over the line that the line won't even be a dot in the distance behind us."

Dan took a deep breath of cold night air. "Freddie Mercury once said that if a thing is worth doing, it's worth over doing."

"I don't think he had something like this in mind," Nick said with his hand still vice-like on his friend's arm.

Dan looked down at the gloved hand at his elbow and smiled grimly.

"Amber is more than reason enough."

Nick relaxed his grip and flexed both hands. "Okay, let's do this."

For as long as Dan knew Allen the latter always took his wife to play bridge at the Garstone and District Bridge Club every

Thursday evening. Dan was prepared to bet that ritual was still in place even though years had passed since he'd last been called on to provide the Garstone CID taxi service to drive them back from the club at 12:30 a.m.

The plan was simple: gain access, look for evidence linking Allen with the Parkers and Ben Binder, look for evidence relating to Amber's investigation and look for anything else that incriminated any of them or may otherwise be useful. The last part provided a very wide spectrum indeed.

If there was anybody at home, the break-in would be aborted. If an alarm was activated they would synchronise watches and spend exactly three minutes inside before making a swift withdrawal. They previously calculated the time for a police or private security company patrol car to reach the house from the nearest main road.

"Amber from Dan, we are approaching the house. Entry in two minutes."

"Got that. All okay here."

When they reached the walls of the house, Dan peeled off left and Nick went to the right, checking windows for any insecurity and also for persons within. Thirty seconds later, they passed each other at the rear of the house, continuing on without acknowledging each other, meeting up at the front door a further half-minute later.

"Looks empty; kitchen door," Nick said quietly.

"Agreed."

The kitchen door was a stable type, being in two upper and lower sections which could be opened separately or together. It was situated at the far back right of the house; the kitchen appeared to lead to a large mainly open-plan ground floor. When they got there Dan took off his backpack and removed a small sledgehammer with a dense, rubber head. Nick called Amber.

"Amber from Nick. Entry in ten seconds."

"Got that. All okay here."

Dan took careful aim at the spot midway between the mortice lock of the lower door and where he imagined the bolt to be on the inside securing the lower part to the upper. The temptation to be quiet was always there, to be gentle and not make a sound. But experience proved one effective strike was far better than several tentative ones.

Dan and Nick ignored the slam of the lower stable door against the inside wall, listening instead for the sounds of disturbed occupants or the telltale beep of an alarm system activating. They waited for thirty seconds without moving a muscle but when they did it was with efficient precision.

"Entry gained," Dan said.

"Got that. All okay here," Amber said.

She would activate her stop watch now. Five minutes to get in, get what they needed, and get out.

"No alarm," Nick said with some surprise, then "study," indicating his target.

"Bedroom," Dan replied, heading for the impressive oak stairway.

Nick found the study just off the main living area. The room was clearly a space for Allen's use: photos, certificates, and magazines on flowers and shrubs were all he required to know he had found his destination. He swung his backpack off and removed two large black rubbish sacks, which he'd previously reinforced with sticky tape.

"From Amber, one minute."

"From Dan, got that."

"From Nick, got that."

The desk drawers were locked but as they were more decorative than functional they opened easily with the help of a jemmy bar. Not bothering to see what the drawers contained, he emptied all the contents into a rubbish sack; it would be far easier to go through everything in a safe location than make a search of it all now. He then went to the bookcase and quickly removed anything from the shelves and lower cupboards that was not a book or ornament.

"From Amber, two minutes."

Nick waited for Dan's reply and then made his own. Scanning the room, he decided there was only one more thing to be collected. At the desk, he deliberately removed all the cables from the keyboard, monitor and printer before sliding under the desk where the hard drive unit was. He responded to Amber's three minute call before he had completed the task of carefully bagging up the hard drive, including all the cables, into the second rubbish sack.

Amber was calling the fourth check by the time he was back at the smashed kitchen door. The temptation to go and search elsewhere was great, but his training made him sit and wait for Dan's return.

Dan found the main bedroom but not before wasting valuable seconds in two others. What proved to be guest bedrooms were so sumptuous they would not have been out of place in a top-end hotel; it was only the empty wardrobes and bare en suites that gave them away. The genuine article was no less impressive, with a modern four-poster bed and matching furniture being the main features. It was tastefully finished with excellent quality bed linen, heavy silk curtains and a huge ornate mirror opposite a large flat-screen TV.

The walk-in wardrobe housed enough hanging and drawer space to accommodate a small theatre company and was also equipped with all the necessary appliances to fit out a ladies' hairdressers. Dan copied Nick in removing two prepared plastic sacks from his backpack, then went to work on the drawers in the wardrobe. Starting with the lowest first because it saved having to close them again while still being able to see into the next one above, he opened them all. Every non-item of clothing, including jewellery boxes, photographs, letters and other documents were removed and put in a sack.

When Amber called in with her three minute transmission he knew he was not going to be able to complete a full search of the bedroom suite. The one thing he was desperately hoping either he or Nick would find was a safe; whether they would be able to get into it or physically take it was another matter entirely. He decided to finish the wardrobe and do the best he could in the bedroom proper.

"From Amber, four minutes."

He had just finished in the wardrobe and was tying a knot in one part-filled sack.

"From Dan, got that," he said, scanning the bedroom.

There was no sign of a safe, so he went to the bedside table nearest the door. Studies showed the majority of men sleep on the side of the bed closest to the bedroom door, a trait dating back to prehistoric ancestors guarding the cave entrance and in his experience of searching houses it proved to be correct. As he emptied the contents of the drawer and the small cupboard space below into his second sack, he took a moment to thank whichever branch of science it was that conducted studies of people's sleeping habits. He was on the stairs again, descending when Amber called in her final transmission.

"From Dan, got that," he replied without breaking his stride.

When he got to the kitchen Nick was crouched by the broken door, his backpack in place and holding a knotted plastic sack in each hand.

"You're late," he said.

"Your bloody clown boots, I feel like I'm wearing diver's flippers," Dan replied.

The purchase had been deliberate. With both pairs the same size 13, they would confuse police investigators as to how many burglars there were.

Nick sniggered. "It's not my fault you have ballerina's feet. Ready?"

"Yes, let's get out of here."

Nick disappeared through the opening and Dan quickly followed. They carefully started making their way back to Amber on a reverse route.

Amber spent the few seconds since her last time check looking in all directions for any sign of activity, but it was as quiet and still as it had been when they arrived. Only nineteen minutes had passed since she last saw her father and Dan, however it felt like hours. She was ready for the next transmission when Dan's voice came over the phone.

"Amber from Dan, we have exited. Are you still clear?"

"Got that. All okay here," she said, hoping it would be the last time.

She checked her book and saw it took them eleven minutes from the time they left her until they got to the house so she started another eleven minute time check, the end of which would precipitate her putting her top coat back on and starting the car's engine. At nine minutes and twenty-five seconds, Nick and Dan appeared causing her to abort her clock watching and gun the engine.

After depositing their sacks and backpacks in the boot, Dan got into the front passenger seat and Nick the rear.

"Home, slowly and carefully," Nick said, resting a big hand on her left shoulder. "You did great, really great."

Dan and Nick were quiet and contemplative for several minutes; in that time, they both used moisturised tissues to clean the camouflage make-up off their faces, putting the dirty tissues in another small plastic bag to be disposed of later. It was vital there would be no clues, not a single shred of evidence to connect them to the break-in.

Amber found it impossible to remain quiet; within a minute she wanted to talk and find out everything that happened in the house.

She pouted when Nick said, "Not now, I know it's hard, but we do our debrief when we are safe. Concentrate on the road, keep looking in your mirrors and watch your speed."

Another excruciating minute later she looked across at Dan. He appeared almost serene, his eyes were closed but the eyelids were fluttering.

"Hey Dan, are you okay?"

Nick answered. "Don't worry, he's just going over in his mind what we did. It's his way of making sure he remembers every single second. If you ask him in a week's time he'll be able to go through it in so much detail it will blow you away. It did me, many times."

When Dan emerged from his semi-trance ten minutes later, Amber was just turning on to the main road back to Nottingham.

"Thanks for tonight Amber," he said, smiling broadly.

"Thanks to me for what! It's you two who have put yourselves in danger for me."

"I meant thanks for the way you did your part. I know your dad will say the same, but I felt very safe with you on the radio, I mean phone. We are only as good as all the team working together and you didn't get stressed. All the time checks were concise and accurate, we knew how we were doing inside all the time because of what you did in the car. When we get home we'll debrief it all, including how you did and what we could have done to make it better."

"Gosh thanks. Can I ask one thing though? If when they get home and discover the burglary, do you think they could come to our house? I was just wondering how safe it would be to take all the stuff back there."

Dan looked over his shoulder at Nick.

"She's got a point. Allen's not the sharpest but he might fluke it and put two and two together," Nick said. "It might be better to go somewhere else?"

Dan thought for a second. "You're both right, but we don't want to be out if they do come to visit because then we will have to explain where we all were late at night. Let me take you home now and I'll take the stuff somewhere safe until we have the time to examine it properly tomorrow."

"Where will you go?" asked Amber.

"The perfect place and somewhere they would never think to look."

At Nick's house, father and daughter quickly changed and handed their black clothes to Dan. It was 12:40 a.m.

"If Allen is still true to form, he won't be home for another forty-five minutes or so, I should be back by then. If anything happens and I can't get back, I'll call. If you need to tell me to stay away, call me. See you soon."

He backed out of the driveway and set off.

"Where's he going?" Amber asked.

Nick put his arm around her shoulder. "I really have no idea. Come on, I need a drink."

As they relaxed in the safety of familiar surroundings, Amber was keen to know what happened inside the house and what Nick and Dan found.

"Sorry, that has to wait. I recorded the local news and a documentary from earlier this evening. We need to watch them now just to cover ourselves. If we do get questioned, we can say we were home all night. Dan will have his cover ready too."

While Nick and Amber caught up their TV viewing, Dan got to his destination.

The street lamps showered the roads with jaundiced light, making Mapperley feel menacing and taking him back in time to a night when his life was changed forever. As with the day before, he could not bring himself to drive anywhere close to Powton Road, therefore, ten minutes later than was necessary, he was finally able to sit back in the comfortable sofa cradling a large brandy, relieved that he was welcome even at such a late hour.

"You were the only person I knew with secure storage and would still be up at this time. It won't be for long. The police will never think to come knocking here."

"What are friends for, Daniel?" Josie smiled benevolently.

Mr. and Mrs. Allen arrived home a little earlier than usual to discover their new home the target of burglars. After screaming obscenities at the absent thieves and then berating himself rather than his wife, for not setting the alarm, Allen called 999 and reported the matter, demanding the immediate attendance of the duty sergeant for the area and also the night-duty scenes of crime officer.

He had a long and painful night ahead of him, waiting for the police investigators to arrive and complete their work. When he discovered the extent of the burglars' haul, first in his study and then from his bedside table, he became wracked with concern. While he was sure there was nothing among the stolen items that could harm his career, the loss of personal possessions and paperwork including bills, bank statements, house contracts and purchase details, not to mention all the emails and documents on his computer, would cause him significant hardship. Thankfully the thieves had not discovered the floor safe in the downstairs coat room where much more sensitive documents were stored. *Small miracles,* he thought.

Dan did not get back to Nick's until 2:00 a.m. He knew they would still be awake as their night's work was not finished.

"Sorry it took so long. Josie loves to talk."

"Josie!" Nick and Amber said together.

"The best hiding place in the country for our ill-gotten gains. We can go over tomorrow, that is, later today, to look at it properly."

"Okay debrief time. I'll do a big pot of coffee and we can get down to it." Nick yawned.

Amber stretched too. "Finally."

CHAPTER TWELVE

Friday morning was a write off for Dan, Nick and Amber. The debrief kept them talking until 5:00 a.m. during which time Amber made copious notes of everything relevant. They all went to bed exhausted but satisfied, agreeing to set their alarms and meet again for brunch at noon.

Penny received the text from Nick when she got up for breakfast saying he would call her at lunchtime. She gritted her teeth and stared at her phone. Not knowing what was happening back home made her feel helpless as only a mother could.

Martin had been as good as Nick's word; in the last two days Rose and Viola learned to quad bike, climb up and down mountains and how to catch and cook wild rabbit. However, she'd stayed behind both days and today was no different.

"So, what have you got planned today?" she asked at the big breakfast table.

"Treasure hunt," Martin said in his usual way of only stating the minimum required.

Viola spoke between mouthfuls of toast. "Something called the Winthrop search technique. It's used by the army. Please come, it'll be fun."

Rose tried to convince Penny too, but with a more diplomatic approach.

"It's not helping for you to sit around and worry about what's going on at home, Mum. Please come, otherwise we'll be worried about you all day long, as well as Dad and Amber."

"Plenty of room in the Land Rover," Martin added, still concentrating on his porridge.

"No. No thank you, they're going to call at lunchtime, so I want to be here for that. You can tell me all about it when you get back."

Martin rubbed a gnarled hand over his chin and looked directly at Penny.

"I'm not a great family man at the best of times, living out here all on my own with the dogs, but I know Nick a little and he would not have asked you to come here if he didn't think it was for the best."

Penny and the twins were taken aback; it was the most their host had spoken in one go since they first met him. When he continued they all looked at him in stunned silence.

"Let him do what he has to. I'll make sure nothing happens to you here. His friend Dan sounds like a good guy too. Being able to focus on their task knowing you are not worrying too much goes hand in hand. I remember when I was active, it helped knowing my missus was getting on with her day-to-day life back home."

"You're married? Rose said, voicing all their surprise.

"I was. She died," Martin said as he started to gather the empty bowls and plates.

"Do you have any other family around?" Rose asked again.

As he got up from the table Martin looked out of the kitchen window onto the wild landscape he made his home.

"No, they are all gone now," he said, leaving his guests to wonder about how many and what he meant by "all gone."

Penny joined him at the sink and started to fill it with hot water. When she looked at him his faraway look was one she felt she should not intrude on. They did the dishes in silence and when the last of the bowls and plates were dried and put away in the overhead cupboards he'd made from locally cut pine, his more usual steely bearing was back in situ.

"If it's okay, I might come with you tomorrow," Penny said, offering him a supportive smile.

When Martin and the twins left a short time later, Penny watched them disappear around the muddy corner before going back to her book, which she left on the chair right next to the phone.

Allen was in his office before 9:00 a.m. and in a foul mood after being necessarily awake until the early hours. The scenes of crime officer's initial report made for bleak hearing.

"No favourable looking prints. There are some black fibres on the outside of the kitchen door and a number of footprints through the house, but they look like new boots. They have a very clean pattern with no apparent wear. Judging by the number of them, I'd say he must have been there quite a while. Sorry Boss, but it doesn't look hopeful."

"He."

"Yes, size twelve or thirteens, maybe bigger."

Allen cancelled the morning's appointments. Having woken in a sweat before 7:00 a.m. with a recurring thought of there being something terribly wrong about the burglary but unable to pinpoint exactly what, he hoped the office environment would cast some light in the dark corners of his mind. The best he could come up with after a cup of strong tea was the sense it was him personally, rather than the house, which was targeted, however there was no real evidence to support the notion. Nevertheless, even after a second cup he could not shake the thought until he was forced to by the ringing telephone.

"Good morning, Allen speaking."

"Good morning James. I heard about the break-in at your house last night. That's bad luck."

Of all the voices he wanted to hear at this precise moment, Ben Binder's was the very last.

"What do you want? I have a lot on this morning and a burglary at my house does not make life any easier."

Binder's reply sounded indignant but at the same time it could also have been thinly disguised pleasure. "I only wanted to see if there was anything I could do. I've got lots of contacts, as you know. What sort of stuff did they take?"

"All the usual; Gwen's jewellery from our closet, personal papers, the contents of my night table and study desk, and also my computer hard drive. I suppose they ran out of time or available free hands to take the keyboard and monitor too."

"I hope you didn't lose anything too sensitive."

"Don't be so fucking stupid. I'm not some wet behind the ears PC who takes files home and then puts them in his wife's knicker drawer. They didn't find my safe and there was nothing else incriminating, even on the computer. If you want to do something useful, find the bastard who did it!"

"I'll do my best of course," Binder replied. "Now what about the other matter?"

Allen snarled at the apparent dismissal. "It's not a problem. The Hetherington girl is still in the frame, no other witnesses to suggest otherwise, not that it matters. She will never see a court room if I have my way, let alone be convicted, but all that matters is your boy won't either."

"Alright then, keep me informed and I'll see you early next week at the meeting."

Allen winced at the thought of having to share more time with him.

"Till then."

He put the phone down without saying goodbye and leant forward, resting his head in his steepled hands to resume his earlier musings. Suddenly he sat bolt upright. Before the call, some details of the burglary did not add up; now perhaps they did. He quickly entered his login details on the computer and searched for the burglary on the internal system; it would have been entered by the constable who came to his house and added to by Scenes of Crime by now. The details of the job instantly appeared on the screen and he read through it all slowly and carefully.

Approach through the garden as electric gates were locked, no signs of a vehicle being used. Entry to the house by forcing the lower section of the kitchen door. Tidy search of multiple rooms. Exit as entry. Departure as approach.

The list of stolen property was extensive.

He next went to the scenes of crime report and gave it his equally intensive attention.

Similar footprints at point of approach and entry later located within premises. Fibre traces at point of entry close to damage and marks consistent with heavy object used to break through door. Smudge marks at point of entry and later in areas searched by offender consistent with rubber or latex gloves. No other marks to assist. Items sent for analysis.

It all appeared to be clean and professional, as if it was a well-planned and executed offence. That meant the burglar either knew the house belonged to him or chose it because of its isolated location and impressive appearance.

If he was known to be the owner, it either did not put the burglar off or was the reason for the break-in. When he returned to the list of stolen property, his unease increased tenfold.

Apart from his wife's jewels, everything else was his, and as her jewellery was in their shared wardrobe, the offender could have easily believed that the contents belonged to him in the haste of searching through cupboards and drawers.

The more he looked and considered the facts the more they seemed to say the same thing. With that in mind, the theft of the hard drive became much more ominous.

There could not possibly have been a lone offender; the amount of property taken would have required at least two people to carry it all out of the garden and away.

Two offenders with the same size feet—possible but not likely. Much more likely was that they were simply extremely clever. Beads of sweat appeared on his creased brow. *Why would very clever thieves want to steal my personal property at this time? What were they looking for and did they find it?*

Anna Rofe was the only significant concern in his work or personal life. "It can't be?" he said involuntarily.

At 1.00 p.m. Dan, Nick and Amber drove over to Mapperley to see Josie once more. She showed them through to a little-used back room of her grand house and left them to it.

With a fresh set of supermarket rubber gloves each they emptied all the bags first and separated the items to be disposed. That included all their clothing and bags from the previous night and the obviously useless articles of stolen property. The potentially useful and obviously useful were put to one side. Dan rinsed everything to be disposed of in a bucket of diluted bleach to destroy any forensic evidence and then put it all into one of the black sacks, which was in turn put inside another to prevent leaks.

They spread the remaining items on the large mahogany table which dominated the room.

"Let's start with the easy stuff," Nick said, shuffling a stack of paper. He shared it out and then said to Amber, "Anything which is to do with you, Anna Rofe, Binder, Parker father and son, or Allen's work."

It did not take long to see there was nothing suspicious in Amber's pile and her initial enthusiasm dulled. "In all the excitement, I suppose I forgot he's a policeman and hardly likely to leave clues laying about the house."

Dan offered support. "Hey, come on, it's only been a few minutes, you never know." He was looking at the purchase contracts Allen had for his house. The A4 sheets were stapled together in order, starting with drawings, quotes and planning applications, followed by more detailed architect's drawings, materials and specifications lists. They looked professionally presented and many of them were on Edward Parker's company letterhead.

"Alright for some," he said, tossing the documents to Nick. "Superintendent's pay must be good these days."

Nick caught the pack and skimmed through the pages, checking out the long list of materials, fixtures and fittings the Allen house was designed to include.

"How much do you think it cost? To you and me it's a case of if-you-have-to-ask-you-can't-afford-it," Nick joked, forgetting about Dan and Tara's combined wealth.

Amber was now looking at some of Allen's bank statements, which dated back several years. "Maybe. According to this it looks like he paid a twenty percent deposit of sixty-five thousand in 2015. How much is our house worth, Dad?"

"About one hundred and eighty. Sorry Amber, we won't be moving out to the countryside anytime soon."

Dan laughed. "You should move out with me. With the exchange rate, you could afford a mansion."

The remainder of the papers offered no assistance and supported Amber's earlier prediction. Dan did not want to say but he too was starting to feel the mission had been a wasted one. What they selected to save and examine was a small percentage of what they took, and it did not take long before the hard drive was the only thing left.

"Do you know anyone who could do something with this?" Dan asked.

"A few people at uni, but I take it that's too risky?" Amber said.

Nick was equally pessimistic. "Not off the top of my head. Do you think Josie might have that sort of contact?"

"Good idea, I'll ask."

They sat back, their optimism from an hour ago very much reduced. Nick gave Amber a fatherly glance. "Hey, don't worry, we'll sort this out. We might not have a three-quarters of a million pound house with oil-rubbed chandeliers, but at least we ruined his week."

She could only offer a weak smile in return and dejectedly answered, "Three, two, five."

Nick paid no attention to the strange remark and it took Dan several seconds before he thought to comment. "What was that, Amber?"

"What? Oh three, two, five. Three hundred and twenty-five thousand. That's how much his house was, not seven hundred and fifty."

Nick stared at the hard drive as if that would make it come to life and provide the answers they were looking for. Dan felt a familiar rush, the sensation he got when he knew he was on to something.

"No, a house like that must be worth at least six or seven hundred thousand."

"I can work out simple maths, you know. He paid a twenty percent deposit of sixty-five, therefore the total cost must be three, two, five."

Dan was stunned. Nick looked up, now completely disinterested in the hard drive.

"Amber, you are a genius," Dan crowed. "I could kiss you."

"I'm going to," Nick chimed, in picking her up and swinging her around by the waist before planting a great kiss on her flushed cheek.

"What? What have I done?" she asked once her feet were on the floor again.

Nick grabbed the documents again and started looking through for the bank statements and house purchase details. When he found them, he laid them on the table.

Dan explained. "You are absolutely right with your numbers and we were right about the price of a house like that. It was a show home from top to bottom, made from the best stone and materials. So, the question is…" He let his comment hang, so she could take the glory of answering.

"How did he only pay three hundred and twenty-five thousand for a house worth two to three times as much?" she exclaimed.

The explosion of mutual self-congratulations was over in a few seconds, replaced by quick fire comments and suggestions.

"What does it mean?" Amber asked.

"It means something is not right," Nick answered.

"And if it's not right then it's wrong. Over half a million pounds wrong and we are going to find out why," Dan added.

"Do you think it has anything to do with Anna Rofe?"

"Small steps Amber, small steps."

Nick was more forthcoming. "Allen's got a deal with Parker for the house. Parker's son is supplying Anna with drugs. One good turn deserves, another don't you think?"

As soon as they separated all the sheets and placed them evenly across the table, Nick stood back a little to look. Amber followed her father's lead and also stood back, passively watching and waiting.

Dan's eyes flicked from page to page, his mind wandered back in time to visualise the scenes. At the building plot prior to construction, at the Parker offices and lawyers' meetings, at Allen's bank and at the various home furnishing stores or builders' merchants. Just as he could remember every detail of the burglary he and Nick committed, so he could also construct a new one about Amber's arrest, Allen, Binder, the Parkers, and now the house-build project from the information before him as if it was a movie screenplay.

When Amber could no longer contain herself, she whispered to Nick, "What's he doing? That freaky stuff you mentioned before?"

Without taking his eyes off his partner he replied, "Yes, but the best part is yet to come."

Dan's meditation continued for another minute or so until he allowed a broad smile to crack his face.

"Oh, you are going to love this, my friends."

Allen stayed in his office all morning going over and over the crime report, desperately hoping to work out what his burglar's real intention was. Once he was finally sure there was nothing in the stolen property, including his computer, that could incriminate him, he allowed himself a little cheer, but it did not last.

Although he could not be sure Dan Calder was involved—and there was not a scrap of evidence to indicate he was—the nauseating feeling in the pit of his stomach refused to go away.

Dan needed fresh paper to detail his conclusions. As always, the clean page acted like sheet music to a composer. He talked as he wrote.

"Tell me if I go wrong. At some point in the past, Allen decides to build himself a new house out in the countryside, somewhere befitting a man of his rank and standing. No doubt Mrs. Allen has a lot to say about it too, which accounts for all the baths. Allen's old and good friend Edward Parker offers his services and a price which is too good to be true and the deal is struck. Of course, for the money he's paying he knows the house cannot possibly be built to the standard he wants unless the materials are less than cost price, and where does a crooked builder find those?"

"Stolen from other building sites or suppliers," Nick stated.

"So, when Amber is set up in a hurry, the fact you are on a squad investigating crimes like that is overlooked at first. Then they realise they need to get you out of the way, hence the real reason to offer compassionate leave." Dan tapped the pen against his pad. "Okay, that was jumping ahead a bit; what are the chances Parker uses that as leverage to get Teddy off the hook when the time comes? Allen is looking at instant dismissal and maybe a criminal charge, but what choice does he have? Amber is in the right place at the right time so far as they are concerned. Allen decides to run the inquiry so he can lead the tasking just enough to have seemingly good evidence against her and control any links to Parker and therefore protect himself."

Nick nodded his understanding. "Bastard," he growled.

"We believe Teddy is the killer and we know he and Binder are connected to each other and likely to be engaged in crime together, so we have Binder's incentive to have someone else take the fall for Anna's death too."

With no warning, Amber slumped to the floor like a puppet with cut strings. Nick was by her side in a heartbeat, stroking her hair. Dan cursed himself. He had been so intent on demonstrating the facts that he neglected to consider the effect it could have on Amber. He offered Nick an apologetic look, which was smiled away.

"I'll get Josie to make some more tea," he said.

As he left them he completed as much of the remaining puzzle in his head as he could, leaving one or two big questions and a plan forming to answer them.

Josie was in the kitchen and Dan was surprised to see she was not alone. A young woman, clearly a prostitute by her clothes and demeanour, sat at the table with a cigarette in one hand and a china cup in the other. She looked at Dan as he entered, summing him up as quickly as he did her.

"Sorry Josie, I didn't realise you had company."

"Oh, Daniel come on in. Estelle dropped by a few minutes ago for a chat. Estelle, this is an old friend."

"Hi, pleased to meet you," Dan said, trying to seem friendly.

"Yeah. Likewise," Estelle replied, taking a huge drag on her cigarette and sounding like Dan's attempt at friendly failed miserably.

Josie smiled broadly. "Estelle works nearby and visits from time to time. She's hoping to go back to college in January. We share an interest in theology so always have lots to talk about. I have high hopes for you, don't I?"

Josie's young friend immediately relaxed and took on a whole new persona, resembling any one of Nick's daughters and a million other young women. The image was made slightly absurd with her cropped pink T shirt, red PVC miniskirt, and matching knee-length boots. Dan wondered about her history and the resemblance between her and another young woman from his past, but did not dwell on the subject.

"What are you studying?" he asked.

Estelle rubbed at a smudge on her skirt. "Politics, economics and philosophy," she said as if she were reading a shopping list.

Dan was taken aback. "Sounds interesting and impressive. What are you hoping to do in the future?"

She looked at Josie first, then quizzically at Dan as if working out if he was actually interested or just being an arsehole. Apparently satisfied, her voice became stronger.

"I'd really like to do something with the diplomatic services, but local government is probably more realistic at the moment."

"Estelle has a younger sister to look after which is how she finds herself in her current position," Josie offered as further explanation.

Dan noticed her blushing slightly at the obvious compliment. He was going to say something about sacrifice and loyalty but changed his mind as it may have sounded insincere. Instead, he asked if he could make some coffee. Josie got up to make it before Dan had a chance.

"Thanks. Can I ask you something? Both of you actually."

"Of course, Daniel."

"If I wanted to see some of the girls waiting for punters and also Teddy Parker doing his rounds, where would be the best place to go?"

Estelle looked wary again until Josie calmed her anxiety.

"Daniel is trying to find out what really happened to Anna. The girl the police are talking to is a friend's daughter and Daniel wants to find who really killed her."

"Is she alright?" Estelle asked. "Your friend's girl."

"As she can be." Dan wanted to ask Estelle if she knew or had heard anything but decided against it; Josie would tell him in any event.

"Powton Road. There are a dozen girls along there and all of them are crackheads. Teddy fixes them all up."

Dan cursed his past and his luck with a resigned smile.

"Perfect," he said. "Josie, I hate to ask but I need some more of your particular help. Before I leave, remind me to give you my mobile number."

CHAPTER THIRTEEN

Wary of spending too long at Josie's house, Nick suggested they all return home soon after Amber recovered. Being home again would be good for her, and he and Dan would be able to work on new ideas.

As soon as they were indoors, and a bit later than he had intended, Nick called Penny and the girls, but only got his wife.

"What the hell time do you call this?"

"Pen I'm sorry; my times are all over the place today."

"That doesn't help me, I've been going out of my mind." She sobbed.

"Oh please don't cry. I'm sorry I fucked up; it won't happen again."

"Yeah right, until next time."

"I am sorry," Nick repeated slowly.

The following minutes were painful for them both; their family's dire situation continued to cast a black shadow across every aspect of their lives.

Penny had intended asking him a few questions about Martin's past but as soon as they started to talk all her attention was fully aimed towards Amber once more.

Nick eventually changed subject. "What are the girls up to?"

"They're doing something called Winthrop searching and they have been gone all day."

"Winthrop searching, excellent," Nick replied.

"I heard Martin telling them about it before they set off. A soldier thought of a way to search based on landmarks because the enemy was hiding explosives and things in remote countryside locations. They only use word of mouth to pass on the locations."

"That's it. No maps necessary."

"Martin's used it for team building exercises and he's got the girls on a treasure hunt," Penny continued.

"You should have gone Pen, it sounds like fun."

He felt Penny bristle again, like static electricity on the other end of the line.

"How can you talk about having fun at a time like this? You don't understand how hard it is for me being sent away from Amber when she needs me most."

"I'm sorry, Pen. That was a bad choice of words. I'm just trying to do what's best for us all. You must believe me, she knows how much you love her wherever you are. The fact is, the police are involved in some sort of cover up like we thought, so you're definitely safer where you are."

"Oh my God, how can this be happening?" she moaned.

"I know, we're only just getting our heads around it too but if I know Dan, it won't be long until all the pieces fit together and as soon as they do it will be sorted, and you can come home."

Penny was silent for a moment. Nick thought he heard another sob, but he might have imagined it. "Okay," she said. "Okay, I have to trust you."

"I love you," Nick said.

"Okay. I have to go now."

She clicked off, leaving Nick alone with his thoughts.

After a frozen fish and home-made chips dinner, Dan called home. Today marked their longest time spent apart since they formally got together, and he missed Tara terribly.

Tara described the events of the previous two days; she and Shelley spent a self-satisfying and pampered time at the spa where they allowed themselves to be waited on hand and foot. He listened with enough interest to keep up with what she was saying, but his attention was elsewhere. He asked how she was feeling baby-wise, and forced himself to focus on her reply.

"Normal I suppose. No sickness which is good, but my hormones are a bit up and down. I thought I felt it move yesterday but nothing since so maybe it was nothing. I'm not getting any bigger either so although I know I am, there's nothing to see."

"When is the next doctor's or hospital appointment?"

"I'm going back in two weeks."

"So, we can go together then?"

"If you're back?" she said. Dan caught the question in her tone, and a hint of doubt or accusation.

"Hey, I'll be back by the end of next week. The weather here is starting to bleach me and I swear the sky feels lower here than in New Zealand. I'm such an idiot, why didn't I think what I was saying the other night?"

"Just being you as usual," Tara replied.

"And now I'm going to be a father! God help the poor little thing, what chance has it got?"

She giggled. "Dan, you're just being you. On the subject of the weather, you're one of those Poms who hasn't become completely acclimatised yet, aren't you? Your glasses are so rosy coloured, you never even moan about the traffic or the weather."

He laughed with her. "And you're one of those typical Kiwis. Any more than ten minutes is a long journey and waiting for two minutes in a queue is a major hold-up. I can't wait to come home again. Do you want to know the sex of the baby?"

"I don't mind. I'm not too old-fashioned that I must let it be a surprise, but there are some advantages to knowing. What about you?"

"Whatever you want. You know me, if someone knows something then I want to know it too."

She laughed again. "I can see you conducting surveillance in the hospital to find out. Perhaps it would be easier for us all to know. What would you prefer, boy or girl?"

"It might be cliché, but it really doesn't matter so long as you and it are okay."

"I miss you. I wish you were here now." Tara sighed.

"I miss you as well. It won't be long, I promise."

"What's your next move?"

"I was thinking about the people involved. I know Allen of course, but the others are unknown quantities to me. I can't see him being the brains behind something like this. He's a useless investigator and makes up for it by being a scheming shit, which is how he's got as far in the job as he has, I'm sure, but he isn't the type to come up with a criminal master plan. He doesn't have the imagination for it."

Dan's scathing opinion came from the heart as well as experience. He had only worked directly under Allen on one major investigation, the one that led to him leaving the police.

"That means one of two things: he is either not the leader and I need to be looking at one of the other three, or all four of them are not as connected as we think they might be."

"Do you want to tell me how you're going to sort it all out?" Tara asked.

"That depends on whether Nick and Amber want to come out to play again."

"I've heard that line before. Does Nick know what you have planned for them?"

"Not yet. I have to work out the details myself first, but it may mean I won't be able to call tomorrow night."

"Just so long as you take care of yourself. It's not just me you need to look after now."

Dan swallowed. He hadn't thought of it like that. "Wow, yeah. You're right. I will, and I can't wait to see you again."

After saying goodbye, Dan switched his attention back to Amber's situation. He took out his A4 notebook and turned to a new sheet. For once he hesitated in starting; he knew what must be done and where that meant going. The desire to help Amber tugged as hard on him as his wish there could be an alternative, but he knew there was none. With a sigh and a sick feeling in the pit of his stomach he began with a list of things he needed for the exercise in Powton Road, Mapperley.

Flick was waiting on a phone call from Teddy. He and a select band of his most trusted serfs were sat in a mid-size delivery truck close to the Garstone South Retail and Trading Park, one of several similar shopping and manufacturing estates which seemed to be the flavour of the present time and sprouted from the ground at regular intervals.

"How much longer we gotta sit here?" Marley Johns asked. "It's as hot as hell in this tin can."

Flick was impatient too, but Marley's constant whining was a greater cause for annoyance.

"Well if you so damn foolish as to wear a leather tracksuit when you know what we doing, then you can sit and sweat! Just do it quietly."

Twins, Ellis (Zig) and Alton (Zag) Bowers sniggered and fist bumped each other while Marley sat back and sulked even more.

"This is top of the range man, you know I ain't lyin'. I didn't know we be stuck here for this long," Marley said.

Flick threw him an, I told you once and I'm not going to tell you again look, which had the intended effect and then glanced at the blank screen of his Nokia for the second time in a minute. The other occupant of the van was the only white member of the group. Kevin Prentiss was Flick's fall guy for every occasion. Everyone else knew it too, except Prentiss himself who thought he must be the coolest kid in the area for being a part of Flick's gang. He was slightly learning impaired, not enough for his struggling parents to get any state help, yet certainly enough to allow himself to be led on and taken advantage of. In the event of any trouble, Kevin Prentiss would be the sacrificial lamb. It had happened once before when a rival gang gave him a beating after he and Flick ventured onto their turf on a scouting mission for another criminal matter. Flick left him to fight them off alone, stating he was going to get help. Even the fractured eye socket, mouthful of broken teeth, and apathy of his colleagues failed to register his true worth within the group.

The van's stereo continued to push out a heavy bass soundtrack to accompany the rap lyrics of America's latest dissatisfied star while Zig and Zag mouthed along to the words like a karaoke mirror image. Their enjoyment only added to Marley's brooding. He looked like he was about to say something when Flick's phone finally screamed into life.

He answered in a whisper, paused, said "okay" once…twice… then ended the call, putting his phone back in his shirt pocket. He turned to face his crew who were all looking on expectantly like sheepdogs awaiting their master's call.

"The Wine Seller on Bennett Road. They got a delivery today of the best champagne, vodka and brandy. That's all we goin' for. Right?"

"Right," Prentiss replied enthusiastically.

"Maybe there be some other stuff just for us?" Zag suggested.

"Mm, bound to be. What you say Flick?" Zig added.

"I said champagne, vodka and brandy. We are the best because you do what I tell you. You even pick up a can of beer and you be pickin' yourself up with two broken legs. You got it this time?"

"Got it," Prentiss replied again with equal fervour.

Flick caught Marley's sly grin as Zig and Zag shrank back.

"Okay then, I'll drive around the back. There is no alarm tonight because the electricity is going to be turned off at midnight for some routine maintenance in the street. It would cause the alarm to activate when it does. You take down the fire door with the sledge and you got two minutes inside. I'll show you which boxes."

Flick did not bother to ask for any questions. He started the engine and moved off.

"Champagne, vodka, brandy. Champagne, vodka, brandy," Prentiss repeated over and over again.

Ben Binder was working late at home. The latest legislation changes needed to be committed to memory before the next round of promotion boards. His converted warehouse apartment close to Nottingham city centre was bathed in soft mood lighting but he also had the bright anglepoise lamp on over his desk to make reading and note taking easy. The CD changer selected another album and he leant back in his leather chair considering his current position.

As the Area Retailers Liaison Officer, he was the point of contact for shop and business owners in the district to direct questions and queries to; it was proving to be a priceless tool for forwarding his grand plan. His call to Teddy Parker about The Wine Seller would undoubtedly be leading to another high-value burglary being committed soon. Only a few more similar incidents needed to take place between now and the next round of force promotions and he would be ready to act.

DI at thirty with Nottingham at my feet, he thought. James Allen was under control, Teddy Parker was at present maintaining his usefulness too, even if he did have to clear up after him from time to time, and his hoodlum friends were committing the crimes he wanted them to. When the time came to dish the dirt on Allen he would be held up as a beacon of police morality in a time when anti-corruption was still a priority for the Home Office super-bosses. Around the same time, he would also single handedly crack the series of high profile burglaries that had been the blight of the force for two years, and if that was not enough, also rid Mapperley of the biggest drugs dealer left in the area and finally clear the streets of all remaining prostitutes. All that as a DI. The particular authority a police officer endowed took hold of Ben Binder early in his career; the greater the rank the more addictive that power. Control over subordinates and suspects, respect and admiration of victims and others in high positions, whatever the field. The ability to determine the lives of others in order to get ahead consumed him now.

They will be falling over themselves to promote me, not just once but all the way. Imagine what I can do as the Chief Constable or better yet, Commissioner in London.

The vodka and the brandy were still conveniently in their boxes; only the champagne had been partly unpacked and placed out on display. Their distinctive gold foil-covered corks made them easily identifiable and despite Flick's team's earlier dissent, once inside they acted with admirable speed and professionalism, forming a chain gang and managing to load the thirty-six cases into the van in well under the designated two minutes. In less than four minutes from the time Marley caved in the fire door with a single blow, they were driving back along Bennett Road and on their way to the gang's headquarters, or Flick's Uncle Herbert's house in every day terms.

"So, what do you think?" Dan asked, closing his pad.

Nick was mostly quiet through Dan's proposal and Amber had been completely silent.

"I don't like it one bit. For one thing, I don't know if I can get to you quickly enough if you get into strife, and I do really question the need for it in the first place," Nick said.

"If you stay on the one-way system Amber got stuck on, you can just keep going around and around," Dan said, trying to sound more certain than he was.

"And that means I can be as close as a few seconds from Powton Road, which is fine, or up to three, maybe even four minutes away, which is not a good scenario if you are getting your head kicked in."

Amber spoke for the first time. "I can always help but I agree with Dad. Is it necessary at all?"

"We need to get more on Teddy Parker. Where better than the place he feels most safe? From what Josie and Estelle told me it's almost certain he will be around at some point to deal to the girls there, and if we can get that, we can use it. Also, we might just find the other girl Amber spoke to before she met Anna and you never know, she might be able to help too. Josie has even found a house close by to assist."

Nick was not convinced. "Sorry, but I still think the risks are too great."

"Have you got another idea?"

"How about trying to get what you need from the father?" Amber asked.

"That's too unreliable and also I think it would be harder to get close to him than Teddy anyway. Try and think what it is we need to achieve and the most direct way of doing it."

"Okay," Nick said. "Say we do it. How can we minimise the risks?"

Dan nodded. "Minimise exposure, maximise escape routes, increase backup plans."

"How, how and how?" Nick said blankly; he was not making this easy for his old partner.

"I used to do test purchasing in the area."

Even as he said it Dan could feel his mouth getting dry. It was all too close to home, too close to Zoe, but he couldn't see any other options.

Amber's expression showed she needed clarification.

"Test purchasing is where an undercover police officer goes and buys drugs to obtain evidence about dealers and premises,"

Dan said. "Sometimes they use hidden mics and cameras, and marked money too. There are lots of derelict houses and doorways for me to sit in and I know how to blend in."

"And what about me? I don't like the thought of driving around in circles all day long. There's nowhere to stop and any number of problems could arise," Nick continued in his most non-committal voice.

"How about you and Amber swap around every few hours? When you're in the car you can be in a position to get to me ASAP, and if you're in the OP you can extract me if the need arises. Both scenarios Amber is on the phone to the local police and stays clear of the street.

Nick's opposition began to waver. "First sign of real trouble and you bail out. First unwanted police contact, you bail out. Any hint of the OP being compromised or the driver not being able to continue… you bail out. This is not a discussion."

Dan knew better than to argue. "Agreed."

Nick was not finished. "Amber, you have to be one hundred percent up for this as well; it's not going to be easy, especially driving around the one-way system for hours at a time. Do you think you can manage?"

"I'm prepared to give it a go. I take it, it means using the phones and log book again?"

"Yes, same sort of thing except a lot less talk from me," Dan said. "When you are in the OP you will be relaying information to Dad."

"That means looking out for any trouble and calling me in to help at the first sign, as well as making sure you are not seen watching Dan out the window for long periods of time," Nick added severely. "This is serious stuff now, Amber."

Her look confirmed her readiness to take part. He gave his daughter a peck on the cheek and raised a submissive palm. "Tomorrow then from 5:00 p.m. We better get some sleep because there's going to be a lot to do to get ready in the morning."

"I'll need to borrow some of your old clothes," Dan said to Nick. "I'll put them out in the garden tonight and hopefully they will be alright to use tomorrow. Can you get me a pillow and a blanket and leave them in the conservatory?"

Amber looked at her father who smiled with a knowledge she did not understand.

"I know, don't ask, right?" she said.

Nick found some of the things he wore for do-it-yourself jobs around the house before he and Amber went upstairs. Dan chose a pair of once-black now ten-shades-of-grey jeans and an argyle sweater which looked like it had lost a fight with a big dog. He added the pair of his own well used running shoes to complete the ensemble and went outside where he threw them all in a puddle on the driveway and stomped them in. When he was satisfied with the look, he took them to the back garden and arranged them on the patio table so they could dry without losing any of the appearance he wanted them to keep.

He then went to the compost bin and stripped down to his boxer shorts. Grabbing a handful from the middle of the large container he rubbed the stinking mulch into his hair and then over his limbs until he felt miserably authentic. It was going to be an uncomfortable night's sleep in the conservatory.

CHAPTER FOURTEEN

"What on earth is that terrible smell?" Amber groaned as she came down the stairs the next morning.

"That will be Dan getting into the swing of things for later on," Nick answered as if it was the most natural thing in the world.

"Oh my God, what's he done to himself?"

"You should see him when he gets back."

"Well if he smells this bad when he's not here I don't want to when he is!"

Nick laughed out loud. "He's one of a kind that's for sure. He slept in some of my old clothes or put them on first thing, and has been playing in the compost heap in the garden. Now he's gone for a short run to complete the look. He won't be long."

"And he's going to stay like that all day?"

"He's very dedicated."

When Dan did return to the house, Amber didn't recognise the man she had seen a thousand times while growing up. His change in appearance was astonishing, from the uniform of the street-dwelling homeless to the lank hair and dirty worn-down fingernails. He even appeared to have hollowed out cheeks and eye sockets. He must have used make-up, it couldn't all have been dirt.

His cheery smile belied his appearance, causing Amber to smile back in wonder.

"Morning, Amber. What do you think?"

"Unbelievable."

"Yes, I always wanted to be in the theatre. So, you reckon I'll pass for a homeless alcoholic?"

"Homeless for the last ten years," she confirmed. "Now if you don't mind, I need to get upwind of you."

Dan seemed happy despite his appearance. "Well I guess it's just you and me for a while then, partner," he said to Nick.

"Oh, lucky me. Come on let's get to it."

While Amber went for a shower, Dan and Nick began discussing the details of what they wanted to achieve and how they were going to go about it.

Allen was heading up the latest and hopefully last briefing regarding the investigation of Anna Rofe's death. Amber Hetherington was due back at the station to answer her bail in four days' time and he did not want to re-bail her again. The sooner this whole matter could be concluded, the very much happier he would be.

His team had tapered down to just three officers. Other cases called for the manpower and his case was winding down anyway. As far as his team was concerned, they had the inquiry all but sewn up. For the first time in his career he was pleased with the lack of numbers. He didn't mind coming in on a Saturday morning either, as the thought of washing his wife's car and then the house windows was not high on his list of pleasant domestic chores.

"Chris, go," he said to his second in command, indicating for him to proceed.

Detective Sergeant Chris Sperry cleared his throat. "Just a few loose ends to tie up before Hetherington comes back on Tuesday next week. We have sufficient evidence to put her at the scene at the time of Rofe's death, forensics matched a hair from her clothes to one of the deceased's and we have a statement from the Ukrainian prostitute, Korlenka. That's the one piece I'm not so happy with. I know none of us here took her statement or have spoken to her, for that matter, but her evidence is poor. It lacks substance and she lacks credibility. She's our only real witness to the confrontation between Rofe and Hetherington; it would be nice to have some corroboration but that doesn't seem to be likely now as all the house-to-house enquiries have drawn a blank, other than the two who saw Hetherington probably in the minutes before the incident.

"Rofe has no known connection to Amber Hetherington, the Hetherington family or anybody Hetherington is associated to. I can't find a motive."

"Dean, how far have you got with Hetherington's background?" Allen asked.

Detective Constable Dean White looked glum. "A complete zero. Amber Hetherington is as clean and white as fresh snow. She has had no involvement with the police at any time in her life. Her dad is in the job, as we know. She's currently studying at university. Medical examiner's report shows no sign of her being in a fight earlier that night; her hands were unmarked and the rings she was wearing are not compatible with the marks on Rofe's head and body. If it wasn't for the evidence of Vera Korlenka, I would give her a fair chance of beating any charge."

Allen was unconcerned. Amber Hetherington was not meant to ever face a jury. Even if she was charged he was sure the Crown Prosecutions Service would put a stop to any proceedings due to the lack of evidence.

"What about you, Andrew?"

"Sorry Sir, but I can't give you much more to assist either," Constable Andy Todd offered. "I've checked and double-checked everything we have on Anna Rofe. I reckon I know more about her than anyone else alive now. She's a typical tom from the area; previous arrests and convictions for possession of heroin and crack cocaine, and also once for assault on police and a breach of the peace to complete the set. She's been in the area for five and a half years off and on, infrequently at first but a resident in Mapperley for the last three. Her bedsit revealed nothing evidential."

"What about friends and associates?" Allen asked.

"She never told police who her supplier was. She seemed to be working for herself, no pimp. Friends wise, just the other street girls and they are as talkative as this table. There was an information report about three months ago, regarding her going in and out of a house belonging to Josephine Lamas in Trenton Grove, which is at the edge of Mapperley Park. Lamas was an old-school madam from what I found out; ran a brothel for years and years but hung up her feather boa quite a while ago. I guess she must still keep in touch with some of the street girls."

Allen's interest was suddenly tweaked by hearing a name almost forgotten. "Old Josie Lamas. Well there's a blast from the past. What did the reports say exactly?"

"No, that was it. Twice on July 29th and twice again just over a week later; Rofe was seen to ring the bell and wait to be let in, no suggestion of her having a key."

"Is it worth a visit?" Sperry asked.

Allen considered the option for a moment.

"No, just funny hearing Josie is still around. It was too long ago, and she wouldn't give us the time of day anyway. She's an old pro in every sense of the word."

"I suppose that brings us to the charges then," Sperry said, opening his binder. "I don't think there's enough for murder. Nothing in the evidence or the pasts of the interested parties, no weapon either."

"Agreed," Allen replied.

"Manslaughter is possible. We can put Hetherington there and arguing with Rofe according to Korlenka, but as I've said before I'm not happy with her as our main witness. Which leaves us with the various assaults under the Offences Against the Person Act. I've brought the legislation with me because I thought it would be good for us all to agree. Sir?"

Allen took the lead role once more; he needed to be seen as pushing for the appropriate charge against Amber Hetherington, although it felt like a sick game of roulette.

"Let's be frank. It is not the strongest case, but we have to work with what we have. We can't show any intent at the time or a reason there may have been intent leading up to it, so we should be counting out Section 18 straight away. Anyone think differently?"

There was no argument. Even Todd, the least experienced of the small group, could clearly see it was a stretch too far to find any intent or malice in the actions of Amber Hetherington.

"So, Section 20 or manslaughter. Dean, you want go first?"

"Involuntary manslaughter for me. She's caused death not intending to kill or inflict grievous bodily harm. The act says she must have committed an illegal act that resulted in the death and a whack on the side of Anna Rofe's head fits no problem."

"Are we pushing too hard? Don't you think we have a better chance of getting a conviction for the assault and also a better chance of Hetherington pleading to it too?" Allen challenged.

"No Sir, with respect, she is dead. Section 20 calls for a malicious wounding and while there have been stated cases about what malicious means, and it does not have to include awareness, it does require a degree of recklessness. I think if we gave the jury malicious to think about it might confuse them, so why take the chance?"

"Mm, I see. Andrew what do you think?"

Todd gulped. "To be honest Sir, this is my first major incident, so I can imagine how a defence lawyer might try to spin it. I did think manslaughter myself and how Dean puts it sounds good to me, so I'll go with him."

Allen and Sperry exchanged a genial look. They'd been in Todd's position a long, long time ago. White made a first-class case and obviously knew his definitions and interpretations. Allen could find no fault in his logic and conclusions and since

Sperry wasn't offering any objections, he assumed he agreed, too.

"Good, Dean. You and Andrew go off and sort a charge sheet out for when she is due back. Put it on the system so anyone of us can give her the good news."

Dean positively glowed as he got up. He drifted across the room like a peacock with Todd in his wake leaving the two senior men at the table.

Sperry waited until he and his boss were alone in the room before speaking. "It's pretty thin, isn't it?" he said, pointing to the main evidence file.

Allen had been expecting this from his 2IC for some time. Chris Sperry was no fool.

"You're right, but we aren't going to get anything else now, so we can only hope that when she is charged, she decides to open up and give us what we need."

"What about CPS?" Sperry probed.

Allen was hoping against Crown Prosecution intervention, but if they did step in, they would probably make him drop the case.

"I'll cross that bridge if and when the time comes."

Nick sat in a wicker chair next to the open French doors while Dan sat outside on the patio like a naughty schoolboy to prevent any trace of him entering the house.

Their plan was a fishing expedition but if they did turn up anything it would in all likelihood be valuable. Nick's concern, which he continued to voice, was Dan's safety. In all honesty, Dan was not overjoyed at the prospect of spending hours in a potentially very volatile situation either, but he could not think of a better alternative. In fact, he could not think of any alternative.

After talking for an hour about the logistics involved they were as happy as they were going to be.

"So, what are we going to say constitutes a success?" Nick asked. What he was really saying was how much is enough before we can get the hell out of there?

Dan understood; detailed comment was not required. "Let's start with the obvious and best and work our way down. Best is corroborated evidence of Amber's innocence, followed by uncorroborated. That includes anything which implicates another, or proves Anna Rofe died in any other way."

"Then information which leads to that," Nick continued.

"Yes, and after that, any evidence and information regarding Allen, Binder and the Parkers. That's probably the best we can hope for and we shouldn't put up anything hard and fast. This is all hit and hope."

Amber had been on the phone to Rose and Viola for fifteen minutes. That was on top of the time she'd spent talking to her mum, assuring her everything was alright, that they were eating and sleeping and looking after themselves.

"Martin is like Action Man and Tarzan all rolled into one," Rose said for the fifth time at least. "We killed a rabbit the other day and ate it for dinner."

"Yuck. That's disgusting," Amber replied.

"Actually, it was lovely. Martin says the best way to eat meat is fresh like that."

The way their voices weren't quite loud enough made Amber think they had the handset between them.

"As you can tell, Rose has got the hots for Martin." Viola giggled.

"I have not!"

They all laughed together as they had a million times before, but not recently.

"Is it scary, Amber?" Rose asked when the laughing subsided.

"Dad and Dan are looking after me."

"That's not an answer," Viola shot back.

"Of course I'm scared, but mostly about what might have happened if we were not taking things into our own hands. Don't tell Mum, but we have done some crazy stuff already."

"Like what?" the twins asked simultaneously.

Amber looked over her shoulder to her closed bedroom door.

"Like fraud and burglary. Later today and tonight we're doing some undercover surveillance."

"No shit," Rose blurted out.

"Don't tell Mum, whatever you do."

"No of course. What did you do a burglary on?" Viola whispered.

"A policeman's house," Amber whispered back.

"No shit!" Rose repeated.

They continued talking for a few more minutes before Nick knocked the door.

"It's Dad, I better go," Amber said.

"Call us again as soon as you can," Rose begged.

"I will. Look after Mum and keep telling her we are okay. Bye." Amber clicked off and went to the door.

Allen could not get rid of his sense of unease. Constable Todd's throwaway remark about Anna Rofe visiting Josephine Lamas would probably have passed without further thought if not for the fact that he knew that Dan Calder had used her for information when he was in the job. One of the benefits of high rank was you got to see many reports and documents you would not otherwise be privy to, and he learned several years after Calder left that he and Josie Lamas were associated.

It was unfortunate Rofe had gone to the old madam's house, and therefore could have told her any number of things about what was happening on the local streets. On its own, he would have let it go, however Calder was back and showing an interest in Rofe's demise. Rofe had been to Lamas' house, and Calder had used Lamas for information. The connections were too close for comfort.

Is it possible he would not think to contact her to see if she could help in some way? he thought. *Not in a million years.*

He decided to call Ben Binder even though he was always the last person he wanted to speak to.

"It's me. I think we may have a problem."

"What sort of problem, James?"

"Dan Calder and Nick Hetherington."

"Who's Calder?"

"Ex job, a great detective and oldest friend of Nick Hetherington. He's come all the way from New Zealand to help."

Binder could not see how this could impact on him. "Go on, I'm listening."

"Did you hear what I said? Dan Calder could cause real trouble."

"I'm sure if we continue to hold our nerve and be careful James, all will be well."

Allen's stomach tightened at the continued use of his first name and at Binder's apparent brushing off of his concerns.

"Rofe was seen at Josie Lamas' home in Mapperley a couple of times in the months before she died. You won't know her, she ran a good class brothel for years and years and she also gave Calder information regularly; he probably did favours for her too. Now that he's back and has got his nose into this, he's bound to go to see Josie at some point. Depending on what Rofe said to her, about Teddy Parker for instance, I can foresee trouble."

"I think you might be getting a bit too excited. Whatever Anna Rofe said to this old bag, I doubt it can cause us any harm, and as for this Calder? He's a nobody now. An ex-policeman with an over-inflated opinion of himself looking to be a hero for an old friend."

Allen could barely contain his rage; to be belittled was one thing, but to doubt Dan Calder's capabilities, skills that Allen had witnessed and admired, was a whole other matter. He could sense the smugness on Binder's face, a face he would never get tired of punching once he started.

"Now just you listen to me. You have no idea who he is and what he's able to do. We came to blows for all sorts of different reasons but I'm telling you, he is the best natural detective I have ever met. He has got abilities that will make your hair stand on end. If you dismiss him, you will be sorry."

Binder was compelled to pause for a second. "Alright, I've got promotion boards to prepare for and I've got to get my timing right for cracking a burglary team so it makes the biggest impact. What do you suggest we do?" he asked.

Allen caught the defensiveness in Binder's voice. He got his point across then, but he could not care less about what Binder was planning.

"I don't know. That's why I called you."

Binder considered the situation for a long moment, so long that Allen felt obliged to speak again. "Well?"

"Well, James, once more I will sort it out. When is the Hetherington girl back again?"

"Tuesday."

"Just make sure you don't balls that up then, and I will handle Calder and the woman."

In his office, Allen twisted the telephone cord in his spare hand and wished it was Ben Binder's neck. Binder was the only subordinate officer who ever spoke to him in the way he did, and it took every ounce of restraint not to tell the smarmy shit exactly what he thought of him. How he ever managed to get himself embroiled in all this would haunt him long after he took his pension to the warmer climes of the Devon coast. He swallowed his pride once more.

"None of us are invincible, just remember that."

After freeing his hand of the mangled phone cord Allen paced his office for several minutes. With every step and every second he became more worried.

Binder spent the next two hours trawling through the police computer's historical records, familiarising himself with all he could about Calder and Lamas. Calder's arrest record was impressive, as was his conviction rate. His disciplinary record was also noteworthy but for the regularity in which he found himself on the wrong side of a judgement. Other than that, the only other thing that Binder thought was mildly interesting was the amount of time Calder was away from his then current posting at different times. When he added it up, it appeared Calder had spent almost two whole years of his service seconded to other police departments, such as Special Branch and T-7, being involved in special operations which were not listed or detailed in any file Binder would have access to until he gained another two promotions at least.

Lamas provided him with more column inches of information but the majority of it was repetitive and boring. She ran a good brothel, if there was such a thing, and kept control of her girls and her clients, judging by the lack of prosecutions in her twenty plus years of business. Since she'd retired, there was almost nothing. Binder did not see anything which ought to give him any cause for concern at all, but he was not an idiot; what Allen said was obviously for good reason and to ignore it would be foolish.

He checked his watch and seeing it was almost 1:00 p.m. he knew it would still be too early to expect Teddy Parker to be awake, which made dialling his number more enjoyable.

The phone blaring out the theme tune from *The Godfather* took thirty seconds to rouse Teddy from his tequila-fuelled slumber. The girl lying diagonally across the bed did not move. Her waist length black hair was splayed out like an oil slick, concealing the whole of her head and chest. Sleepily, he reached out and grabbed the phone, finally stopping the noise.

"What?" he said sourly, using a foot to move some of the girl's hair so he could see her breasts.

"Sorry Teddy, did I wake you? It's Ben here. I need you to do a job for me," Binder said pleasantly.

Teddy held his eyes tightly shut for a few seconds, hoping to be more alert when he opened them again.

"Hey Ben, what time is it. Can't it wait till I'm up?" he replied, imagining what he would be using that long black hair for shortly.

"I want you to do a job for me now!" Binder bawled.

Teddy was instantly wide awake. He kicked out with his foot until the girl stirred and pushed a great handful of hair out of her face.

"Get up and fuck off!" Teddy growled.

The girl failed to register. "Huh?"

"Now. Piss off, go on, get the fuck out!" he bellowed again.

The girl dragged her supermodel body off the bed and slunk away with her dress and high heels tucked under her arm.

"Make sure you close the door on the way out," Teddy yelled after her. He waited for the chunky click of his solid oak and steel front door before lifting the phone to his studded ear again. "Sorry Ben, I had a late one. What do you need doing?"

"Have you ever heard of a woman called Josie, or Josephine Lamas of Trenton Grove? She used to run a whorehouse in Mapperley a long time ago."

Teddy added 'confused' to his other current sensory states.

"What? No, I mean yes, yeah, I think so. Never met her I don't think. Why?"

"Because I want you to pay her a visit and see what she and Anna Rofe talked about when she visited her a couple of months ago, and then I want you to convince her to make sure whatever they did say she forgets permanently."

"What? I don't get it."

"You don't have to get it Teddy, you just have to do what I tell you to do. I thought you understood that by now."

"Shit Ben, take it easy. I'll do it, I've just woken up for fuck's sake."

"And while you've been sleeping I've been sorting out yours and everybody else's crap so don't talk, just listen and then do what I tell you. Josie Lamas had the Rofe girl at her house at least four times and she is obviously someone a lot of the working girls know and talk to. Since you could not control your temper and you created this whole situation, you can do some of the work to fix it. There's an ex-policeman named Dan Calder, a friend of Hetherington's father and also an old acquaintance of Josie Lamas. Can you put the rest together, Teddy?"

"You don't want Lamas talking to Calder," Teddy sulked.

"No Teddy, *you* don't want them talking."

"Yeah okay."

"So, go and talk to her. Even you should be able to do that, and with your way with the ladies I'm sure you can convince her to keep whatever she knows to herself if Calder does come calling."

Binder didn't bother giving Teddy Lamas' full address before he hung up; he would be able to find it without any problems.

With the girl gone, Teddy's plan for her was gone too. He went off to the toilet disappointed.

By 4:00 p.m. Dan, Nick and Amber could wait no longer. Dan's enforced banishment to the garden had bored him into such a stupor that he had spent the last thirty minutes on the old swing Nick made for the children years before. Nick used the afternoon to school Amber over and over again as best he could until his jaw and her ears ached. He could not shake the feeling that although their intentions were good, it was also too dangerous a plan, and no amount of quiet self-affirmations could hide his discomfort.

"Let's just get on with it," Amber said as they stood around watching Dan struggle to his feet.

Nick couldn't help himself. "Are you sure you want to?"

"Oh, for God's sake Dad, this is worse than waiting for the police."

Dan finished shuffling over to them. "It might not feel as bad once we're there, Nick. Give it an hour and see how we feel then. If we're still not comfortable we can reassess," he said.

Nick wrinkled his nose at the smell. "Alright alright, I'll get the car."

The journey into the city was unpleasant for them all and uncomfortable for Dan as well. Wrapped in a blanket in the boot of Nick's car to try and minimise his odour travelling through the vehicle, he rolled around like a Saturday night drunk, occasionally knocking elbows or ankles on something hard or sharp. Inside the car, Nick and Amber wound all the windows down fully and could not help exchange smirks and grins every time a muted *ouch* floated through from behind them.

They were still a mile away when Nick pulled over on the side of a quiet street to release Dan from his captivity. The smell hit him like a wrecking ball as he lifted the lid. Dan grinned up at him from his cocoon.

"You're actually enjoying all this, aren't you? You are crazy, one hundred percent, off your head."

"Just like old times. Do you remember that time…"

Nick silenced him with a raised palm and a look of friendly amazement.

"Get out of my car you smelly bastard. If we're all in one piece at the end of this, we can get pissed and reminisce all you want."

Dan heaved himself into a sitting position and then manoeuvred out of the boot still wrapped in his blanket.

"Can I keep this?"

"Be my guest. I'll tell Pen I ruined it if she ever asks. It won't be a lie."

For all their horseplay, their invisible bond was as solid as always.

"Take care. Remember, always be one step ahead," Nick said, extending his hand without thinking and regretting it when Dan took it.

"I'll be okay. After all, you're my backup. See you out there."

Dan shuffled off down the road like any one of the thousands of destitute souls seen but never noticed on the streets of every crowded city in the world. It took a quarter mile and two corners before he came across another person, a couple in fact, probably on their way home from a busy day in the office, just desperate to be inside their comfortable house with the TV on and a microwave meal burning their lap. When they saw Dan they both became hyper-interested in the pavement or their briefcases, anything but the filthy halfling approaching them. They visibly took a breath as they passed, as if they could make themselves smaller and whatever conversation they were having was suspended until they were out of contamination range again. Dan noticed their eyes never even came close to making contact with his and that was just what he wanted. He smiled and continued onwards, in the near distance was the next corner where he would turn onto Powton Road.

Nick tested Amber's knowledge and patience one more time before he dropped her outside the house Josie lined up for their use. It was a single fronted terrace, identical in appearance to the ten either side of it. The net curtain in the ground floor window flickered for a second and then a moment later the front door opened by half an inch. It was Amber's cue to move, to approach the house as a regular occupant and be inside in a seamless movement.

When she closed the door behind her, Nick moved off once more. He set the tripmeter to zero and felt behind for one of the two full petrol containers he'd put there. By the time he got to the end of the road the silence was deafening, so he switched the radio on. As the presenter finished the local weather forecasts, the next song started. "Billy don't be a hero" was a hit when Nick was a boy.

"Oh, give me a break." He breathed heavily, reaching for the tuning knob.

Powton Road had not changed. His first steps into it after the long absence were as painful as the last ones Dan took out the morning he woke up next to Zoe. The rows of terraces on either side of the pitted tarmac strip may have grown a few shades greyer due to the nearby industry and winter chimneys, but the feel was the same and the sound of his footsteps on the ground were as guilty today as they were then. Now that he was back in this place again, all the emotions he so carefully stifled most of the time came spewing out of him like a bad genie from a dark and ugly bottle. He managed to keep putting one foot in front of the other as he got ever closer to number 22 and with every stride, the memories of that night became bigger and bigger in his head until there was no room for anything else.

It was just another test purchase job like so many before and yet, when Zoe offered him her can of warm cider he took it and drank without a hint of hesitation. The rest of the night was a total blank.

The next morning he was aware of many things even before he was awake. The smell of age and dirt associated with the run-down house was strong but could not compete with the sweet, acidy and unmistakable stench of human vomit, which felt like it was burning the inside of his nostrils. He could feel the springs of the worn-out chair he had occupied the evening before sticking into his backside and his ears buzzed with the sound of flies which were obviously attracted by the free regurgitated meal close by. All that before he opened his eyes. The job dictated that he was not carrying anything in his pockets other than the marked bank notes to purchase a wrap of heroin with, so he was not concerned about checking for his wallet or ID. An obstruction against his straightened legs had stopped him from sliding further across the threadbare carpet. When he saw what it was, his brain could not place enough cells in order to fully comprehend the scene. Zoe's head was at a slightly unnatural angle to her neck and shoulders, which resulted in the rest of her body appearing to coil around the side of the chair. Her lifeless eyes were open wide and staring directly at him as if she had been waiting hours for him to wake up and see her. His boots were wedged into her neck and shoulder.

Dan's whole body ached with a particular brand of discomfort he had never experienced before—the pain of the morning after a drug-filled night. For a man who prided himself on the way he could exercise such control over all his senses, this was a wholly new sensation and it filled him with a dread of monstrous proportions. When he tried to move his bones felt brittle and likely to shatter into a thousand pieces at any moment. It took a second—but felt like an hour—before he was close enough to be able to reach out and touch her. Although everything he could see and feel told him she was dead he still needed to confirm it and make it real. Her body radiated cold. When his fingers came into contact with the skin of her neck, it was dry too. Like a fallen leaf she still looked alive in some ways and yet completely dead in so many others.

The flies continued to circle and feed. The sight of them behaving normally, just doing what flies do outraged him. Their lack of respect for the recently deceased girl suddenly turned him into a raging animal, swinging wildly at them with no hope of making the slightest contact. The burst of physical activity revived him mentally and he adjusted to the situation he now found himself in.

He began wracking his brain for any memory of the last twelve hours. Zoe was there before he was; she had come from the kitchen when he arrived and sat with her skinny back against the arm of his chair once he settled. The open can was in her hands already.

How could you have been so fuckin' stupid? he silently cursed. It was the look in her eyes which made him do it without any thought of the consequences. She had begged and beseeched him without a word being spoken and he thought in that look he understood.

What else happened, he had no clue. What he did know was the previous evening was not filed in his head, as if it did not happen, or rather, as if it had happened to someone else. Reality slowly dawned on him. He dragged his sleeves up to reveal bare forearms and studied both quickly but expertly for puncture or tourniquet marks. He was relieved to see they appeared unmolested.

He had now been sitting with Zoe on the floor for a few minutes, the unreal slowly normalising and making logical thought possible. His work with T-7 necessitated risk and the ability to operate unsupervised; he went to Powton Road the night before without reporting it to his handler. The previous night was just another of several he wanted to complete before leaving it to others in uniforms and suits to use all the intelligence and evidence he obtained to arrest, prosecute and convict the purveyors of so much destruction and misery. Obviously, a lot had gone very wrong.

In the years that passed after his decision to leave poor Zoe there to the flies, Dan mentally revisited the scene a thousand times, each time hoping but not believing he would remember what really happened. At that time on that morning, what he did next seemed rational. He was probably still under the influence of whatever residual poison remained in his body from the contaminated cider and God knew what else. He subsequently came to know that what he did next was the worst decision he had ever made. Then as now he could not believe he would be responsible for her death. Then as now he could not discount the possibility he was.

A few hours later, his actions made it far too late anyway. During active operations, he always painted his finger tips and palms with a mixture of clear nail polish and baby oil to prevent leaving fingerprints; he then dirtied his hands so no one could tell. He had the clarity of thought to check himself and Zoe for traces of a sexual connection between them but they both appeared to clear in that regard too. The cider can was gone, so he knew he could walk away from the house leaving no forensic evidence link from her to him.

His duty report submitted on official T-7 documents stated he was at another address the previous evening and had then gone back to his own flat before midnight. If it was ever known that he had taken an illegal substance without prior authority during this operation his undercover career would be over, and since at the time he prized work above everything else he was somehow able to legitimise the decision he made. The moment he deposited it into the dead letter box his fate was sealed, and the rest of his life would be contaminated by this lie.

Now all these years later, Dan continued passed number 22 without looking, but he felt conscious of it looking at him. Amber was in trouble this time; another innocent. He could not afford to get another decision so badly wrong in Powton Road.

Estelle suggested from the lamp post outside number 104 and the bus stop by 138 would offer a good vantage point to meet and talk with people. Josie's friend was at 127 and from either of the front windows there, Amber would see both landmarks.

She saw Dan approach, only recognising him because she knew what he looked like from less than an hour before. "Dad from Amber, I have a visual on Dan now. He is approaching the area."

"From Nick, got that," he replied, glad the comms were ten out of ten.

Dan's acknowledgement was to wipe his nose with his right sleeve. Amber reacted as they agreed.

"From Amber, Dan copies."

Nick was already circling in the car like a vulture and he was doing once more what destiny seemed to ordain for him, and what he loved most in the world and hated at the same time. Staring into an abyss of uncertainty and putting his safety and that of those he cherished most up for grabs.

At the farthest point away from Powton Road he made a mental note to time himself back to the nearest.

Dan willed his mind to stick to the task at hand and scanned the area of the road ahead for hazards and also for suitable places to stop. At this time, he did not expect to see any working girls on the street but would not be surprised if there were either. The lamp post identified by Estelle was a lonely figure, its single grey limb scratched and tattooed with marker pens by innumerable teenagers who stood under it over the last fifteen years. The road between it and the bus stop was also apparently deserted but just as Dan was deciding on one of two prospective doorsteps to make his OP, he noticed a pair of silver stiletto shoes visible under the wall of the bus shelter. Quickly evaluating the pros and cons, he selected the nearest of the doorsteps, the entry to the now dilapidated number 120. With movements like a battery operated sub-human whose power was fading he sank into a dirty blanketed huddle on the step and dissolved into the doorway.

If Amber wasn't watching she might not be able to see him now. After another moment of wonder she messaged through to Nick.

"Dad from Amber, Dan is now established at one two zero Powton Road."

"From Nick, got that."

"From Amber, Dan copies," she said again at the conclusion of another nose wipe.

In their different ways Dan, Nick and Amber settled and tried to prepare themselves for an unknown near future.

Dan's eyes flicked up and down the road, taking in any change since the last sweep. The owner of the silver stilettos was actually waiting for a bus and had departed some forty-five minutes before. Since then activity was minimal and there was no hint of an evidence gathering opportunity. He allowed himself to look up at number 127 across the road. There he noticed Amber in the upstairs window. The house was in a good spot. Nothing made it stand out. Nothing about it would draw the attention of passers by. She would be fine.

By contrast he thought if anything, Nick would have the hardest time of all, navigating the one-way system during the peak hour traffic, worrying about Amber and him and with too much time just to think of anything and everything that could go wrong.

At 6:00 p.m. Powton Road burst into life as if all had been waiting for the hour. A green and white number 625 bus came from Dan's right and stopped; four girls in sequins and Lycra stepped off like extras from a burlesque show. They chatted at the bus stop for several minutes before two walked away in the opposite direction, leaving the other pair to finish their conversation.

The older girl was in her mid to late forties, with thick black hair in a ponytail and bright pink lipstick which seemed to make her mouth work independently from the rest of her face. She wore a black miniskirt and a purple vest top which barely contained her enormous breasts, both featuring tattoos of Disney characters. Her chosen look was completed with pink flip-flops to match her lipstick.

The younger girl wore cut-off denim shorts and a gold and silver sequinned tube top. She was in her teens, Dan guessed older than fourteen but younger than nineteen although he knew he could be wrong by a couple of years in either direction. Her sandy hair was gelled and spiked, resembling a young punk rocker. Not for the first time, he regarded both prostitutes and wondered how any man could find either attractive, but then reminded himself there was no accounting for taste. Under his stinking blanket and argyle jumper he smiled and thought how about long he should wait and how best to approach the girls.

Amber reported the new arrivals to Nick and took an even greater interest in the street below.

As he watched the girls, Dan's thoughts were once again invaded by what happened at number 22 years before. He found being back more difficult to deal with than he imagined it could be. Part of him was annoyed at being unable to concentrate on the matter in hand, however another part was, if not happy, at least grateful to be human enough to still feel emotion. For once he did not try to force out the memories of Zoe and warm cider; instead he allowed his mind to drift away on the remorse and guilt that he had stored away.

The subject of his unfinished book's chapter fourteen, written but not included with the other pages, remained a secret, hidden away from everybody, including Tara. Only Katrina Mallinder ever noticed and questioned its existence, the cold-hearted murderer seeing something in Dan's history nobody else did and thereby forming a bond with him from which there was no escape. He still remembered their brief meeting in Auckland Prison's Remand Centre and her final words to him at her trial when she made certain he knew that she had glimpsed inside his soul.

When he looked again the picture had changed completely. It was almost dark now and the younger girl was gone. He had no idea how long his mind had been occupied elsewhere and the surprise he felt was uncommon. At times in the past when he did not perform to his absolute best the self-recrimination was often painful. On this occasion he only felt quiet and peaceful, suddenly aware that he was changing.

An hour and a half had passed since the four working girls had gotten off the bus. Now the only one left was patrolling the pavement between the bus stop and lamp post like a soldier outside Buckingham Palace. Amber watched, fascinated by the measured way the woman walked, the economy of movement probably based on years of doing the same thing day after day. The streetwalker noticed Dan in the doorway of number 120 but paid no interest in him. Amber wondered if, in this other world she had been dropped into, there was an understanding or set of unwritten rules between the homeless and the whores and if their lives ever overlapped.

Dan seemed to have taken root, she knew he would be watching and planning his next move with the precision she witnessed first-hand over recent days and she tingled inside with expectation.

Now his mind was back on the job again Dan decided to see if the girl, he used the word in the loosest sense, might have something to say. When he started to move and stand, his back and legs protested. He was not cold because under the vagrant exterior he wore thermals and the best insulated socks money could buy, but the pain made him realise how long he must have been motionless for. The resulting disjointed movements to a fully standing position was as good as he could manage.

The working girl was on her latest slow walk towards him. Business had been non-existent up to this point, so he was hoping boredom might persuade her to talk. When she saw Dan emerge onto the footpath she looked unfazed and disinterested. When they were close enough to talk, Dan began.

"Hi, I'm sorry to disturb you." He deliberately chose his own voice and hoped it would have the desired effect.

"Well don't then, love." It seemed it did not, but he persisted.

"I don't think it's because of me things are so quiet, but would you prefer it if I went?"

Now that got her attention. She seemed not used to being spoken to like that by anyone, let alone someone like this. She stopped, fortunately for both of them upwind.

"No, you're alright," she said slowly.

Dan removed enough of his blanket to reveal his face and put on his best and most open and friendly look. "I'm new."

She cocked her head, her smile halfway between a smirk and a grin.

"New to what love? The area or the way of life?"

Dan relaxed into the role and into the moment. "Is it that obvious?"

"You're not from round here, darling, but you still have your local accent. Are you running away from something or just fallen on hard times?"

Dan recognised the maternal instincts in the old tom. She had probably been on the game for years, seen and heard it all, watched younger prettier girls come and go and more than likely had a family to go home to at the end of each shift. Now that he could see her properly he revised her age to forty. "I bet you have a few stories to tell too."

Her initial reply came in the form of bright pink lips curled into a wide smile.

"What exactly are you after? I don't do freebies or charity cases."

Dan laughed, long enough to appear genuine, he hoped. "I'm Dan. Would you believe I want some information?"

Just as quickly the smile disappeared and her eyes narrowed. She looked up and down the street before returning to Dan.

"I definitely don't do police."

It was what he was expecting. For the purposes of his objectives, there was little risk in being more or less honest. Now he had seen and talked to her he knew she was no druggie; her bare arms were devoid of the telltale marks, the veins in her limbs were not constricted by the abuse of heroin, coke or amphetamines, and all the other speech, hair and sensory signs normally associated were absent. In a few moments, Dan worked out her life story; she was unlikely to have any allegiance to Teddy Parker. Her look and manner also convinced him she was also independent and strong willed enough to look after herself. She was just a good old-fashioned, hard-working and honest prostitute.

"I don't do police either, but I do try and help my friends out. It's Anna Rofe I need to know about."

"Anna wasn't a friend to you looking like that."

"True, but the young woman the police say killed her is though. I'm hoping to bump into a few people she might have known."

He watched the street-smart streetwalker combine what he said with how he looked and come up short. "Sorry love, I think you better ask someone else."

"Do you think I'd be here like this if I did have anywhere else to go and ask? Please give me a minute. Look, I don't even know your name, but we've both been around the block enough times and understand how this shitty old world works."

"Why do you think I won't just give you a load of crap, or worse, call up some of the locals to come and sort you out?"

She crossed her arms. "It's Purdy," she added after another moment.

"Purdy. Hi. You still might, that's why I'm wearing my running shoes."

She glanced down. Dan's worn out Adrenaline's looked like they had seen a lot of action but did not look like they were ready for another Olympian effort.

"Well hopefully." Dan offered shooting her a smile and taking a quick glance across the road. He visualised Amber watching the silent movie unfolding in the gathering gloom below, the yellow sodium lights along the road turning the scene vaguely macabre. When the girl rolled her head back and laughed he hoped Amber would too.

"Go on then darling. Let's hear it," Purdy said, placing a ring-covered hand on her hip.

"I heard Anna wasn't killed by another girl but by her supplier. If that's true I'd really like to meet him soon. You must have been around here for some time and seen it all, but I can tell you're not like Anna was. I am guessing you would be as pleased as me to see the likes of him disappear from around here. Josie Lamas would."

Straight away he noticed Purdy recognise the plain truth in the face in front of her and Josie's name was well known also. Dan decided to go for broke and continued before she could speak.

"You probably have kids of your own at home, a daughter maybe. Of course you don't want her down here doing what you do but I expect your old lady never expected you to either, so what would you do to protect yours?"

Purdy bristled. "Watch it."

Her veiled threat only served to tell Dan he was on the right track.

"Come on, help me and you might just help yourself too.

There often came a time during an interview of a suspect when a war of silence would determine the outcome. Dan knew it, but the suspects mostly did not. Purdy didn't either, she spoke next after an awkward silence.

"Anna wasn't a bad sort, but she wasn't cut out for this. The poor little bitch never had two pennies to rub together," Purdy said.

"What was it, crack?" Dan asked, sure he would get a reply.

"Darling, I would not be surprised if she was on everything. All she wanted to do was get the hell out of here. That's how she did it I suppose."

"How much longer do you have to keep coming down to Mapperley?"

"My youngest is fourteen. He'll start an apprenticeship when he leaves school in two years."

Dan felt assured a relationship had been established and pressed on.

"Purdy, what have you heard?"

"The only dealer around here and supplying the girls is Teddy Parker. I stay well clear love, clear of the gear he's pushing and clear of his temper."

"What about the competition?"

"There isn't any now, used to be a few to fight over them but all the girls get their stuff from him these days. I don't know how he managed it because he is such a little prick." Purdy paused for a second and then added aimlessly, "But he does have this creepy habit of quoting from books and poems. Probably thinks that makes him the dog's bollocks."

Dan stiffened as he confirmed the connection to Teddy's university course and what Amber told him the first time she described her meeting with Teddy.

"I was going to hang around here to see if he turns up tonight. What are my chances?"

"Not until after nine. I'll be gone by then but there will be a few other girls who will want to score and he always has what they need."

"Thanks a lot. Perhaps we can have another chat sometime?"

"You'll have to have a bath first darling, you stink like a dead cat. Show me your hands."

Dan held out his palms so the tired street worker could examine them. She smiled an all-knowing smile as she let them drop.

She would make a better scenes of crime officer than half the fully trained staff in the force, he thought.

"Yes, alright my love, maybe once you've scrubbed all this off."

"How about Josie's place? You name the day and time."

"No Dan, you give me your number and I'll give you a call."

He recited his latest pre-pay number without a second thought, which she seemed content to commit to memory. She then wrote a number on a scrap of paper and handed it to him. With that she expertly completed an about turn and headed off back to the bus stop once more. Dan returned to his doorstep and gave his nose a wipe.

"Dad from Amber, Dan has resumed at the house."

"From Nick, got that."

It was 7:10 p.m.

There was some activity over the next two hours but nothing worthy of another approach. Purdy continued her patrol until 8:15 p.m. when a dark green Volvo turned up and whisked her away after a short verbal interlude with the driver. By that time two new girls had taken up positions under the lamp post. They seemed more interested in each other's fashion than the occasional punter who cruised up the street from one direction or the other and his sixth sense told him they would be no use.

By 10:00 p.m. Amber was starting to tire and struggle. As previously arranged, she called up Nick and Dan.

"From Amber, I need to call Dad."

Dan wiped his sleeve across his nose. "From Amber, Dan copies. Calling you now, Dad."

"Amber from Nick, got that," he replied startled by the sudden request. "Hi, how are you doing? Is there something wrong?"

"I'm exhausted, Dad. I can't believe you and Dan did this for days on end sometimes."

"It does take a bit of getting used to. Do you want to have a break?"

He realised Amber was suffering from the nervous excitement her maiden surveillance operation generated, and feeling guilty. The combination of recent events and exertions would feel like the straw which was making the camel buckle at the knees.

"Sorry Dad, I just never expected it to be this hard."

"Don't worry," Nick said. "I'm not surprised at all. I'll come and take over from you, but I want you to go to a burger bar or something. Take an hour or as long as you need to, have a hot drink and something to eat and just rest your eyes and your mind. When you're ready you can either come back to the house or take over in the car."

"But what about the plan?"

"Forget it, Amber. You're no good to me in your state and Dan and I can look after ourselves."

"But Dad?"

"No, Amber, do as I say or I'm going to tell Dan it's all over and we will all leave."

Nick concisely passed the details of the change of plan to Dan and ten minutes later he approached the house on foot and went in.

Amber then appeared moments later and set off along the road to recover Nick's car. They both watched her carefully until she disappeared from view.

Nick came on the line within the next minute.

"Hey buddy, how is it?"

Dan stretched a leg out slowly as if cramped. A leg movement was always a positive answer.

Nick understood, the body signals they used a thousand times in the past were as fresh in his mind as the day they last used them.

"Got that." Then, "Was the old tom helpful?"

Dan retracted his leg.

"Got that. I don't suppose you want to call it a day? The first pint is on me."

Dan stretched an arm out, the agreed negative response and extended his fingers as if releasing the tension from sitting in one place for so long.

"Got that. Why am I not surprised?" Nick joked, knowing Dan would be grinning from ear to ear.

For the next hour, Nick watched Dan watching the street, occasionally talking in their mixture of his questions or comments and Dan's limb movement replies. The next burst of activity coincided with the local pubs closing and at 11:00 p.m. bringing more people onto the street than there had been at any time during the previous six hours. The two working girls were picked up, the first by a passing car and the second by a middle-aged man walking by. Dan was mostly ignored, and Nick's attention remained alert.

When Amber called Nick at 11:20 p.m. he told her to go home and get some sleep. Now that they'd been in the job for a few hours and gotten a feel for the place, his danger and safety rating was now only a three out of ten.

She sounded dejected but Nick was insistent.

"Give me a call when you come back in the morning. Tell you what, if we need to call you back, I promise we will, okay?" He said by way of a peace offering.

The steady stream of pedestrians up and down Powton Road continued up to and past midnight. The sight and smell of takeaway fried rice or kebabs accompanying some of them teased and tantalised Dan and left Nick complaining just like old times.

As with earlier in the day Dan occasionally allowed his mind free reign for a few minutes at a time, which invariably led back to Zoe, 22 Powton Road and chapter fourteen. The change he noticed in himself during the afternoon now made him think in greater detail about the whole subject. Zoe's body was discovered two or three days later by a new band of druggies who saw 22 Powton Road as ideal for their needs until her decomposing body swiftly convinced them otherwise. He then sweated for the next week as the inevitable police inquiry was launched and developed a life of its own. He continued the T-7 job for another ten days then returned to Garstone to resume his normal duties. As he remembered and relived some of the key moments he winced at his stupidity, cowardice and plain bad luck.

Months later the inquest found she died from physical asphyxiation, strangled in other words. The dietary contents of her stomach were limited presumably because she had thrown up. The news devastated him further as he still did not have any recollection of whom, why or how. In the weeks after that tragic day, he deliberately tried not to investigate the matter at all for fear of drawing attention to himself, but he was interviewed by one of the Major Incident Team detectives assigned to the job since his undercover duties at the address were made known to them. He shrugged through the few questions and said as he hadn't been to that address that night he couldn't help, and he had never come across the girl before.

Then as now, all he really remembered with certainty was that she called herself Summer on the night. It was not unusual for people in and around the drug scene to use an alias. What made it all the more tragic was Summers was Zoe's real surname.

Nick's call at 1:10 a.m. wrestled the images away once again.

"Dan from Nick, there are three undesirables approaching from your right."

In a second Dan's full attention catapulted back to the present and he crossed his legs in front of him for Nick's benefit.

"Got that," Nick replied.

Dan heard them before he saw them, and before they saw him. They were drunk certainly, the type of drunk that brings on language from the gutters and thuggish behaviour never completely disguised as bravado. He lowered his head a little to limit the chance of the street lights illuminating him. As the men reached him he saw they were little more than youths and he tried to shrink a little more.

"And fuck me if his sister didn't come in right then." Dan labelled the voice as yob number one for the time being. All three roared with laughter.

Dan then saw their shoes crossing his field of vision, two pairs of white tennis shoes and one pair of unidentifiable work boots. As he willed them to continue, a pair of tennis shoes stopped abruptly and was accompanied by another voice.

"Hold up boys, look what we've got here."

That will be yob number two, he thought. *Go on keep walking, just this once. Come on God, make me a believer.*

But something else told him this was not going to be his lucky night.

"Dan from Nick, say the word," his earpiece whispered.

The appropriate word or body movement would result in Nick appearing from across the road like Captain America in a matter of seconds, but he had been in tighter situations than this many times before. He remained quiet and still.

Yob number three was still to give voice to his footwear. Dan imperceptibly lifted his head enough to see more. One of the pairs of tennis shoes belonged to a white, eighteen-year-old with sandy coloured hair, the other pair to a black youth also in his late teens whose head was as bald as an egg and shone like a black pearl.

"Hey, have you got the price of a cup of tea?" Dan said quietly, lifting enough of his face again for them to get a better look at him.

He tried to display an I'm-not-worth-you-bothering-with and a don't-mess-with-me-look at the same time.

"Man, you stink. I've never seen a pile of shit talk before."

Ah number three. How nice to meet you.

Yob Two laughed out loud again.

Dan mentally assessed and adjusted. His brain was razor sharp and even though his body had been still for so long he spent a lot of the time invisibly flexing muscles in case there was a need to move quickly.

"Just fifty pence?" Dan begged again.

Yob One came into full view again, giving Dan his first look at all three together.

"Get a job, then you can get your own tea. Waster," Two said venomously.

In a perfect representation, Dan withdrew into his blanket again like a hedgehog going into a protective ball.

"Maybe we should give him something," Three joked to his associates.

"Fuck that," Two said again. "I wouldn't piss on him if he was on fire."

One sniggered this time and Three took a step towards Dan.

"Yeah but he's not on fire is he, and I could do with a leak."

Dan considered his options, the objectives of the job and the risk/reward balance of his immediate situation. He hunkered down as far as he could, making sure he was protecting his face, genitals and the mobile phone.

One and Two cheered and laughed as Three undid his button-fly. A few seconds later a hot stream pattered down on top of Dan like a smelly waterfall. Unfortunately, Three was very accurate with his statement of needing to relieve himself and was being equally accurate with his aim. By the time he finished, Dan was soaked from head to foot.

"There you go shit pile. How's that for a hot drink?" Three said, refastening his jeans.

As they walked away Dan sat very still, hoping they would not decide to return for more fun and games. The phone was dry, but his face was not so fortunate.

A minute later confirmation was received.

"Dan from Nick, they are away. Please tell me what I think just happened didn't?"

Dan extended two wet legs.

"Shit. Got that partner."

It was four miserable hours later when Dan finally gave in to the obvious. Teddy Parker was not going to make an appearance. He wondered if Purdy was yanking his chain and decided not. Whether Teddy met his customers elsewhere or had other business which prevented him making a stop in Powton Road, the information he hoped to find out would have to wait for another time.

After thirteen hours of personal phone silence he made the call he was sure Nick had wanted to hear all along.

"Nick from Dan, stand down. Watch me clear the area and I'll see you back at yours."

CHAPTER FIFTEEN

After Ben Binder called, Teddy stewed on the short conversation for some time before he made an executive decision not to rush around to Josie Lamas' house immediately. Ben always seemed too concerned with every single detail and Teddy knew well enough the old woman posed no threat to them. She might have been something in Mapperley once upon a time, but Teddy was the main man these days. The detective might believe he oversaw their relationship, but Teddy held the real power in the area now. If need be, he could dissolve their partnership and continue to build his business the way he wanted.

So instead of following Binder's instructions, he went back to sleep. Josie could wait until tomorrow. When he woke again it was 3:00 p.m. He wished he hadn't kicked the girl out of the house earlier on. They'd had sex the night before but he hadn't finished his business with her. He intended giving her a hard fuck again in the morning and then finish her off in his favourite and disgusting way so that she was completely humiliated when he got rid of her.

He made a triple espresso, which acted like a punch in the face, and by 4:00 p.m. as Dan, Nick and Amber were leaving home for Powton Road he was at the snooker club where he remained until late into the night.

Allen spent the day up to his neck in the biannual meetings with the various groups and departments under his command. Photographic, Scenes of Crime, and Victim Liaison took all morning, during which time they argued back and forth over budgets and overtime.

"So much for a modern police service for the twenty first century," he griped to his uniformed counterpart over coffee in the senior officers' meal room after lunch.

The afternoon was even more tortuous as it involved all the divisional heads of CID similarly squabbling over who was most deserving but with ten time's greater voracity. What made this meeting so much worse was that DI Ben Binder was there as a divisional head and Area Retailers Liaison Officer for Nottingham Central.

Since Binder discovered, presumably through Teddy Parker, the arrangement Allen stupidly and unwittingly entered into with Edward Parker Sr. to build his new house, the gentle and predictable slide into retirement with a fat lump sum and commensurate pension had become a scary ghost-train ride where he did not know what might lurk around the next corner. If it weren't for the money, he would have jumped and taken early retirement as soon as Binder first approached him. But the combination of Gwen's insistence that they enjoyed what they had when they had it, and Binder's new influence meant that he had no choice but to stay and see his time out. It was no surprise therefore, that as soon as the meeting was over, Binder approached him.

"A word James, if that's okay," he said. "I'll get us a tea."

Allen slumped back down into his seat at the head of the large oval table while Binder fetched two cups of tea from an urn at the back of the room and returned, taking the seat immediately to his right. The large conference room was now otherwise deserted, the weak sun magnified through huge windows made it warm and stuffy. Allen removed his jacket and loosened his tie.

"So, how are things?" Binder asked, placing a cup and saucer in front of him.

For a moment, he tried to imagine that all the crap that was happening to and around him wasn't.

"Same old, same old. I'll be glad when it's all over and the likes of you can deal with it, you might appreciate things a little differently then. You would not believe how much the job has changed even in the last five years, let alone ten or twenty."

Binder regarded him as a dinosaur and thought. *The sooner the likes of you do go and modern thinking men like me take over the better.*

"Times change James, and we all have to change with them. No, I was actually meaning how are things with Amber Hetherington?"

Reality bit back causing the old detective to hover his cup at his lips and then put it back down on the table.

"It's all wrong, and you know it as well as I do. I've cut an odd corner here and there over the years, but getting myself involved in anything like this makes me sick."

"Well of course James, it is very unfortunate. We've both found ourselves in a difficult position. Look at the positive side of things. Anna Rofe will not be missed, she was one of life's misfits any way. And it doesn't matter if Amber Hetherington is convicted or not. We probably believe she won't be, but from the job point of view, justice will have taken its course. Edward Parker has got us both over a barrel, you about your house and me helping Teddy out when I met them in Durham."

"I hope to God she does get off long before she sees the inside of a court. What then though? Parker will have us even more over that barrel."

"Fortunately for you James, you'll be able to retire soon enough. I may have to move away from Nottingham altogether to get some respite."

Binder's continual use of Allen's first name set Allen's teeth on edge, but he tried his best to ignore it.

"There must be a way you can apply some pressure to counter what he's doing, I don't see the bugger at all anymore and have no wish to start again," Allen said.

"Like what? We've been over the same old ground many times. We cannot change the past so just how would you suggest we do that?" Binder asked. Then he leant forward. "You know Josie Lamas talked with Rofe before she died?"

Allen frowned. "Yes, so what?"

"Well after you told me I got to thinking, we should really find out what it was the two of them discussed."

"You think I should go and see her?"

"I actually decided to get someone else to do it for us. If it becomes necessary later, you can then manage the situation."

Allen stiffened. The moment he did he also knew Binder had noticed.

"Just a quiet word, so we don't have to become involved unless absolutely required. After all, if their meetings were innocent then we don't want to arouse suspicion, do we?"

"Who do you have to go and see Josie?"

Binder knew better than to tell Allen it was Teddy. "An acquaintance, no one you know."

"I don't like it. Josie won't say anything to anyone, it's always been her way."

"Anyone? What about Dan Calder?"

Allen shrugged. He was sure Josie Lamas was as discreet now as always but not sure enough to say so.

A few hours later, while swilling his whiskey and ginger around in one of the crystal tumblers he and Gwen bought on a recent trip to London, he could not help but feel he should have been firmer with Ben Binder about someone going to see Josie. He nearly put in a call to Binder at 10:00 p.m. but poured another double instead. That night he could not sleep.

Dan spent two hours washing off most of his disguise but there was a lot more below the skin that could never be removed with soap and hot water. Everything he wore was burned in Nick's back garden, including his well-loved running shoes. The thick black plume rising from the metal brazier Nick used for such occasions was a dark reminder that time was running out to save Amber from an appointment with a judge and jury.

It was mid-morning when they convened in the kitchen again. Amber was still apologetic about not being able to last the duration. Dan and Nick agreed not to tell her about Dan's episode with the three youths but admitted that Teddy Parker hadn't made an appearance.

"So, what are we going to do today?" Amber asked, pouring milk on some cereal.

For once Dan did not have a ready reply. That very question had been foremost in his mind as he showered earlier, and by the time he'd dried off, he still didn't have an answer.

"There are a few more people to go and see," he said as he did not want to appear without hope. "I think you should just rest for the day as we may be very busy again tomorrow."

Amber seemed placated, but Nick knew very well what his friend was thinking.

"I should give Tara a call as well," Dan said changing the subject.

CHAPTER SIXTEEN

Unusually, Teddy was up by 10:00 a.m. He remembered yesterday's phone call with Ben Binder and decided it might be better to go and see Lamas sooner rather than later. He called Flick but got no answer. By midday Flick still hadn't called back. He couldn't wait any longer, so he called Marley Johns. Marley was only too pleased to step up and fill Flick's Timberlands.

"I want to find out what she and that Anna talked about when the skank came to visit her," Teddy explained on the way over.

"Everybody knows of Josie. She used to be the only game in town when you was looking for girls, but she been out the game for so long. Shit Teddy, that was when I was still in short trousers an' long socks," Marley said. "You think she was tryin' to get back in the game?"

"I doubt it. She probably just let her house be used as a drop-in centre so she could still feel involved."

"What would she and Anna Rofe have to talk about other than the price of condoms that could affect you?"

"Again, probably nothing but I do not like loose ends." Teddy pondered his own words until he found a suitable line from Macbeth. "That calls upon us, by the grace of grace, we will perform in measure and in place," he said for his own satisfaction.

Marley's glassy eyed silence proved to Teddy once more why it was him who drove the BMW and wore a Ben Sherman suit while the likes of Marley were in ridiculous bright red basketball boots.

His cockiness of the day before had waned, and though he would never admit it, such was Binder's influence over Teddy that he was determined to follow Binder's instructions to the letter and gain every scrap of information. When they arrived at Josie Lamas' door, the alcoholic and narcotic influences that usually influenced his state of mind were long gone and he was thinking with a spiteful, dangerous, and clear head.

The old-fashioned doorbell half buzzed, half rang inside the long hallway of Josie's home. She was well used to visitors at all hours of day and night and thought nothing of checking to see who it might be before she pulled the elegant wooden door open. Her surprise at what she saw was only temporary.

"Hello, what can I do for you gentlemen?" she asked, pulling her robe fully across her front.

"You must be Josie. I'm Teddy Parker."

Josie was not impressed. "That does not answer my question, Mr. Parker."

"Well if you invite my friend and me inside I can tell you."

Josie went to close the door, but Marley's red boot made an effective stop.

"Looks like I'll have to invite myself in, then doesn't it?" Teddy said.

Josie could fill a phone book with the list of men who thought they could intimidate her, however she recognised now was not the time to attempt a physical response. She held the door open wide and allowed the two men to enter. She deliberately left the door open after they both walked along the hallway towards her kitchen and living room. Parker was sat at the breakfast bar when she caught up with them.

"Nice place, if you like this sort of thing," Parker said.

Josie switched on the second bank of lights over the kitchen area to accompany the softer ones which were already on. The new harsh brightness showed up the crows' feet around her eyes she usually worked so hard to conceal but at that moment her appearance to Parker and his puppet was the least of her concerns.

"If you want something from me Mr. Parker, I suggest you ask and then go."

"You know who I am?"

"Of course."

"Then don't mess me around. You got anything to drink in this time capsule?"

Marley snorted a laugh displaying the big gap between his two front teeth.

"Mr. Parker, I am an old lady now but an old lady who has seen bigger and braver men in her time than you could ever aspire to be. The last thing I am going to do is offer you a drink, so please, make your threats and ask your questions and then go back to wherever it was you came from."

Marley's smile disappeared as quickly as it had arrived. Josie felt the tension build in Teddy's shoulders and the sudden electricity in the room. She guessed young Edward Parker was unused to being spoken to like that.

Teddy was jolted too. He sniffed the air like a wild animal as he contemplated his next move; instinctively he thought of violence first and then a line popped into his head though its origin escaped him.

"A fool shows his annoyance at once, but a prudent man overlooks an insult," Parker said, narrowing his eyes. "Once anyway. Don't test me again, I get bored easily."

As Marley giggled like a schoolboy on heat Josie was in no mood to demonstrate fear of the jumped-up son of a one-time client. She walked across to the small table next to her sofa where she kept some odds and ends and her Bible. Picking it up and flicking through the pages for Parker's benefit, she wanted to appear nervous and in need of something to do. She turned away from him, apparently gazing out of the French doors to the garden.

"What do you want, Mr. Parker?"

"What I want is to know why Anna Rofe came to see you back in July and August. What I want are concise answers and what I want is them right now."

Suddenly Josie was extremely afraid although she did not allow it to show. She underlined a line in her Bible with a red pen she kept on the table before turning back and putting the open Bible back down on the table.

"Why would an important man like you want to know about what Anna and I talked about over a cup of tea and a slice of cake?"

Moving with the speed of a cobra, Parker slapped the side of Josie's face with the back of his right hand. Josie's head spun around and she nearly lost her footing altogether. Forever the lady, Josie slowly returned to a forward-facing position with eyes like stone despite the bright red patch over her left cheek and the trickle of blood from her nose. She reached into her robe pocket and withdrew a lacy handkerchief which was folded into quarters. Very slowly, and with her eyes still on Parker, she opened it out and dabbed her face, spotting it in crimson.

"Mr. Parker whatever you came here for, you're not going to get. Now be a good boy and get out of my house before I lose my temper."

Even as she said it Josie had a fair idea of what might follow. In all her years of business she was no stranger to the occasional drunken slap or even an angry punch, but she always maintained her self-control and dignity, never giving way to threats or compromising a friend. That her and Anna Rofe's innocent talks about the Bible and psychic phenomena were as relevant to Edward Parker Jr. as the time in Venezuela did not matter a jot now.

Parker hit her again, this time with a clenched fist, sending her crashing to the floor. Before she could move to get up he brought the heel of his shoe down on her right temple and followed that with a kick to her stomach.

Marley could only look on in shock. Teddy continued his vicious assault while he tried and failed to get a word out. He had never seen anything like this and for all his usual bravado, seeing the defenceless old lady's skin tear open, her blood on Teddy's shoes and her refusal to beg for mercy, he became the weak, unconfident individual he tried so hard to disguise every day with garish clothes and glib lines. By the time Teddy was finished, Marley had tears in his eyes and rising bile in his throat.

Dan spent the rest of the day at the local library. Throughout his police career libraries were always a haven he could go when he needed a neutral venue to think, or hope for inspiration. Whether it was from scanning through the rows of author's names and titles until something clicked, or reviewing old newspaper articles on the microfiche machine, the library never failed to deliver something. Until today.

He went back to Nick's at 6:00 p.m. feeling disconsolate.

"Where the hell have you been?" Nick nearly yelled as he opened the front door. "I've been trying to think where you might be and calling half the town for an hour."

Dan stood on the step gawping. "The library. I left my phone here to charge. What's up, is Amber okay?"

"It's Josie. I'll tell you on the way."

"On the way where?" Dan asked very slowly.

"If it's not too late already, the City Hospital."

After leaving Josie Lamas' house Teddy drove home to wash and change, depositing a shaken Marley in the city centre en route. Later he went to the snooker club. He was drinking neat vodka when his mobile rang.

"It's me," Binder hissed.

"Hey Ben, I was just about to give you a call."

"Have you got any idea what you have done, you malignant cretin?" Binder whispered.

"What the fuck, Ben."

"What the fuck is right. Guess where I am?"

"What's up man? Why are you so quiet?"

Binder almost exploded, almost. Teddy heard the sharp intake of breath instead. "I am at the City Hospital where we were called an hour ago, after Josephine Lamas was admitted. If she lives, and there are no guarantees that she will, we will be interviewing her about who the hell beat her up so badly that she ended up with more bruises than skin. If she dies, it's a murder inquiry."

Teddy was quiet. For once there were no classical lines which came readily to mind.

"You are a contemptible fuck who just became more of a liability to me than a use. Give me one good reason why I should not hand you over on a plate right now. I expect her house has more than enough forensic in it to do that without my help anyway."

"You told me…"

"I told you to talk to her, that's all, but obviously, you decided that meant beating up and almost killing a seventy-year-old woman in her home."

Teddy was starting to shake with fear and a renewed rage of his own. "I did talk to the fuckin' old whore but she wouldn't say anything. I didn't mean to go all Rambo on her, it just happened when Marley started laughing. Remember you're involved too. You got me to go, we're in business together, Ben."

"You and Marley!"

"Yeah. I couldn't get hold of Flick, so I took him along."

Binder planned every association with Teddy down to the smallest detail. His life was made up of getting all the small details right in order to succeed and achieve the position of power and authority that was his destiny. When Teddy blurted out his last remark, Ben Binder knew it had all been worth it. He had his realisation back when he had first met Teddy at Durham. He had handled that incident with such consummate professionalism that Teddy was in his debt. When advancement in Nottingham became possible, it made sense for Binder to go and have that debtor available to use.

His micro-management of Teddy sometimes felt overcomplicated, but now it had proved priceless. He was untouchable. The phone he used to communicate with Teddy was an untraceable pre-pay, he and Teddy never met in the company of another person, he had not been to his home. Teddy knew nothing of his personal life other than what he fed him, which was a carefully designed ruse in any case. The payments Teddy made to him were all in cash and he placed them in a safety deposit box rather than an account, even an offshore one. In short there was nothing which tied him to Teddy other than Teddy's worthless word. Any threats or allegations Teddy might make, he could refute. With all the evidence he engineered against Teddy for the burglaries and drug dealing, Ben Binder knew he was on the safest ground imaginable. He terminated the call without another word.

The phone clicked off. Teddy screamed obscenitics into his mobile and then threw it viciously across the room where it smashed against the wall. He popped the lid of a small medicine bottle and washed four blue pills down with a swig of vodka.

Remembering how Marley was when he ejected him from the car in town he now regretted his haste. With his phone smashed, he headed back home to call Marley. He had already drawn the attention of some of the snooker club patrons and didn't want to risk anyone else learning what had happened. As he drove home, the combination of pills and vodka kicked in with a vengeance and he was only semi-conscious by the time he climbed the stairs to his plush abode. Once inside all thought of making a phone call was gone, replaced by the world spinning uncontrollably. He collapsed onto one of the white leather sofas in the lounge and passed out.

CHAPTER SEVENTEEN

En route to the hospital Nick explained that Estelle found Josie lying unconscious in her living room covered in blood and bruises. She called 999 first and then the number Dan gave to Josie on a previous visit, it seemed Estelle's memory for phone numbers mirrored Purdy's. Nick picked up the call.

They didn't know what to expect when they arrived.

"Are you a family member?" the admissions clerk asked.

"I'm as close as anyone can be. Josie has no real family still living," Dan explained not quite lying but not telling the whole truth either. "I'm the one she would want you to contact," he added, now lying properly.

"I see. You better sit over there and I'll find a doctor to come and talk to you." The clerk sounded doubtful as she pointed them towards a waiting area where a dozen assorted men, women and children were sitting in three rows like bored zoo animals.

In the back row, partially hidden behind a tatty magazine was Estelle, wearing the same pink T shirt Dan saw her in at Josie's, although tight blue jeans replaced the miniskirt. As if by magic she lowered her page to meet Dan's look. Her stare conveyed her concern, anger and fear all at once.

"Estelle. Hi."

She put the magazine down on her lap when Dan sat next to her; Nick remained standing.

"I didn't know who else to call," she said in a low voice.

"No, you did exactly the right thing. This is my friend Nick. What happened?"

Estelle looked at Nick in the same way she did when she summed Dan up at Josie's house a few days before. Apparently satisfied, she turned back to Dan.

"I called around at about 5:00 p.m. The door was closed but not locked and when she didn't answer, I went in and found her in the front room."

Dan and Nick looked at each other.

"Have they told you anything since you've been here?" Nick asked.

"No, but the police were here up until a few minutes ago."

"That's standard procedure. Can you tell us what you told them?"

She looked at Dan again as if needing permission; he gave her a gentle smile and a nod. "Not much else. Josie was unconscious when I found her and she never made a sound until the ambulance men took her off to come here, she moaned when they lifted her onto the stretcher but that was it. They wanted to know if I saw anything else at her house, but I didn't. All the lights were on but there was no sign of it being ransacked or anything like that."

"Did they want to know anything else?" Dan asked.

"No. Really it was just if she said anything."

"What about you having to make a statement?"

"No."

Dan and Nick exchanged another look. That was not right.

"How many police were there, Estelle?" Nick asked.

"I saw two but there might have been more. Only one talked to me, an inspector."

"Did he tell you his name?"

"Binder. Detective Inspector Binder."

Dan fixed his gaze on her face. "Did he say anything else to you, anything at all?"

Estelle's head bobbed like a duck on a pond. "Not really, he asked two or three times if Josie said anything at all and told me not to talk to anyone until I heard back from him again. He wanted Josie's house key, but I told him I didn't have one."

Nick sighed loudly. "Oh shit." There were still some of the stolen items from Allen's house securely hidden away there; both he and Dan thought much the same thing. "That's a shame; we could do with one ourselves," Nick said.

Estelle flicked the magazine off her lap and onto the floor, then reached into her little shoulder bag and fished around for a moment.

"Josie told me I could trust you. Here." She handed Dan a single brass key. "I must have forgotten I had this when he asked about a key," she said, allowing a hint of a smile.

"Thanks Estelle. What are you going to do now?"

"I'm not going anywhere until I know how she is."

Nick read Dan's mind. "It's okay I'll go back to Josie's. You stay here with Estelle. After, I'll go on home; I have to call Penny or she will have my guts."

"Thanks, mate." Dan paused and decided to say what was on his mind. "Hey, I don't want to sound like I'm teaching you the obvious but…"

Nick grinned. "As if you would, leave it to me."

After Nick disappeared Dan settled down for what could be a long wait.

"What was that all about?" Estelle asked.

"Old police habits die hard. Nick will have a look around when he gets there as well as retrieving what I left the other day. Thank you again for doing what you have."

Estelle blinked twice and for a fraction of a second Dan saw the emotion behind the tough exterior she was doing her best to control.

"Josie has been so good to me and to my sister, our guardian angel. What do you think happened to her?"

"I can't be sure yet. When she wakes up let's hope she can tell us."

"It was not a random attack. Everyone knows or knows of her. She wasn't a threat to anybody. I think it's got something to do with you."

Dan did not believe it was coincidence either and Estelle giving voice to his own suspicions sickened him. If he was somehow responsible… Before he could think about it any more, a serious-looking doctor approached them.

"Mr. Calder?"

"Yes."

The doctor hesitated, looking at Estelle.

"My niece," Dan said in explanation.

All three knew it was just a means to continue the conversation.

"I'm Doctor Flynn, can you follow me?"

Dan and Estelle stood and followed in single file. Dr. Flynn was a perfect replica of every TV doctor: long white coat, stethoscope around his neck, tired looking and with no fashion sense. Dan fought against the feeling he knew what was coming. Once in a quiet room off the main waiting area Flynn offered them a seat on a sofa; Dan and Estelle sat.

"I'm so very sorry to tell you that Ms. Lamas did not regain consciousness and she died a few minutes ago."

Estelle took in a sharp breath and held it. Dan nodded.

"The savagery of the assault plus her age, I'm afraid she was just not strong enough."

Estelle gripped Dan's hand. "Oh no."

"I really am very sorry. There are certain procedures which have to be followed and there will need to be a post mortem to establish… well it's one of those things which happens in a case like this."

"Is it possible to see her?" Dan asked. He did not want to but knew he must.

"Ms. Lamas was very badly beaten. Some people prefer to remember a loved one as they were," Flynn offered.

"Thanks, but I want to. Estelle, you should stay here. Please."

A few minutes later Dan was shown into a cubicle in the accident department.

"I'll give you a few minutes," Flynn said, withdrawing and closing the curtain behind him.

Dan had been in this position too many times before, in the presence of a death linked to something he had said, or done, or been involved with. The contours of the white sheet which covered Josie's battered body could have been his mother's, Zoe or Tara's brother Neil. Their ghosts now crowded into the small cubicle making him feel like he was trapped in a lift with them.

He stepped forward and drew back the sheet.

"Jesus fucking Christ."

The words came involuntarily. Josie's face was a puffy mix of blue and purple, her deformed nose and swollen lips and eyes made her head appear twice the size he remembered. He had seen many victims of assaults before and he knew what she must have gone through.

"Oh Jos', I'm so sorry," he said, touching a cool, blue cheek.

Her hair, which she always took so much pride in, was in an insulting mess and Dan used his fingers and palm to try and smooth it into a style she would find more acceptable. He then pulled the sheet down further, so he could see the rest of her broken body. He took a deep breath and found himself apologising again before he lifted one of her arms so he could examine her hand; the limb was starting to stiffen already. He then repeated it with the other arm, taking in the injuries and bruising patternation as well as every other unnatural mark.

Job done he stood back so he could see all of her; spending another minute committing his old friend and confidante's features to memory. When he was finished, he found her personal effects in a paper bag next to the bed and took them with him.

Estelle was crying. Dan went to her and put a fatherly arm around her shoulder. She did not object.

"I'm sorry you found her like that, Estelle. Come on let's go."

Against his wishes, Estelle insisted on being taken home. An hour later Dan was back at Nick's house waiting for his return and with time on his hands to think.

Nick was unsure if he would have to wait, or even go away and come back again, if there was police activity at Josie's house when he got there. All scenarios were possible depending on how the police were proceeding at that moment. What he found and did not expect was an empty house and no activity at all. After a moment's thought he decided he should take advantage of the current situation. Scenes of crime would have been and gone, and so there was no need to be concerned about leaving traces. He was inside the house a few seconds later.

First priority was the recovery of the items from Allen's house which Josie had offered to store for them. The false wall in the cupboard under the stairs came away easily, revealing sufficient capacity for anything up to two fully grown adults. He wondered who and what had been secreted in there in the past as he removed what they needed before carefully replacing the wall panel.

Conscious of the time, he switched on his phone's video function and held it in front of him as he walked through each room looking for clues to what happened there a few hours earlier. The dried pool of blood on the lounge carpet was nearly a metre square and its metallic odour filled the room. He guessed the attack began and ended there because of all Josie's many ornaments, the only disturbed ones were in close proximity; an overturned chair and small table, which once stood at the end of the sofa according to the indented footprints left in the carpet.

He slowly walked through the lounge a second time, making sure his phone's video captured every detail. After thirty minutes, he felt that he had pushed his good fortune as far as he could. Collecting up the retrieved items, he looked both ways out of the front room's big window before exiting.

When he got home, Amber was looking very worried.

"Hi, Am. What's up?"

"It's Dan. He's been on the computer upstairs for ages. I think he's talking to Tara, but he sounds in a terrible state. I've been trying not to hear but I can't help it."

"How many more times are you going to keep doing this to yourself? I've told you a hundred times, I am not going to stroke your hair and tell you it's all okay every time you blame yourself. It is not your fault!" Tara was initially concerned for Dan for another reason when he called her at 6:00 a.m. New Zealand time but after he explained what happened she spent the next forty five minutes doing what she could to make him see sense.

Once again, his mother, Zoe and Neil Danes' deaths were at the forefront of his mind, playing Russian roulette with his sanity. Josie Lamas successfully navigated her way through a lifetime of potential confrontation with the skill and expertise of a veteran politician and now within days of him dropping into her retirement she was gone in the most disturbing possible way.

"She's dead because I went to see her and asked for her help. How can it not be my fault?" he said again.

In the last two years, they spent many nights having similar conversations. Tara was desperate for him to find a way to see what happened to his mother and her brother differently but to no avail. He readily accepted the debilitating effect his guilt had on him, but maintained that it was the truth of the situation.

"So, what would you rather have done? If you stayed here where would Amber be right now? If you didn't take on Katrina Mallinder, the chances are Neil would still be dead, as would how many other people?"

"I know, I know. Maybe that just goes to show I tried to do the right thing but got it wrong both times, and now a third time. She was an old woman Tara, she helped me out so many times before. When I saw her in the hospital I could tell what had happened. It would have taken several minutes for her to accumulate all the injuries I saw."

They sat in silence looking at each other's image on their computer screens until Tara shrugged.

"So, what are you going to do?"

"I don't know. If I stay, more people could end up getting hurt but I can't just tell Nick and Amber hey sorry I'm leaving, good luck."

Tara thought momentarily. "Why don't you go to the police then? Go to another police station or even another police area if it would be safer."

"Because there's not enough evidence in Amber's favour or against Parker to make an allegation stick. If we go now and get no joy, we won't be back to square one, we'll be ten times worse off."

"Be honest Dan, will you be better able to live with yourself if you see this through to the end or if you walk away now?"

He shook his head. "That's just it. I'm not sure I can take the responsibility of doing either."

"Well, I am sorry my darling, but only you can decide."

"I know. But what would you do if it was you?"

She searched her head and heart for an answer.

"I'd give anything to have Neil back, but the fact is he died. It happened. You blame yourself despite what I think but that apart, I'm glad you resolved it. You did, Dan, and nobody else could have done. Maybe the question you need to answer is, if you don't, who will?"

"Thanks, you always know what to say." Dan felt empty, he touched the screen where Tara's cheek was, and then traced his finger down to her belly. "Now how are you feeling today, any more baby movements?"

Her face softened. "No, nothing again. I did go into town today to look in the baby shops, but I really want us to do it together. There is so much cute stuff, I even saw a camouflage tracksuit and thought of you."

"I still can't quite believe it myself. I wish I was there," he said honestly.

"Yes, me too. Just so long as you come home safe, I'll be happy."

When Dan came downstairs Nick and Amber were reviewing Nick's video footage of Josie's house on Amber's laptop. After the events of the last week none of them thought twice now about Amber watching the images or her being any less a part of their team.

Dan's mind was still on the conversation with Tara and the dilemma he felt he was facing as he absent-mindedly looked over their shoulders at the screen. The video showed the large blackened blood spot—the last part of Josie still in the house—and it made him gulp. He was about to look away when something caught his eye.

"What's that?"

Nick hit the pause button and looked up. "What's what?"

Amber shuffled along the sofa so Dan could sit between them with the laptop on his knees. He shifted the video back a few seconds and pressed play again.

"That." He pointed with one finger while pressing pause with another.

Nick squinted at the screen. "Oh, it was a Bible. I think it must have been on a table and got knocked off in the melee."

"And that?" Dan pointed again.

"What?"

"That there on the page, look." Dan did not want to put words in Nick's mouth or mind.

"It looks like a red line on the page," Amber stated innocently, frustrating Dan.

"Oh, yes I see it. Yes, it was open but I didn't notice the underlining at the time."

Dan's mind was completely back in the moment. As with countless times in the past his inner troubles were placed on hold, allowing them to bubble and fester but not interrupt.

"Try and enlarge it or print it. I want to know what it says. I've got to make a call."

He disappeared leaving Nick and Amber staring at each other and the screen.

"What is it?" she asked.

"I haven't got a clue but that's not a first. Can you do something with this?"

"Hopefully, let me take it upstairs and see what we can print off before Dan comes back."

Dan went to the kitchen where his mobile was still plugged into a power point.

"Hi Estelle, it's me Dan, how are you doing?"

"Still in a state of shock to be honest. Is everything okay?"

"Yes, I'm sorry to bother you, I just need to ask you something about you and Josie. You said you talked about theology, is that, right?"

"Yes, a shared interest although her knowledge was much greater than mine. God was a big part of her life; she liked to talk with all the girls."

"Did she keep a Bible at home?"

"In the living room, why?"

"I was just thinking, did she ever write in it?"

"God no! Sorry, that wasn't meant to be a joke. No, she would never do that."

Dan felt a familiar rush once more. "And you said she was quite knowledgeable?"

"She could quote hundreds and hundreds of verses by heart. Are you sure everything's okay?"

"Fine Estelle, yes you've been a big help. Can I call you tomorrow?"

He was back in the lounge before Nick and Amber. As he waited for them to return he played over what he saw at the hospital earlier in his head, so he was one hundred percent sure by the time they came back in five minutes later.

"How did you get on?" he asked before they had a chance to sit down.

"Good and bad. We were able to print the page off but it's too distorted to read properly when we enlarged it," Nick replied.

All three studied the sheet of A4. There was a line which was clearly underlined but the words were unreadable.

"I think that's sixteen," Amber said pointing to the far left of the page. "So that makes it verse sixteen."

She and Dan squinted again but could see no more. Suddenly Nick slapped his knee. "Of course." He was looking at the laptop screen again, not at the underlined section but at the top of the page. "Look, Proverbs Chapter Twelve."

He quickly minimised the screen to perform a search. Amber read the top answer.

"'A fool shows his annoyance at once, but a prudent man overlooks an insult.'"

The significance hit Dan head on. Amber read a few other versions. They differed slightly depending on which Bible the phrase was taken from, but the meaning remained constant.

"What does that mean?" Amber asked.

"I'm a bit lost too. Would you care to explain?" Nick added.

"When I was at the hospital I went to see Josie. I saw some red marks on her hand, but they weren't blood because she had been washed, they were pen marks. I talked to Estelle a minute ago and she said Josie would never have written in her Bible, so it must have been something very important to make her do this."

Amber read the line again. "'A fool shows his annoyance at once, but a prudent man overlooks an insult.' I still don't get it."

"I do," Nick said. "Who do we know who has a liking for quotations?"

Dan returned his stare. "Exactly. And if Teddy Parker said that to Josie, what was he doing at the time to make him come up with that line in particular? If I know Josie she wouldn't have been intimidated by him turning up and shooting his mouth off. More likely she would have told him to take a hike."

"Him!" Amber said. The anger in her voice struck Dan, but there was a note of panic, too.

Nick put an arm around her. "Of course, we should have guessed straight away."

Amber shrugged his arm off and went to Dan. "Oh Dan, I'm so sorry. This is all my fault."

Amber's words struck Dan like lightning. In that moment, as she looked at him with utter despair in her eyes, Dan knew that this wasn't her fault. And he knew it wasn't his either. He felt a renewed sense of clarity. The pain that had weighed him down for three decades shifted and melted away like ice in springtime. He placed his hand on her arm and embraced her gently.

"Don't you ever think that, and you listen to me really carefully. I have had the same thoughts you are having now for far too long. Josie was killed by Teddy Parker because Teddy Parker either wanted to do it or could not control his temper, just like Anna Rofe. You do not have to think of it in any more complicated terms than that."

"But if I…"

"Amber, Amber. I have been saying 'but if I' for as long as I can remember, and it's finally taken hearing it from you to make me realise other people do things regardless of what you think you have said or done. Take it from me, it's not a burden you want to carry with you. Let it go, please."

Amber breathed in deeply. "We have to stop him, Dan."

"We will, I promise you, but right now, I have to make another call."

Tara was initially surprised to hear back from Dan so quickly and then a little sceptical when he told her of his recent epiphany. Finally, understanding and relief flooded through her.

"I'm so sorry Tara, for all this crap I've put you through," Dan said for the fifth or sixth time in as many minutes.

"It's alright. I am so glad you called back. Going back to England was obviously meant to be for you to work it all out."

"I don't know about that."

She laughed. "Yes, I know you don't but that is alright. It means I still have to work on you to get you right. Does this mean you're staying?"

"I have to. Is that okay?"

"Dan, I would not have you any other way. Be careful though."

"I will. I love you, I love you both. Give Jet a pat for me."

CHAPTER EIGHTEEN

When Dan woke the next morning, he was a man divided. His heart ached for Josie and she dominated his thoughts, but perversely he felt refreshed and good for another reason. After years of bearing his painful past like a cilice, now at least his mother and Neil Danes were finally resting in peace in his mind. Amber's misplaced guilt had opened his eyes to his own, clearing the way for personal absolution and an understanding of what must be done. The seed of an idea about Zoe Summers and that night at 22 Powton Road also implanted itself into his subconscious, but that was a matter for another time.

Right now, he still had to figure out what to do about Allen, the Parkers, and Binder, but try as he might, he still didn't have a plan. He was genuinely concerned all the investigative avenues had turned into dead-ends.

Allen could hardly believe his eyes as he read the daily bulletin, the summary of noteworthy crime in the force area over the previous twenty-four hours. He had to place his tea cup on the desk as he lacked the strength to even hold it steady. He stared at the monitor as the name of Josephine Lamas burst from it and he felt like the wrath of all the gods was within him as he read the short passage over and over.

Discovered in her Trenton Grove, Mapperley Park home by a visiting friend. Multiple injuries. Taken by ambulance to Nottingham City Hospital for emergency treatment. Detective Inspector Binder making the early crime assessment. Died of injuries one hour after admission. Crime suspected although motive not yet apparent. Officer in case Detective Chief

Inspector Raye, Serious Crimes Unit, internal extension 4087. Media release pending.

Josie Lamas was attacked and killed within two days of him telling Ben Binder of his concerns over her dealings with Anna Rofe and her connection to Dan Calder. The facts of what must have happened were as clear to him as daylight. The possible consequences were just as clear.

He read the brief report again before burying his face in his hands and wishing with all his might he had not said a word about Josie to Binder. For once he was clueless as to what to do. The whole situation was so far out of hand now he felt like his brain was a ball of unravelling string and his future was no longer his own. The thought of a view from a prison cell rather than the Devon coast at his retirement home sprang to mind.

He considered calling Binder but decided on a text message instead. Deleting what he really wanted to say, he sent a more restrained 'My office NOW' and sat back in his chair to further consider the awfulness of the situation.

Staring into the dark grainy swirl of his walnut desk, the patterns slowly morphed into pictures of faces and places from his past and present. As he continued to gaze, the clouds of his current predicament parted, revealing a clarity in the highly-polished wood surface. His reflection stared back at him and he knew what must be done.

"Sheila, I'm going out," he said curtly to his secretary as he strode from his office and headed for the lift.

When Ben Binder arrived fifteen minutes later Sheila could not assist when he asked how long Allen would be or where he had gone. He waited for a few minutes and then left.

Dan sat alone at the breakfast table. He was glad Nick and Amber were yet to put in appearance as it gave him more time to think in desperate hope for an idea to come to mind. The toaster popping reaffirmed his sorry state and he considered phoning Tara again. She understood him better than anyone and was regularly able to say just the right thing at any given moment. Much as he did not want to admit it, the prospect of failing was looming very large indeed.

He was just about to reach for the phone when there was a knock on the front door. His first thought was, *why knock when there is a doorbell,* and his second was, *I used to knock on doors when I was in the police regardless of there being a bell or not. It always seemed more… appropriate.* Therefore, his shock was mildly tempered when he opened it to see who the early caller was.

"You've got a bloody nerve. Don't you think you have done enough already?" Dan said.

James Allen stood before him. It took Dan several moments to fully notice how strained he appeared.

"Listen, if all I wanted was a verbal ear-bashing I could go to a hundred other places and be very adequately catered for," Allen offered with open palms. "I'll understand if you don't want to but is there any chance we can talk?"

It took a lot for Dan to be surprised but his ex-boss had managed to leave him completely at a loss.

"Please. You need to hear what I've got to say, and I need your help."

Dan stiffened as Allen's words sunk in and when he replied it was almost involuntarily. "Not here. Let's take your car."

"Where to?"

Dan didn't know why but there was only one place which seemed right.

"The library, it will be open by the time we get there."

Allen's car was warm inside but the atmosphere between the two men was as cold and frosty as any winters' day. As they drove along Dan reflected on the dozens of trips they had taken in the past where he was the chauffeur. He noted that Allen had turned off the police radio and the only noise was that of the traffic around them. He tried not to think of what Allen wanted; it would become apparent soon enough.

Allen's stare remained resolutely on the road. He seemed to nearly speak on several occasions but then thought better of it. Dan felt no desire to help him out with some meaningless chatter and so the whole journey was made in deafening silence.

When they arrived, Allen let out a mighty sigh as he exited the car. He followed Dan inside. Despite the library opening just a few minutes earlier they were not the first visitors by any means. Three men who could have been triplets in their mid-sixties with grey hair and plain coats were reading the free newspapers and a female student dressed from head to toe in black with headphones under her wool hat was scanning shelves in the modern history section. None of them paid any attention to Dan and Allen.

Dan was focused on his chosen path and headed straight for a corner of the ground floor with a few scattered tables and chairs, some for working at and others for more relaxed reading. He saw Allen paid little attention to where exactly he finally came to rest. The two low chairs with no dividing table immediately below a large sash window were deliberately selected. Dan sat, leaving the other chair for Allen. When he sat, the morning sun shone through the window straight into his face, making him squint to see. Dan smiled inwardly.

Dan was about to say, "Well, what the fuck do you want?" but Allen beat him to it.

"I bet neither of us imagined the day was going to start like this when we went to bed last night. Why don't you just hear me out, let me get what I have to say done and then you can have whatever fun you want with me. We are both too old and too long in the tooth for much else."

Dan sat back comfortably and mimicked Allen's open palms from earlier. In order to see without the sun blinding himself, Allen was forced to sit leaning forward.

"I don't know how much you have worked out already," he began, heaving another great sigh. "Probably a hell of a lot knowing you. I suppose what you're most interested in is Amber Hetherington. I know she had nothing to do with Anna Rofe's murder."

Dan shifted slightly in his seat but remained quiet. For once he could not think of anything useful to say, and in any case, he had no idea where this was leading or even if Allen had an altogether unknown agenda.

"It's a long story and a right shitty mess now. I've royally buggered up the last couple of weeks and I want to get it sorted before things get worse, if they possibly can. I'm guessing you know about Josie Lamas by now too?"

Dan frowned darkly.

"Of course, you do. You must believe me when I tell you I had nothing to do with that. I knew her back in the day, I liked the old girl. Oh, Christ Dan, let me just start at the beginning."

Allen was visibly sweating and wringing his hands like some end of the world prophet. As much as he disliked the man and wished him nothing but ill will, Dan could not bring himself to crush him completely.

"Start with Amber."

Allen appeared genuinely pleased and relieved to get something out of Dan that was not undisguised contempt.

"She was in the wrong place at the wrong time. He needed a suspect."

Dan did not intend to speak. He intended to listen to all Allen had to say but once again his mouth moved and words came out in an involuntary reaction. "Why did you need someone other than Teddy Parker? Surely putting away the real offender is much simpler than constructing a whole new story," he spat.

"By the time I got involved it was already too late," Allen caught himself mid-sentence. "Sorry, that's a load of bull. I should have done something, but circumstances made me make a series of bad decisions and before I knew it, it was too late. There's this other bloke in the job, you don't know him, DI Ben Binder. A real flyer but an obnoxious toad. I just wanted to get to retirement and then I would be shot of all this forever, but now I might have fucked up my retirement full-stop."

Despite himself, Dan found he was engrossed by what Allen was telling him. He could tell it was all true and that made everything better and worse at the same time. He mentally amended his previous assumption of Allen and Binder being best buddies, willing and equally complicit participants in whatever their deal was.

Allen paused, gaining some composure as he got more into his story.

"It doesn't matter if Amber Hetherington is convicted or not. Think about it. We both know how many times a new suspect is identified let alone charged and convicted when someone else has already been before the courts: practically zero. If she is put in front of a judge, Teddy Parker is in the clear. He would never be put in the frame even if she is found not guilty. It will all just go cold and be forgotten because there is no one to remember Anna Rofe enough to make a fuss."

This time Dan bit his tongue and waited for more.

"I found out about Josie this morning when I got into the office. Whatever else I've done or got involved in, I won't have her blood on my hands. Anna Rofe was a nobody. No family, no friends, no one to mourn her. Not putting away her killer isn't going to affect anyone. That's what Binder convinced me of and that's why I went along with it." He paused again for oxygen. "That was what I allowed myself to think anyway. Until now. There isn't a name you can call me which I haven't called myself but enough is enough."

Dan added what he was hearing to his knowledge of the facts plus his virtually infallible sixth sense and computed it all into rational thought. It did make ugly sense except for one obvious thing.

"So why are you telling me?" His tone was still contemptuous, his opinion of Allen unchanged. "Just do the right thing and you can retire in a blaze of glory by locking up a double murderer."

"Binder has got me by the balls Dan, Edward Parker senior too, to a lesser degree. A couple of mistakes, bad decisions, have come home to roost and I can't risk losing it all now."

"So, it's cowardice then?"

"Fine, however you want to put it. You who has never made a wrong move in your whole life, you who has never made a mistake or tried to correct something when it's all gone pear-shaped. I forgot who I'm talking to for a second, obviously. I'm telling you because I need your help, because I recognise it might already be too late. Can't you see how far I've fallen just by the fact that I am talking to you after our history? By Christ, you are your father's son alright."

Although he could not possibly know it then, in two sentences Allen just gave himself a lifeline to cling on to. Dan inwardly recoiled as the old detective's words hit home like a combination of heavyweight punches, and he saw him for the first time as someone other than the man and supervising officer he detested for so long.

His voice cracked a little as he spoke. "So?"

Allen took a deep breath and continued. "I want to make it alright with Amber Hetherington and I want to put Teddy Parker behind bars where he belongs, I really do, but is it too much to ask that I also want my career to survive for just a few months more, so I can get out intact? Not for me so much as for my wife. Think of me what you want, but she is a saint with all she has dealt with."

"You are asking the wrong man about that considering how my career ended and your part in it."

Allen looked incredulous. "Well, I deserved that one as well didn't I. We're not going to get into all that again are we? You must look back yourself and see how I was trying to help you, son."

Dan's attention was momentarily taken by another thought and he did not register Allen's last remark properly. By the time he refocused, Allen had moved on.

"Cards on the table Dan, am I right in thinking you already know enough to stir up one hell of a mess? I reckon so. Call it self-preservation or whatever you like, but I want to make things right and I know I can do it a lot quicker and more effectively knowing I'm not battling against you."

"So, you want me to trust you to do an about turn on everything…"

"Have you not heard a bloody word? It's me who's trusting you not to throw me under a bus and report everything you already know, not to keep digging on your own and finish me off for good, not to use all our past differences as ammunition for your latest personal mission of destruction."

"All I care about is Amber and Josie. Watching you crash and burn would just be an added bonus."

Allen threw up his arms and spoke with a raised voice. "Like I said, you are your father's son and no mistake."

Heads now lifted and turned from newspapers and modern history towards them. Dan's mind raced back through Allen's previous comments as Allen himself returned a sheepish look to a clearly angered librarian. When they locked eyes again, Dan was confused.

"You don't know anything about him and me."

"I know he made my life a bloody misery and you did the same. I did everything in my power to get you on my division in Garstone when you came off the Surveillance Unit because I'd heard such good reports about you."

Dan couldn't hide his obvious surprise.

"You were the best investigator I ever had work for me, but you always thought you knew best, always needed to have it all your own way. I served under your father for the first years I was in the job. He didn't like me from day one, who knows why, maybe he just didn't like my face or that I was from the poor side of town with the accent to go with it. That's all water under the bridge now, but I fought for every scrap of success I've achieved. I got out of uniform and his area as soon as I could and into the investigations department. Having you years later turned into a poisoned chalice. I thought I could do better by you than he did of me."

Dan's surprise rapidly grew to consternation as he was forced to reassess much of his past, leaving him feeling defensive. "So that explains why you were so happy to hang me out to dry, does it?"

"When you left the job, it was your decision. The fact you were disciplined before that because of what you said outside Garstone courthouse is also all your own work. I can still remember it word for word and let me tell you, it took a lot of getting over. Shit always sticks regardless of how accurate it is. You may still think I was at fault over that case, but I followed the rules and made the decisions I did in accordance with them. If you want to remember it at all correctly, then remember that you never came to me before, during or after. You went home and sulked and then left. I've regretted your going ever since, regretted not being able to get it into your thick skull that I was always on your side, wanted to help, wanted to be a better boss to you than your dad was to me, and wanted to help you reach your full potential."

Dan was reeling now. What started as a conversation about Amber was now a very uncomfortable personal trial.

"But you were always against me," he stuttered.

"Was I? Was I? How about you ask anyone who has worked under me in the last thirty odd years if they feel the same. Apart from your friend Nick, I'll stand by the general consensus. Why do you think you could go off whenever a course or an undercover job came up? Did I ever say no? When did you last look back with an open mind?"

Dan shifted uncomfortably as Allen's truths hit close to home.

"Listen Dan, we may never be best friends, but we need to have a very long and serious talk some day, not about Amber Hetherington and Josie Lamas, let's get that sorted first and I promise you we will, but about our careers and lives, son, because somewhere along the line things have gone way off the rails."

Son. That is the third time in ten minutes he has called me that, Dan thought, *and not in a bad or condescending way.*

"Amber first. Starting right now," he said, struggling to regain the initiative.

The turmoil within him failed to dissipate as he watched Allen take yet another deep breath before speaking. Suddenly unable to cope, Dan held out his open hands once again but this time as a signal to pause. Without another word, he got up and walked away. He meandered as if in a maze with no way out, desperately trying to process the new information and make it fit with what he knew already, or rather, what he thought he knew. This new load added to the recent revelations Amber brought to the fore and was almost too much to take. Could he really have been so wrong for so long about so much?

A full five minutes passed before he returned to settle in the low chair to focus in on Allen once again. The detective reached across the small gap between them to place a gentle and fatherly hand on Dan's shoulder. Dan did not attempt to remove it.

"Listen Dan, there's nothing good in making mistakes if you don't learn from them or take the chance to put them right. I want to try and put mine right. I believe I can't do it without your help and I'm asking you for it."

Although he was the one asking for Dan's assistance, Allen sounded like the authority figure Dan remembered from all those years ago, and in that moment, he felt the security of being in the police family again. Almost.

"If you think after that little speech I'm going to roll over and tell you everything I know," he said guardedly, "you can think again."

"There's no need to say anything at all. If you can stop working against me and just start working with me I'll tell you all you need to know, starting with Nick Hetherington's girl. Come on Dan, what have you got to lose?"

Nothing. Everything, he thought, pausing to regain his composure. "Go on, I'm listening."

It was 11:30 a.m. when they left the library together, going their separate ways at the main doors. Dan needed the fresh air to think so he declined Allen's offer of a ride back to Nick's. A plan was forming, but he knew he would have his work cut out for him convincing Nick and Amber to go along with it.

Sure, enough Nick's first reaction was to tell Dan, "You might be my best friend, but you and Allen can go and fuck yourselves if you think that!"

"Well that's what he's prepared to do, drop all charges before the first court date if we help him dig himself out of the hole he's in, and at the same time try to deal with Binder and Parker."

"No Dan, not a chance. I want all investigations finished now and I bloody want a letter of apology from him and the Chief Constable for what they've put Amber through," Nick said, banging the table repeatedly.

"I know it's a lot to ask and Amber has been through more than enough already, but maybe a few more days and we can get Parker and Binder."

"No. That's final."

"Don't you think I should get a vote?" Amber interjected. "After all, it is me we're talking about, isn't it?"

"Sorry, of course," Dan replied, holding up submissive palms.

"No, not a chance Amber," Nick blasted. "He knows you're innocent. If he has got himself in the shit because he's a bad cop then let him suffer the consequences. I thought you would have known better too, Dan, after all the crap he's sent your way over the years. Christ, you make it sound like he's doing us a favour. Well, you can forget it."

"Dad, I'm not a baby!"

"What do you think your mother would say if I allowed you to play his bloody game?"

Amber frowned. "What I was going to say was, I don't want to do it either, but it's my decision not yours, okay?"

Nick went silent.

Dan waited a moment. "I promised myself before getting to the house that I wouldn't try and change your minds if you were against the idea. It's a lot to ask, continuing to use Amber as bait so we can build a case against Teddy and Binder. I'll be honest, I am a bit disappointed but alright, I'll tell Allen no deal and he will have to live with that, which means winding up the case against you. I suppose congratulations are in order then, you can relax and consider yourself off the hook."

Nobody felt like celebrating; Amber went back to bed while Nick phoned Penny to tell her and the twins to come home. When he told Dan how pleased and relieved Penny was they hugged like long lost brothers.

Dan sniffed as they came apart. "I better get back to Allen and let him know. Can I use the car?"

"Sure. You understand, don't you?"

"Of course. I suppose it's just a bit weird that it's all over with a whimper. Hey, I can make some plans of my own to go home too. I've got a nursery to decorate."

"Well, I'm not complaining this whole episode is over. You have to remember that all this cloak and dagger stuff doesn't happen to us mere mortals like it does for you. That's why I've still got all my hair."

"So here we are again," Allen said, pulling up a chair. "It's obviously not good news for me at least, seeing you again so soon."

Dan shrugged. "Depends how you look at it. You're not investigating an innocent person anymore."

He pushed a pint glass of Allen's favourite ale across the table and lifted his glass in an apologetic toast.

"You even remember what beer I drink?" Allen said.

Weekday lunchtime at the country inn was a quiet time and they had the bar to themselves. The barman was fully concentrating on polishing glasses, so they were free to talk.

"So where does that leave you?" Allen asked after his first sip.

"Happy for my friends and looking forward to going home."

"For what it's worth, can you pass on my regards and sincere apologies? They must be delighted."

"Just relieved. What you put them all through was a nightmare. The last thing they feel like is having a party, and they don't care less what you think."

"Of course, sorry, that was a stupid thing to say. I can't say I'm surprised. Nick's got a family to look after, why should he give a stuff about my situation? I suppose I'll have to deal with it as best I can. You can tell Amber to call me on my office number anytime in the next few days to come in, just a formality and a couple of signatures."

"Sure."

"You look disappointed, Dan."

"No, Amber's in the clear and Nick will calm down in a few days, especially with his wife home again. It's just what we talked about earlier. I would love for Teddy Parker to be brought to justice for all his crimes and for this Binder bastard to be accountable too. His type in the job is no good for anyone."

"We don't always get what we want. I've got some hard decisions to make, the trouble is even if I come clean there's a very real chance I'll not be able to prove Binder's part in all this and with what he has on me, it would just be seen as an attempt to cover up my failings by slinging mud at him. Look, I brought it all on myself so that's just what happens. I asked you a minute ago, about what you're going to do now, and you said you'll be going home. I would really like to have that talk with you before you do so I can at least have a clear conscience about something."

Dan stared into his beer. Tara was waiting at home with a new baby on the way and life was looking good. He had learned to live with his past, despite the lack of closure in some areas, and the last thing he wanted was more complications. He thought about being on a plane, landing in Auckland to be met by her then going back to their house, finishing the new deck, having a barbecue, playing golf with Paul, and even playing with Jet on the beach.

"All that stuff before, you and my father, me and you, is that how it really was?" It seemed what he wanted and what he needed were two different things.

"It was, son. I often thought that if I stopped you from going off on those undercover jobs you might settle down a bit and be more content. I thought they did you more harm than good."

"I loved all that, getting away from everything and pretending to be somebody else."

Allen shook his head. "See, that's what I mean. You were never yourself for long enough to get to know who you were and what you wanted. To me, you were almost schizophrenic. Do you remember that last time, God you were like a different person altogether and before I knew it you were screaming and shouting at the top of your voice outside Garstone Crown Court."

Dan's mind went back to that day, and the previous days and weeks in Powton Road. When he refocused Allen was still talking.

"…What options were there? Headquarters went into damage control mode and I had no choice but to tow the line. The organisation is more important than one disgruntled DC."

"Can I be honest with you? I thought you and my father were out of the same box."

Allen raised his glass and his eyebrows. "Funny thing, perception."

"I was so sure. I'm more confused now than I was back then."

Allen took another sip. "Listen, son," it was becoming a habit that Dan found himself having no objection to, "time can do strange things, some good, some not so, but given enough of it, generally it does deliver clarity. I think I could have done more to help you, made you a better policeman and maybe you would still be in the job, but then, who knows. I would certainly have done things differently for myself with my time over. I might not have a big house in the country, but I wouldn't be in the mess I'm in now. That reminds me. Can I have the stuff you stole out of my house back?" He said it with no animosity.

They looked at each other over the table with fresh understanding and respect. Dan felt no need to answer the question directly. Instead he asked, "Is there anything I can do to help you before I head off?"

"I don't know. What I said earlier was all I know. I'm sure there is more history between Ben Binder and Teddy Parker than I'm aware of, but right now that doesn't do me any good. Binder has definitely got a plan. He's not here to stay a DI. He wants to go all the way and the next lot of boards are coming up in three weeks' time. Another promotion and he'll be controlling a whole division. The sky's the limit after that."

"Why so?"

"At the moment, he's still in the business of preventing and detecting crime, actually locking bodies up. Once he's got the big office all that goes out the window and he becomes a manager responsible for everyone else who does the locking up, and providing he doesn't make any complete fuck-ups, further promotions become a treadmill of regularity."

Dan pondered the whole mechanics of Binder's strategic approach to promotion, rather than simply being an effective police officer. It was an alien concept to him and scary to imagine anybody would think that way.

"Are you involved in the boards?"

"No, not this time. It's the Deputy Chief and a couple of his cronies, including the new civilian personnel and discipline executives. They know nothing about police work but can count pencils and analyse the shit out of the smallest risk. Nowadays it's more important to have the least potential trouble maker rather than the best candidate."

Dan's brain was working again like a machine.

"I've seen that look before, Dan," Allen said.

"I was just thinking, is he the type to want to know he's got the promotion before he goes in the room?"

"Without a doubt. It's a modern thing."

"What would be the best way to do that?"

Allen clearly had no idea where Dan was heading with his line of questioning but had the good sense not to stem the flow with unnecessary questions. "Have a big gold star next to your name with whatever is current procedurally."

"What's current?"

"In the last review, it was better implementation of search powers and use of informants. The time before that was reducing the rates of violent crime, sexual offences and burglary."

"And what has he been doing most recently in those areas?"

"I'm not sure. To be honest, I try to avoid contact with him as much as I can. We have to see each other at the regular divisional heads meetings."

"What's his role?"

"He is the Area Retailers Liaison Officer for the city, including all other businesses who sell or supply. He oversees the crime unit Nick was on, not hands-on, more administrative."

Like tumblers in a lock, Binder's ambitions fell into place in Dan's head.

"Hold on, Nick is on a countywide burglary team, which he was conveniently removed from when you offered him compassionate leave. He told me he thought he was onto something but didn't say what."

Allen's eyes widened. "Binder asked me to get Nick off the job. I assumed it was because of his relation to Amber and the Rofe case, but what if it was about his work?"

"And burglary is a hot topic. What if Binder has a plan of his own? What if he's just waiting for the right moment to make his big splash?"

"Dan, they would be falling over themselves to lick arse. Hold that thought while I get us another pint."

"It almost beggars belief," Allen surmised two pints later.

Their conversation kept developing through the afternoon. They scrutinised and concluded Ben Binder's actions were calculated to get him to the top of the police hierarchy and he possessed the distorted skill set to do just that. What his long-term objectives were they could only guess at.

It was clear to them Binder must have some knowledge of the burglaries Nick and his team were investigating, and that somehow Teddy Parker was involved too. Why his involvement was so important to Binder that he was prepared to compromise a murder investigation to keep Teddy out of trouble, they could not explain.

Allen remembered a recent meeting he had with Binder.

"He said something once about cracking a burglary team just before his promotion board interview, but I didn't take any notice at the time. I was more worried about you, believe it or not."

"Obviously the timing is vitally important to him."

Allen rubbed his chin. "That just makes the whole thing, worse, doesn't it? Deliberate and measured."

They explored the possibility of Teddy, or even Edward Parker Sr., being the mastermind but dismissed the notion out of hand. This was all Binder's work; he was the puppet master and he seemed to have a whole cast of characters dancing to his tune.

"Have you got any evidence against Teddy for Anna Rofe's killing?" Dan asked.

"Not a shred. Only a Ukrainian prostitute can actually put him at the scene and her evidence is poor at best. She's already made a statement dropping Amber in it, if she recanted now and put Teddy in the frame any first year lawyer could tear her up for toilet paper. Teddy is sure to be alibied up as well. Like I said, I've royally screwed it all up. Not only that but Amber's friend Stacey's evidence, whilst completely honest, only implicates Amber. We have to face facts. Teddy Parker is free and clear so far as Anna Rofe is concerned."

While it went against everything he believed in, Dan conceded what Allen said was true.

"So how can we prove he killed Josie, presuming Binder is going to be looking out for him again?"

"That calls for another beer. Same again?"

CHAPTER NINETEEN

While Dan and Allen were trying to find a way to prevent Ben Binder from covering up another Teddy Parker murder, Binder wasted no time in making sure he couldn't be implicated an any of Teddy's mistakes. Cracking the spate of commercial burglaries blighting the county would result in his promotion to Chief Inspector, he was sure, and adding the arrest of poor old Josephine Lamas' murderer using a registered confidential source would be an extra bonus.

He'd fulfilled his duties, arranging for a constant uniform presence to attend Lamas' home until further notice and included the hospital's report in his initial assessment. There was sufficient foul play involved in the woman's death to warrant a full-scale investigation by the Serious Crimes Unit rather than local detectives. The wheels of a police major investigation would soon be rolling with professional ease and in no time, there would be enough evidence on top of an eye witness account to ensure that Teddy Parker would spend the rest of his life behind bars. Foolishly he said Marley was with him when he killed Josephine Lamas, therefore Binder's next port of call was at the home of Marley Johns in Lampwick Road, Hyson Green.

As he came to a stop outside the dilapidated semi-detached he felt grubby curtains twitching on all sides and was sure one of Nottingham's worst areas had come to a state of high alert with the appearance of his marked police car.

The doorbell obviously last worked years before; its exposed wiring was colour coordinated with the Rastafarian bumper sticker covering the broken glass pane at eye level and conveniently prevented visitors from being able to see inside. When he rapped loudly on the tired door, paint flakes floated to the ground and it seemed the whole thing might collapse out of sheer exhaustion. Muffled voices came from inside but Binder could guess the conversation taking place on the other side about who brought the police to the address and for what reason. He was about to knock again when scuffling footsteps negated the need. The door creaked open and two big brown eyes peered around the frame.

"Marley, is that you?"

The eyes blinked.

"Marley, I am Detective Inspector Binder. I want to speak to you about something which happened yesterday in Trenton Grove. We can do it here or at the station."

Marley's eyes bulged.

"It's up to you Marley. I'm not going to stand here all day. You can either help me and help yourself at the same time, or look forward to twenty years in a prison cell. I'll give you three seconds. One, two…"

"Okay, okay. You promise you can help me out?"

"I don't need to make promises to you, now open the door and let me in."

The inside of the Johns' house was as depressing as the outside. Threadbare carpet which was once a painter's palette of green hues looked more like the bottom of a dried-up riverbed and the walls and ceiling were the colour of dust held together with antique cobwebs. Binder followed Marley down the dark hallway into a kitchen where hand-painted cupboards clashed with the dirty black and white linoleum floor tiles. A wooden table with plastic garden chairs set around it stood in the centre of the room. Binder sat and indicated for Marley to do the same.

"You were with Teddy Parker yesterday at Josephine Lamas' house, weren't you?"

Binder knew the weight of what happened to the old lady would be crushing down on Marley Johns after sixteen hours to think about it. He only needed to press the right button.

"It was Teddy, it was all him, you gotta believe me."

As he went to continue a small boy appeared at the door dressed in pyjamas.

"Get the fuck out you nosy little prick!" he bellowed, causing the boy to turn on his heels.

An older woman's slurred voice drifted into the room from somewhere back along the hallway. "Don't you be shoutin' at your brother. Why you bring the police to my house anyway?"

"Fuck you too, stay outa my business," Marley shouted. Turning to Binder he continued as if he just paused for breath. "Honest Mr. Binder I never touched her, and I couldn't have stopped him it all happened so fast. What's going to happen?"

"That's up to you. You can either make a statement about what happened or get charged with being an accomplice. If you make a statement, I'll guarantee to look after you."

Marley recoiled. "He'll kill me if I rat him out. What he did to the old lady will be like playtime in comparison."

"Well, if you would rather take your chances with a judge and jury that's up to you, but there is something else you might want to consider."

"Oh yeah? I can't think of anything more important right now," Marley spluttered.

"Well in a few days' time I'm going to be making a name for myself when I arrest the gang who have been committing burglaries all around the area over the past year plus."

Marley gulped. "So why you tellin' me?"

"Felix Pope, Ellis Bowers, Alton Bowers, Kevin Prentiss, Justin McCrory. I can go on if you like, including you, Marley. All the names, all the burglaries including the most recent one at The Wine Seller on Bennett Road. The way I look at it Marley, is one name off that list won't do me any harm. Felix and his gang are all going down. You can be with them or not. It might mean you end up as king of what's left or decide to get away from Nottingham altogether and find somewhere for a new start. Either way, you are going to be all the way in or all the way out. So, what's it to be?"

Binder wasn't playing games now. From his position, it was difficult to tell what the gibbering fool in front of him was more scared of.

"Come on, if you have to think about it then you are more of an idiot than I thought. Just do yourself a favour and I'll see you alright."

"How, how can you?"

Binder did not fear repercussions. His security was rock solid and as things were turning out, he would be able to manipulate the circumstances to even greater personal advantage.

"I can get the Prosecutions Service to draw up a document assuring you of immunity from prosecution in return for you providing the evidence they require about Josephine Lamas' murder and the burglaries. You will be safe and sound, I give you my word. We'll even draw up the agreement before you provide your statements and you can have a solicitor present if you want."

He had left Marley with nowhere to turn. Binder noted his king of the area remark resonated with Marley, but it quickly seemed to become as distasteful a prospect as his current surroundings. A fresh start somewhere far away appeared a lot more inviting.

"What do you want me to do?"

Binder nodded and smiled. "Come with me now. I'll explain on the way."

Teddy Parker emerged from his latest alcohol and barbiturate haze at closer to dinner time than lunch. He stumbled to the bathroom, unbalanced and groggy, and pawed at the light switch. Even before he stepped under his state-of-the-art-shower, he felt like he was submerged. As the water hammered down on him he slowly reconnected with reality until his memory of the last day and a half was hideously clear. After drying and putting on clean clothes he went to call Ben Binder but soon realised his smashed mobile would never be making a call again. Circumstances demanded he break his own rule about using the home phone for business only to find it failed to get through to Ben's number three times in succession. Rather than call Flick he decided on a more direct approach and grabbed his coat on the way out to the car.

Flick and Alton 'Zag' Bowers were playing pool when he arrived at the club. Kevin Prentiss sat close by, jabbering away in his peculiar breathless way.

"Yo, Teddy," Flick exclaimed as Teddy threw his coat across the table, ending the game.

"Get me a drink." Teddy snorted. "Where's Marley?"

Flick nodded to Zag, who scurried off towards the bar.

"Don't know, not seen him for a few days. Got some missed calls from you yesterday, sorry I was out of town doing some business. I called you when I got back last night but your phone was turned off. Is everything okay with you, Teddy? You look pretty stressed."

"No. Everything is pretty fucking not okay. I need to talk to Marley. Now."

"Hey man, I can help you out, you don't need that fool. What you need Teddy?"

"Less of you trying to sound like a gangster for a start. If you know where he is, get him, and if you don't, find him."

Flick bristled but stayed quiet, even Kevin Prentiss held his tongue at that moment. When Zag returned with a glass Flick gave him further instructions and he disappeared again with Kevin trailing behind.

When they were out of sight and earshot Flick joined Teddy, who was now sat at an elevated bench seat with a view over the pool tables.

"I'll get him Teddy, what's so urgent though?" he asked.

Teddy drained the glass in two gulps, unblinking eyes staring into the gloom of the club.

"I mean, perhaps if you told me what the matter is. I can keep a secret," Flick said.

Teddy thought for a second. "Three may keep a secret, if two of them are dead," he replied, quoting Benjamin Franklin.

Flick took a second of his own to think. "Let me get you another drink," he said wisely.

Zag first called his brother and then other members of the gang to spread the word. Teddy and Flick wanted Marley found ASAP. Failing would not be a good idea.

Despite the rest of the afternoon and evening spent calling, visiting and searching Marley's known hang-outs, his whereabouts remained unknown. Snatched phone conversations between group members became more frenetic. As time increased so did their anxiety about Teddy's reaction to failure and what exactly Marley might have done to warrant such attention in the first place. Chinese whispers became Chinese screams and by midnight when they were all called back to the club, most were afraid but still had no idea why.

Teddy spent most of the time using Flick's phone but for all his efforts, he drew a blank too. In his experience, no one could remain undiscovered in a place like Nottingham unless they were deliberately trying to. If none of his contacts could locate Marley, then clearly Marley did not want to be found, and if that was the case, then there was a reason. Teddy's bluster was replaced by an altogether different persona. He prowled around the pool table with a cue in his hands as he addressed the group.

"You bunch of halfwits have had all day to find that little shit Marley and what have you done? Fuck all, that's what! I look after you all day in and day out, get you out of the police cells even when you're stupid enough to get caught," he glared at Justin McCrory who had still not fully recovered from his encounter with the Taekwondo champion, "and what do I get in return." It was not a question.

"He's just dropped out of sight," Flick offered lamely.

"He's just dropped out of sight," Kevin Prentiss mimicked.

Teddy whirled on him and swung the cue at his right leg. Prentiss screamed and buckled to the floor. He lay mewing on the beer-stained carpet with Teddy stood over him like an ogre complete with a hickory staff, but otherwise kept his trap shut. The gang made no move to help him. All eyes and attention were on Teddy and the cue.

"Anyone else got something useful to say? No, I thought not. I'm going to make this as clear as I can so that even you losers understand. Nobody goes home until he's found, nobody sleeps until he's found, and when he is found, you call me on this," he said, holding Flick's mobile aloft. "I want some good news soon."

He dropped the cue on the floor and stalked out of the club, leaving his band of amateur soldiers bickering amongst themselves.

Outside, the cold air acted like a slap in the face. Teddy was starving; he hadn't eaten for almost a whole day and hoped getting some food inside him might also bring a change of fortune. He wandered across the road and into an all-night kebab shop. The greasy mixture of bread, meats and salad he scoffed down a few minutes later only satisfied a small percentage of the hunger burning within him. Although the Lamas woman's smart mouth was the reason he was in this position, he did not care about her death; all he cared about was making sure Marley Johns did not make matters any worse for him.

While Teddy was stewing, Marley was relaxing. Detective Inspector Binder was as good as his word and with amazing speed. After the brief discussion at Marley's mother's house they went directly to the police station at Kimberley in the southernmost part of Nottinghamshire, just off the M1 motorway.

This was hardly Marley's first time in a police station, but it was the first time he was not under arrest in one. He was impressed by what he saw. It was small but very modern, and it even had a nice lounge and kitchen in the area for questioning witnesses not suspects. Marley was well fed and then spent two hours talking to a solicitor he picked out of the Yellow Pages until he was satisfied that the deal Binder was offering him was indeed so good he dare not pass it up.

By the time Teddy was wiping the last traces of chilli sauce from his lips and fingers, Marley had been interviewed once regarding the murder of Josie Lamas and his signed copy of his confidential informants' contract was in the solicitor's safe. Now he was resting more peacefully than he could have dreamed of the night before, in a bed with clean sheets, and under the protection of a police station full of officers.

Dan and Allen were also in comfortable surroundings. They stayed at the pub until closing time, taking advantage of the bar menu as well as the endless supply of beer. They talked more than they drank, the food helping them to remain focused on the matters in hand without succumbing to the alcohol.

Dan called Nick to say he would not be back until the next day but lied about why, saying it would be best for him and Amber to have the night together. When the barman called last orders, Allen suggested they continue back at his house, which is how they came to be in the two large leather armchairs when Allen received a call on his mobile at just after midnight.

"It's always the job and never good news at this time," he said, trying to free the device from his jacket pocket.

Dan smiled. "Perks of the rank."

"This is Allen," he said into the phone. "Yes. You're bloody kidding me Frank… When? When did this all happen… Who authorised it… Well tell them I want the report on my desk in the morning and I'll want to speak to both of them tomorrow, too. Thanks for the warning, Frank."

Allen put the phone down on the coffee table and looked at Dan. "Not even you could guess what's just happened."

He was right. Dan thought the call was to inform the county's senior detective of something major occurring in the area as a matter of protocol, he was partly correct. Allen was about to blow his mind.

"Binder has got an informant in protective custody. He's supplied information about burglaries all across Nottingham."

Dan was about to congratulate himself and Allen on their detective skills when Allen continued.

"The same informant has also given a statement saying he was present when Teddy Parker beat Josie to death yesterday. He has traded immunity from prosecution to assist police. Binder's been interviewing him all afternoon, Serious Crime is being tasked to obtain warrants on about ten addresses and an arrest operation is being planned for tomorrow. What the hell is he up to?"

Dan was assimilating the incredible facts as fast as Allen was talking.

"He's good. He's bloody brilliant actually."

"What? I don't understand," Allen said, blowing out his cheeks.

"It's easy. He was always going to burn the burglars, like we said before. Maybe he was going to sacrifice Teddy at the same time but I'm thinking probably not."

"As we guessed, yes, so we're Starsky and Hutch, big deal," Allen said.

Dan laughed out loud. "When he killed Anna Rofe, Binder still needed Teddy to complete his plan."

"You've lost me, Dan."

"According to the timetable he set for the promotion interviews, it was too soon, he needed to be the hero closer to interview day. When Teddy killed Josie, that was the last straw and one complication too many. You said there was an eye witness right? Well if Teddy was going to be the informant for the burglaries then this new one for Josie's murder can do both roles. I'll bet he was one of the burglars. Binder must think it's Christmas, burglars *and* informants! He'll be expecting your job by the end of the month."

Allen reached for the brandy bottle but put it down as soon as he picked it up. "No, this is too bizarre, it's all too much."

"No, it isn't, just look at the facts. To you and me this is too fantastic to imagine only because it's something we could never comprehend doing. But to him it's just a matter of planning and execution. You are only limited by your imagination."

Allen sighed. "Well it's game, set, and match to him then, isn't it. He doesn't give a toss about Anna Rofe, it's not his inquiry and although we know what his involvement was in keeping Teddy in the clear, only Teddy can highlight it and he's not going to do that now, is he? Binder is going to take the credit for solving the burglaries he probably helped plan, and arresting Josie's murderer too. God knows if he had a hand in that because I for one would not put it past him."

"And he's got you by the balls because he knows about your house?" Dan added.

Allen threw his arms up in despair.

"Bugger me Dan, is there anything you don't know? Old Ed Parker said he was doing a mate a favour. I honestly didn't know it was built out of stolen materials until it was too late. By that I mean too late for my wife not to want it and me to tell her what a mess I was in. I thought once we sold and moved away it would all be… you know, just all be better."

"Don't worry, your secret is safe with me. Like you said, we have all made mistakes. What are you going to do about Binder? He may feel that you know too much."

"I can't see it. For one thing, he doesn't know how much we do and I am still his boss. He knows I'm just biding my time until I can go. Once Teddy Parker is off the streets and he gets a shiny new desk hopefully he will leave me alone. Unfortunately, that means he goes on his merry way and Rofe becomes a cold case."

Dan momentarily remembered Zoe Summers once more. Hers was a cold case as well, an unresolved crime of such long standing it was now frozen in time.

"Where's the justice? How can we allow him to get away with all that and Parker not be responsible for Anna Rofe?"

"There you go Dan, listen to yourself. It's your crusader attitude that's the real difference between us. The legal and justice system we have is not perfect, not by any stretch of the imagination, but it isn't all bad either. I have always thought one of its better traits is the burden of proof being set so high. It means a conviction has to be properly earned with compelling evidence. The downside of that is without the evidence, sometimes guilty men stay free. It's not right but it is better than the alternatives. I know what you're going to say, so how does Amber Hetherington fit into that equation right? And I accept there have to be exceptions because we are all human with human strengths and weaknesses."

Dan drained his glass. "I wish we could have talked like this years ago. I want to apologise for being such a prick. I've made some very wrong decisions over my time."

"No need son, and why don't you call me Jim. Did I ever tell you there are no such things as wrong decisions?"

Dan looked at him blankly.

"We all make decisions which sometimes turn out to be bad, but they are never wrong. Take your little outburst at Garstone courthouse."

"I wish you wouldn't."

"Yes, well, certainly a bad idea at the time and worse afterwards, but I bet you could absolutely justify it to yourself for whatever reason at that precise second. It's the same with everything. Whatever we choose to do, even if it is completely illegal, you can find a reason for doing it even if nobody else in the world would agree with your thinking. What is the worst decision you ever made?"

In the context of the conversation and the spirit of their much-improved relationship it was an innocuous question and Allen only meant to emphasise his point. However, faced with the prospect of deciding which among the raft of 'oh shit!' moments in his life was the gold medal winner, Dan shied away from the whole truth. Instead he proved Allen correct about decisions.

"My skeleton cupboard is big and full but that day in Garstone would be right up there." The words tasted like acid as he spoke them.

Allen looked at him for a second and Dan felt sure he saw the lie.

"I thought as much. Does it prove my point?"

"So, what do you suggest? We just let Ben Binder go and Anna Rofe's death is on our conscience forever?"

"It may be bad, but it wouldn't be a wrong decision Dan, not for me anyway, here and now."

"I'm not sure I can."

"If you had your time over again and could go back to Garstone on that day, would you do the same or would you do it differently?"

Dan allowed his mind to access the memory again, but the memory was of Zoe Summers, not the Garstone courthouse steps. The detail swirled in bright Technicolour around his head.

"Honestly, I don't know. I wish I did."

"So, there is our dilemma, even years after and all that time to think about it, you can't say if you were right or wrong, good or bad, so how can we know now if letting Binder get away with it is going to be a good thing for us or will haunt us for the rest of our lives? Life can be shit and it's only the depth which changes." Allen stifled a yawn. "I need to sleep now; I've got another hell of a day coming up. Come on, I'll show you where you can sleep, although you already know your way around the place don't you?"

They both laughed. "Now that was a good decision. We might not be here tonight otherwise," Dan said as they climbed the stairs.

CHAPTER TWENTY

Penny and the girls drove back with Martin early the following morning. He had some work-related matters to do in Derby, and so could drop them off on his way. Dressed in a suit for the day, it was the first time she and the twins had seen him out of his usual fatigues. With his hair combed and face shaved he looked every inch the city gent. He was even wearing a pair of stylish glasses instead of his usual contact lenses, which he matched with a caramel coloured silk tie. Nick tried to persuade him to wait and meet Dan but his schedule did not allow for such a delay.

When Dan arrived back, it was to a very different household. The Hetheringtons were united again, together as a happy family and not one divided by fear and uncertainty. When Penny embraced him on the driveway her tears were full of joy, her gratitude boundless.

While Dan, Nick and Penny took coffee in the garden, even the weather was in celebratory mood, being pleasantly warm. Amber and the twins were holed up in Amber's room. Nick had made her swear to not divulge some of what they'd seen and done in the past week upon pain of death, and she could be trusted. Rose and Viola were sated with the details she provided, thinking Amber's account was more than cool and scary enough. Amber also wanted to know what they had done and so every now and then they would break into fits of laughter as the stories unfolded.

Out in the garden, Penny put down her mug.

"I can't believe it's over," she repeated. "We'll never forget this."

"I'm glad things turned out as they did, the poor kid should never have been in that position in the first place. She's strong though Penny, she will be alright." Dan smiled.

Nick squeezed his wife's hand as tears welled up in her eyes, which were still red and puffy from her most recent bout of crying.

"I just can't help thinking of what might have happened if you and Nick hadn't been able to do what you did."

Dan smiled but it was a tired effort; the exertions of the previous week were making themselves apparent now with the pressure gone.

Penny reached over and touched his hand.

"I'm not trying to get rid of you and you are welcome to stay for as long as you want, but I expect you'll be wanting to get home as soon as possible."

"You should all come out and visit us sometime, the girls would love it and it would be nice for Tara to meet you in person."

"Maybe we can make it my retirement present," Nick suggested. "I'm going to seriously look at leaving. The job will never be the same again, not after all this."

Dan nodded. "I don't envy you going back, have you thought when you will?"

"Well actually I thought I'd drag it out for as long as possible. They wanted to get shot of me. Putting me on compassionate leave was just a means to an end so I'm going to make the most of it. I'll see my doctor and get him to sign me off, maybe even see the Force Welfare Department and lay it on thick with them too. I've got no enthusiasm for it at the moment."

"I'm sure Jim Allen would help with whatever you wanted. He is feeling much the same."

Penny bristled. "That gutless bastard," she blurted, surprising Nick and Dan with her vehemence. "I hope he rots in hell for what he has done to us all."

"He is genuinely sorry, Penny."

"I'm still amazed how you have changed your opinion of him despite his about-turn on Amber after what he did to us *and* you in the past," Nick said, saving the need for Penny to swear again.

Dan did not tell them all the details of his conversations with Allen, it was still so raw so instead he concentrated on Amber's issues.

"People change," he replied, leaving them to guess whether he was talking about Allen or himself.

Allen's early meeting with Ben Binder and Detective Chief Inspector Keith Raye was brief and professional. Raye was heading up the Josie Lamas murder investigation as senior officer on the Serious Crimes Unit; it was all under control. The evidence was already piling up against Teddy Parker; fingerprints and other forensics obtained from Josie's house and the hospital were being compared with national databases as they spoke. Added to Marley Johns' ongoing cooperation and statements, for which Raye thanked Binder again, Parker's continuing liberty was now only a question of time. Raye was in and out of Allen's office in fifteen minutes, leaving him and Binder alone.

Allen buzzed through to Sheila and sent her on a pointless errand to be sure they would not be overheard and as soon as the outer office door was closed he turned on Binder with loathing in his eyes.

"I wish I'd told you to go fuck yourself the day we met. You and I have both got blood on our hands," he roared.

"Don't give me all that," Binder shouted back.

"You're a bloody disgrace," Allen fumed. "I've got a good mind to arrest you myself. Teddy Parker is not long for this free world, the bastard is going down for bloody years, if not life, and won't be needing any more of your 'protection' so what's to stop me wrapping up the Hetherington case as insufficient evidence right now?"

"Spare me your sanctimonious bullshit, James. I had no idea Teddy Parker would murder the old girl." Mellowing significantly, he added, "Look. What's happened can't be undone, but it's all turned out alright in the end."

Allen's rage ratcheted up another notch. "What the hell! I don't believe I'm hearing this! Josephine Lamas is dead. Anna Rofe is dead. What in God's name is alright about that? And by the way, you will refer to me as sir or so help me..."

"Calm down or you'll give yourself a heart attack. Okay, that was a poor choice of words, but Teddy Parker is going to be convicted of murder. He's going to get life, he wouldn't do more time for the Rofe girl's killing as well. You've got your way with Amber Hetherington. One way or another the bad boy gets locked up, the innocent girl is off the hook and we can move on from the whole sorry episode."

Allen was sorely tempted to take Binder by the throat and see him out of his office by the plate glass window. "You cold hearted bastard."

"I got the job done, what had to be done. Parker's going down, what more do you want?"

The temptation to scream back that he knew all about Binder's promotion plans, the burglaries, Teddy Parker, and Marley Johns being the unwitting informant slash fall guy was almost over powering, but Allen bit his tongue. He was well to take Dan's advice, and not give that away for fear of becoming an obstruction to be removed in Binder's relentless drive to fulfil his aspirations. Instead he invaded Binder's personal space and pushed his forehead hard into Binder's.

"This is it, no more. I don't want to see or talk to you ever again, have you got that? You come to me again for anything and I'll go to the chief and tell him everything. As God is my witness I will see myself go down in flames before I ever do another thing for you. Do you understand me?"

Binder was taken aback. Allen watched him diplomatically retreat a step.

"Please that's enough."

"Please, sir," Allen roared.

"Sir, I'm as sorry as you it got this far but it's all over now. In a few weeks' time, I'll be out of your way for good and in a year or so all you'll have to worry about will be your roses and daffodils. So, let's just leave Teddy Parker to be dealt with by the Serious Crime boys and we can just get on with our lives. Teddy's father will want to distance himself from his murderous son, so you can forget about him too." He took a breath before continuing. "You do need to sign the G19 regarding Johns. Keith provisionally signed but it requires your counter signature."

Allen had taken as much as he could bear, the G19 Confidential Sources document was the final insult.

"Leave it here and then get out of my sight," he said, turning from Binder and concentrating on the far distance out of the window.

Binder quickly and quietly left the room.

Allen took several moments to calm down before he went back to his desk. Reaching down he picked up his Dictaphone, which had been on and recording since before Binder and Raye arrived and clicked it off. He then used his mobile to call his most recently added contact and waited for Dan to answer.

It was 8:30 a.m.

For Teddy Parker, the night passed without incident, which was a very bad thing. His instructions for Marley to be found went unfulfilled and in the last hour he resorted to more desperate measures.

He called Oliver Treave, the acquaintance and previous owner of his new BMW.

"Your sister is in the police isn't she?" he demanded. Treave knew better than to prevaricate. "Yes, a civilian analyst at Mansfield's District Headquarters."

"I'll give your car back car in exchange for cast iron proof of where a shit I know called Marley Johns is." He gave Treave a few more details and left him in no doubt this was not a polite request.

Teddy desperately hoped Marley may have done something stupid like get arrested, but the nauseous feeling in his stomach betrayed that wish. The combination of drugs, alcohol and rage made thinking about anything else impossible, so he paced his living room like a caged lion, waiting for something to happen. When the landline finally rang, he jumped to answer it.

"Who is it?… Yeah go on, I'm listening."

When Treave was finished, Teddy just hung up.

Like a dormant volcano whose pressure was building until it could not be contained any longer, Teddy exploded. The large mirror above the fireplace shattered into a thousand pieces when his new phone hit it. Next, he ripped the fifty-two-inch plasma TV off the wall and threw it as hard as he could across the granite bench-top separating the lounge from the kitchen. It smashed on the Italian-tiled kitchen floor and came to rest against the shiny and little used steel oven. Teddy's rampage continued through the living area and into the hallway where two pictures and another mirror suffered irrevocable harm. Finally reaching the front door and with nothing else close to hand to break, he punched the wall to the right of the door as hard as he could with both fists until the painted plasterboard succumbed. Collapsing to the floor with blood on his knuckles and plaster powder all over him he shuddered and started to moan the same word over and over.

"Bastards."

Treave's sister could not find out much but what she did was more than enough. All information regarding Johns was now only accessible with permission of a Chief Inspector or above. The last memo was authorised and signed by Detective Chief Superintendent Allen.

It took some time for him to pull enough of his senses together to think again. Finally, when he, did he snorted a great lump of mucus from his nose into his throat and spat it out on the parquet floor.

"Bastards," he repeated for the last time in a new and menacing tone before hauling himself upright and staggering into the bedroom.

While throwing random clothes from his wardrobe onto the bed, his mind continued to race. The names of Marley and Allen in the same sentence could only mean one thing: big trouble.

That whore bitch Anna, he thought, grabbing a Gucci holdall and stuffing a handful of brand new polo shirts inside. *If it hadn't been for her and her big mouth none of this would have happened. Josie Lamas also brought about her own demise. What is it with the whores in this town?*

In his mind, he killed them, and was right to do so, or at least understandable. Now it looked like he would have to answer to the police because of Marley and Allen. It was all wrong, they were nothing but worthless slags.

"How's it fucking murder?" he asked himself out loud. "How can it be?"

As he shoved another crumpled handful of clothing into the bag a phrase came to mind.

"Kill one man and you are a murderer, kill them all and you are a god."

CHAPTER TWENTY-ONE

"So, that's it then, son," Allen said.

With a bin liner full of his returned property at his feet and an apology for the stolen things that were damaged beyond saving, Dan and Allen's business was more or less complete.

Dan nodded. "I guess so, Jim. I'm most glad for Nick and the family, but us making our peace has been a great bonus for me. Thanks again."

The busy café they met in was close to the library where Dan had spent the previous couple of hours to give the Hetherington family a little extra time to find their path once more.

Allen blew on his tea. "Good idea for an insurance policy," he said, tapping the Dictaphone on the table. "You never know."

"If he's got any sense he'll realise his good luck and stay well away from you from now on. Have you given any more thought to retiring early?"

"I'll talk to the Police Association people and also Personnel Department to see if I can do something. I haven't got the heart for it anymore. I feel I'm here under a false pretence. How did you find it, being a civilian, I mean?"

"Rough. I hated your guts and the job in general, but there were a million times when I would have done anything to be back in again. I can't say how long it took to feel better because of how I left, and I changed everything so drastically by going to New Zealand and all."

"At least you're settled there."

"Absolutely. The country, Tara, and now a new baby on the way. I can't imagine being here anymore."

"When are you going back?"

"Two days."

"Can I ask you something, Dan?"

"I reserve the right to answer or not, but go ahead."

"What would you and Nick have done if things continued as they were a few days ago?"

"Anything and everything it took. Gone to the press, reported the whole matter to the Chief Constable in person. We were reaching that point the other day when you knocked the door."

"I wish we could have resolved our differences a long time ago without any of this recent pain and suffering, son. If there is anything I can do for you, you only have to ask. I don't forget friends either."

"Be careful what you wish for and offer. I might just need a hand one day. I'd better go."

Dan stood and extended his hand, which Allen took warmly.

"No, I mean it. Being in my position has some benefits, for instance I get to see documents and reports other people don't even know exist. There will be a lot I can remember long after I leave the job but before I do go, there is an awful lot more I can do for a worthy cause."

"You obviously know something I don't."

"Just something you said about your skeleton cupboard being full. I'd like to help empty it if I could. Think about it."

"Maybe I will. One day," Dan replied.

"Okay good. All the best Dan, see you around."

They both knew it was unlikely they would ever meet again, and they were both sad because of it.

Dan walked back to Nick's in good spirits. Life had taken an unexpected step forward in the past week. He thought himself somewhat happier, or rather, more at peace, with the world than before and believed he was a better person for it. To maintain his good mood, he decided to buy a few gifts for Tara and the baby and took a bus into the city centre.

Allen went back to his office. His mood was decidedly mixed. The great pleasure he wanted to feel about mending bridges and burying hatchets with Dan were well and truly tempered by a large dose of self-loathing for what he was previously a part of, anxiety about the time he still had to serve, and concern regarding what Ben Binder might still be capable of.

The disquiet Teddy created within the gang over Marley rapidly snowballed into panic and delirium. Flick went to Marley's house and finding his mother in her usual drunken stupor, finally got some sense out of Marley's young half-brother Simeon. A plain clothes policeman took Marley away the day before and they had not heard a word from him since.

Flick summoned the members together at the club. He was as anxious as any of them to find out what happened.

"So, has that fool been playing Lone Ranger and been doing stuff on his own?" he asked aggressively.

Nobody knew.

"I was with him a couple of days ago, but he was just like normal," Justin McCrory said. "If he was doin' some stuff on his own he couldn't keep it quiet, he's got a mouth that won't stop flapping when he gets going."

Flick could not deny the fact Marley was no more able to keep a secret than keep his hands off some of the girls at the local sixth form college.

"So, what does Teddy want him so bad for?" Zig asked, speaking for many in the group.

Teddy Parker's legendary temper was one thing but the way he was about Marley the day before was something new to them all. What made matters worse for Flick was he tried all morning to get hold of Teddy, but he too had disappeared, not answering the home phone or Flick's own mobile, which he still possessed.

"What we goin' to do man?" Zig asked, once again speaking for them all.

"Keep cool, stay cool. Teddy's got our back and he's got a bitch cop too, remember," Flick said.

"Why would Marley go off with some police then? It's no good us being cool if he's fuckin' us over."

"I just need to talk to Teddy, then find out what's happening," Flick replied.

"So where is he then? He's gone AWOL as well. Maybe they're cookin' something up all together and we the ones goin' to be dumped on," Zag said.

Flick had no idea what to do next.

"It's all okay, it's sweet," he said. "We'll just keep cool like I said and wait for things to equalise. Till then we stay out of any trouble."

As he spoke he was also thinking it may be time for a change of scenery. Nottingham was way too hot all of a sudden.

Marley's day picked up where the previous evening's left off. True to form, once he began talking he found it impossible to stop. The freedom to speak in the knowledge he was not going to get into any trouble not only loosened his tongue but improved his memory. As the interviewing officers presented him with crime files relating to different burglaries, he filled in all the details of who was present on each occasion, what was stolen and importantly, what was left, thereby adding further credibility to his story.

Teddy Parker planned the jobs, every one of them, but Flick was the leader of the burglars and he took responsibility for moving all the stuff on with the help of his Uncle Herbert. The gang members were all paid in cash and only a few times was some of the stolen property divided between them. Teddy was always adamant about that, for security reasons he said, but Marley didn't know if he sanctioned the odd diversion from it.

In all, Marley accounted for almost fifty raids on shops, offices, builders' merchants and residential homes all across the county and into adjoining force areas over a near two-year period. The investigators were extremely happy; it looked for all money as if they had an open and shut case against *all* the offenders.

Ben Binder kept in touch with Marley Johns' inquisitors as a matter of courtesy. Considering that Johns was his source there was nothing unusual about that, but for him it was the perfect way to keep his finger on the pulse and stay several steps ahead of the game. The conversation he now needed to have with Edward Parker was not going to be such a pleasant experience though. He waited patiently for Parker's secretary to connect them.

"Ben. This is a surprise."

"Mr. Parker, I'm sorry I couldn't visit you in person. I've got some terrible news for you about Teddy and I can't get away, but I wanted to tell you myself before you heard it from someone else."

"Jesus, Mary and Joseph. What's the bloody idiot done now?"

Binder needed information first. "Has he been in touch with you in the last two days?"

"No, not a thing."

"When did you last hear from him?"

"About a week ago, or more, when he came to our house for dinner. You know what he's like."

"I do Mr. Parker, I do. I'm sorry to tell you that things have got well beyond my control now. There's no easy way to say it. It appears Teddy went to the house of an elderly woman called Josephine Lamas in Mapperley two nights ago and assaulted her. She died as a result. Teddy will be arrested as soon as the police can locate him."

Edward Parker was silent. For a moment, Binder thought he must have hung up, but then there would have been a disconnect tone.

"Mr. Parker, are you still there?"

"Yes, Ben, I'm here. What the bloody hell is wrong with that boy? He'll probably be the death of me, and his mother too, one of these days. What happened? What the hell happened?"

"All I can tell you is I was called to the hospital when she was admitted. When she died the police investigation automatically commenced and then out of nowhere a witness came forward who has put the blame squarely on Teddy's shoulders. I don't know how this person knows, but apparently with what he or she said plus the forensic evidence at the scene, there's little room for manoeuvre. I can't help Teddy on this one, but I wanted to be the one to tell you."

"What can we do, Ben? There must be something; what about if I call Jim Allen?"

Binder was ready for this and replied immediately. "I thought about that too Mr. Parker, in fact I did call him, but he made it very clear to me in no uncertain terms. Let's face it, we managed to convince him Anna Rofe's death would not be mourned for long, but Mrs. Lamas is a different matter altogether. From what I understand the whole area is up in arms. Mr. Allen's right, there's no way we can get Teddy out of this mess. If I were you I'd be looking for the best defence lawyer I can find. It's his only hope now."

"But surely if we can put enough pressure on him…" Parker begged.

"You forget we're fellow conspirators with him about the Rofe girl. He wasn't slow to remind me. I think whatever our leverage was before has been used up. To be honest with you Mr. Parker, I think we have both stuck our necks out for Teddy for long enough. I don't want to get you or me into something we have no hope of controlling."

"It's just that he's my son, Ben."

"I know, I do understand. If there was any other way… Can you think of a reason he might want to harm Mrs. Lamas?"

"No. What should we do now?"

"Nothing. If Teddy gets in touch I would get him that lawyer and tell him to hand himself in."

"Are you sure there's nothing else we can do?"

"I'm sorry to say no."

"Okay. I'd better go and tell his mother. Thanks for calling. I appreciate what you've done for him, or tried to anyway."

"As I say, I'm sorry there's no other way. I think it's best if we don't communicate again, not for a while any way. I hope you understand."

"Of course, you couldn't have done any more. Thank you, Ben, thank you."

Ben Binder breathed out a big sigh of relief. Now he could get on with some of the day's other work.

The working day held no pleasure for Allen whatsoever. As he perused a number of budgetary reports relating to undercover operations in progress and planned for the next quarter, his mind wandered back to the days when he was simply a detective with nothing to worry about other than investigating and detecting. Right now, he would have given a lot, including his Chief Superintendent's pension package, to be in that position again. His senior status was why he now had the problems he did. By 2:00 p.m. enough was enough though. Even his new home, the cause of some of those recent problems, was better than being at work so he put the files in his briefcase and headed for the door. As he reached for the handle he was struck by an idea. Turning to his long-time and ever reliable personal assistant, he said, "Sheila, do me a favour before you go today. Contact Personnel and also Force Admin. I want everything there is to know on Detective Inspector Binder. Arrest records, courses, informants, the whole shooting match. Have them send everything to my secure account so I can read them at home."

Sheila offered a small smile of acknowledgement. She was, as usual, dressed in a dark two-piece skirt suit, one of several she owned for work. Her well-manicured hand jotted down her boss's request without question.

Once in the car he put on Vivaldi's "Four Seasons" and drove off towards the countryside where he hoped to get an hour in the garden before it was too dark and at least be free of Ben Binder and Teddy Parker for a short while.

When Dan got back he was ready for a rest and glad his business class ticket offered a larger luggage allowance. Amber let him through the front door as both hands were full of presents for Tara and the baby.

"Looks like someone's been having fun."

"I think I went a bit over the top," he confessed.

"A bit! Did you leave anything in the shops?"

"I got you something too, here in this bag, the yellow one."

Amber unhooked a bag from his fingers and opened it.

"Ha ha very funny," she said.

"Well, you were so good at surveillance I thought they may come in handy one day."

Amber held her new binoculars up to her eyes then went to Dan and hugged him.

"I'll never be able to thank you enough."

"Hey, they're just binoculars."

"No, you know what I mean, everything."

"It's okay, might be a good idea to stay out of Mapperley in future though."

"I will, don't worry about that."

Dan sat and indicated for Amber to do the same.

"Actually, there is one thing you can do for me."

"Anything."

"I'm not going to be here when Josie's funeral takes place. Would you go for me? I'll ask your dad too, but I would like it if you could."

"Of course. Are you really going to go so soon?"

"I think it's for the best. Tara wants me home and you can all get back to normal as well."

"I don't think we will ever be normal again. I've decided when I finish uni I'm going to apply to the police, not here though. What do you think about the Met in London?"

Dan cracked a huge smile. "I think it would be a great idea. The job can always use the best people possible. Nick will be so proud."

Amber beamed. "After all this I can't think of anything more useful, I really want to do something worthwhile with my life. Maybe I'll end up on the surveillance team too."

When Allen arrived home, he glanced over to his rose garden and did not notice the car partially obscured behind the garage. He parked outside the front door and dropped his mobile phone into his jacket pocket before rummaging for his keys. The door was not locked when he inserted the key.

"Gwen, how many times do I have to tell you to lock the door, even when we're home?" he called out as he stepped across the threshold.

If she was able to reply he would not have heard it. The steel poker from the fireplace in the lounge crashed down onto the back of his skull, knocking him out cold and he crumpled to the floor with blood oozing from the wound like a small crimson oil slick. Teddy stood over the motionless older man holding the poker as if it were a conductor's baton. A drop of Allen's blood fell to the floor, making him smile. He regarded the fragment of bone, matted hair and more blood on the end of the steel rod with mild interest before dropping it next to the body.

CHAPTER TWENTY-TWO

It was dark outside when Jim Allen came to. He groaned as a wave of nausea rolled through him. His headache was a soul splitting pain that seemed to get worse when he tried to think. When he opened his eyes, he found them looking into those of his wife. She was sat on the floor, leant against the lounge wall with thick green tape over her mouth. She looked terrified.

He tried to move and found his ankles were tied together, as were his hands behind his back. When he went to speak he realised he was gagged too. He felt himself being roughly grabbed from behind and hauled into a sitting position next to Gwen. Looking up he found Teddy Parker staring back—whack!

The shock of the slap hurt more than the slap itself, but the force of it threw his head back into the wall and the pain intensified. The wound had started to congeal and dry in the time he was unconscious. It opened up again now. Teddy wrung his hand and for a moment Allen thought he was about to strike again.

"You awake now?" Teddy bellowed.

Gwen Allen whimpered next to her husband. Despite having no idea of the time or his condition, he tried to cast an encouraging look her way but his view of her was unfocused and seemed to do little to calm her. She mumbled as if trying to speak but the tape made it impossible. Teddy raised his hand once more in her general direction and as she cowered, Allen tried his best to shout through the adhesive. Teddy ripped the tape from his mouth, causing more pain.

"Leave her alone you fucking animal!"

The insult calmed Teddy immediately. Where it would have enraged others he merely understood someone talking his language. Allen's nature came to the fore and he spoke again with as much authority as he could muster. "Untie us both now. Who the hell do you think you are coming to my house?"

When Teddy ignored him and glared at Gwen again, Allen's rage took over.

"You worthless piece of drugged up shit, I'm going to make sure you get arse fucked every day for the rest of your miserable prison life."

Teddy seemed to ignore this comment too, but Allen saw Gwen nearly faint at the prospect of how he might react. Teddy bent down in front of Allen so their noses were almost touching.

"A fool shows his annoyance at once, but a prudent man overlooks an insult," he said, pushing a finger into Allen's head wound.

Allen's acute pain intensified. He flicked his head up, which made it even worse. Wincing, he said, "Is that what you said to Josie Lamas just before you bashed her brains in?" Dan had provided him with all the details he could regarding Josie's murder and he remembered very well the salient points. He took satisfaction seeing how Teddy was taken aback for a moment as the memory returned.

"This is all your own fault. You better start thinking how you're going to save your own skin instead of threatening me," Teddy growled.

"Give me a break." Allen snorted. "You must have lost all your senses coming here. What the hell do you think is going to happen now?"

"You're going to tell me what you and Marley Johns have been playing at and then you are going to fix it or I'm going to fix you and your old lady for good."

"Me and who! You must be bloody joking. I haven't had a thing to do with him. I've never met the bugger."

"Fucking liar!" Teddy screamed. "You've got him stashed away somewhere making deals. See, I know as much about you as you do about me."

Allen shot a look towards his wife again. It seemed it was all too much for Gwen, beneath the tape she heaved and gagged. Sick flooded into her mouth but with nowhere to go she automatically swallowed it again.

Allen leaned towards her as her inner organs revolted, and she seemed to want to explode from within. To Allen and Teddy, she appeared to be in the throws of a major heart attack.

"Please," Allen implored. "For Christ's sake do something."

Teddy pulled the tape away from her mouth. With her access way now clear, Gwen heaved violently again and a stream of stinking, hot vomit rushed out of her and onto the expensive Turkish rug. She gagged three more times and with each convulsion the puddle grew around her. When she was finished, she had so little strength left that she was unable to move or speak. Looking utterly defeated she slumped sideways along the wall until she reached the floor. There she lay, in a semi foetus position looking at Teddy.

"Let her go, Teddy. Just let her go and I'll do whatever you want."

"It's too late for that old man. Too late for you and too late for me. Whatever you and Marley have arranged has sealed your fate."

"Didn't you hear what I said? I've never met him. You should be asking your friend Binder all these questions. It's him who's been doing a deal with Marley for information about the burglaries, as well as Josie."

Teddy shook his head slowly, a malevolent smile playing about his lips.

"It's your name on the paperwork. You signed the deal with him this morning."

Allen mixed disbelief that Teddy knew about the G memo with a sickening appreciation of how it appeared.

"I swear to you on my life, Ben Binder brought Marley in as a confidential informant and he's been playing us all against each other from the beginning."

"Bullshit. You're pathetic, you know that? Ben's got me out of strife and looked out for me. We are *partners*. I bet you never knew that, did you?"

"That's just what he wants you to think. All he cares about is himself. Even now he's planning to take all the credit for getting you convicted of Josie's murder as well as the brains behind all the burglaries Marley and his mates have committed going back years. He's fucked you Teddy, right from the beginning to now. I can prove it."

Allen saw the briefest hesitation in Teddy's eyes and desperately seized the opportunity.

"I can prove it. Let me show you."

Teddy unclenched his fists.

"Let me get my computer. I have all of Binder's files on it to show he's Marley's handler. When you see that perhaps it will convince you."

"Just trying to save yourself. You make me want to puke," Teddy said, looking at Gwen and the sick on the floor.

"So, what have you got to lose? Please, Teddy just take a look."

"Where is it?"

Allen sighed inwardly. "I left it in the car when I came in."

Teddy grunted. "Stay there, I'll get it."

Alone in the room for a few seconds, Allen tried to reassure his wife.

"It's alright love, I'll find a way to get us out of this, just try and hold on."

All she could do was manage a look of disbelief. As he struggled to a more upright sitting position his only thought was to hope Sheila had done what he had asked earlier because if for some reason he could not show Teddy the G memo, they were as good as dead.

Sitting more comfortably he felt a lump pushing into his side and remembered his mobile was in his jacket pocket. There was still no sound of Teddy returning so he grabbed at another unlikely chance for assistance. Wrestling to get his taped hands in a position to get to the phone felt like he was about to dislocate a shoulder, but the pain was inconsequential. He muffled a cry as he made a final effort and managed to get both hands inside the pocket and pulled out the phone. As he did the front door slammed closed and heavy footsteps got louder and louder. With no time to place an emergency call and unable to see the key pad because his hands could not get far enough forward, he guessed where the last number redial button was and hit call. In the instant before Teddy re-entered the room he got the phone back into his pocket again.

Allen was always a confirmed atheist but now he prayed to high heaven for a miracle. Teddy looked at him suspiciously. "You have got five minutes or it's goodbye Gwen."

Penny came into the lounge holding up a beeping mobile. "Someone's phone is ringing."

Nick and Dan looked at each other confused. Neither could think of a reason for one of the pre-pays to be ringing now.

Dan took it from Penny and answered. "Hello."

The display showed number withheld. Almost as he said it he could sense there was something wrong. In the time it took for his brain to send the first electrical impulse of concern his whole body became an antenna to receive information. Nick was watching closely, Penny too, although Amber's attention was elsewhere.

"Sshh." Nick said in a loud whisper.

Penny and Amber looked in surprise. "What's the…"

"I said sshh," Nick repeated, cutting Penny off.

Dan slowly placed the handset down on the coffee table in the middle of the room, lowering his head as he did and keeping his ear to it until he found the speaker button.

He looked up but kept his attention fully on the phone. Penny's concern almost made her speak again, but his look and Amber's hand on her arm stopped her. Nick followed Dan's lead and quietly knelt by the table. Amber pulled Penny down so all four of them surrounded the table with the phone set between them.

Dan's entire focus was on the muffled noises emanating from the phone. Penny and Amber looked from him to Nick and when their eyes met he indicated to the phone with a look so serious it could have stopped a clock.

There were voices; they were indistinct but clearly there was a conversation taking place. They all listened as hard as they could.

Teddy powered up the laptop but was halted by the password.

"Well?"

"Gallica, G.A.L.L.I.C.A." Allen answered, and then as if to justify it said, "It's a variety of rose."

Teddy punched in the letters and waited. A moment later the laptop buzzed into greater life and the screen displayed the star and crown crest of the Nottinghamshire Police above a login window.

"Login?" Teddy growled.

Allen spelled out the appropriate letters while looking at Gwen and trying to impart calm. "C.A.N.I.N.A."

Once again Teddy punched at the keyboard and they all waited.

Gwen started to cry.

"It's alright love, look at me. Look at me Gwen. It's going to be okay," Allen said.

Teddy was not so reassuring. "Shut the fuck up!" he yelled at her. "By the way, it's not going to be okay for either of you."

As Gwen lost all control and began to wail, her husband took the opportunity to raise his voice, not for Teddy's benefit but for an old enemy and new friend he hoped might just be on the other end of his mobile phone.

"You nasty bastard, Teddy. Isn't it enough you've come to our house? Can't you see she's scared witless."

Teddy ignored him and stared hard at the laptop.

"How does this work?"

"It's my work machine, it accesses the force systems. I'll have to show you."

He saw Teddy was reluctant to untie him. Although he was younger and fitter, and Allen was badly injured, it seemed Teddy still much preferred overwhelming odds.

Teddy grabbed Gwen's hair making her cry out. "You so much as blink the wrong way and I'll break her neck."

Allen nodded vigorously. "No, I promise."

Teddy peeled back the tape securing Allen's hands and dropped the computer into his lap. "Get a move on."

Allen started working the machine with a distinct lack of proficiency.

"Sorry Teddy, I'm not good with these things at the best of times," he lied.

He needed to show Teddy the G memo, but just as importantly, he needed time. Keeping up his amateur appearance, he quickly scanned his inbox, but could see there was nothing concerning Binder.

He fought back the urge to look up and instead went to the special operations folder where details of confidential sources and registered informants were located. He knew the G memo application, contract and authority would be there and also knew very well that while his name would be on the authority document, Ben Binder's would not be as the police handlers were identified by code number only, and even he could not access the files where Binder's name would be located.

He stole a glance at Gwen and tried to think of a way to protect her from what he guessed would follow.

Teddy watched over his shoulder. When he could prevaricate no longer he finally brought up the contract and held up the machine for Teddy to see. Marley's details took up the first few lines of the pro forma document, followed by the contract wording, and then a box marked special conditions. Teddy's eyes widened so far Allen thought his eyeballs may fall out of their sockets.

The following is agreed by the Nottinghamshire Constabulary and Crown Prosecutions Service of England and Wales:

A1. Marley Clifton Johns DOB. 06/09/1995 will provide such information that is known to him regarding burglary offences in the Nottinghamshire Police area and other police areas between 01/01/2015 and 19/10/2017. Information will include written statements, contemporaneous notes of interview and evidence given under oath until such time that police investigations and any subsequent court proceedings are complete. Marley Clifton Johns will be immune from prosecution regarding any and all burglary offences described by him covering the period as above providing his cooperation with Nottinghamshire Constabulary and Crown Prosecutions Service of England and Wales in the above matters continues.

A2. Marley Clifton Johns DOB. 06/09/1995 will provide such information that is known to him regarding offences committed at 44 Trenton Grove, Mapperley Park, Nottingham in the Nottinghamshire Police area between 16/10/2017 and 19/10/2017. Information will include written statements, contemporaneous notes of interview and evidence given under oath until such time that police investigations and any subsequent court proceedings are complete. Marley Clifton Johns will be immune from prosecution regarding any and all offences described by him covering the period as above providing his cooperation with Nottinghamshire

Constabulary and Crown Prosecutions Service of England and Wales in the above matters continues.

Signatures and witness endorsements were made in the sections below. The section marked 'Confidential Informants Police Handler' contained the number 62/A145 and a corresponding repeat of the same number hand written in the box marked 'signature'.

When Teddy got to the bottom of the page he looked blankly at Allen.

Allen was desperate for more time and to do whatever he could to protect himself and Gwen. "Don't you recognise his handwriting? That's it there."

Allen's wish evaporated as Teddy threw the laptop across the room. Although his ankles were still bound together making useful movement impossible, basic human instinct took over. He lunged for Teddy, grabbing him by the knees and dragging him to the floor.

"Go Gwen. Help me, son," he screamed at the top of his voice while trying his best to climb on top of Teddy and punch any part of him he could get to.

Gwen acted on sheer impulse. Screaming and crying her husband's name she slithered away from the scrapping men like a wounded lizard. Her sweat over the past hours moistened the tape around her wrists but it was still strong and unforgiving. By the lounge door a brass ornament of a Greek soldier holding a spear provided a sharp enough point to puncture the tape three times before in rent apart and she wriggled her hands free. When she looked, back Teddy appeared to have regained enough of his faculties to grab Allen's arms and was struggling into a position of ascendency.

"Go," Allen shouted again.

She ripped away the tape holding her legs together and ran for the kitchen without looking back. Her car was unlocked and fortunately new enough that it included an electronic ignition.

Still wailing for her husband, she got in and pressed the button to start the engine. The thought of what was happening inside blinded her and she was unable to steer the car through the large ornamental gateway, instead crashing like a fairground dodgem into one of the great stone pillars before bouncing sideways onto the road. She drove on regardless towards the main road—the nearest house was a mile away.

All Allen wanted to do was give Gwen sufficient time to get away. How long that needed to be he had no idea but within a few seconds it was completely academic.

He knew for sure he was about to die.

They all heard the raised voice at the same time. Penny jumped and Amber cried out. Dan was concentrating so intently he could even hear the electronic buzz of the mobile phone. He could also hear the ambient noises surrounding the spoken words and quickly worked out whoever was calling could not be holding the phone in a normal way.

His brain forced all but his aural senses to step aside, leaving it free to absorb every detail of each sound. It was almost impossible to make out specific words; all he could tell for sure was there was at least one male and one female voice, and they were both borderline hysterical. Sounds of movement and brushing or rubbing punctuated the conversation. Somewhere, deep from his subconscious, came the thought that this might be what it was like to be a ship in a bottle, and it became instantly obvious that the phone he was listening to must be concealed within something. The noises continued for a minute and a half, still too indistinct to be sure and then there was a moment of quiet.

Dan redoubled his efforts, knowing there would be something more, knowing it would be all important and somehow knowing it was a matter of life and death.

And then it came, amidst more brushing and rubbing so as to make it any more unintelligible: "Go…en…lp me…on. Go."

Then silence.

When he was sure there was no more, Dan picked up the phone and studied the display again. Number withheld, call duration two minutes, sixteen seconds.

"What the hell was that all about?" Nick said, but he was already too late.

Dan was replaying the whole episode over again in his mind, trying to access the one detail which would answer that and all other questions. Other conversation in the room meant nothing.

His eyes were mostly closed. He could hear it all again. A man's voice, a woman's voice, crying, more voices again, rubbing, brushing. *"Go."*

He shook his head trying to remember better, filtering out the unwanted brushing sounds to just hear the voices.

"Go… help me. Go."

No, that wasn't it. He started again, going through the two minutes and sixteen seconds as if watching a DVD one frame at a time.

Finally, on the third run through he got it. *"Go Gwen. Help me son. Go."* Dan opened his eyes and stared at Nick.

"That's it. 'Go Gwen. Help me son. Go.' That's what he said."

"That's what who said?"

"Who's Gwen?" Penny asked, eyes wide with panic.

Nick looked from Dan to her, and then to Amber. "No idea. Dan, what is it?"

Dan's head was throbbing with the effort. It took another moment for his brain to fit the pieces together and when he did he cursed the delay. "Not Gwen, you stupid bastard Calder. Son!"

"Son?" Amber and Nick said together.

"Yes son, son. 'Help me, son'."

Their blank looks were understandable; he was the only person in the room who had been called son recently.

"It's Jim Allen and he needs help."

"You're not making any bloody sense, Dan. What are you on about?" Nick asked.

Dan was already on his feet.

"There's no time. Penny, call the police. No, police and ambulance. Tell them it's urgent. Get them to check Allen's office and home. Nick, come with me."

"Where to? How do you know it was him? I couldn't understand a word."

"There's no time, I'm driving."

Dan rounded on Penny who was still dumbfounded. "Pen, get on the phone now!" he shouted.

Amber grabbed the landline and dialled 999. Before she was connected Dan and Nick were gone.

Considering the horror of his current situation, Allen was, if not happy, at least content. With every blow he was sustaining, Gwen was getting farther away and would make it to safety. The ridiculous thought occurred to him that her plaintive cries of his name as she managed to escape were her greatest display of love he could remember throughout their whole marriage. And he loved her too, she was the love of his soon-to-be-over life.

Teddy's brutality reached new heights. What started as retaliation in order to overpower Allen shifted to furious beating and then morphed into the calculated deconstruction of another human life. He took his time stalking around the prostrate policeman before delivering another massive blow with the steel poker to all parts of Allen's body. Head, arms, torso, legs, and even his genitals, over and over. Allen could feel his life's essence draining away.

The fact Teddy was sometimes talking, sometimes shouting in between blows was no longer relevant, and his burst eardrum made hearing redundant anyway.

Teddy paused between striking Allen with as much power as he could, to espouse pearls of wisdom he felt germane. Quoting from poets to politicians he mixed violence with a sickening one-way conversation.

Delivering another bone crunching blow to Allen's right arm he shouted.

"To die and part is a less evil; but to part and live, there, there is the torment."

A minute later another furious strike across a knee was followed by, "Nor is there any law more just, than that he who has plotted death shall perish by his own plot."

After a particularly vicious blow, Allen realised Teddy's beating had passed from just being a personal attack into torture for torture's sake, and in that moment he felt release, like his mind detached from his body, and the pain he suffered stopped intensifying with each new blow.

Never once in his long service did Jim Allen think he was a particularly brave police officer; he did his job, got into a number of physical altercations, sustained a few minor injuries, and protected members of the public who themselves were under attack. As the room started to become quiet and dark, he was glad he had had the chance to do something heroic before he died: he had saved his wife.

Then there was nothing.

Nick's car screamed at the treatment it was receiving. Dan hadn't driven so aggressively in a long time, and that had been in a vehicle that could take the punishment he was now inflicting on Nick's family saloon. They almost lost the front bumper on the driveway in the first three seconds and once clear of the tight residential streets, Dan pushed the gearbox to it limits to get to the Allen home before it was too late.

"Tell me again," Nick shouted above the engine noise. "Right here then next left."

Dan swung the car around the corner oblivious to other traffic; fortunately there was mercifully little.

"I noticed he was calling me son. It was one of those things and I knew it was affection not condescension. The phone call, it was him, he said 'help me, son'. I know it was him."

"But when and why was he calling you son?"

"The other day, I don't know, a few days ago, when we got talking."

Even though they were both sat in the car, they both sounded out of breath.

"How long until we hit the motorway?" Dan asked, sounding the horn while completing a dangerous overtake of a double-decker bus.

"A mile, ten minutes to junction twenty-three and then maybe another ten to twelve minutes to get to Allen's at this speed."

The offended bus driver hit his main beam, causing the light to bounce off the rear-view mirror and into Dan's eyes.

"Shit!" He knocked it aside with his left hand.

Nick laughed nervously. "It's not as if you need it tonight anyway."

They sped on through the city outskirts until the big roundabout forming the motorway junction came into view. There was a small queue of cars waiting at a red light to join the slip road southbound but Dan was in no mood to wait. With one hand on the wheel and the other pressing down hard on the horn, he mounted the kerb on the nearside of the queue and drove through knee-high grass regardless of any hidden obstruction. It was only by sheer luck that he missed a steel post set in concrete as he bounced back onto the tarmac again at the front of the queue. As he tried his best to push the accelerator pedal through the floor, the car gained momentum down the slip road. With no rear-view mirror to assist he took a brief glance in the door mirror as he entered the motorway proper at ninety mph. Flashing lights and horns from other vehicles met their arrival but Dan ignored them as he bullied his way across three lanes into the fast lane and hurtled onwards.

Dan looked in his side mirror and then Nick's before catching sight of Nick with his phone by his ear. He nodded his approval. "Good idea."

"This is Detective Constable 1917 Hetherington, Notts Police. Put me through to motorway control urgently," Nick barked. "Motorway, this is Detective Constable 1917 Hetherington, Notts Police. I'm in a Green Ford Mondeo index Bravo, Mike, Five, Six, Mike, Sierra, Sierra. I'm southbound on the M1 between junctions twenty-four and twenty-three just passing marker one, six, three. I am en route to the private home address of Detective Chief Superintendent James Allen at speed."

There was a silence Dan knew would be filled by somebody in the control room saying, "What the fuck!" or words to that effect.

Nick continued in a loud but calm voice. "Speed one, one, zero." He looked at Dan and raised his eyebrows. Words were being said at the other end. "So, sue me! I believe Detective Chief Superintendent Allen is in mortal danger at this time. Request urgent assistance of all available units to the address at Plovers Cottage, Lees Lane, Tinsley. I repeat Plovers Cottage, Lees Lane, Tinsley. My ETA is ten minutes, ambulance is also required. I will call treble nine again when I reach the address if there is no other police presence. Out."

"I bet they weren't impressed." Dan had to shout above the noise.

Nick dropped the phone into his jacket pocket. "This junction, three hundred metres," he yelled back.

Once off the motorway driving became easier even though the roads were progressively more narrow and winding. Dan broke Nick's time estimation by a full minute, he had no intention of making a quiet approach.

Entering Lees Lane, he noticed car lights behind.

"Got to be police behind us, blues and twos."

Nick took a look back and confirmed at least two marked cars bearing down on them fast, blue lights flashing and two-tone horns screeching into the early night.

"You want to let them go in first?"

Dan grunted.

"Sorry, stupid question. This is it. Look out, someone's taken out the stone pillar."

Dan skidded the car to a halt next to Allen's and flung open his door. The only voices he could hear were coming from outside, where Nick and a number of uniformed police hurried to follow him. Inside, he could not hear a sound.

He ignored one of the uniforms who called out for him to stop and stepped through the open doorway. Inside, the house felt cold. He went to the left and towards the kitchen. The stable-style back door had been replaced after Dan and Nick's break-in but hadn't been painted yet. It was also open, allowing the cold air in.

Then he heard a shout behind him.

The first uniform inside had gone right. He found Allen.

"Je-sus!" It took a moment before he could say more. "Control from Tango Charlie Two Seven; I need ambulance to Plovers Cottage. One male with serious injuries. Two Seven."

As Dan made it into the lounge he was aware of a radio conversation but the sight he was met with made it fade into the distance. The mass of blood and exposed flesh was barely recognisable as human, let alone a human he was in the company of a few hours before. He went to bend down, but Nick held him back.

"No Dan, not this time."

They hugged like brothers again for the second time in as many days, but this time Dan needed his friend's arms to keep him upright. He burst into loud, uncontrollable sobs, each one contorting his body as he descended into a new type of hell.

They found themselves being ushered out of the room by another officer while still embracing and as a result could not fit through the door. Dan struggled to release Nick's grip as sounds of feet stomping into the house made him look up. Two paramedics in garish fluorescent jackets pushed past them.

Nick dragged Dan into the large hallway where they both sat down heavily on a dark brown leather Chesterfield. Dan's convulsions dwindled and he wiped the tears away. By the time he could breathe normally again, he was still unable to speak. A torrent of emotion flooded through him about the man that a week ago, he would happily have seen in his current condition.

He was so overcome that the commotion in the lounge barely registered. Even when Nick stirred and left, he still could not think rationally. He remained like a statue, until Nick ran back and shook him by the shoulders. Dan looked and for a second only saw Nick's lips moving. Nick continued shaking him, moving his lips until one word penetrated the fog in Dan's mind.

"Alive."

As he shook the fog away Nick repeated his last sentence again.

"He's still alive."

An electric current passed through Dan. He bolted upright and came to attention.

"He's still alive," Nick said again.

Through the door, the back of one of the paramedics appeared, pulling a stretcher. As if on a conveyor belt, Dan watched his frame pass and the full length of the stretcher came into view. There was Allen, more spread over it than lying on it, utterly motionless except for a small amount of blood still flowing from open wounds and seeping from bandages. What was left of his face was covered by a clear plastic mask and bag the other paramedic was rhythmically squeezing.

One of the police followed next, carrying some of the other medical equipment. Dan went towards them but was prevented by another officer.

"We need to talk to you."

Nick intervened. He flashed his warrant card and identified himself as police too.

"I can tell you everything. Please let him go," he pleaded.

Dan shrugged the policeman's hand off his arm and followed the paramedics out onto the stone chip driveway.

"Are you family, are you coming?"

"Son," Dan said.

Once they had carefully loaded Allen into the ambulance, Dan climbed aboard. He went to the left of the stretcher as the paramedic with a name badge on his chest, Phil, it said, continued working, feverishly attaching wires while still squeezing the bag attached to Allen's face mask on the opposite side. The driver took off with lights and sirens screaming, and Dan also heard the different sound of police horns behind them.

The driver was using his radio to call ahead to the nearest hospital. Dan only caught a few words. "Inbound… critical… trauma."

"You should hold his hand and talk to him. Here wear these," Phil said, dangling a pair of latex gloves at Dan.

"No, it's fine," he replied.

He reached down and gently wrapped fingers around Allen's right hand. His index finger was badly dislocated and stuck out over his thumb. The whole hand was swollen and bleeding; for all the world he could have just pulled it out of a grinding machine, but Dan held it like a baby bird.

When he bent forward this time there was no one to stop him. He rested his forehead on the stretcher's sidebar with his face as close to Allen's as the mask would permit. The smell of blood filled his nostrils, and blood filled his vision, too. He tried to locate the spot where Allen's eyes would be, but they were also obscured by swollen tissue, bandages and more blood. Clearly Phil considered the blood loss to be a secondary concern at that moment.

The ride was remarkably soft despite the speed of the ambulance. Dan tried to think of something to say but there seemed little point in trying to think about anything. Instead he just talked in soothing tones with no regard for the words themselves.

"Hey Boss," he whispered. "It's me, I got your message. Sorry it took me a bit too long to find you, but I'm here now."

Allen did not stir. If he was breathing beneath the mask, Dan could not detect it. He looked at Phil, who smiled encouragingly as he continued doing his best to keep his patient alive. Dan put his spare hand to Allen's forehead, which was soaked and matted with blood and hair, and stroked it backwards and forwards.

"Gwen's alright." He worked out the snatched line Allen got out on the phone before it went dead. He had no idea if she was alright, or even where she was, but maybe if Allen could hear it somehow it would make him feel just a little better.

"She's safe. She'll come to the hospital to see you there."

Phil's body language became animated.

"We're losing him," he called to the driver. "Here, carry on doing this," he said urgently to Dan, grabbing his hand and putting it on the bag attached to the mask. "Count to five and squeeze gently. Don't stop, whatever happens, don't stop."

The driver used the radio again, something about "the crash team" and "three minutes."

"Come on Boss, stay with me please."

Phil injected something into Allan's arm and waited.

"Crashing!" he yelled at the driver.

"Don't go, not now, please don't go now," Dan whispered again.

It was the longest three minutes of his life. When the ambulance stopped, the rear doors flew open.

"Move," a voice shouted.

Dan felt hands on him. "You, move," the voice said again.

As the stretcher slid out, Phil unfastened the mask. Dan was left alone in the ambulance, still squeezing the bag as Allen and his entourage disappeared through large sliding doors.

CHAPTER TWENTY-THREE

Teddy drove on into the night. After leaving the Allen house, his first thought was to somehow find Marley Johns, but he soon realised he had no idea where to start. Accepting his time as a free man was very limited, he was now determined to try and make the police work overtime to apprehend him.

During the time he was at college and university he was interested to learn that the famous Scarlet Pimpernel play written by Baroness Emma Orczy at the beginning of the twentieth century was first performed in his home town, at Nottingham's Theatre Royal. Thinking of escape brought this knowledge back. He passed a few seconds recounting the most well-known phrase from the story.

"We seek him here, we seek him there, those Frenchies seek him everywhere. Is he in heaven? Is he in hell? That damned, elusive Pimpernel."

Escape was not such a bad idea; he still had Oliver Treave's passport in the glove box and there were regular channel ferry crossings to France.

Phil came back to Dan after handing over custody of Jim Allen to the hospital staff.

"You better come in as well, we need to get you cleaned up." He helped Dan out and put a comforting arm around him.

"Your dad's a real fighter. It's not good but don't give up hope. I heard your mum is on the way too."

Nick went home after giving an initial statement. Once there he explained to the family what happened without being able to fill in all the details or answer many of their questions.

"What about Dan?" Amber asked.

"He went with him in the ambulance. I guess he'll still be at the hospital."

Penny beat Amber to the next question. "Should we go?"

"No. I know him. He'll be better on his own."

When Gwen Allen arrived at the hospital, Dan was still in the Accident Department being checked over. To look at him it appeared he'd been severely beaten too because of the sheer volume of Allen's blood he was soaked in, but as it washed off the staff were more inclined to believe he was okay, as he kept telling them.

Suddenly the privacy curtain parted and a nurse said, "See your son's right here," while ushering a confused looking middle-aged woman through and sitting her down.

They both looked at each other in stunned silence until Dan was able to summon a few words.

"Hello. Gwen, is it? I'm Dan, I can explain." He hopped off the bed and sat next to her. "I used to work with him. I think he must have called me while you were both… while you were both in the house."

Gwen started to shake uncontrollably; fresh tears appearing in her eyes. The nurse called for help and Gwen took Dan's place on the bed while he looked on helplessly. Gwen's glassy stare never left him as she was treated to calm her shredded nerves.

It took some time before the staff were prepared to leave her alone again but when they finally did, she sat up on the bed.

Dan shifted his seat forward. "How are you feeling?"

"Like I need to be told what's happened to us," she said coldly.

"Jim called me and I came as soon as I could."

"I don't mean that. Who are you to start with, and why did you tell them you are our son?"

"No, I didn't, that was a misunderstanding. I used to work with Jim at Garstone. I've been back in the country this past week from New Zealand and we've caught up. I don't know if it's a habit of his, but he called me son a few times while we were talking, and I remembered it when he called tonight. The ambulance guys thought we were related when they got to your house and I was there. I suppose you would like to know who that maniac in your house was?"

He regretted his choice of words as Gwen paled.

"Sorry, are you okay?" When she nodded, he continued. "His name's Teddy Parker, you may or may not know his father?"

"I know that! His father used to be a friend of ours until he built our house and he and Jim had a big falling out."

"Oh, sorry I didn't realise. Teddy Parker is wanted by the police for some serious offences and in his twisted mind he thought it was all your husband's fault. That's why he came to your house. Jim did what he did so you could get away. He knew what would happen, I think."

Gwen crumbled in front of him and for a second he didn't know if he should go to her or not, but seeing her descend into despair again was too much. He stood up and wrapped her in his arms.

"I'm so sorry. So, so sorry."

Allen was not in the ICU. He was on an operating table in Theatre 1 where a cast of nearly a dozen highly trained and experienced medical personnel were keeping him alive by artificial means while trying to repair enough of him so he might have a remote chance of surviving through to morning. Only the soles of his feet were injury free.

The surgeons started by opening his chest cavity to find all the major organs haemorrhaging. His spleen and kidneys were ruptured, one of his lungs was collapsed and his pancreas and liver were not functioning properly. Under all this stress, his heart unsurprisingly gave up.

"It looks like someone's put it all in the blender for five minutes," the chief-surgeon commented.

To make matters worse, his skull was so smashed up it had not been possible to run a brain scan to see what activity was present. Nevertheless, two specialists worked on his head at the same time.

When Dan finished explaining as best he could to satisfy Gwen's first barrage of questions, she seemed only slightly less wary of him. It was clear she did not know the full extent of her husband's injuries and Dan did not feel he was the right person to tell her, but when she started asking direct questions about how he was, Dan was backed into a corner.

"When I got there, he was in a bad way. I think Teddy Parker must have given him a severe beating. I came in the ambulance, but he didn't wake up at all and they took him straight in. I haven't seen him or heard anything since then."

"Why did he call you? He's never mentioned you before."

"I wish I could answer you. I was and still am as surprised as you."

"I should find out where he is," Gwen said.

"Do you want me to go? I think it's better if you rest. You have been through a hell of an ordeal too."

Dan thought Gwen might put up a fight, but fortunately, she flopped back, clearly drained. He ducked out from behind the curtain, glad to get away from her questions.

The A & E department was humming, just how he remembered every A & E when he was in the police; worlds of their own with a heartbeat and a soul. The nurses' station was manned by four uniformed staff, all of whom looked as if they had put in a long shift already.

"Can you tell me about James Allen please? I came in with him earlier. He was rushed straight through triage."

After a few quick keyboard strokes the nurse looked up.

"He is in theatre now. I can't tell you any more than that."

Dan was not surprised. "Where can I go to find out more?"

"He's in Theatre 1 so you will need to go to the General Surgical Unit on the fourth floor. They will have as much information there as you will be able to get, although you may have a wait because information does filter through slowly up there, only because it's the nature of things," she added apologetically.

When Gwen was given the all clear they took the lift up to the fourth floor. She was still suspicious of him and he could feel her eyes boring into him as he looked straight ahead.

"I still don't understand why he would call you," she said.

"We met and talked a bit over the last two or three days, maybe I was just the first person it occurred to him to ring."

Gwen offered a small non-committal nod, and Dan hoped she would not want to know more.

"Did you have anything to do with what happened?" she asked.

Dan gulped. "Honestly Gwen," he started, but was saved by the lift doors opening. "We're here. Let's see what they can tell us."

The Surgical Unit was the opposite of where they just came from. Quiet and calm filled the air. The nurses' station here was immediately in front of them as they walked out of the lift; a young nurse in pale blue scrubs looked up from a computer monitor.

"Can I help you?"

"I'm Mrs. Gwen Allen, James Allen's wife."

The nurse stole another look back to the monitor, which did not escape Dan's attention. "Mr. Allen is still in theatre."

Dan quickly calculated two hours and thought, *okay not too bad.*

"He will be in there for several more hours I'm afraid," the nurse continued. "All his injuries will take a long time to be attended to."

Shit. Dan understood enough hospital speak to understand what that meant.

"When will you know more? Can we wait?" he asked.

"Of course, there is a family room halfway along the corridor with coffee and a TV. I'm here until midnight. I'll come and tell you any news when I have it."

The coffee was surprisingly good, sofas and chairs populated the room. However, the TV seemed to insult the reason for them being there at first. Dan was on his second cup before Gwen had finished blowing on her first to cool it enough to drink. "You didn't say if you had anything to do with why Jim is here?"

Now he wished the TV was on and showing something interesting.

"Teddy Parker badly assaulted at least two other women recently and another young woman was set up to take the blame for one of them. I know her family and that's what Jim and I have been talking about. The other day one of Teddy's friends decided to make a deal with the police and now Teddy is going to get arrested and charged with enough to send him to prison for the rest of his life."

"So, you are police then, you said you used to work with him."

"Not police any more."

"So why would he be talking to you about a current case he's working on? That's not normal."

Dan admired the way years of being married to a detective had sharpened Gwen Allen's wits to a fine point, and now it seemed the coffee was having a reviving effect too.

"I was trying to help. I had no idea it would end like this. Teddy must have just flipped and decided to exact some revenge on the person he thought was to blame."

It was difficult to tell her enough to sound convincing, he did not want to lie but saying her husband firstly got himself into a hole over the house and then tried to get himself out of it in the way he did would be too painful, not to mention open the way to a lot more difficult questions.

"I'm sure he will be able to tell us both when he comes out," he added trying to sound a lot more positive than he was.

Gwen was tired, the trauma of the day caught up with her now she was in a sedate environment with nothing to do but reflect on what happened.

"Why don't you try and get some sleep? I'm going to stay so I can wake you if there is any news," Dan said.

She looked cautious. "He obviously trusted you enough to call when all that was going on, so I suppose I could do."

"I don't blame you for being suspicious of me. All I can tell you is he and I are on the same side in this," Dan said, pleading to her better judgement.

Gwen rested back in her chair, not quite closing her eyes. "Make sure you do wake me the second anything happens."

It did not take long before the need to sleep overcame any other emotion. When he was sure she would not stir if he left, Dan got up to use the payphone he'd seen as they were shown in to the room earlier. Nick picked up on the first ring.

"Hey how are things?" he answered Dan's tired greeting.

"As bad as they can be. He's still in the operating theatre and Gwen Allen has just given me a grilling. I don't blame her either."

"Well at least he's still alive, that's got to be a good thing."

"I suppose. They didn't even stop for a look when he arrived. I don't like his chances, Nick."

"Are you going to stay?"

For a moment Dan was not sure if Nick meant stay at the hospital or stay in England. All he could say in reply was. "Can you do me a favour and call Tara? I've missed my call tonight and I don't want her worrying."

"Sure. Is there anything else we can do here?"

"No, we just have to wait and hope. Did you learn any more from the police?"

"No. The bastard was still on the loose when I finished giving my statement; they were getting ready to do his flat and a couple of other places he frequents. I think we can safely assume Teddy Parker is top of the police most wanted list right at this moment."

"I'm on a payphone. If you need to contact me can you call the General Surgical Unit on the fourth floor?"

"Of course. Hey Dan, try and get some rest yourself and one more thing, none of this is your fault."

"You should take up mind reading."

"Not really, if you hadn't guessed and we got there when we did, he would not be alive now, would he?"

"Thanks for that. I'll talk to you later."

Gwen was still asleep. Dan lay down on a sofa and closed his eyes but all he could see was a row of people he knew who were no longer alive. His mother, Zoe Summers, Neil Danes, Anna Rofe, and Josie Lamas. Before his eyes snapped fully open again and he sat up straight, the image of James Allen floating into view.

Gwen woke up unassisted at 4:00 a.m. She blinked and looked around, finally seeing Dan. He had barely slept. Haunted by the ghosts of his past still.

"What time is it? Have they said anything yet?" she asked.

"No, I'm afraid not. The nurse came in at midnight to say she was going and there was no new news then. It's very late, just gone four. Would you like a coffee?"

They sat in silence drinking and deep in thought until Gwen spoke.

"I do know you, don't I? When you said you worked under Jim at Garstone I couldn't remember you at first, but I do now. Just as I was waking up it came to me. You occasionally drove us home from the bridge club when you were on a late shift."

"That's right," Dan replied, expecting more awkward questions.

"He always said out of everybody he trusted you the most."

Dan was amazed.

"Didn't you know? He always said there was nobody else he would trust with my safety apart from himself. You resigned didn't you, it's all coming back now. You resigned, and he was upset for a long time afterwards. He said it was like losing a family member."

"I never knew. When I left we weren't on great terms. Probably all of my own doing."

Gwen smiled for the first time. "That's why he called you tonight, he knew he could trust you and he was right wasn't he, you got there in time to save him."

Dan's exhaustion prevented him having a stronger answer. "Oh, Gwen I'm sorry, he was in such a bad way when we got there, it might be too late."

He looked at her, her smile remained in place and she even managed a look of reassurance.

"Do you believe in God, Dan?"

"I don't think so," he replied honestly.

"Nor me, but I believe in Jim and he believes in you. Maybe you should believe in yourself a bit more. We have been together a long time and I've never wanted for anything, he always said he would look after me. I'm a bit demanding to tell you the truth, but he loves me the way I am, and I love him for it. We're going down to Devon when he retires, did you know?"

"Yes, he said."

"Well let me tell you, however many broken bones he's got he won't give up because he will want to be able to look after me down there. So don't you go and give up either. If he called you son it wasn't an accident. He values family more than anything."

Dan felt an inner warmth in the core of his being replacing a coldness which had been there for a very long time.

"Did he ever tell you about our family?" Gwen asked.

"No, as I say we never talked like that, like people who are close."

"It's funny isn't it, thinking about it all again now I can remember as clear as day. He didn't talk about you much at home either but when he did it was always how good and safe you were. We had twins you know, a boy and a girl. She died after only two hours."

"I'm sorry. I wish I'd known you all better before."

"Thank you Dan, that's a sweet thing to say. Bradley our son, he was more like me in many ways."

Dan noticed the way she spoke about their son in the past tense and steeled himself for more bad news. Gwen continued as if confiding to a close friend.

"I think Jim would have loved him to go into the police too, but from an early age it was obvious he would not have suited that life at all. Bradley was very artistic but was also quite demanding. He liked nice things and didn't like to wait for them. When he was eighteen he got involved with this group who promised him the world if he invested with them and he went off to South Africa to find diamonds."

Dan was trying to guess at the timings of these new revelations. "When was all this, Gwen?"

"Bradley left in 1983."

Dan waited for more, expecting a continuation of the story but that was it. Gwen looked into the open space of the room and back in time. She sipped her coffee and smiled benignly.

"It must have been very hard for you both," he finally said, hoping he sounded caring and interested.

"It still is. It never goes away. Jim doesn't like to talk about it, but I know he thinks about him all the time. What hurts him most is that Bradley just lost contact with us so soon after leaving. We talked a few times about whether he might have died too, but as his mother I always thought I would know, do you understand?"

Dan nodded, he had no words.

"The last we heard was in January of 1984 when he sent a letter asking for some money. We sent a wire transfer, but it was never collected."

Dan calculated all this happened before he even joined the police and two decades before he met Allen. He felt honour and despair for and towards a man he never really knew anything about and accordingly had dramatically misjudged.

They continued to talk. There was nothing else to do. Dan told Gwen about his life in New Zealand and what happened two years before with Katrina Mallinder. He talked about his and Tara's new house, the coffee table and their upcoming parenthood. Gwen was delighted with the news.

"How wonderful for you both, I do like a happy ending."

Neither of them noticed the sun rising and when a nurse knocked and entered the room, they were both taken aback.

"Good morning, did you get some sleep?" the nurse asked.

"Not much," Dan replied. "Is there any news yet?"

"That's what I came to tell you. Mr. Allen will be out of surgery in the next thirty minutes and will stay in Intensive Care. Someone from the surgical team will come along to see you and tell you how it all went. Would you like some breakfast? I can get some toast brought up."

"Thank you. I don't think either of us have eaten for well over twelve hours," Gwen said.

After eating Gwen went to freshen up as she wanted to look presentable for the doctors.

Dan looked at his reflection in the bathroom mirror. He felt he'd aged ten years overnight. He splashed water on his face and patted down some random hair. When he got back to the family room Gwen was not alone.

Two doctors in green surgical gowns were sat on a sofa opposite her. She held out her hand to Dan and he joined her.

"I was just saying, I'm Patrick Collison and this is Greg White, we have been with James."

"Okay, go ahead," Dan said.

"Well it was a very long and hard night for James. He has undergone four procedures to repair and stabilise major organs, plus a procedure to reduce swelling to his brain. He needs time to rest before we operate again. I'm afraid it was one of the worst multiple injury cases I have ever seen." Gwen squeezed Dan's hand. "It really is remarkable he got to the hospital at all." She squeezed again.

Greg White then spoke. "He's as stable as he can be at the moment. We have him heavily sedated, so his brain and body can rest. We will look at him again this time tomorrow and decide when we can operate again. You'll have to excuse us, it's been a long night for us too. I think you should go home and we'll see you again another time."

"Can we see him?" Gwen asked hopefully.

"He's in ICU. You'll be able to look at him through a window for a few minutes but that is the best we can offer for now. James is still in a terribly bad condition. All we can do is hope he becomes a little stronger so we can do more. I'll send a nurse to take you."

Gwen and Dan thanked them for what they had done so far. When they were alone again it was Dan who needed to be comforted more than Gwen; she maintained a steely resolve about her, a countenance he could not match.

"Do you mind staying here while I go to see him? I won't be long," she said.

Dan had no choice, he wanted to see Allen too, but could hardly decline Gwen's request.

He resembled an Egyptian mummy more than her husband. What little she could see was swathed in clean, white bandages apart from narrow slits for his eyes and mouth. Wires and tubes ran in all directions to and from him. He was still more broken than mended, his life was still more likely to end in the room than not.

She rested her forehead against the glass and said a small prayer. Before leaving again she silently sent him another message.

You hurry up and get better. We've got a lot of planning to do and I can't do it on my own. Get better love, Dan's going to need you too.

CHAPTER TWENTY-FOUR

"You look terrible."

"Thanks Amber, nice to see you too."

When Dan got back to Nick's he flopped down in a chair completely shattered. Amber brought him in a coffee and sat down next to him. Nick and Penny were out shopping but would be back soon, the twins were at friends. He wanted to call Tara, but the chair had an unbreakable grip on him at that moment.

"How is he?" Amber asked.

"Not good at all. They said to hope and pray was the best we could do at the moment."

Dan explained a little more as he struggled to finish his drink, the effort of swallowing was almost too hard.

"I'll talk to his wife again later and go back."

Amber looked slightly embarrassed. "I don't want to sound horrible, but how will this affect me?"

"That's alright. I expect your dad will talk to them and get it sorted out. None of this affects you."

"Are you sure? I mean, he's the one in charge and is making all the decisions."

"Yes, honestly." Dan was so tired, it was all he could manage.

"Really." Amber understandably was not wholly convinced. "It's been so unconventional, how is anybody else going to make any sense of it? Half the time I still can't believe it's actually all happened. It's more like a book or a movie than real life."

Her trembling voice and teary eyes revitalised Dan a little and they continued talking. He explained how the investigation of her would be formally closed and as they finished, they heard the sounds of a car returning outside.

"You look terrible," Nick said entering the room.

"Not you as well. Amber was just as subtle when I got back. Let me call Tara first and then I'll tell you the latest."

Having assured Tara he was okay and spent time making sure he talked about her and the baby too, he eventually went back downstairs an hour later. He went through a more detailed version of the events of the previous night once more with Nick and Penny and by the time he was finished all he wanted to do was sleep. Penny agreed to wake him up at 5:00 p.m. Once upstairs, he undressed and was asleep within seconds.

Ben Binder's feelings were very mixed. He was upset and disturbed initially to learn of the brutal assault and injuries Allen sustained at the hands of Teddy; the hospital accommodated him with the latest on his condition and prognosis. Now in the cold light of day he thought it might be better if Allen did not recover; Teddy was on borrowed time and with Allen gone a number of side-issues would go with him.

Marley Johns' statements would soon be in the hands of the Prosecutions Service. A dedicated task force had also been set up from members of the Serious Crime Unit to deal with both Teddy Parker's violence and burglary offences. His own invaluable input was over but the kudos of bringing it all together was already becoming legend.

Teddy Parker was in London. He still intended to head for the coast but needed a day or two to realise some assets before leaving for good.

His first call of the day the next morning was to a back-street barber where he had his head shaved to a number one. Next, he went to Wimbledon High Street and visited a dozen ATM machines, making the maximum daily withdrawal from each on several cards he had in his wallet. At the final one he went into the branch and opened an account in the name of Oliver Treave, using the passport for identification and stating his new hairstyle accounted for the difference in appearance.

"Bullshit baffles brains," he said to himself as he left.

At a BMW dealership, he got a good price for the car and then went to buy something a little better suited to blend in on the continent.

By lunchtime he had almost twenty thousand pounds in his pocket, more in the bank, a 2008 Citroen and a future that was looking rosier by the minute.

He grabbed a quick meal at an Internet café where he booked another hotel in Canterbury for that night and the next, and then booked a return journey on a cross-Channel ferry for Friday night, although it was only going to be a one-way trip.

Feeling refreshed, he spent the early afternoon pawning his watch and jewellery before driving down to Canterbury before rush hour.

At 4:00 p.m. Dan was still fast asleep but he was happy to be woken from his unwanted dream.

"It's Gwen Allen on the phone for you," Nick said, passing the handset. "He's awake."

"Hi, Gwen."

"Hello, I heard your friend pass on the message. I wanted to let you know as soon as they called me. They couldn't tell me too much over the phone so I'm going in at six."

"Great news, can I come in as well, if you don't mind?"

"No of course, I'll see you there."

Dan got up and woke up properly under the shower. He was still overcome with anguish about Allen's condition and how he still had so much to say to him. The events which led to Allen's hospitalisation formed yet another layer of emotional baggage to top the mountain he carried as a matter of course, however, the intensity of his feelings for his old boss, which had somersaulted from a deep rooted and prolonged loathing to a genuine liking and respect in just a few days, was a wholly new concept. He knew he could not possibly go home now until Allen's future for the better or worse was more understood.

Once he was dry he sent Tara a quick email promising to call later and to make a request. He was surprised to hear the phone ringing downstairs a few minutes later was for him again, and even more surprised when Tara's voice replied to his "Hello."

"Hi honey, what are you doing awake at this time?" Dan asked.

"Something in the garden made Jet bark so I got up to let him out, and saw I had an email from you on the way back to bed. How is your old boss doing?"

"Not good, I'm going in again in a while. Sorry the message was a bit cryptic. I was going to explain when I called later."

"Yes, 'email your book over'. What is that all about?"

"I thought it would be an idea to read some of it to Jim. You know they say unconscious or sleeping people can still hear so I wanted tell him something of my past." He hesitated before adding, "In case I don't get the chance to explain more in the future."

"So, it's still touch and go?"

Dan sighed. "Very."

Tara sounded relaxed. "Hey, no problem, he must have made quite an impact on you."

"He has, I'll tell you all about it soon. There is one other thing though, I need you to go to my desk and take out the middle drawer. Taped to the underneath is another envelope with some more pages. Maybe I should have mentioned it before, but there is another chapter to the book which I've never let anyone see, but it relates to the time when I was at Garstone with him." Dan waited for a reaction.

"I wondered why there was no chapter fourteen," she said. "I didn't want to ask in case there was something you wanted to write but hadn't got around to. I didn't think you had already. You are a strange one, Dan."

He was embarrassed, feeling like a child caught with a pocketful of chocolate.

"And you are wonderful, I thought you never noticed. Sorry, it was put away long before we met and I suppose it was easier to leave it there."

"Don't worry. I'll get it now and scan it onto the PC in the morning. I'll send it along with the rest of the book then. I take it I still can't read it?"

Dan detected a hint of disappointment in her tone but because of the content he could not bring himself to tell her yes unconditionally.

"I should know better by now, shouldn't I? You can read it if you want to, but to be honest I'd prefer for you to wait until I get home so I can explain before you do. You might not like what you see."

Tara hesitated for a moment, but it was long enough for Dan to become more uneasy. "Tara?"

"Yes, I'm here. Jet was barking again, that's all," she said with no conviction.

"I will explain, I promise."

"Yes of course. You get on and call me when you can."

"I love you Tara, you and the baby."

Tara mellowed. "We love you too. I hope your friend is better."

Tara went to Dan's desk straight after breakfast, found the brown envelope where he said it would be, and removed the few pages it contained. The top page read Chapter Fourteen. It took all Tara's will power not to read on. She understood Dan well enough after nearly three years together to know how to scale his degrees of importance. Also, having read the rest of his first manuscript numerous times it was glaringly obvious that these pages must contain something altogether different for him not to have included it with the rest. With Jet by her side she scanned them onto her PC and emailed them as a folder with the other manuscript.

How many more secrets has he got? she thought as she put the sheets of A4 back in the envelope again.

By the time Dan was properly dressed, it was time to go. Nick dropped him at the hospital entrance.

"I'm going back into work tomorrow to see the Divisional Commander and someone from Personnel. If I don't see you, I'll call and let you know how I get on," he said as Dan opened the car door.

"Okay, sounds good. I'm not sure how long we'll be here for, so see you whenever."

Gwen was already in the family room with a new doctor. As Dan entered it was clear the doctor had only just arrived too.

"This is Dan," Gwen said as a full explanation indicating for the doctor to proceed.

"Right, hello, I'm Andrew Morgan. I was saying that James has had as good a day as we could hope for. He came around a while ago and was able to answer a few basic questions such as his name and address, but he has no recollection of the assault. He was able to confirm he has feeling in all four limbs."

Gwen and Dan exchanged looks of relief and delight.

Morgan continued. "While all that is very good, James is still critically ill and we need to operate again soon. Pressure is building in his cranial cavity, which is our biggest concern, but he also needs more surgery on his major organs, both legs and probably both arms too. He was incredibly lucky to survive the attack."

"So, what happens next?" Gwen asked.

"As I said, the pressure on the brain is our primary concern. We would like him to be stronger before we proceed but time may be against us. I need to ask your permission to operate now rather than wait for an improvement which may or may not come."

When Gwen and Dan looked at each other again there was no pleasure this time.

"It doesn't sound like I have a choice. What do you think Dan?"

He was surprised to be involved in the conversation. "What would he say if it was you?"

Gwen turned to Morgan. "Yes, right. Yes of course you should go ahead. Can we see him again now?"

A few minutes later she and Dan stood at the same glass where Gwen saw her husband hours earlier. He appeared not to have moved. Dan struggled to take in the sight without becoming overcome once more.

"He is as strong as an ox. He is going to be alright," Gwen said.

They stayed looking at Allen until a flurry of nurses in blue came and unhooked him from the various tubes and wires and wheeled him out of the room.

"Round two," Dan said coolly.

In the family room, again they poured a cup of coffee and sat together on a sofa.

"Why don't you put the TV on?" Gwen suggested.

They made small talk for a few minutes, though Dan was just working up for a way to ask Gwen a particular question. When the chat ran out, he shifted in his chair.

"I want to ask if it would be alright with you for me to read to Jim sometime. I wrote a book a while ago based on my life and some of the things I did in the police. I thought it might be good for him to hear something familiar, well, sort of familiar, when he wakes up, or even before that. They say it's good for unconscious patients to be talked to, don't they," he said feeling uncomfortable broaching the subject.

Gwen studied Dan, increasing his discomfort.

"That would be wonderful. Jim loves a good book. Are you sure you want to?"

"I really would. I think I owe it to him in light of how I used to think of him and why." Dan wanted to add he was desperate for Allen to be his confessor and hear his words even if he was not conscious, just in case his injuries won the battle and he might never be able to tell him in the future.

She patted his arm. "Well let's hope you can do soon."

At 9:00 p.m. Andrew Morgan appeared again.

"Hello there, good news we think. We've removed a clot and there was an instant reduction in pressure around James' brain. He is resting again now but hopefully we can have him in again in the morning for a more extensive procedure to increase the function of his kidneys and pancreas. Would you like to see him?"

Instead of the glass barrier, Gwen and Dan were escorted to a private cubicle within the ICU where Allen lay wrapped in more clean gauze.

"We've sedated him again, but you can have as long as you like," Morgan said before leaving them.

Gwen put both hands to her face and then touched her husband on the back of his left hand between two thin tubes.

She looked at Dan. "He's so warm. Is that usual?"

"I'm sure it must be."

Allen was still breathing with the aid of a respirator, his rising chest the only movement Dan had seen him make since seeing him in his lounge. His eyes were not bandaged but the swollen skin and severe bruising made them invisible. To Dan it was incredible to think he managed to survive the attack at all. He rested a hand on Gwen's shoulder while she continued stroking the two inches of Allen's hand with a finger.

"Should I talk to him now?" she whispered.

"Why not, it will be good for you both. I'm going to go and talk to the nurses for a minute, so you go ahead, and I'll come back soon."

Outside Dan needed to take some deep breaths before continuing. He went to the nurses' station to ask a favour.

"Hi, I was wondering if you have Internet connectivity here and if so whether I could use a terminal and your printer. I am happy to pay."

As he settled at a computer a minute later Gwen was having a one-way conversation with her husband.

"Then Carole came over to help with the clean-up, but I think that rug has had it. When you're better we should definitely look at getting away to Devon as soon as we can and sell a load of the stuff we've got. You know me, I like things too much, but let's make it easy for ourselves in future, less cleaning as well."

Gwen talked about the house and moving for several more minutes until she could not think of anything else to say on that subject.

"I wish you would have told me more about Dan before now. He's feeling very bad for you and he is desperate for you to get better soon too. There is obviously some history between you isn't there? But he seems to be a lovely boy who needs a bit of TLC as well. He was telling me about his family in New Zealand. Him and his wife or girlfriend are having a baby around April time, he didn't find out until the other day. He also said he has written a book which he wants to read to you and I said how much you liked reading. He's here somewhere, he just went off to talk to the nurses.

"Oh, Jim what am I going to do until you get home safe? You know I'm hopeless on my own."

Gwen continued talking until Dan returned with a sheaf of paper held together with a bulldog clip. "Sorry. It took a while to print all these."

"Is that it, your book? I was telling Jim about it."

"Oh, right well maybe when he's a bit stronger and…"

"No Dan, no time like the present. I need the toilet and could use another drink so why don't you sit here and make a start."

Before he could think of a way out Gwen was on her feet. She ushered him into the seat she vacated and offered him an encouraging smile. "Go on, you will be fine, both of you."

A minute later Dan was still thumbing the pages, suddenly sure this was the worst idea he ever had. Allen continued to breathe, seemingly waiting for something to happen. When Dan became so uncomfortable with the near silence and could not think of a word to say he took a deep breath and began.

"There's no title yet." He waited for an answer, but none came. "I hope it will make things a bit more understandable for you, about me, about how I was.

"Chapter One. I killed my mother. I did not pull a trigger or thrust a dagger or even swing a heavy object, but I killed her as surely as if I had done any of those monstrous acts.

"When she needed my help, I turned away, when she was too scared to call for assistance I did nothing. When she died, I cried with pain, regret, remorse and sheer bloody anger.

"I was an only child, son to the perfect mother and a father who probably resented the attention I received from her and he made sure we both knew it.

"He was an important man with an important job; he knew lots of other important men too. When I first became aware of his status I mistook his beastliness for something which was a by-product of his work. I call it beastliness because my father was a beast; more of that in due course."

Dan took a great big gulp of air. He had managed to read the first passage without taking a breath and he felt exhausted.

He looked at the still figure of Allen; he was calm, non-judgemental. Dan suddenly felt relief flood through his body. He relaxed cleared his throat and continued.

Through the glass, Gwen watched the last few seconds. When Dan seemed to settle and sit comfortably on the seat rather than perch on top of it she smiled and sighed.

"Alright, you boys have a good time," she said and walked back to the family room.

Gwen watched one of her regular soaps and then a wildlife documentary occasionally looking at the door or her watch. At 12:30 a.m. she went back to the ICU.

"Well look at you two," she said, breaking a spell.

"Hi." Dan looked up from page ninety-nine. "Sorry what time is it? I must have got carried away."

"How are you both doing?"

"Fine. I mean I've just been sat here rabbiting on."

"For more than three hours," she joked.

"Oh, I had no idea. I guess I got a bit carried away."

"Do you feel better?"

It seemed an odd question to ask him with her husband lying on the bed but when he thought about it and looked at her again, Dan knew she had a greater understanding of his situation than he considered before.

"I do Gwen, thanks to you. You are a very clever person."

"Well you live with a detective for long enough and something has to rub off. I'm going to sit with him for a while now. Why don't you come back tomorrow and carry on?"

"Okay, I'll call first to see what their plans are. Can you call me if there is any update?"

"Alright Dan, see you soon."

Once again it was another late arrival home but when he saw all the downstairs lights were still on he guessed someone must be still up and for a reason.

"Hi. How is he?" Nick said as Dan walked into the lounge.

"Hey. It's hard to say. There's so much wrong with him that an improvement here or there hardly makes a difference at the moment. What are you still doing up?"

Nick grimaced. "Teddy Parker has gone missing."

"Missing?"

"Yes, the type where police don't know where he is or where to start. All enquiries have drawn a complete blank."

They both knew the first forty-eight hours, but especially the first twenty-four, were crucial in an inquiry of this type. Find them quick or you might not find them at all was a lesson they learned many times over.

"Banks, credit cards, vehicles?" Dan asked automatically.

Nick nodded, answering them all at the same time.

"That's exactly what I said and that's the worrying thing. Before two nights ago, he's using multiple credit cards all day every day, yesterday two dozen large withdrawals in South London but since then nothing. The search of his home was inconclusive. He has so many clothes you can't tell if he's taken a suitcase load. His passport was there though so we can discount overseas travel.

"So, he was in London yesterday, maybe because it's the easiest place to get lost in, but something still doesn't add up. I can't help thinking he should have come to notice by now wherever he is. He's also got three cars in his name, a Porsche which is kept in his garage, an old Ford Escort which has been renovated for racing, and a Land Rover. They're all unaccounted for."

"Teddy is not the type to stay out of sight for long. Tell me about London."

"At least ten ATMs and maximum daily withdrawals from each, but nothing else on the credit cards and no sign of any vehicles belonging to him on the registration identification system over the city. One thing I know for sure is he is not a public transport sort of person. Their system is world-class and covers every main road. If one of his cars came into London we would know about it by now."

"Adding Teddy's access to those types of funds into the equation makes me very nervous," Dan said.

"I've been talking to Tim Traynor this evening, do you know him?"

"The name rings a bell, was he on Special Branch when I was at Garstone?"

"Yes, that's him. He's a good guy and says hi. Anyway, Tim is document liaison on the Teddy Task Force as well as a friend. He's brought me up to speed.

"It seems one of Teddy's thieving mates called Marley Johns has turned into supergrass and is the prosecution's golden witness, he was there when Teddy killed Josie. It's his statements which pretty much ensure Teddy's conviction, although the forensics at Josie's are very compelling too. Apparently it makes for interesting reading. Tim gave me some details."

Dan was wide awake again.

"No, something isn't right. Teddy is the going-out-in-a-blaze-of-blood-and-glory type. If he hasn't surfaced yet it's because he's either not ready for his O.K. Corral moment or he's got another plan altogether. What did Tim say exactly?"

Nick appeared to pump out his chest in pride.

"You will be pleased to know I am actually ahead of you. Like I said, Tim is a friend, he emailed me Marley Johns' statements earlier. You can read them for yourself."

Dan smiled as Nick produced several copies of official police documents.

"If you were that far ahead you would have the coffee on by now."

Nick grinned back. "Ah there you go, Dan Calder, always one step ahead. Here make a start and I'll get some on."

Dan read voraciously; devouring every detail and occasionally silently chastising the police interviewer for failing to develop a point that he would have. Nick brought the coffee back and placed Dan's cup in front of him, which earned him a nod of thanks.

Dan took a pen from his pocket and made notes in the margins as he worked his way through the pages while Nick sat back with his cup and waited.

Marley Johns gave a detailed account of the events leading up to the sudden and vicious attack on Josie by Teddy. In his mind's eye Dan saw the incident develop and found no flaw in Johns' account. His final comments about what happened after when Teddy dropped him in the middle of town in his new car also rang true.

When he finished his first read through he turned to Nick. "It's pretty good stuff. If this Marley Johns repeats this in the box with a modicum of credibility, Teddy's a dead duck. I'll need another cup to get through the burglary statements though." He put the first handful of papers down and reached for the next.

Nick got up and stretched. "Your wish is my command."

As Dan reset his brain, storing the first statement details in readiness for the next, something stopped him and made him reassess. It only took a second to access the scrap of information he needed and when Nick returned he could hardly contain himself.

"New car, he said new car!"

"What?" Nick replied, nearly spilling the drinks.

"Teddy dropped him in town in his new car. Is that one of the three we know he has, or a new, new one? I need all the notes from his interviews, can you swing it?"

After mulling the pros and cons of calling Tim back at such a late hour Nick decided their friendship could withstand it.

"Hi Tim, it's Nick Hetherington again, I'm really sorry to call so late."

Dan went to the toilet while Nick grovelled over the phone. When he came back Nick gave him a thumbs' up signal.

"Tim, thanks a million. I owe you big time for this one. Yes, I'll wait now and call you at a more decent time in the morning. Thanks again. Goodnight." Nick hung up and turned to Dan. "He didn't appreciate being phoned in the middle of the night but he's going to get up and send the stuff to me now."

Dan felt a little bemused. Nick picked up on it.

"Been away a bit too long haven't you, Mr. Calder," Nick said with a certain satisfaction. "Like me, key staff on major crimes are issued laptops nowadays. Tim is going to fire his up and we'll have it in a few minutes."

For once Dan was pleased to hear of a small advancement that made a big difference to investigators. When the email arrived on Nick's machine a few minutes later he ran upstairs to print the pages off while Dan wrote down some questions he wanted the answers to on a fresh page in his notebook.

When Nick bounced back into the room he resembled a child on Christmas Eve. "Right here you go, do your stuff. I was going to bed but there's no way I can now."

Dan settled with the papers, ridding his mind of superfluous data. He knew time was of the essence. Every passing minute could mean Teddy Parker was getting farther away and just maybe the key to his whereabouts was contained in the pages at his fingertips.

Unfortunately for him, every police officer had a different and preferred way of taking notes, and it took him some time to get used to the style and find a rhythm so he could read without effort and allow his concentration to focus on finding exactly what he was looking for.

He read page after page, making notes of his own, underlining words and lines and scribbling addenda in the margins.

Occasionally he nodded or shook his head, but through the whole process he remained silent.

Like a snake charmer and a cobra, he had a hypnotic effect on Nick, who hardly noticed when Dan finished his first read through and went back to the beginning again.

Dan continued on, refining his notes until he suddenly stopped and looked up. Nick caught his breath as Dan quickly flicked back through a number of pages, then returned to the spot where he stopped a moment before.

"Gotcha!" he said, underlining several lines and making a final note in his book.

Nick got up and stretched. "I don't know how you do it but I'm really glad you do."

"I need coffee," Dan replied, slumping further back into his chair. "And a change of scenery. Come on, I'll tell you in the kitchen."

The kitchen table and chairs were not as comfortable as the lounge, but the change was welcome. Nick pulled his seat around so they were sat next to each other.

"I won't bore you with the details, but the bare facts are pretty straight forward," Dan began as Nick poured the latest steaming brew.

"Marley said that Teddy dropped him off in the city in his new car. While we still can't completely discount the chance Teddy's using his Porsche, Ford or Range Rover, I think he is in another.

"During Marley's initial interviewing he told police about how Teddy used to go to a snooker and pool club to see his gang of burglars, it seems that was the meeting place. A few weeks ago, or maybe a bit more recently, Teddy was bragging to them about getting a new car in lieu of a bet he won playing poker with some yuppie or other with more money than sense. I went through the notes twice, but Marley doesn't say what sort of car it was but, and it's a big but, when he got dropped off in the city he said some other guy said to him 'why are you getting out of it and leaving the white man in a black man's car?'

"It took me ages to find the name because the interviewer must have gone over his own notes later and seen it was question worth asking, even though he forgot to ask about the car. It was right at the end; Marley said it was a posh name like Olly or Ozzie."

Nick was struggling to keep up. "A little help please? It is very late."

Dan was enjoying being sure he was right.

"Oh, come on, black man's car, known to all as black man's wheels. BMW, right?"

"Of course, sorry, how come you can still function like this at stupid o'clock?"

"Fun isn't it! I'll bet there can't be too many white Olivers or Oswalds in Nottingham who are within Teddy's associate age bracket and own Beamers. Find Ollie or Ozzy, Nick, find him and you'll have the car Teddy's driving. I guarantee it."

It was almost 7:00 a.m. and Nick thought he could risk another call to Tim. After telling him of Dan's findings and confirming again that they both considered Dan to be something other than human, Nick followed Dan upstairs. On the landing, he patted his friend on the shoulder.

"'Thanks' seems to be so inappropriate after everything you've done."

Dan shrugged. "We just do what we can."

"You know if you needed anything?"

"Yeah, I know. Hopefully it never happens."

CHAPTER TWENTY-FIVE

Dan woke up having dreamt of Tara and Jet. One small blessing with the recent dramas that had overtaken his life in recent weeks was the almost-suspension of the recurring dream of Zoe Summers and Powton Road.

When he got downstairs he could hear Nick in conversation with at least one other male.

"Here he is now," Nick said as a greeting.

There were, in fact, two other people, obviously police, at the kitchen table. Tim Traynor he recognised but the female officer was new to him.

"Hi Tim, good to see you again," he said, shaking Traynor's hand.

"You too Dan, it's been a long time. This is Detective Inspector Katie March. Katie is second in command of the Parker Task Force. She wanted to come and say thanks too."

"A pleasure," March said, also shaking Dan's hand.

He could not help but think she must have joined the police when she was nine to be a DI now.

"I didn't even get this much love when I was in the job," he said, slightly embarrassed. "I take it what we did was useful?"

March made it clear she was in charge, even in Nick's house. "Very, even if it was a somewhat unorthodox method. When Tim told me what he'd done in sending you and Nick all that material I was not best pleased to begin with. We won't be making a habit of it, but nevertheless, I did want to come and thank you as well as remind you that this is a strictly one-time thing and we would prefer you not to advertise the fact."

"Understood. I only want to help. So, can you tell us what's happened?"

Traynor took his lead from March.

"You were spot on Dan. Fortunately the list of BMW owners with the first name Oliver is very short. Oliver Treave, twenty-six years, handed Teddy the keys to his seven series a little over two weeks ago. It seemed it was that or lose the use of his legs after a game of cards got out of hand."

"That's great."

"It's not all so good I'm afraid. We talked to Treave this morning and he confirmed the details. He also said that his passport was in the car at the time and he never got it back. We were working on the assumption Teddy is landlocked in the UK, but now there is potential for him to travel abroad."

March interrupted. "We have an all ports bulletin out and the vehicle has been circulated along with Treave's details. No news at the time we left the office but by the end of the afternoon we should know if an Oliver Treave has left the country in the last thirty-six hours."

Nick was disconsolate. "So, he could be out of the country already? London alone has got multiple airports."

"He could be," March replied. "But let's stay optimistic for the time being at least. If he hasn't but is trying to, what do you suggest we do? I only ask because it seems you two know Teddy Parker a lot better than we do at the moment. That is, you might know what he's thinking of doing."

Dan and Nick exchanged a look.

"You go," Nick said.

"If he hasn't gone yet and if he intends trying to leave the country using this Oliver Treave's ID, he will want to go soon, but where to I have no idea."

"That's as far as we got in guessing," Traynor added.

As he, March and Nick all talked at once about their next move, Dan considered Teddy's options and put himself in his position.

When Nick said London had multiple airports, something fired in his mind and he tried to connect it to what it had to do with Teddy. Suddenly he snapped his fingers, remembering a line on a sheet of paper a week ago.

"It's not an airport!" he exclaimed, silencing the others.

"What? How come?" Traynor asked.

"Teddy's afraid of flying. It was in one of his school yearbooks I saw. He went to Brazil and got a special mention because he flew despite having a fear of flying. If he is heading abroad and if he went south from here to London, you need to check all sea ports in the south and south-east first."

March was flabbergasted. "Are you sure?"

"I am," Nick answered.

It was March and Traynor's turn to look at each other.

"Okay let's do it, Tim. Nick, thanks for the tea. Dan, it has been an experience meeting you," March said, rising from her seat.

"My pleasure, good luck. Just one other thing. Teddy won't come easily. If I were you I would use overwhelming force when the time comes."

"Thank you. I'll remember that when we do the operation order to detain him."

Nick saw them to the door while Dan sat and finished his coffee. When Nick came back he was laughing.

"You are such a freak."

"What? They asked." Dan laughed back.

"Just another morning in the life of Dan Calder. Tara must be a saint. What have you got lined up for the rest of the day?"

"Nothing. Maybe hospital later."

As Dan forecast Teddy was indeed in the process of finalising his departure from Dover later that night. After a quiet night in a local hotel, which reminded him of his grandparents' house, he could not wait to get out in the morning.

Even after a short time away from his more nocturnal lifestyle he was missing the buzz. Drug free by accident as he forgot to pick up his stash from home when he left, the last two nights he relied on vodka and tequila to dull his senses enough to get through the boredom.

He paid cash for a two week return channel crossing for him and the Citroen at the office of P&O Ferries in Dover and once again only raised a moment of staff indecision when he offered Oliver Treave's passport. It seemed shaving his hair off had the effect of disabling people's ability to look at the rest of his face. Ordinarily his was just a passing resemblance to Treave at best, yet this simple technique had worked like a charm on three separate occasions in as many days.

There was nothing else to do for the rest of the day but wait. The ferry departure was for 11:30 p.m. and he needed to be at the terminal for loading an hour before at the latest, which meant almost twelve hours of dullness. What he really wanted was a hit of something chemical and a girl. He had not had sex for four days and next to an unnatural high, that was the thing which got him off most.

As he wandered along High Street then Biggin Street, which the receptionist at the hotel assured him was the shopping centre, he felt depression enveloping him. Any thoughts of Anna Rofe, Josie Lamas or James Allen were distant memories now. The fact he killed two women and probably the traitorous detective too was as insignificant to him as the faded memory of a TV programme he might have watched a few days ago. The shops, like everything else in Dover, appeared trapped in a time warp and he could find no trace of the twenty-first century.

In frustration, he kicked out at a telephone box causing an old man riding a mobility scooter to curse his loutish ways.

"Fuck off cripple!" Teddy spewed back. He would have said more if his attention hadn't been drawn to the numerous cards stuck to the inside walls of the phone box. He opened the door to be met with an overwhelming stink of urine, which in a disturbing way was almost a comfort to him and a reminder of things closer to home. The bright blue, green, orange and red cards had all been placed by prostitutes advertising their services. Most included a cheaply copied picture of a girl and a phone number only, but there were enough that also included an address too. After a moment's study, he realised there was one street in particular that could potentially satisfy all his current desires. It took a minute to find a male of his own age to get directions to Wardle Road and then another twenty minutes to walk there, each minute increasing Teddy's excitement at the prospect of finding some bitch he could unload into and get his hands on some meth, trips or coke.

Kings Avenue, Mackie Road and Gloucester Road became progressively more natural to him as he closed in on Wardle Road. Their socio-economic status descended with each stride and he could feel the air in his nostrils start to fill with the scent of misery brought about by high crime and low expectations. Other foot traffic became more familiar too: young men of different colours wearing ridiculous bright, oversized clothes inhabited street corners; middle aged women who looked like middleweight boxers, half-walked, half-ran between shops and home or vice versa; and more and more younger females fitting his requirements leant on gate posts.

"Let us be grateful to the people who make us happy; they are the charming gardeners who make our souls blossom," he said quietly to himself.

Wardle Road was a long, straight, and busy road of terraces and semi-detached brick houses; some wore painted façades, all of which seemed to be long in need of a fresh coat, but most were the original red brick dulled by dirt and time. None had a tidy front garden; broken motorcycles were far more frequent than flowers.

Teddy now strolled along in comfortable surroundings. He exuded a primal air of knowing his place in the pack as did everyone else. Girls he passed eyed him like fresh meat and he stopped to talk to a few who commented on his accent and his clothes. He felt secure enough to ask where he could buy cocaine and meth and there was no shortage of knowledgeable replies.

One girl with peroxide hair and cut-off denim shorts stopped him. "Hey doll, how about some fun?"

She could not have been older than twenty and despite the cold day seemed oblivious to the temperature, relying on a cigarette to keep her warm. She wore a T-shirt with a picture of Snoopy on the front, and her nipples protruded like rivets through the thin cotton.

Teddy openly admired her breasts but she was not quite what he was looking for. "Another time babe. I'm looking for a girl with long hair, real long you know?"

"You don't want long hair. I've got plenty on top for you but none down there. Twenty pounds? Come on, doll."

"Sorry, got to have the hair today. But if you've got some acid, I could use some."

She was not upset; the chance to make a small amount without opening her legs or mouth was okay with her.

"Alright, I have got some. Maybe we can have a little party some other time?"

"Sure, why not." Teddy smiled back taking a few notes from a pocket.

The girl poked two fingers into the waist band of her shorts and pulled out a small plastic bag with four pink capsules inside. "Fifteen each."

Teddy was happy enough not to haggle. "I'll take them all." He handed over three brand new twenties, which she shoved into her back pocket.

Teddy popped a capsule before putting the others in his pocket.

"Thanks. What about a friend you may know?"

"You can try Crystal further along near the next corner. She's got hair down to her waist."

She gave Teddy further instructions and he moved away starting to feel the trip kicking in already.

Just after 2:00 p.m., Tim Traynor struck gold. He had used the phone book to get the numbers and therefore his enquiries of the cross-Channel ferry companies were in alphabetical order. P&O Ferries' computerised system made short work of identifying the booking made earlier in the day at the Dover office and soon he not only had Teddy's Treave booking but also the full details of the previously unknown Citroen.

"Good job, Tim," March said when he gave her the news. "Times might be a bit tight but if worse comes to worse we can always get the boat delayed. I want a department heads meeting in ten minutes and an arrest team ready in an hour. I'll call Keith Raye now. Can you get the others in here ASAP?"

Traynor hurried off to round up various personnel while March called her boss and head of the task force. Fifteen minutes later she began a briefing which was going to be brief in time too.

"Okay, we haven't got long so let's get a move on. You all have an Op Order in front of you relating to the intended location and arrest of Edward Parker later today.

"Parker is known to be in Dover as of nine fifteen this morning and is believed to be attempting to leave the country by channel ferry tonight at eleven thirty. Our intention is to allow Parker onto the ferry where he will be in a secure environment and then facilitate his detention and arrest at the soonest opportunity, which may be on the car deck or within the boat proper. After his arrest, he will be driven back here under escort for interview. Any questions so far?"

There were none.

"Good. Next, method. Four vehicles with four officers in each will leave here as soon as this briefing is over. One of each of us will be in each of those four vehicles to brief the others on the way. Three of the four vehicles will board the ferry. I'm going for overwhelming manpower here, I want him to give up like a mouse but us to be prepared to batter him if necessary."

She looked at Traynor who offered a sly grin in return.

Over the next half hour March detailed what she required. The best operations were those with the simplest and most effective methods; this one was basic personified and at just after 3:00 p.m., they were on the road.

Teddy found Crystal to his liking, however the room she used in the house was a hole and the bed appeared to be on the verge of collapse.

Even before they got upstairs he was pawing at her top with a roughness she should have realised was an indication of what was to come. Money first was not a problem to Teddy, the fifty pound note he threw on the dressing table was as new as the twenties he gave to Snoopy earlier.

"I do everything except anal," Crystal said matter of factly, wiggling her hips out of her jeans.

Teddy grabbed a handful of her hair and twisted it around his fist locking her head.

"I do whatever I want."

The contents of the pink capsule had now dissolved into his blood and he was feeling good, in fact he was feeling invincible. With his free hand, he groped at her breasts, squeezing a nipple so hard it made Crystal shout an objection, but he ignored her. He pushed her backwards onto the bed, falling on top of her. Immediately his hand went from her breast to her pussy and he shoved two fingers hard inside her, rotating them violently until he could feel them moisten.

In his experience, Crystal would be used to rough sex, it was all part of the job and she had probably become desensitised to it over time. She should be prepared for an uncomfortable session, not that he cared one way or another.

With his hand still controlling her head there was a limit to which she could move and no limit to Teddy's feeling of dominance. He removed his wet fingers and drew them across Crystal's face, forcing them into her mouth. By this time, he was fully erect and ready to vent several days' celibacy on her. He entered her like a battering ram and pummelled her so hard that he started to froth at the mouth.

Crystal watched a spider crawling over the ceiling and hoped the bald brute on top of her would be finished quickly.

Teddy's orgasm made him judder and he loosened his grip on her hair, freeing Crystal to move her head. When it was over he allowed his weight to rest on top of her, completely disinterested in how it would make her feel. As was his way the sex act was just the first part of the entertainment and he needed a moment to recover.

She pushed him off and went to get up, but he grabbed her by the arm and pulled her down again.

"Hold on sister, we're not finished yet."

"If you want anything else it's going to cost you."

Teddy laughed out loud. "No shit, I don't think so." He slapped hard on the cheek, making it sting and colour instantly. "Just wait, I'm almost ready."

He glared at her to negate any thought to fight. It was just as well, for if she had tried to resist Teddy he would have made the slap a mere appetiser for a far more violent main course.

Sufficiently rested Teddy stood up on the bed so his head was almost touching the bare light bulb hanging above it. His trousers were still around his ankles.

"Shower time," he said.

She tried to move but his lower legs and ankles either side of her and his trousers across her waist pinned her to the bed like a giant staple and prevented her from doing so.

She had the good sense to remain quiet. As she waited, Teddy's face took on a new concentrated expression and by the time she realised what he was doing it was too late.

Teddy got off the bed smiling and grabbed her hair again. Street smart as Crystal was, Teddy's next and final act of wiping his backside with her flowing locks brought stinging tears to her eyes and his ultimate satisfaction.

Dan got to the hospital in the middle of the afternoon unaware of developments concerning Teddy Parker. Allen seemed like he was the night before; the on-duty nurse told him his condition was slightly improved, but he was still not able to breathe unaided.

Gwen had been in earlier on in the day but was now at a prearranged appointment with the police, meaning she would most likely be away for several hours.

Dan settled in the bedside chair again, instantly feeling at ease.

"Hi, how are you? It is a crap day outside, so you're not missing anything. Where were we?" He found the last page from the previous night.

"Chapter Five. The Summer of 1976 was the best I can remember…"

Dan looked at Allen's still face and smiled before continuing.

CHAPTER TWENTY-SIX

Katie March's four car convoy blasted down the M1 motorway assisted by a marked traffic car leading the way with lights and sirens persuading everything in the outside lane to move aside. The M25 junction was a blur as they continued south and east towards the M20 west of Maidstone and by the time they were on the A20, they had completed the usual three-hour journey in a fraction over two hours. With time on their hands March thanked the traffic unit for their help and called them off. She and the convoy slowed to within the speed limits, which gave them time to come down from the high of the journey in the final miles before they hit Dover.

She wanted another meeting with all her staff and directed her driver off the main road and into the car park of the Black Bull pub in Church Hougham.

Fortunately, it was very quiet, and they were able to take over an entire end of the lounge bar after she introduced herself to the landlord and ordered sixteen assorted soft drinks, crisps and peanuts.

"Everybody should be up to speed, this will be the final full briefing of Operation Spear, but are there any questions before I begin?" she asked after a sip of lemonade.

"Is there any update on Parker since we left?" Detective Constable Paul Kerry asked.

"The information is unchanged. I talked to the Port Police and the ferry company en route and we have a plan to take Parker on the car deck as he boards. Port Police will act as P&O loaders and will be using one of their spare radio channels so there will be no chance of interference. Parker will be directed into a space where there is a large bulkhead in front of him, with the nearest staircase up to the passenger desks behind him. Team One will have three personnel in P&O fluorescent jackets in the area of the bulkhead and two more by the staircase led by DS Linton. Port Police is supplying two armed officers who will take direction from him and will on his command approach Parker as he opens his door, take control of him and get him face down on the floor. Once he is under control, DS Linton will direct as many of Team One as he feels appropriate to secure Parker with cuffs; only when he is cuffed will he be searched. If for whatever reason Parker cannot be approached by the armed officers, the two on the stairs will block him being able to get up and the three by the bulkhead will follow him and secure him, leaving the armed officers to take control of the vehicle. Any questions so far?"

"What if there is anybody else in the car with him?" Tim Traynor inquired.

"There is no reason to believe he is going to be accompanied. The booking is for himself only. Should he have a companion or companions then they will be identified by the two of us forming Team Two who will be with P&O staff at the landside boarding point checking passengers and vehicles onto the ship and they will act as the advance warning group for Team One.

Traynor and several others nodded their understanding.

"Team Three will be a vehicle and four who will board immediately behind Parker but will remain in their vehicle unless everything goes pear-shaped. As I said to the team leaders before we left Nottingham, if needs be we will adopt an overwhelming show of force to make him comply.

"That leaves Team Four, another vehicle and four who will remain in the parking area for cars waiting to board just in case he gets off the ship. In that very unlikely event, Team Four will detain him land side.

"DS Linton has team lists. It's all deliberately simple. I don't anticipate a problem but let's be prepared for any eventuality. No heroes please, I don't want anybody getting injured, even Parker unless it becomes unavoidable, but I'd much rather it is him than any of us. Remember, he is a nasty piece of work who's killed an old lady and almost killed Mr. Allen."

There was a general murmuring around the group.

"Oh, one last thing. If Team Three's and Parker's cars gets stuck on the ship, two volunteers are going to have to go with them and come back on the next available, presumably tomorrow morning. If that happens we will rent a replacement car to get the others back to Nottingham. There's no overnight stay for us. I want Parker back and in one of our cells by morning."

"And that means if anyone wants duty free you better make a list and choose your volunteers beforehand," Detective Sergeant Ed Linton said seriously to everybody's amusement.

March made to absent herself but stopped.

"Okay. Ed will do the honours with the teams, I've got some calls to make. We'll leave here at nineteen thirty, and convene at the Port Police Station at twenty thirty. Please remember we don't know where he is now so let's not do anything that he might possibly be able to see between here and the port. I do not want us compromised before we get to the ferry port."

Teddy hung around in a grotty café in Kings Avenue. Despite the hour, he ate a full English breakfast which seemed to come with an extra portion of grease. Nevertheless, he finished every morsel with gusto due to the latent excitement rush of his interlude with Crystal. The café owner seemed surprised to see his plate empty and even more so when Teddy demanded more tea and toast.

He had no desire to go back into the town centre until the last minute, so he sat with a copy of the previous day's newspaper and waited, occasionally reliving the meeting with Crystal.

Dan was still reading when Gwen arrived. She told him about giving her statement to police regarding the night of the attack and also relayed back to him the small amount they told her.

When Dan explained what he and Nick got up to earlier in the day and how it led to the Parker Task Force to start looking for an Oliver Treave heading overseas she was amazed.

"You have got all sorts of hidden talents haven't you? I'm beginning to understand what Jim meant when he used to talk about you. How is he? Have you been reading to him again?"

"Yes, for what it's worth. I don't know if it's helping or not but it's making me feel better. Tara would be very proud of me. Not so long ago I would have been charging around the country, hunting down this Teddy Parker by myself."

"I'm sure she knows what she's got."

Dan changed the subject. "Jim is not a lot different. The nurse said there was a slight improvement in his overall condition. They haven't said to me, but I think they may want to wait a while before operating again now the pressure on the brain has subsided."

"I just wish he would open his eyes or say something, even for a second." Gwen sighed. "A little thing like that would mean so much rather than the continuing beeps of all these machines being the only thing telling us he is still alive at all. Don't let me stop you if you want to carry on."

Dan baulked at the idea. "Please don't take this the wrong way but this is the first time I've read it to anyone and I couldn't read it to anybody else but him. Another one of my oddities, one day Tara will tell you about the rest of them."

"No, it's alright, I think I can understand. I've been talking to him as well, but about me. Funny how I, or we, rather, can discuss things with him when he's asleep we probably wouldn't if he was awake."

"I know I've said it before, but you are a very clever lady Gwen."

They went for coffee but chose the more worldly environment of the public cafeteria on the floor below rather than the solemnity of the family room. For the first time, they discussed everyday subjects not related to recent events and got to know each other a little. When they went back upstairs Operation Spear was about to reach its climax two hundred and fifty miles away.

"Op Comm to Team One, receiving?" March called smoothly from the back seat of her car. They were positioned in cover but with a view over most of the passenger car park.

"Loud and clear, Boss. In position," Linton replied.

March continued through the teams and got the same reply each time.

"From Op Comm with Team Four, very good. The time by my watch is twenty fifty-five. The information is unchanged. We are eyes up for a green Citroen C5 hatchback, index Alpha, Bravo, One, Zero, Delta, Echo, Charlie."

At 9:15 p.m. March repeated the process and did the same at 9:30 p.m. and 9:45 p.m. All they could do was wait. At 9:58 p.m. she was getting ready for her next call out when Paul Kerry, who was sat next to her, spotted their target.

"There! Green Citroen, directly in front of the big white artic with a picture of red apples on the side."

"Got him," March replied, bolting upright in her seat and dropping her mobile in the footwell. "From Op Comm standby, standby. Target vehicle is within the vehicle loading area. Wait for more."

Everybody stopped what they were doing and listened. Ed Linton's watch seemed to tick at a thousand decibels.

"From Op Comm, confirming the green Citroen C5 hatchback index Alpha, Bravo, One, Zero, Delta, Echo, Charlie is in the port. One male occupant not yet identified. Wait for more."

Linton unconsciously touched his pocket where his handcuffs were secreted. Tick, tick, tick went his watch.

"From Op Comm. Male occupant is the only visible occupant. He is a white male, bald head, clean shaven, no spectacles, aged between twenty and thirty. From Op Comm, I am calling this male our target. Team One receiving?"

"Team One. Loud and clear, Boss."

"From Op Comm, target is in lane six. There is a white Vauxhall Astra immediately in front of the Citroen and an articulated unit immediately behind which is displaying a picture of red apples on the side of the trailer. Team Three receiving?"

"Team Three loud and clear. We are in lane seven now."

"From Op Comm, wait for the P&O loaders to position you."

"Team Three received."

March reached down and grabbed her phone.

"Okay here we go," she said to her colleagues in the car.

Five more agonising minutes passed as she updated the slow progress of the Citroen towards the loading ramp.

"From Op Comm, the target is approaching you Team Two."

"Team Two received. Wait."

Linton's watch continued screaming.

"From Team Two, single male occupant has ID and boarding pass in name of Oliver Treave. Op Comm?"

"Op Comm received. Towards you Team One."

"Team One received. Ahead and waiting," Linton replied.

"Op Comm to Team Three, how are you doing?"

"Team Three, wait please Boss."

Tick, tick, tick, tick.

"Team Three to Op Comm, we are loading behind the target vehicle now. We are walking pace and are within the ship. Target is proceeding. Still proceeding. Still proceeding. I can see the passenger stairway to my offside now, still proceeding. Brake lights on the target vehicle, he has stopped by the bulkhead. Team Two stop any further vehicles."

"Team Two received."

"Team Three to Team One, have you got him?"

Linton did indeed and just as well because he was about ready to throw his watch into the sea.

"Team One has the target. Car doors are still closed; wait."

As Teddy pulled the door handle to open it, the interior light came on. Linton tapped the shoulder of the Port Police officer dressed like a ninja and armed with a Heckler and Koch MP5 semi-automatic machine gun who similarly tapped the colleague ahead of him. They raised their weapons and moved forward.

"Team One is striking! Team One is striking! Wait," Linton said into his radio.

As March held her breath, all hell let loose on the car deck.

Teddy emerged from the car vaguely aware of movement around him. Other passengers were getting out of their cars too and everybody was looking for the stairways.

"Armed police, stand still! Armed police, stand still! Edward Parker, stand still!"

The ninjas advanced with weapons at the ready, safety catches still on. Teddy heard his name and turned automatically to see what looked like the SAS coming towards him with two guns pointed at his head and chest.

"Armed Police, stand still! Edward Parker, hands above your head!" the first ninja repeated over and over as he got within near touching distance.

He laughed and raised his arms in front of him with extended middle fingers. "Fuck you!" he roared.

Ninja Two, careful to avoid encroaching into his partners arc of fire, moved to Teddy's right side, allowing his weapon to drop on its sling. Without any warning he smashed an armoured boot into the side of Teddy's knee, buckling him in a seamless movement.

"On the ground, on the ground. Do it now, do it slowly!" Ninja One continued to yell despite having his H&K eighteen inches from Teddy's forehead. Ninja Two grabbed the back of Teddy's collar as he continued to fall and dragged him forward so he was instantly and involuntarily face down on the steel floor. Teddy writhed like giant fish but was no match for the ninjas who trussed him with large, black cable ties in seconds.

Linton broke the radio silence. "The target is contained, Op Comm."

March blew out her cheeks as her car heaved a collective, elated sigh even though they could clearly hear the sound of Teddy screaming vicious obscenities at the world over Ed Linton's open radio.

"Op Comm received. Good job Ed, great job."

"Wait for confirmation he's cuffed and in custody," Linton said in a more relaxed and steady voice.

March got on the phone to Keith Raye in Nottingham to give him the good news as Teddy went from his knees to a fully prostrate position on the cold steel floor. With the ninjas still bearing down on him, Linton called in two of his team to make the formal arrest, handcuff him, then search him. Operation Spear had their man.

Fortunately, the full resources of the P&O collective were able to manoeuvre sufficient vehicles around to extract Teddy's Citroen and Team Three's unmarked without too much hassle. Teddy was placed in the back of the Team Three car, squashed in between the two biggest officers March had while the shifting took place, therefore eliminating the need to walk him anywhere. During the whole process, he did not let up with his tirade of threat-filled bile towards the police, often spitting at the officers. In the end they obtained a balaclava from one of the local police motorcyclists and put it over Teddy's head.

At a little before 11:00 p.m. March's convoy departed Dover Port and started their long journey back to Nottingham, noisily escorted by a marked police car and two motorcyclists. Teddy kept up the abuse for as long as he could until the heat generated under the balaclava reduced him to a more manageable level of obnoxiousness. Nevertheless, it was four very uncomfortable hours for his car's occupants, who spent the whole journey on high alert for the next verbal volley, sudden attempted headbutt or kick.

Dr. Morgan was examining a chart at Allen's bedside when Dan and Gwen returned. "Hello, that was good timing. How are you, Mrs. Allen?"

"Good thanks. What good timing is that?"

"I have just finished looking over James and I'm pleased to say he seems to be responding very well so far. All his vitals have improved, and his heart is functioning especially well now there's less strain caused by his other organs. We may take him off the respirator tomorrow morning if there's no relapse."

Dan put his arm around Gwen's shoulder. "Thanks, doctor."

"Well it is still early days, but we may find that he also starts responding to stimulation too. He won't be running up and down the corridor for weeks, if not months, yet, or even hold a conversation for more than a few seconds but any sign of his cognitive state returning will be very well received."

Gwen was unable to contain her happiness. She hugged Dan and then the doctor. "I knew it, he's going to be okay, Dan."

"Please don't misunderstand me," Morgan said. "Your husband is gravely ill and we still regard him as being in a critical condition. What I'm saying is hopefully he has taken a small step towards a recovery, his first small step."

Gwen was not going to be dissuaded. "Then that's a beginning."

Morgan finished his notation on Allen's charts and bade them good evening.

"What great news," Dan said echoing Gwen's thoughts. "You might get your wish sooner rather than later when he opens his eyes and answers you back."

She beamed. "And what will you do if he wakes up while you're in the middle of reading to him?"

Dan feigned pleasure at the idea but his heart skipped a beat. Up to that point the prospect had not been real.

Although the use of mobile phones was prohibited in the ICU, Dan's was on silent mode in his pocket. When it buzzed against his leg he went out into the corridor to read the incoming message. When he returned, his grin was as wide as Gwen's before.

"Can you handle some more good news? That was a text from Nick; Teddy Parker has been arrested down in Kent as he was trying to get on a cross-Channel ferry. Apparently the police are bringing him back to Nottingham now."

"Did you hear that, Jim," she said, leaning close to Allen's bandaged right ear. "Now you have even more reason to get better, so we can have our day in court with the little beast."

CHAPTER TWENTY-SEVEN

The next morning the sun reluctantly dragged itself up over Nottingham but by 10:00 a.m. the city still appeared dark.

It was darker still in Teddy Parker's cell where he was placed after March's team returned to their base in the middle of the night. When he was booked into custody he loudly demanded to speak to a solicitor and Detective Inspector Ben Binder. The Duty Solicitor called back from home a few minutes later and only half listened to what Teddy said, as calls at that time of night hardly ever required attendance there and then. That only made Teddy angrier.

"Get your fuckin' arse down here now," he bawled.

"There's no point Mr. Parker. The police have to let you rest, so it may be lunchtime before they want to talk to you. Try and get some sleep. I or someone else will come and see you in the morning." He quickly ended the call before Teddy could unload another foul mouthful.

Teddy's rage was incandescent, he stared at the receiver and then at the Custody Sergeant, Dave Bell, who simply held out his hand for the phone.

Teddy was no more successful a minute later in getting Ben Binder. Bell smiled. "You've made your lawyer's call. I'm not waking up DI Binder at four in the morning, so you can forget about that. I'll pass on a message to him that you have requested to speak to him. He will contact you if and when he wants to."

"He'll want to see me," Teddy spewed.

"Forget it." Bell turned to his jailers. "Put this noisy runt in cell one. No interviews before ten thirty."

The jailers manhandled the squealing Teddy out of the charge room and along the corridor to cell one at the far end. It didn't take Teddy long to realise he was not going to get to speak to Ben Binder or anyone else in a hurry. After a few minutes bleating at the top of his voice and being told to shut up in no uncertain terms by the occupant of the cell next door he laid down on his plastic covered foam mat. Ben Binder was his only hope now.

Binder arrived for work fifteen minutes early as he did every day. Dave Bell's internal email was the second he read. He knew this day would come ever since Teddy went too far with Josephine Lamas, and he mitigated the discomfort of the situation as best he could. He decided to let Teddy wait. He was in no rush and Teddy wasn't going anywhere. Instead he called the city hospital to get the latest on Allen's condition.

Allen, he was informed, managed another comfortable night all things considered, which gave him mixed feelings.

As usual Gwen arrived at the ICU shortly after breakfast. She adjusted the already immaculate bed then rearranged the fruit in the basket on the bedside table. She then got straight down to the business of telling her husband about his favourite two programmes he missed the previous day. In this most impossible scenario she wanted to keep whatever normality there was in their lives going for as long as she could.

"Carla and Archie got lost in the mountains on their honeymoon. Why on earth they decided on the Canadian Rockies is beyond me. Anyway, by the time the rescuers found them they already had more domestics than us in thirty years.

"Oh, you would have loved the garden show. It was all about old roses making a comeback. There were some called 'Duke of Wellington' and others called 'Captain Haywood', which I thought you would like especially."

As she continued Gwen was aware of a nurse entering the room but took no notice. When a second appeared and asked her to move, she obediently complied and only then properly heard the higher pitched beeping coming from one of the machines attached to her husband by a thin blue wire.

"What is it, what's the matter?" she asked as panic started to rise and spread through her.

When neither nurse replied, her concern deepened. "Please, what is it?"

A third nurse gently took her by the arm and led her outside. "Give us a couple of minutes and I'll come back. Why don't you go down to the family room?"

The nurse left her standing by the glass screen and hurried back to join her colleagues. Within another minute Doctor Morgan also appeared and hustled by her without his usual greeting. Gwen started to shake.

She could not tell how long it took for Doctor Morgan to finish doing whatever it was he was doing, but when he did come out he looked a lot better than she was feeling.

"Are you alright, Mrs. Allen?"

"No of course not! What's going on?"

"Can you tell me what you were doing just before the nurses and I came in?"

"Nothing! I didn't touch him I promise," Gwen replied, feeling suddenly guilty too.

The doctor moved to allay her obvious confusion. "No, I mean were you talking to him or something like that?"

Gwen was still none the wiser. "I was telling him about the roses on the garden show on TV yesterday. It's his favourite."

"Right ho, that might explain it. As you were doing that James set off three alarms monitoring his heart, pulse and brain. I think what happened was he must have heard what you said and reacted. He might not be able to talk to you about your roses, but this is the next best thing."

Gwen's own pulse also quickened at the news.

"If I were you I would keep talking to him like that for as long as you can. I'm going to have the staff replace his oxygen mask with a nasal tube, that way if he does try to speak, he will be able."

"I must call and tell Dan," she said without thinking. Much later she would reflect on the strength of the bond developing between the three of them.

At 10:30 a.m. Teddy was woken and given a breakfast nearly as bad as the one in Dover the day before. The acid he'd taken then was well out of his system now and he hadn't had a drink for eighteen hours either; for him this was the nearest to being alcohol and drug free for six years and it did not agree with him one little bit.

At 10:45 a.m. his cell door opened and March looked in. Teddy Parker's smell, added to that of the Custody Centre's usual overpowering combination of floral room spray and disinfectant was a pungent cocktail. Teddy looked up from his mat and took note. "Bet you wish you'd skipped breakfast." He laughed hoarsely.

"Good morning, come with me please."

Teddy shuffled to the door, glad to be out of the cell and blinked into the brightly lit corridor.

"Put your shoes on. It's time for us to talk," March said.

His shoes were on a low shelf outside the cell door; he kicked his feet into them without untying the laces and followed March down to the Charge Room.

The day time Custody Sergeant, Mick Martin was as long in the tooth as Dave Bell; he knew all he needed to know about Teddy from his computerised custody record and the wildfire conversation that had flown around the station and the force when the news broke that James Allen's attacker was locked up.

He looked down from the elevated desk as they entered the room and took a quick glance at his watch.

Teddy stopped in front of the big desk next to March and prepared to list his first set of demands but even as he opened his mouth March and Martin ignored him completely, entering into a conversation of their own.

"Morning, Mick. Long day and night yesterday but no rest for the wicked. I'm ready to interview stinky here when you are."

"You look as lovely as ever to me, Katie. He hasn't spoken to a brief yet this morning and apparently he wanted to talk to Ben Binder last night when he arrived."

Shocked he was being overlooked Teddy tried to command some attention. "Fucking right! And I still do."

Martin and March looked at him like an alien and then carried on as if he was not there.

"I heard that. I'm sure Ben will have got the message and will come down if he wants. I'm going to need an interview room with cameras as well as recorders please, but not number six; it's right next to the generator and I have to scream to be heard half the time."

Martin laughed. "No problem. I'll set number four aside for you all day today and tomorrow."

"Thanks Mick, you are an angel."

Teddy's frustration meter was in the red: he banged his fists down on the desk like a petulant child. Martin's reactions were lightning fast, and he lunged forward, pinning Teddy's hands to the Formica surface. He glowered at Teddy and whispered so as not to be heard on the CCTV capturing every aspect of the Charge Room 24/7.

"You are in my house now and it's my rules here, you scummy little bastard. You will behave yourself, especially in front of this lady. Do you understand me?"

Teddy struggled to move his arms but could not. "All fucking right," he conceded.

"By the way I heard you wet yourself when you got arrested. Is that right?" Martin added, releasing his grip.

March could not contain a laugh completely but did well to stifle it as well as she did.

Teddy whipped his hands back off the desk, temper ignited, but Martin's stare changed his mind. "I want a lawyer and Ben Binder," he said quietly but venomously.

"Katie, what would you like to do first?" Martin said ignoring Teddy once more.

"Best he has his brief first, I can't talk to him until then."

"Alright. Leave Mr. Personality with me and I'll call your office when we're ready."

As March left, Martin nodded to his duty jailer. "Thanks, Tom."

Tom led Teddy into a holding room with a large glass partition where he could be monitored by the Custody Centre staff.

"Wait here. Do you want the Duty Solicitor or one of your own?"

Teddy had not needed representation for such a long time; he did not know any names.

"Duty," he replied. "But I still need to talk to DI Binder as well."

"Just wait. I'll let you know."

Teddy dropped down onto the metal bench seat. If his situation was not bad enough already, the Sergeant had just humiliated him in front of a woman.

And where the fuck is Ben, he thought.

As if by magic Ben Binder walked into the Charge Room at that very second, a moment after passing March in the corridor.

"Good morning Katie, I understand your boy wants to see me. Any idea what that's all about?"

"Morning Ben," March replied, wondering how it was Binder always seemed to look like he was just heading for photo shoot. "I was hoping you could tell me."

"Sorry, no can do. I've met his father a couple of times but that's it. Perhaps he thinks he's special because of that. Is there anything you want me to say to him?"

"No, as murders go this is one of the less difficult ones to prove, but I'll be interested to hear what he wants to talk to you about."

"I'll come and tell as soon as I've finished with killer."

"So, Teddy, I got your message," Binder said, entering the holding room. He was happy to talk there. It was soundproof to allow those in custody the ability to speak to their legal representatives unhindered but still be visually monitored for safety reasons.

"Ben, it's good to see you. I really need your help."

Binder watched the Charge Room staff in the window's reflection.

"I thought you would have gotten the message the other day. When you killed the old prostitute, you went way past the point of me risking my neck for you, but you weren't happy to leave it there. You then went and almost killed the head of Nottinghamshire CID."

"But Ben, you have to."

Binder remained calm. "I do not have to do a single thing for you. Not now, not anymore." He watched Teddy's growing agitation with no interest.

Teddy stood up, so he was above Binder causing a jailer to move, but Binder indicated to him it was all under control.

"Go on, I dare you," he whispered at Teddy. "Make me even more of a hero."

Teddy sat back down again. "If I go down, you will as well. Remember what you've been doing for the past year or more," he said with little sign of confidence.

Binder was more than ready. He'd expected that Teddy's last hoorah would be to threaten him. "Oh, yes and what exactly have you got? Phone calls to an untraceable mobile, a few meetings with no witnesses, cash only transactions. Think about it Teddy, you have nothing. Anything you say will be taken as desperate mud slinging.

"They have got you bang to rights for Josie Lamas' murder and James Allen's attempted murder, hell, this time tomorrow he could be dead too. Even Marley Johns has given you up. Flick and all the others will be next. Face it Teddy, you are fucked. Thank you and goodnight."

"Please Ben, we're partners." Teddy's tone was now that of a beaten boxer. "I've got more money stashed away, loads more. I'll do anything."

Binder smiled, he was done with Teddy.

"Do anything? In that case, do yourself a favour, get your father to find the best lawyer in the country, plead guilty and don't ever ask for me again." He got up and strode to the door. With his hand on the handle, he turned back and looked Teddy straight in the eye. "I mean it. Not ever."

"What did he want?" Mick Martin asked as Binder completed his entry on Teddy's custody record to say he spoke to him.

"I know his father. They don't get on too well these days and he wanted me to ask his dad if he could get the best lawyer he knew. I told him there was no better time to build a bridge and he was going to need all the family support he could get."

"He's going to need divine intervention let alone a bloody good lawyer," Martin joked.

"Yes, he wasn't impressed. He made some stupid threats saying he would try and ruin me if I didn't help him out."

"Charming. I wouldn't worry about anything he has to say."

"Oh, don't worry about that Mick. I couldn't care less what Teddy Parker has got to say."

As if to add extra credence to Binder's comments, when Teddy was brought back into the Charge Room he asked rather meekly, "Can I call my Dad please?"

Dan was pleased to hear the latest news from Gwen when she called. He arranged to go in later in the day.

"That was Gwen Allen," he said to the massed ranks of the Hetherington clan as they were about to set off on a week's holiday at Nick's parents' timeshare in Spain. "He reacted to her this morning. Gave her a fright initially but the fact he is responding to stimulation is the best sign yet."

"That is good news," Penny said. "I hope this means he can recover. For all he did to Amber at first at least he tried to make amends, and paid a high price for it."

Nick was not so forgiving. Over the past month, Allen had played a major part in transforming the job he loved into something he wasn't excited about any more. His holiday was an indictment. It could have been a working day if he wanted it to be, but he was determined to make the most of the Personnel Department's offer for him to take all the time he needed before going back to work.

"Well, you know where everything is, I've checked Pen's car is all good too. Have you got any plans other than going to see him?" he said to Dan.

"No, it's not often I haven't got much to do."

"Alright, well try and stay out of trouble. We'll see you in a week."

It was the day of Josie Lamas' funeral. It turned out Dan was here for it after all, so there was no need for Amber to go. He remained uncharacteristically vague when she asked if he would be going. The truth was, Josie did have family, on her mother's side. They appeared soon after her death and took on the appropriate duties. He never knew about them before and thought it best to leave them to their grieving as the prospect of explaining who he was might cause more unnecessary heartache for all concerned. She was gone, and she knew in life how much he cared for her. In all honesty, he wanted to be among the living as well. Josie would understand. He sent flowers, and reading to Allen on this day was a fitting tribute to her.

"Morning Gwen, you're looking better, too," Dan said as she came into Allen's room.

"Jim's better so therefore I am as well," Gwen explained happily. "I'm going to see if they will let me bring in a little player, so I can show him some of his favourite DVDs. How is your book going?"

Dan grinned. "Well, judging by the lack of response I get I'm thinking he doesn't rate my authoring skills very highly. But while I've got him as a captive audience I'm going to make him tell me to stop if he doesn't like it."

"Is it working for you? Reading your book to him, I mean."

"Hard to say. Apart from Tara he's the one person I feel I owe it to, so I suppose that should be a good thing for me."

"Yes, well let me get out of your way so you can. I've got a lot to do, there's not a scrap of food in the house and it hasn't been cleaned for a week." She caught herself and they both thought back to the bloody scene she had to clear up a few days before. "Well, you know what I mean."

When they were alone again Dan took a few minutes to settle ready for another instalment; he was already up to chapter twelve.

Henry Talbot-Kerr's suit cost more than Mick Martin's monthly wage and his briefcase was made from the hide of something on the endangered species list. Even for Martin, who was normally unflappable in any company, Talbot-Kerr exuded an impressive aura.

"Sergeant, good morning," he said, handing over a white card with gold and black writing. "I'm here to see my client Edward Parker. I would also like to see any advanced disclosure the senior investigating officers have and to speak to one of those officers. It matters not in which order."

The advance disclosure document package of information and evidence which all defendants and their representatives were entitled to was in a white envelope March delivered when she came down to the cells earlier. Martin handed it over to Mr. Talbot-Kerr while noting the card included Queen's Counsel in Talbot-Kerr's title. To his knowledge, it was the first time in his career a QC had appeared to see a person in custody at the police station at such an early stage in the process.

"Mr. Kerr, straight to the point I see."

"Talbot-Kerr."

"Excuse me, Mr. Talbot-Kerr, Parker is in his cell. Would you like to see him there or in an interview room?".

Talbot-Kerr sniffed. "We shan't be long but not the cell, I think."

He was shown to a sparsely decorated and furnished interview room where he draped his mohair coat across the back of a chair and waited for Teddy to be brought to him. He scanned the disclosure while waiting. When Teddy walked in a few minutes later he sniffed again, but at the tramp-like aroma which entered with him.

"Mr. Parker, please sit. I am Henry Talbot-Kerr," he said handing out the second business card of the day. "I don't have long so I will be brief and you will listen. Do we understand each other?"

Teddy went to answer but nodded instead, indicating he understood perfectly the way things were going to go.

"Jolly good, Mr. Parker. You will undoubtedly be interviewed later on today and when you are you will answer the introductory questions about your name, address, date of birth, etcetera, but thereafter will respond by saying 'no comment at this time' to each and every question. Okay so far?"

"Yes."

"I have an associate who will be attending in my place and he will sit with you during the interview process, but he will not speak to you or the officers about the matters for which you are here. When the interviews are finished, he will make an application for bail, which will be refused. You will probably remain here until you are charged and then you will go directly to the Magistrates Court where my associate will again ask for bail, which will again be refused, and you will be remanded to prison until your next appearance. This could all take up to three days."

"If you're supposed to be the best, get me out of here."

"Mr. Parker, I am the best but let me make this very plain to you. You are going to spend most, if not all, of the rest of your life in prison. Even at this very early stage I can tell you that the facts are as plain as the nose on your face. Witness testimony, forensic evidence, motive, opportunity, and your previous history." He waved the disclosure pages. "We will discuss your plea options another time but between now and then all you have to do is say nothing. My associate is called Adam Smith. He will see you soon but now I must go."

Talbot-Kerr rose and swooped his coat off the chair leaving Teddy without another sideways glance.

After a minute alone Teddy started to cry.

He did not have a clue how much time passed before the door was unlocked from the outside and Katie March stuck her head in.

"Your brief is here, let's go."

"This interview is being recorded. I am Detective Inspector Katherine March. I am interviewing Edward Francis Parker. The time is two eleven p.m. on Sunday October 28, 2017. This interview is being conducted in interview room four of Nottingham South Central Police Station."

March continued with the necessary formalities of introducing Ed Linton and Mr. Smith before turning to Teddy for the first time. As she did Linton and Mr. Smith scribbled in notebooks.

"Edward, will you tell me your full name and date of birth please?"

"Edward Francis Parker, first of February 1991."

"What is your current address?"

"8B Canal Apartments, Nottingham."

"Thank you. People call you Teddy, what would you like us to call you today?"

Teddy shrugged.

"Okay, Teddy," March continued, giving him the impression she was going to call him whatever she liked regardless.

"I must remind you that you are still under caution and that means you do not have to say anything, but it may harm your defence if you do not mention when questioned something which you later rely on in court. Anything you do say may be given in evidence. Do you understand?"

"Yeah."

"Very well, you have been arrested on suspicion of committing murder, also on suspicion of attempting to commit murder and conspiracy to commit burglary. I wish to talk to you about all these matters, but for now I want to talk to you only about the murder of Josephine Lamas. Do you understand?"

Linton continued to scribble; Mr. Smith paused and looked blankly at Teddy, triggering the pre-arranged reply.

"Fuck you. No comment."

So, this is how it's going to go, March thought. "I have many questions for you and this is your opportunity to tell me what you know. Now, Josephine Lamas, do you know her?"

Mr. Smith took advantage of the split second of quiet to loudly clear his throat while maintaining his vacant look at Teddy.

Teddy took another moment to refocus. "No comment at this time."

Over the next ten minutes March asked a dozen more questions and got the same reply. It was not wholly surprising, but it was disappointing. She looked forward to the day when a jury could take an inference from a suspect's continued silence during interview. Ed Linton had had enough by that time too. He drew an asterisk in his book and showed the page to March. In light of the circumstances she agreed it would be best to wind things up but wanted to put a few direct accusations to Teddy just in case they might elicit something different or useful.

"Well it's clear you understand you have a right not to comment, but can I ask you if you are saying no comment because you wish to, or because you do not understand the questions?"

She happily noted Teddy's reaction to her backhanded slur on his intelligence.

"No comment at this time," he said very deliberately.

"Then Teddy, I put it to you that we have overwhelming evidence to say you deliberately and maliciously killed Josephine Lamas. What have you got to say about that?"

"No comment at this time."

"Evidence that you were in Ms. Lamas' house and beat her to death with your bare hands."

"No comment at this time."

"Evidence you cannot explain away, mitigate for or refute. You murdered Josie Lamas didn't you, Teddy?"

"No comment at this time!" Teddy roared at the top of his voice, sending spittle across the table.

Lovely, that will look great on the video, March thought.

"I see no point in continuing this interview. It is now two thirty-three p.m. and I am turning the recording device off."

Linton took Teddy back to his cell while March and Smith went into the Charge Room.

"Thanks for nothing," she said.

"My client has a perfect right not to comment," Smith replied. "Shall we get on with the formalities?"

"You know we have to interview him again?"

"And I'll look forward to seeing you then as well. I imagine you are considering three days' local custody and charges at the end, if not before? You have my contact details and I will be available at any time with thirty minutes' notice."

When Smith was gone Mick and Martin offered March a look of solidarity.

"Fuck them Katie. At the end of the day you go home to a warm bed," Mick said.

"I know. It just pisses me off. The law is a bit too fair sometimes."

CHAPTER TWENTY-EIGHT

Prior to reaching this moment Dan wondered how he would feel or whether he could do it at all, but the moment turned out to be something of an anticlimax. His audience remained silent and willing.

"Chapter Fourteen," he said without concern. "The opportunity to get away and do something different was always one of the best aspects of the job. I would often say if you were bored then you must be doing something wrong.

"I had been doing undercover work with Special Branch, other forces and my own force for six or seven years when I was tasked with running as the UC operative in a major test purchase operation to identify drug dealers in Mapperley. I'd done test purchase jobs a hundred times before and I was comfortable in the role.

"This one was slightly different in that it was set up to last between six and eight weeks during which I would remain in character for the whole time and only have limited contact with my handler. As I said, I'd been there and done that so many times before. I was reliable and the less contact with the real world the better.

"I sat in a load of disgusting houses and flats in the first two weeks building up trusts and relationships with the lower end of the food chain before the chance to get to some of the major players. In that time, I bought a shop full of cannabis and some harder stuff too with my marked bank notes and reported back. On days I did not see the handler, I made a log entry of what I'd done for evidential purposes and dropped it in a dead letter box for collection. A dead letter box is a prearranged secure point for items to be left and collected; ours was a metal fence post outside a disused petrol station with a false fascia plate we could remove to conceal and retrieve log books and messages.

"As things got more exciting and I got closer to the people we were most interested in, the contact with the handler lessened but that was fine; I felt I was in control, my constant risk analysis was always acceptable."

Dan took the glass of water from the table and downed a long sip. Allen remained quiet and still.

"One day I was taken by a new friend to an address I had not visited before, 22 Powton Road. At first I thought it was just another horrible hole but I soon realised this was the Mecca I'd been searching for. Inside it was dark and dirty but there seemed to be a lot more activity here than any other house I'd been taken to up to then…"

BEEP BEEP BEEP. Dan stopped and looked to the machine on his right and then to Allen's face. He noticed a change.

"Nurse!"

When he last looked at Allen, it could only have been ten seconds ago, Allen's eyes, nose, and lips were all that was visible on his bandaged face, but ten seconds ago, his lips were only fractionally apart. Now they were parted a full centimetre.

"Nurse!"

Dan got up, dropping the pages on the floor. "Jim, it's me Dan," he whispered, leaning forward so he could feel gauze strands on his cheek. "Jim?"

He listened as hard as he could, tuning out the ambient noises in the room. It was so quiet Dan almost believed it was a thought he was having but when he heard it again he knew.

"Sorry, son. I didn't realise."

"Jim, Jim."

He was suddenly pulled back as two nurses took control. He did not know what to do. He considered trying to talk to Allen again, or running to find Gwen, but he was overcome with a stronger emotion that needed satisfying first.

"Sorry son, I didn't realise. Sorry son, I didn't realise," he repeated over and over.

The doctor told Gwen Allen had reacted to what she was saying or doing at the time. He snatched up the manuscript and went to the last paragraph he read before the beeping started. He read it over again to himself.

One day I was taken by a new friend to an address I had not visited before, 22 Powton Road. At first I thought it was just another horrible hole but I soon realised this was the Mecca I'd been searching for. Inside it was dark and dirty but there seemed to be a lot more activity here than any other house I'd been taken to up to that point in the operation…

He stored the information and raced out to the payphone to call Gwen.

When he came back the sight that greeted him almost made him cry: Allen's eyes were open.

Gwen came in before the doctors and nurses finished checking, testing, talking to and writing up the latest on Allen. It was torture for her and Dan to be forced to wait in the corridor but worth it a hundred times over when they were allowed into the room again.

When Allen saw his wife for the first time in days he managed the weakest of smiles. When he saw Dan there too, a tiny tear nobody noticed seeped from his bruised eye and disappeared at once into the bandages.

"Oh, Jim," Gwen gasped, holding his hand between hers.

Dan stood by the door. For once he could not find any appropriate words for how he was feeling but he could not remember when he last felt such joy.

A doctor he didn't recognise stopped as he left the room.

"He is quite a character."

Dan was nonplussed until he saw Allen's mouth was moving very slightly in between Gwen's overtures and realised they were having a conversation. When she turned and he could see her, Gwen's face was flushed.

"Come over here, Dan."

He placed his head close to hers so Allen might see them both in his restricted field of vision.

"It's good to see you again. You gave us a real fright there," Dan said.

Allen smiled again although his face clearly ached with the effort. His fingers managed a slight movement in between Gwen's palms and she gently placed Dan's hand in between them so they could both feel. They leaned in even closer and could just make out his words.

"You saved me."

Dan's eyes filled for a second time in as many minutes.

"No Jim, you saved Gwen and yourself. It's so good to have you back with us again."

"Dan has been here every day, Jim," Gwen told her husband. "He's been reading his book to you."

"I heard love, it woke me up."

"He's got to finish it before he can go home so you better make plans to be awake a bit more over the coming days."

They felt his fingers move in a faint squeezing motion and then he closed his eyes again. When it was clear he was sleeping once more they withdrew so as not to disturb him, but in the family room they hugged and cavorted like lottery winners until Dr. Morgan found them there. For the first time, he spoke with some confidence, still tempered with words of caution but enough to give them genuine hope Jim's future was among the living.

"Whatever it is you two are doing, just keep doing it. Medical science is a wonderful thing but there are some people who seem to gain strength from other forces I certainly cannot explain. Clearly, he's heard you. It would be much better for him to be awake a lot more than he has been, so I suggest you spend as much time as you can with him to continue the stimulation."

Gwen looked at Dan. "Can you stay, just a little longer?"

"Yes, you'll have to drag me away now."

CHAPTER TWENTY-NINE

The next few days became a procession of opposites.

Teddy found it increasingly more difficult to hold his tongue when he was interviewed by police; the evidence seemed insurmountable even to him. Forensic evidence at Josie's house matched that on his clothes, his home and crucially DNA testing found traces of his skin under her fingernails and between her teeth. She had died as she lived, fighting to the last for her friends and her self respect.

During each interview, Adam Smith sat alongside Teddy being of as much use and support as roller skates on a fish. It might be Henry Talbot-Kerr's idea of a strategy but to Teddy, who was used to dominating everybody, it was like waving a white flag.

When he was asked about the burglaries his "no comment at this time answers" tasted more like capitulating "yeah whatever's". The police now had phone records linking him to Flick's mobile just minutes before a series of offences and at least two other members of the gang rolled over hoping to cut a deal and minimise their prison time.

The final straw came when March handed him a statement to read made by Flick himself an hour before. Teddy didn't bother reading past the first few lines; Flick screwed him over too. He leapt up and struck out at whatever was within range shouting and cursing. Fortunately for the police and the recording equipment, the king hit Teddy delivered to Smith's nose was captured perfectly. It took a short time to restrain him with the assistance of uniformed jailers summoned by the emergency assist alarm, and when he was led back to his cell Teddy was still raging.

"Et tu, Brute?"

Across town in another secure room filled with altogether different monitoring and recording devices, Dan and Gwen continued to give Allen little respite. They took the doctors advice literally and spent hour after hour talking to him and getting reward for their efforts.

As time passed Jim showed more signs of regaining mental strength and soon he was awake for several hours a day and communicating exponentially better.

He asked Dan to go back to the beginning of his book and start again but this time as he read, they shared moments of conversation and also silence as Dan laid bare his soul to the man whose name he cursed several times in the pages. For the first time he could remember, Dan felt he was sharing a problem and it was halved, not doubled as a result. The torture he endured writing it in the first place was more than offset now by he and Jim experiencing it together.

When he got to Chapter Fourteen on the Wednesday afternoon Jim was strangely quiet and did not make one comment or interjection through its entirety. As he finished Dan blew out his cheeks. "Remember you asked me what the worst decision I ever made was? Sorry I didn't have the guts to tell you then."

It was bizarrely normal now to accept Jim's bandaged head as his everyday appearance. His speech was vastly improved and there was only a slight slur remaining, but it did not hinder Dan's understanding of him.

"Christ almighty. I can't say I remember too much of it at the moment, but I definitely remember the address and having some dealings with it. Maybe I just read the reports once."

"I was in a real mess, it doesn't excuse my actions now, but I've been paying for it ever since," Dan said.

"I don't know what to say, son. We all make mistakes, and some are bigger than others, but you have to be the potential prize winner." He managed a quick laugh before it became another painful cough. "All this time you've kept it a secret?" He spluttered.

"It's easier to live with a secret or a lie sometimes. Box it off and try to exist around it."

"Well I can't argue there, look what happened to me when I confronted mine."

"Sure, but how do you feel inside knowing you tried to put it all right and Parker is locked up now?"

"Better I suppose. Better that me and Gwen can retire with me having a clearer conscience. It will never be completely clear though. Ben bloody Binder is still out there and he's way more despicable than Teddy."

Dan answered without thinking. "The really bad ones are often good enough they never get caught. I learned that lesson a long time ago."

"I refuse to believe that. One of these days he will get his just deserts."

"We'll see."

Jim more happily changed the subject. "We might not be able to do anything about him right now, but we might be able to do something about you. If they let me out of here in the next hundred years what say you and I take another look at Powton Road?"

Dan shrugged. "That must be the drugs talking. I think I'm beyond hope or salvation so far as Zoe Summers is concerned."

"No seriously, don't say no now. Think about it. Think what I could do for you."

He looked like he might cough again and Dan waited. When nothing happened they exchanged a glance in which Dan demonstrated his concern and Jim tried to placate him.

"I know you're not talking from the point of view that we can fix what happened, but I've been over it a million times and the one question I cannot answer is what would I do if I found out I did kill her. What happens then, Jim?"

Before they could talk more Gwen arrived with more bananas, grapes and another load of gardening DVDs to watch and discuss.

Henry Talbot-Kerr was educating Adam Smith in the ways of dealing with scumbag clients. "Think of it as an important part of your learning. Most of them will be vermin."

Smith was not happy being told he must go back to sit with Teddy for all his interviews.

"But sir, my nose."

"Do you think with your nose? Do you speak with it? No, so there is no reason you cannot continue acting for Mr. Parker." He made the Mr. sound like a profanity.

"I really think it would not be appropriate."

"If I were you I would think about the one hundred and forty an hour instead. You will find it has significant painkilling qualities. When do they say they intend to speak to him next?"

"After dinner, that is, their dinner time, so around six p.m."

"Very good. Be there, Smith."

"Yes sir."

"The police will have no choice but to charge him by the end of tomorrow, then he can sit on remand until his trial. Just think, one more day then you can have up to six months free before you'll have to see him in court again."

Gwen spent the afternoon talking to her husband as they both watched recordings on her handbag-sized laptop. Jim had been awake since breakfast and although he was with her in body his mind seemed elsewhere.

"Are you alright sweetheart?" she said during a break between programmes. "You're so much better already but you're away with the fairies this afternoon."

"Yes love, did I ever tell you how much I like you calling me that?"

"Don't you start that answering-my-question-with-one-of-your-own trick on me. We have been together far too long for that to work."

"Gwenny love, you get me every time."

"Yes, and you being in a hospital bed doesn't let you off. You've been funny since Dan went, are you really okay?"

"He has had it so hard. I had no idea what he's been through in his life. We both badly misjudged each other."

"You both look like you have affected each other."

"I think we have, love. You know I said that I won't go back and will take early retirement if they don't offer me a deal to finish early rather than go on sick leave?"

"Yes, so?"

"If I do, I need a few things first. The other night when Teddy Parker came to the house, did he break my work computer do you know?"

"I don't know. When Carole and I were tidying I just put it in your study."

"Can you get it next time you go home and bring it in?"

"What are you scheming, Jim?"

"Ask me no questions and I will tell you no lies, love."

Teddy's final interview commenced at 6:10 p.m. March wanted to give him one last chance to speak before she was ready to charge him. She brought all the paperwork with her so that once the interview was over they could go straight to the Charge Room and he could be processed.

Adam Smith sat to Teddy's right in a state of high alert. Teddy himself perched on the front of his chair with his elbows on the table and his eyes on March's shirt somewhere south of her collar. As she spoke he tried to imagine her naked and with much longer hair.

With the introductions over March began with a searching question, expecting Teddy's usual reply.

"Did you go to James Allen's house intending to do him harm?"

After the standard momentary pause, she got what she expected.

"No comment at this time."

"Did you go intending to kill him?"

"No comment at this time."

"It looks like he is going to make a good recovery, what do you think about that?"

Smith sniffed uncomfortably.

Whether Teddy was put off by the noise or just finally had enough, he answered without thinking. "Bad news travels fast. I can't remember who said that."

March and Smith were equally shocked by the response but fortunately for her March reacted quicker.

"What do you mean by that?"

Having gone off script once, Teddy could not contain himself. He let days of frustration out in one go.

"Because I wanted that piece of shit dead. I left him for dead, but he couldn't even do that right," he roared.

Smith was almost catatonic. "A moment with my client," he pleaded hopelessly.

"Do you want to stop the interview to talk to Mr. Smith, Teddy?" March pressed.

"Fuck all of you. Charge me now, I've had enough of this."

"I want to ask you more questions Teddy, about Mr. Allen, about Josie Lamas and about the burglaries."

"No comment bitch, just charge me or get across this table and suck my dick."

March tried for two more questions but in reality, she was as happy as Teddy to finish it there and then.

At 6:45 p.m. March read the first of a long list of charges. At 7:00 p.m. Teddy was back in his cell.

CHAPTER THIRTY

The next morning Dan went in to the hospital and was amazed to see Allen sat up in bed, albeit supported on all sides by pillows.

"The doctors reckon he's trying to break some sort of record," Gwen said, walking in right behind him with yet more fruit.

"Morning, Dan. How are you?" Jim said in a gruff voice.

"I'm good but not half as good as you by the look of things. When did you decide to become mobile?"

"Don't be fooled son, it took me an hour to get here from lying down and I was exhausted by the end of it."

"I can't believe just a few days ago you were at death's door. Sorry, I didn't mean to be crude."

Gwen answered. "No, you're right. I think it's amazing what you can do if you have a reason, and I also think it was you who gave him that reason more than anyone else."

Dan went to object but Jim stopped him. "I've got something to show you. Can you pass it over, love?"

Gwen pulled out a black laptop from a bag on the floor and handed it to Dan.

"You better do it," Jim said. "Turn it on and I'll give you the passwords."

Dan was bemused but followed the instructions Allen gave him until he was looking at a page headed "CID Archive."

"Type in 'murder' in the search box. Right, now, search for Zoe Summers in the same box."

Dan felt his heart quicken and his palms became sticky. "I'm not so sure this is a good idea."

"Trust me Dan, have you got it yet?"

Dan nodded. He was looking at another header page listing contents relating to Zoe's unsolved death. It looked like there were hundreds of documents in all.

"What is this?"

Gwen found a reason to leave them alone again and disappeared.

"She's a wonderful woman Dan, I don't know what I would do without her. That there is the whole shooting match. Every inquiry, every statement, every memo ever written. A couple of years ago we followed the lead of some other regions and computerised many cold cases so they could be looked at again at any time."

"But why are you telling me now?"

"If you're going to investigate it, you're going to need it all."

"What! I mean what, are you crazy? You can't let me have this and I sure as hell can't go off and investigate it."

"Can't or won't. I don't think you have a choice, not anymore, son."

Dan felt the laptop trembling in his hands. "You must have got a knock on the head the doctors haven't found yet. I can't."

"Just listen to me for a minute. You have to for a number of reasons. One, you are probably the only person I know who can find out what happened because you are the best detective I've ever met. Two, you have the advantage of knowing there was a witness the police didn't know about before, namely you. And three, you have a vested interest in discovering the truth. The other thing is you won't be on your own, not anymore."

Dan's head was swimming. He looked at Jim with utter disbelief and confusion.

"I want to help," Jim went on. "It gives me another reason to get well. I want to be your partner and help you to finally get this monkey off your back and whatever the outcome, we'll face it together."

"But Jim."

"No buts, son. There should be some flash drives in the bag too; copy the files and keep them safe until I'm fit enough. That may be several months, but it will give you time to read it all and have a think about how you want to go about it. Not a word to Gwen though. When you have what you want, I need you to break the laptop. I'll say Teddy Parker did it on the night and no one will be the wiser."

"Don't we have to think about this?"

"No, we don't. Trust me Dan. I won't let you down again."

Gwen came back in. "What are you boys concocting?"

Dan could not find a suitable answer. Jim simply replied, "How I'm going to spend my retirement. Can you break up a banana and feed it to me please, love?"

While Gwen was there Dan had no choice but to stay quiet but it gave him time to think about Allen's extraordinary proposal. He found himself feeling scared in a way that reminded him of his childhood and the fear of what was coming from the tongue or belt of his father depending on what he said or did. It was a fear which frayed his nerves and tested his resolve about the things most precious in his life; Tara and the baby and the relationships with a few people he considered friends.

But of all the things that came to mind, one stood above the rest: his unquenchable desire to find inner peace and to lock the door on his skeleton cupboard once and for all. When Gwen left the room again he went and sat by Allen.

"What you said earlier, do you really want to open that can of worms?"

"Take my word for it. Find a way to get rid of your demons, not just for yourself but your family too," Jim replied.

"What if we find something we don't like?"

"Let's cross that bridge when we come to it. I believe it will be alright in the end."

"Okay but I want to tell Tara everything first. She deserves to know."

"That sounds like a good start."

Dan rested his hand on Jim's, sealing their contract. Neither could have any idea where it was going to lead them and what they might find along the way.

CHAPTER THIRTY-ONE

Teddy Parker's second court date coincided with Ben Binder's interview with the promotion board. Adam Smith requested Teddy's bail. The judge wasted no time refusing.

Binder took the three days prior to the interview off to hone his final comments to the panel at the end of what he knew would be a successful session of questions and answers.

His sun was at its zenith after months leading up to this day. He sat quietly outside the interviewers' office waiting his turn and reflecting on the events of recent past.

Finally, all my hard work is about to pay off, he thought.

The interview went even better than he imagined. The board members were so full of praise for his recent achievements they almost ran out of time to ask all their questions.

Binder easily navigated his way through the procedural stuff and let them in on several ideas he was working on to further modernise the force over the coming years, with a particular focus on subjects that happened to be associated with next year's force objectives.

"I want to be at the spearhead of developments, I am a man who gets things done."

As he rose to leave at the end, he was already mentally going over the upcoming postings he preferred, pleased that he would be moving on from James Allen, Nick Hetherington, their pest of a friend Dan Calder, and Mapperley.

Dan left for home the day after Nick and the family got back from their holiday. They appeared normal although in reality, the scars would remain for a long time to come. He called Tara from Los Angeles to confirm what time his plane got into Auckland.

"I can't wait to see you. Let's not do this again. Have you started to think about baby names?"

Tara was joyfully surprised by Dan's choice of topic. "Yes, I can't help it, I even have a list. Have you got something in mind?"

"If it's a boy I quite like Bradley. It came up in conversation recently."

"Bradley, that's nice. Conversation you say?" she mocked.

He grinned. "Yeah you probably don't want to know, but from now on everything will be different."

She laughed out loud. "If I thought you were remotely capable of being able to keep your word on that I would tattoo it on your backside. You might not go looking for trouble, but it does seem to have a habit of following you around."

Dan fingered the flash drive in his pocket and considered Jim's proposition about Zoe Summers. He knew he was not done with all things Mapperley just yet.

Ian Austin was born in 1963 in Southampton, England. His very unremarkable school life ended at 16. Drifting into and out of several jobs including hotel porter and photocopier salesman he eventually found his salvation in the Hampshire Police. A career as first a constable and then detective in the UK followed, where he also served as a tactical firearms officer, covert surveillance operative and National Crime Squad trainer.

He transferred to the New Zealand Police in 2003 having visited several times before and falling in love with the country and the Kiwi way of life.

He now lives in Auckland with his artist partner Sallie.

The Dan Calder series initial trilogy began with The Agency published in 2016. Its runaway success included several appearances in the Nielsen Best Sellers List and universally positive reviews from critics and reviewers at home and abroad.

The Second Grave published in 2018 has been eagerly awaited. The third and final chapter of the trilogy, Frozen Summer, will follow very soon.